For
One Night
Only

For One Night Only

A *Glitter Bats* BOOK

JESSICA JAMES

Berkley Romance
NEW YORK

BERKLEY ROMANCE
Published by Berkley
An imprint of Penguin Random House LLC
penguinrandomhouse.com

Book design by Daniel Brount
Interior art: Microphone and bass guitar © Lemon Workshop Design/Shutterstock.com

Library of Congress Cataloging-in-Publication Data

Names: James, Jessica, (Jessica M.), 1990- author.
Title: For one night only / Jessica James.
Description: First edition. | New York: Berkley Romance, 2025.
Identifiers: LCCN 2024014176 (print) | LCCN 2024014177 (ebook) |
ISBN 9780593817711 (trade paperback) | ISBN 9780593817728 (ebook)
Subjects: LCGFT: Romance fiction. | Novels.
Classification: LCC PS3610.A44252 F67 2025 (print) | LCC PS3610.A44252
(ebook) | DDC 813/.6—dc23/eng/20240329
LC record available at https://lccn.loc.gov/2024014176
LC ebook record available at https://lccn.loc.gov/2024014177

First Edition: January 2025

Printed in the United States of America
1st Printing

For Andrew
I'm so thankful music brought us together

AUTHOR'S NOTE

This book deals with emotionally difficult topics, including biphobia, misogyny, brief discussions of toxic diet culture, emotional abuse by a parent, parental neglect, and depictions of generalized anxiety disorder that include panic attacks. Any readers who believe that such content may upset them or trigger traumatic memories are encouraged to consider their emotional well-being when deciding whether to continue reading this book.

For
One Night
Only

1

✦ Valerie ✦

When you become famous, everyone claims you can control your own image—but it's the media that decides if you're a darling or a diva. I've been stuck in the diva category since I was seventeen.

Every day there are headlines like, "We Liked Valerie Quinn Better When She Was Making Music," and there's nothing I can do to change the narrative. It's not even accurate, but I guess "We Liked Valerie Quinn Better When She Was in a Band and Not a Musical TV Show" doesn't have the same vicious ring to it.

Poor word choice is the least of my problems today, because there are photos everywhere of me all over my castmate Roxanne Leigh. With my aching head in one hand and my phone in the other, I sit at my cold marble kitchen counter, scrolling through one clickbait article after another with growing horror.

Last night is such a blur that the grainy images bring it back in fragments.

The lights were low and I was with someone beautiful, and I hadn't been out since Theo dumped me, so I let myself forget about the consequences. There's a pic where we're too-close-for-friends in a booth at a club I don't remember, another of us on a crowded dance floor with my hands gripping Roxanne's waist, and one of me licking salt off her hand to do a shot. The photographer even managed to capture the horny spark in my eyes in that last one.

God, how embarrassing. At least I looked hot while breaking my one-drink rule. (The rule in question was my idea four years ago, after I threw up on John Mayer in front of the paparazzi at that Grammys after-party. Not my finest moment. In my defense, it's hard to stay sober-ish when so much of this industry involves parties full of booze.)

Still, the only truly incriminating photos are outside Roxanne's building, the two of us sharing a heated kiss and going inside together. And yeah, I know what it looks like, but we didn't hook up. I was so drunk that I crashed on her couch.

This morning, I woke up in a cold sweat, threw up in her toilet, and awkwardly asked to borrow some clothes to make it back to my apartment. I'll be lucky if she texts me again.

The photos imply a lot more happened. But the media's job is to tell a story, and it's rarely the whole truth. I accepted long ago that these invasive assumptions about my personal life are the cost of my moderate fame—I just can't figure out why the internet is so angry today. I slam my phone face down on the counter, forcing myself to look away before the real self-loathing kicks in.

Sure, Roxanne and I are both actresses, but the headlines are singling me out as the problem. I can't make sense of it with my tequila headache, but obviously it's not good. Why else would my manager be knocking on my front door?

My stomach drops as Wade Ortega and I make eye contact through the window, and I launch myself off the barstool, hurrying to let him inside. Nausea roils my gut from moving too fast.

"Good morning," I cough out, trying not to heave again.

"Hey, Valerie, you weren't answering your phone," Wade says.

Even on a Saturday morning, he's dressed impeccably in a gray suit, which is unsurprising. He likes suits. He's Puerto Rican, with warm brown skin and black hair with a splash of silver that's trimmed in a perfect fade.

Palming my forehead, I groan. "I left it on Do Not Disturb after the club last night." I had so many notifications this morning that I didn't even check who they were from.

"I'm assuming it's too much to hope that you haven't been online today?" Wade asks. I cringe at the question and usher him inside, bracing for the worst.

Wade is a former MLB outfielder turned talent manager, and he's damn good at his job. His team has been tirelessly working for years to further my career and maintain my image, and he's worth every dollar. But the thing about Wade is he prefers to do business in writing—text, email. I even got a postcard with an audition reminder that one time he was on a family ski trip without cell service.

If he's showing up unannounced, something is horribly wrong.

"Let me get you some water," I say, stalling for time. I head over to my fridge to get him a glass, then get one for myself after he cocks an eyebrow. With my hangover raging, it's not a bad idea to hydrate.

Fortunately, Wade doesn't comment on the ghostly green tinge of my skin. "Valerie, just tell me what you've seen."

"I've seen photos, haven't read too many articles . . . yet," I admit. After the last time I made headlines like this, I became obsessed and fell into a total depression spiral. My therapist gave me homework to *scroll past* the bullshit, but I'm not very good at homework. At least today, my headache is preventing a deep dive.

"Well, I can give you the SparkNotes," he says, letting out a huge sigh. "Has Theo Blake reached out to you at all?"

I freeze, confused. This question is "out of left field," to use one of Wade's favorite metaphors. Maybe I was drunk, but I'd definitely remember if we ran into my C-lister ex last night—even if it was only by the suffocating aura of Calvin Klein Eternity.

"What does Theo have to do with this? Aren't you talking about the photos of me and Roxanne?" I ask.

He sighs, running a hand over his hair. "Theo is spinning . . . something. Y'all broke up, right? You haven't rekindled anything and forgotten to tell me? No judgment, I just need to know what's going on so we can start damage control."

Damage control? More nausea makes my head swim, and I clench my jaw to fight it back. Nothing makes sense today.

"Not even a little. It's been more than a month since we split and we haven't had any contact."

"You should probably go to his page."

My jaw clenches even more, but I do what Wade says and grab my phone. I don't really care about anything Theo has to say at this point—we ended things when he signed on for a fantasy franchise in Spain, after we decided our relationship wasn't worth long distance. He was kind of a jerk about it, actually.

I set down my water and open the app, where Theo has posted a thirst trap on the beach that makes me grumble in irritation. He's shirtless, showing off that CrossFit-cultivated six-pack in the sunrise, and his blond hair swoops over his strikingly gray eyes.

But this post is unique for Theo, because it has a rambling caption instead of emojis:

I'm sure you've all seen the photos by now—they took me by surprise as much as everyone else. This isn't how I wanted to learn Valerie wasn't committed to our relationship, but I'm not going to beg her to stay with me, especially after cheating like this. I have some pride. And honestly, I'm so grateful to be free of the toxic

relationship we were in for more than a year. Some
people are so self-centered they don't care who they
hurt. I'm going to spend some time working on myself,
seeking happiness, and diving into creative pursuits
while I'm overseas to film my next project. I can't
pretend I'm not heartbroken, but I'm surrounded by
people who love and appreciate me for who I am,
and I know my heart will heal from this pain.

XO, Theodore Anderson Blake

The absolute *nerve* of this asshole. I didn't realize you could be
gaslit from halfway across the world, but I *know* we broke up last
month. I was there.

WE'RE AT A GLAMOROUS EARLY-HOLLYWOOD TRIBUTE RESTAURANT
*in Malibu—one of Theo's favorites, since he thinks worshipping Frank
Sinatra and Errol Flynn is an admirable personality trait. It's the kind
of place with warm lighting, no prices on the menu, and paparazzi lurk-
ing in the shadows outside.*

*Theo's been staring longingly at my New York strip ever since our
orders arrived, obviously resentful of his boring kale salad. He keeps
talking about getting "movie-star fit," even though we both know his
real plan to shape up for those shirtless scenes is diuretics. Theo looks great
naked already, but if I insist he doesn't need to lose weight for the role . . .
he's just going to roll his eyes and tell me I'm lucky to have my superhero
costume to hide any flaws.*

*He pulls out his phone, takes a litany of selfies with his vodka soda,
and posts his favorite while I take another deliciously tender bite of steak.
Apparently satisfied, he puts his phone face up on the table so he can
watch his notifications, then reaches for my hand. I don't really want to*

stop eating, but I guess I should at least try to connect with him tonight. He's been so different lately, but we used to have fun.

I put my hand in his. He smiles at me, and I do my best to return it.

"Valerie, baby," he says. "This role is a huge step in my career. I think bringing any baggage with me to Spain is just bad energy, you know? Long distance will only hold me back. We've had a good run . . . but we should break up."

NO ONE KNEW WHO THEO WAS UNTIL WE DATED. HE WAS A COMPE-tent television jobber with dozens of credits on IMDb that no one remembers, hustling for his big break . . . and he started getting loads of auditions once our relationship made "Who is Theo Blake?" trend. Now that the buzz about his new gig has faded from the media cycle, he needs me again.

"He's making this up for press," I say, groaning. Our relationship was never anything really special, but we had fun for most of the six months we were together. I thought he cared about me. Things were starting to grow sour before he dumped me, but I never expected he'd outright lie for engagement.

"For the record, I never liked him," Wade says.

"I know." I close my eyes and sigh, because I know what's coming. It always does. "They're running with his side of the story, aren't they?"

Wade grimaces. "Someone called you 'Hollywood's Heart-breaker' and it's starting to stick . . . so that's the gist of it, yeah."

"*Shit.*" I'm used to this, but it doesn't mean it's not exhausting. When you become rock-star famous as a teen, no one gives you the grace to make mistakes and grow up: every wrong move is rehashed and reviled. I pissed off a few important people, forgot to bite my tongue in interviews, was a little too loud about my sexuality . . . and then some of my intimate photos ended up online. Suddenly I wasn't a person—I was kindling for the media, and they loved to watch me burn.

Anxiety churns in my already-queasy stomach as I trudge over to the espresso maker, suddenly desperate for caffeine. Does everyone really believe Theo's lies? What does Roxanne think?

I scroll through my endless notifications, and sure enough, there's a text from her:

> **Roxanne:** Look, I had a great time last night, but didn't realize there was still something between you and Theo. I think it's best if I take myself out of the equation, so I told The Network I'm no longer interested in coming back for season 3. I've been considering a different offer anyways. Please don't call me again.

Damn it. The Network is the streaming service that owns *Epic Theme Song*, the show I've been lucky to star in for two seasons after years of struggling to pivot from music to Hollywood. Fans loved Roxanne's character. Now she's never coming back, and it's my fault.

I'm not completely heartbroken about losing a "relationship" with Roxanne, because this was just our first time out after she filmed a half-season arc on my show more than a year ago. But we had a good time. There was possibility. And Roxanne isn't even giving me a chance to explain; but we barely know each other. If our positions were reversed, I'd . . . probably handle it the same. This business is cruel: you have to look out for yourself first if you want to survive.

Guess I'll chalk last night up to one more mistake in my scrapbook of regrets.

"You still here, kid?" Wade asks, frowning over at me. I realize my hands are shaking as I try to set up my coffee shots, and decide I should just keep hydrating instead. I down my glass of water, wincing as the cold liquid hits my pounding brain.

"Unfortunately, an anvil hasn't fallen on my head yet, so yep, still standing," I say, grimacing. I could really use an anvil right about now.

He settles onto one of my barstools and gestures for me to join him. "Look, I know this must be upsetting, but you made me swear on my Boxster that I'd tell you the second we heard from The Network."

My stomach drops as I return to my earlier seat at the counter, folding my legs into a pretzel and hoping I don't look too eager. We've waited on renewal news for nearly a year. Our small but loyal fan base is holding strong, but they're getting ravenous for updates. And honestly, so am I, because my entire career is balancing on this.

"Just tell me."

He purses his lips. "They're not happy Roxanne took another offer, and the bad press doesn't help."

I blink, truly stunned. "They can't actually believe that bullshit too." You'd think a streaming service would be used to handling the media—especially stories that aren't true. First *Gossip Daily*, then Roxanne, now The Network—is no one going to give me a chance to tell my side of the story?

Wade runs a hand over his hair. "Roxanne was slated for a series regular promotion, and you cost them that possibility."

My nails dig sharply into my palms as I ball my fists. "They would have to actually renew the show to get series regulars. I don't see why one embarrassing night has anything to do with it."

"You know as well as I do that image is everything when you're promoting a teen-adjacent show."

"They don't worry about that for *Young Sherlock*."

"You didn't want to be on a sexy teen drama. If you get on the *Young Sherlock* cast, you can do whatever you want."

I huff, because we've had this discussion before. While *Epic*

Theme Song and *Young Sherlock* are technically aimed at the same eighteen-to-thirty-four demographic, they could not be more different. *Epic Theme Song* follows a mediocre squad of not-so-superheroes navigating college by day and thwarting the minor villains the real heroes can't be bothered with by night. It's campy and fun with lots of dynamic queer characters, and the music is incredible. I auditioned for *Epic Theme Song* because it's a musical, and it gave me a chance to work with Broadway legend Patricia Turner, who plays my mentor.

Young Sherlock, on the other hand, is closer in tone to *Gossip Girl* and *Riverwood*. It's a great show, but the last thing my image needs is more sex appeal. As if I could play a teenager who acts like a thirty-year-old when people already write think pieces to explain why I'm such a bad role model . . .

Epic Theme Song really took off with teens, and they're not exactly our originally intended audience, but our marketers have taken the fandom to heart. I love our fans, but the pressure to keep a low profile to remain palatable for *parents of teenagers* is stifling. It shouldn't matter what I do in my private life.

I fold my arms on the counter and press my forehead into my wrists with a groan.

"I didn't do anything wrong!" I say, the sound muffled by my hair.

"You didn't, but the damage is done as far as The Network is concerned. They lost a high-profile star who was bringing in a new audience, and now the show is in the headlines for the wrong reasons."

Of course he's right, and bile stings the back of my throat. We've been hanging on by a thread. *Epic Theme Song* has been critically acclaimed, but our numbers aren't good enough. Despite our loyal fan base, we aren't getting the views The Network wants from a show like ours, at least according to the mysterious metrics they won't even disclose to our showrunner. It's been eleven months since season two dropped.

As a cast, we did everything we could to keep the renewal hope alive—livestreams with different actors, conventions, fan art contests . . . I even filmed a series of video tutorials for acoustic covers of my character's songs. The fans loved it all, but we still haven't heard a thing. Nothing has been good enough.

And now I might have killed the show by being the Internet's Main Character.

"Is there anything I can do?"

Wade hums. "The Network is pretty concerned, but they haven't made a final decision. If anything, I think they're afraid of the fans reacting negatively to a cancellation, so they're waiting for the right time to move forward with a decision. If you want them to change their minds, you'll need to drum up good press, and fast."

As if it's that easy. I've been fighting a battle with the press for years.

Ever since the band I started in high school went viral and we signed a record deal, it's been all I can do not to make everyone hate me. It all started when I got caught on a hot mic telling indie darling Hunter O'Brien to "get the fuck away from me" when we shared the stage at Bonnaroo.

In my defense, he insisted on "helping me arrange guitar pedals more efficiently" when we were already on the damn stage. I'm perfectly capable of managing my own setup, thank you very much, and he *completely* jacked it up before our set. But the details didn't matter to the tabloids. From that day forward, I was branded a diva.

The rest of the Glitter Bats didn't have the same problem—everyone loves angel-on-earth Jane Mercer, our keys player. She's literally the nicest person alive, and she's one of the most talented people I've ever worked with. These days, Jane composes and produces critically acclaimed music for TV and video games.

Riker Maddox, our rhythm guitarist, has kept busy as a touring musician with the hottest bands. He only ever makes small headlines for kindnesses like quietly leaving massive tips at restaurants, or taking time to talk in depth with fans after shows. He's a human golden retriever, and everyone likes golden retrievers.

Keeley Cunningham, our drummer, is in demand for every studio pop, rock, and folk artist aiming at the awards circuit. She can be blunt, but people care more about her work than her attitude—and when she parted ways with her big-name pop star ex after three years, the headlines only said the split was "friendly."

And, well . . . I'm pretty sure Caleb Sloane is still beloved by the entire internet, even though he hasn't been seen in public in years. Caleb never had to try for good press—he was a darling from day one, the kind of person with such innate *goodness* it could never be denied. If the media sees me as a thunderstorm, he was always the sunshine streaming through the clouds after the rain, light shining on everyone around him.

And *oh my god*.

That's it.

"Caleb!" I say, raising my head and whirling to face my manager. For the first time all morning, I don't feel a hint of nausea. This could work.

Wade raises his brows. "You'd better not be saying Caleb is back, because I cannot handle another of your romantic entanglements today."

I flush, because I mean *ouch*, but fair. Things between Caleb and me are complicated, and it's the kind of complicated that stays firmly in the distant past. It would take a miracle for him to talk to me again, but a miracle might be my only chance to save our show.

And saving our show isn't just for me or my costars—it's for the *fans*. Of course I want to make another season, but after the cliffhanger at the end of the last episode when my character lost her powers, I know our fans deserve more than they got. More than me ruining their beloved show, at least.

But there's a way I might be able to fix my reputation—and make a lot of other fans really happy too. I just can't do it alone.

"What if I could pull off a Glitter Bats reunion?"

"Yeah, and what if I could win *Hollywood Idol*?" Wade famously can't carry a tune, so I don't need to hear the laughter in his voice to know he's not taking me seriously yet.

I pop off of the barstool and start pacing, mind spinning as the idea falls into place. "I'm not joking. Everyone loves a good reunion."

He folds his hands together on the counter. "Fine, I'll humor you. *Hypothetically*, I think a Glitter Bats reunion would guarantee some excellent press very quickly. But you need to be realistic here."

Caleb was Wade's client too back in the day, so Wade knows just how adamant he was about leaving the industry behind. But I wouldn't be asking Caleb to come back permanently; it would just be temporary. A reunion concert.

My throat tightens, and I swallow thickly. This isn't a door I ever planned to open again, but I'm desperate. I just might have to grovel. "I think I might be able to make it happen. Could you reach out to the label and the rest of the band?"

I haven't had the courage to talk to the band in years, and the label, well . . . after everything that happened, it's better if this comes from him.

Wade nods, already making notes on his phone. "Sure can—that's my job. You know the others won't agree unless Caleb is on board, and I don't want you to get your hopes up. It's not going to happen."

Yesterday, I'd have said he was right. But it's been six years, and I have nothing to lose.

"Leave Caleb to me."

Glitter Bats Take the Internet by Storm!

BY MARY KATE HAMPTON, COLLEGE INTERN

If you haven't heard "Midnight Road Trip" yet, you might be living under a rock. Glitter Bats, an indie pop-punk-inspired band hailing from Seattle, is going viral with a homemade music video of their debut single, which has been featured on an episode of *Riverwood*. And who can resist that bridge? *"I'll take any road / as long as it's with you . . ."* is destined to live on in social media captions for years. The harmony Caleb Sloane sings over Valerie Quinn's melody gave me chills the first time I heard it.

Started by best friends Quinn and Sloane (who co-lead, sing, and play guitar and bass, respectively), Glitter Bats also features Keeley Cunningham on drums, Riker Maddox on rhythm guitar, and Jane Mercer on keys and synth. The group first connected two and a half years ago at an exclusive summer camp for standout high school music students, and when they realized they had magic on their hands, the band was born. Before they went viral, they earned local praise playing in coffee shops, opening for groups touring the PNW, and winning a Battle of the Bands fundraiser for an animal shelter. All the band members are in their teens—Mercer and Maddox are nineteen, and Cunningham and Sloane are eighteen, with Quinn coming in youngest at seventeen—but they seem remarkably grounded for kids finding success at such a young age.

When this reporter reached out to the band for comment, both Quinn and Sloane were eager to talk.

"All this attention is so much more than we ever dreamed of!" said a wide-eyed Quinn in a video call earlier this week. She wore all black, with her signature pale pink hair styled in messy curls. The excited energy she brought to our conversation was palpable, and it's no wonder she connects so well with an audience.

"I agree—it's all about music resonating with people, and we couldn't have imagined this response. We're so grateful for our fans. God, I can't believe we have fans," Sloane added. He wore a Blink-182 T-shirt and eyeliner, his brown hair falling to his shoulders in a mop of haphazard curls. When I asked about plans for an album, the two shared a conspiratorial look.

They didn't confirm anything, but rumor has it that Glitter Bats was recently signed by Label Records, so stay tuned for updates. I know I'll be one of the first to preorder anything new the band puts out.

The band can be found all over social media at @Glitter BatsMusic.

2

✦ Caleb ✦

When you used to be famous, people recognize you in the most inconvenient places.

It would be worse if I was still in LA. My appearance has changed a lot since I stopped wearing all the leather and eyeliner and cut my hair, but the superfans are too smart to fall for my Clark Kent act. I mean, I'm not nearly as recognizable as my former bandmates these days, but I still have my own Wikipedia page.

Wikipedia is forever.

"Oh my god, you're Caleb Sloane, aren't you?"

I smile politely at the barista handing over my iced matcha. She's tall, white, and lanky with dyed red hair in two long braids and a name tag that reads "Betty." Closer to my age than some of the usual staff—which is probably how she recognized me—she looks every bit our fan base with ripped jeans, heavy makeup, and black nails.

My mouth goes dry with panic, and all I want to do is forget my order and run like hell out the door. But I don't want to be a jerk, and I can't afford to alienate the only dog-friendly coffee shop in town. I'll go anywhere I'm allowed to bring Sebastian Bark, the pit bull I adopted after I finished school, who sits impatiently at my side for one of the treats on the counter.

So even though it kills me, I lean on the thick slab of butcher block that makes up the espresso bar for strength and confirm Betty's suspicions with a small smile.

"Yup, that's me." Since the ticket to a record deal for my old band was a viral video, fans tend to recognize my face. I square my shoulders, resisting the urge to duck my head. Sensing my discomfort, Sebastian Bark licks my free hand. I scratch his warm, silky ears in silent gratitude.

Betty's eyes go wide. "I *knew* it! Are you still in touch with the rest of the band?"

My heart hammers—I've never been good at answering questions like this, especially since I know the truth just lets our fans down. The fans were the best part of my Glitter Bats days. They were so kind and supportive, and they did amazing things like draw incredible art inspired by our music and tattoo *lyrics I wrote* on their skin. They even wrote fan fiction, which I swore to never read again after the first one made me blush.

I owe every moment of success to people who were so inspired by my art. But I don't have anything to offer anymore.

Suddenly, this quiet, spacious coffee shop I usually find so much comfort in, with its bare warehouse ceilings and walls bedecked with cheerful local art, feels stiflingly claustrophobic. Fortunately, I'm not alone this Saturday morning, so I don't have to navigate the awkwardness by myself.

"Caleb is late for an appointment, but we love fans!" Leah, my sister-in-law, says. Somehow she manages to wrap an arm around my shoulders with a cold brew in one hand and the leash for Strawberry, her bouncy red border collie, in another. Sebastian Bark huffs for good measure as Leah steers all of us out of the shop.

"Thank you," I say.

"Anytime," Leah says, brushing her ponytail over her shoulder. She's Korean, with almost-black hair and freckles across her face, and even though she's fairly petite, she can easily sling an arm around my shoulder since I'm only five seven. As a PE teacher and track coach, she's used to wrangling people—and teenagers are a much bigger challenge than harmless fans.

"I don't know why I always freeze up," I mutter as I squint against the late-spring sunlight.

"You don't like letting people down. It's cool, I'm happy to help." My older sister, Cameron, is an ER nurse with intense work hours, so Leah's kind of adopted me in her spare time, including for regular Sunday hikes like the one we're coming back from. I'm only five years younger than Cam and Leah, but it's enough that they both think they have to take care of me.

To be fair, I had a lot of growing up to do after becoming a rock star at eighteen. And now that Leah and I teach at the same school, we get to work together a bit—as much as PE and choir cross paths. (It's more than you'd think.)

"We should have gotten drinks *before* the mountain. I'm parched!" she says as we open the rear doors of my Subaru for the dogs. It was a cool enough morning that Licorice Mountain wasn't too hot, but I hum in agreement as I sip my own drink. Once everyone is situated—us with drinks and the dogs with treats—I pull out onto the road.

Leah plugs in my phone and turns on the stereo, and I try to just ignore my feelings and drive. My entire music library starts to shuffle.

"Taylor Swift?" Leah asks as something from *1989 (Taylor's Version)* plays.

"Taylor Swift is an incredible lyricist and I will not invite any slander in this car."

She raises her hands, chuckling. "I wasn't going to slander her. It's only that your collection always surprises me."

"I wish I could write songs the way she does," I admit, clenching the soft leather of my steering wheel. It's the closest I'll get to confessing I've still got a notebook full of verses I'll never record.

While I loved sharing my music with the world, there was something so raw and vulnerable about putting it all out there for public consumption. When people hear your lyrics, they make assumptions about your personal life, and it's hard to navigate what's safe to share and what needs to be kept locked away in your chest. There's no going back now, so I'll stick to helping the next generation find their voice.

The sun is getting unseasonably warm, but it's such a nice day that I roll down the windows instead of blasting the AC on the drive back into our part of town. The dogs like it when I do this, because it means they can smile out the windows, tongues lolling in the wind. Still, the heat makes sweat bead down my skin as I drop Leah and Strawberry off at their condo. When I pull into my own driveway, I decide to hose Sebastian Bark off in the yard. Since he thinks the water is a toy and goes squirrelly with the hose, I strip my shirt off and change from running shoes to slides before beckoning him over to the spigot.

The water is a cool, crisp respite from the warm weather, and my anxiety trickles away as I maneuver eighty pounds of wriggly muscle to rinse off the dust from the trail. But he behaves, and I spend a few minutes taking pics of him being a good bath-time pup to post tomorrow. After I left the industry, I swore off social media, but Sebastian Bark's account (where I never show my face or reveal my name) has almost one hundred thousand followers. Maybe that means I'm still an entertainer, but dog videos make the world better.

I used to think our music made the world better too, but that's in the past.

By the time Sebastian Bark is clean, I'm soaked but sweaty, so I dunk my own head under the water. It's almost freezing, but after a long hike it feels amazing. I start to think through my afternoon plans as I curl up the hose when a familiar voice makes my mouth go dry.

"Hey, stranger."

Every muscle in my body tenses—like I'm waiting on a particularly jazzy chord to resolve into a smoother sound. I never expected to hear from her again, and definitely not in my front yard in an Oregon suburb. She's been haunting me for years, a steady presence in magazines and TV shows and on the back pages of my songwriting notebooks, reminding me of our unfinished business.

Now she's here on my doorstep, so I turn around to face Valerie Quinn for the first time in six years.

Despite the years of zero contact, I have to fight the instinct to pull her into my arms. She's as gorgeous as ever, standing here in a faded T-shirt and leggings with platinum hair piled into a haphazard bun on top of her head. There are dark circles under her ocean-blue eyes, the tentative smile on her lips betrayed by an obvious exhaustion that still makes my stomach twist with concern. Something about her unkemptness reminds me of late nights writing music until the sun started glowing on the horizon.

It's unsettling.

"What are you doing here?" My words are so harsh I can *feel* her flinch, and I almost want to take it back. But what was she expecting—a hug? After so much time apart, my brain is short-circuiting in her presence.

"Would you believe me if I said I was in the neighborhood?" she asks.

Calling her on her bullshit isn't my job anymore, but based on the very non-Valerie Toyota Corolla parked on the curb, she came straight from the airport rental lot. She's obviously here to talk, and

I don't think I'm going to like whatever made her travel a thousand miles to get here.

"How'd you even find me?" I ask.

Valerie clears her throat. "I'm sorry if this is a bad time . . ."

"No, it's fine." I sigh, running a hand through my wet hair. As much as I want to tell her to get back in the car and leave forever, I don't have the heart to do it, even after all the horrible things we said to each other that last night. Now that she's here, I know there's no getting rid of her until she tells me what she came for. "We'll go inside."

Sebastian Bark chooses that moment to bound over to Valerie, flopping his wet torso against her legs and begging for scratches with the kind of puppy-dog sweetness that can't be denied. Valerie crouches down and gets flat pit bull kisses all over her hands for the effort, and I can't help but soften a little at the sight.

In a different life, he might've been hers too.

"Oh my god," she says, staring up at me with heart eyes. "What a sweetheart." Valerie beams, like it's love at first sight. It's hard not to make the comparison—the last girl I dated, Morgan, was terrified of any dog bigger than a Pomeranian. Our relationship was brief and casual, but if I had to choose, I would have chosen the dog.

With Valerie, that wouldn't be an issue. She's always adored dogs.

I clear my throat. "Yeah, Sebastian Bark loves everyone."

Her smile brightens, and damn it if it doesn't make the ice in my heart thaw a bit. I've never been good at resisting this girl. "*Gilmore Girls* or Skid Row?" she asks.

I bite back a chuckle. "Both."

When we were touring, it was hard to sleep on the bus, so we picked TV shows to binge until we fell asleep. *Gilmore Girls* was a particular Glitter Bats favorite because of the band, especially once Sebastian *Bach* showed up. I'm pretty proud of the terrible pun.

"Great name," Valerie says. I call for Sebastian Bark again, and he bounds through my front door without further delay.

My jaw tightens as we head inside. The condo is small and bare, and all of my furniture is secondhand or straight from IKEA, obviously cheap. I live on a strict budget, and I can't help but wonder what Valerie thinks as she takes in the space. It's a stark contrast to the kind of places she's used to staying.

At least the place is clean. My bare feet take comfort in the fresh vacuum tracks I laid down before our morning outing. Still, the carpet of my rental is as cheap as the rest of the place.

Most of my Glitter Bats money is long gone. After the first big paycheck, we bought designer clothes and paid for fancy hotel rooms and found the best instruments money could buy. Since I was still used to having a certain amount of (what I thought was) disposable income when I left the industry at twenty-two and went to college, I didn't know how to manage my money. I blew through my remaining cash and couldn't cover basic living expenses, which meant crashing on Cameron and Leah's couch while I finished my degree.

If I could do anything over, it would have been putting all my Glitter Bats money in the bank. Maybe then our younger sister, Carrie, would have a college fund—because Mom sure as hell didn't plan for her to be a piano prodigy. But there's not much I can do to help on my teacher salary. Between the cost of rent and my staggering student loan payments, I live paycheck to paycheck, and it shows.

"Like what you've done with the place," Valerie says, and I can't tell what bothers me more—the fact that she can still read my mind, or the fact that she's using it to get in a jab.

"It's what I can afford." Despite the tension coursing through my veins, I try not to sound super defensive. I don't want her to know she can still hurt me. Desperate to do *something*, I walk over to the slider and let Sebastian Bark into the backyard to air-dry, keeping an eye on him through the windows. Then I realize I'm still shirtless. Neck heating, I scramble to tug on a T-shirt from the laundry basket I forgot at the base of the stairs last night.

Seemingly oblivious to my discomfort, Valerie wanders around my sparse living room, scrutinizing every inch. She pauses at the one personal item I have out—a photo of me and my sisters at Cameron and Leah's wedding a few years ago. At the wistful look in her blue eyes, I can't help but wonder if she wishes she'd been there.

Cameron was like her big sister too.

"You look happy here," she says.

"I was." It was a small wedding on the lake, but it was perfect for those two. Mom was actually mentally present for once, Carrie was happy-crying all day, and Strawberry was a very enthusiastic flower girl. It's the best day I've had since I left the Glitter Bats behind.

Suddenly, I'm desperate to figure out what the hell Valerie wants and get her out of here, before I do something stupid like tell her how often I still think of her, or press her up against these god-forsaken beige walls and kiss her into oblivion just to see if she still tastes the same. Instead of hovering around the living room like I'm doing, she drops her purse on the floor and sinks into my armchair, draping a knee over one side like she owns the place.

And in that moment, I know why she's here: she wants something.

Perching on the edge of the couch against the other wall—as far away from her as I can get without being rude—I clear my throat. "So, Valerie . . ."

"I want to put together a Glitter Bats reunion," she blurts.

My head swims as I try to register the words, but I feel like I'm hallucinating. She's out of her mind. "You're joking."

"Please, just hear me out."

Crossing my arms, I scramble to think of the fastest way to get her to leave. I can't believe she would come here after all this time and ask me for *this*. "Nothing has changed. I said I was done."

"I need this, Caleb. My reputation is a disaster. I don't know if you've seen . . ." she trails off, face flushing.

"Whatever it is, I haven't seen it." I've muted everything Glitter Bats for years, anything I can do to keep these old feelings from stirring in my chest again. In Valerie's presence, they come crashing back like a tidal wave. Suddenly, I can't remember if I took my medication this morning, and I tap out a subtle rhythm on the cheap suede of the couch to ground myself.

Valerie shifts in the chair almost violently, tucking her feet under her and clasping her hands under her chin. "The Network won't renew *Epic Theme Song* as long as I'm getting bad press. We can do a couple shows in LA, or just one night. Whatever it takes to get them to say something *positive* about me." Even after all this time, I can tell when Valerie Quinn is trying to keep her voice steady. She's fidgeting, agitated, clearly upset. It's deeper than the press.

Still, I don't know why she could possibly think this is the answer. My stomach knots. "So all of your reasons for doing this are what, some last-ditch effort to save your career?" At least she's being up-front about wanting to use me this time.

The color drains from her face, and she straightens her shoulders, placing her palms on her thighs. "It's not just about me. Ever since Glitter Bats broke up, the fans have begged us to do a reunion. The rest of the band is already in. They're just waiting for you to say yes before they sign," she says, pulling her phone out of her pocket. "You always said our fans were the reason for our success, and this would make them so happy. And the label is offering us all a huge check, so it's not like you'd be doing this for nothing."

"If I wanted the money, I'd have stayed in the industry," I say. Of course the label is offering us a check—anything to get their hooks back in. Still, my resolve wavers, just enough to pique my curiosity.

"I know what you're probably thinking—but it's a good contract. My mom has nothing to do with this deal. Wade vetted everything, and so did Jane's agent. Please at least read it before you say no," Valerie says, crossing the room and thrusting her phone at me. It's pulled up to a draft of a contract, and my eyes glaze over all the legalese until I find the payment.

It's a big check. Big enough to pay off my student loans . . . or I could use it to start Carrie's college fund so she doesn't feel all that pressure to get a scholarship. That alone might sway my resolve to stay away from the industry forever. There's even a bonus if tickets sell out.

But is the money really worth going back to everything I ran from? Saying yes feels like a deal with the devil.

I stare around my sparse apartment and think of the times I've had to tighten my own belt because my mom needed money. She's not intentionally a bad parent, but Carrie is on her own too much—Mom's lucky no one has ever called child services. When Mom finds a new boyfriend, she ignores all of her responsibilities, including work. She spends money on the strangest things to impress these guys, like three-hundred-dollar salon visits or a new set of golf clubs; but then she can't always pay the bills that matter . . . because she can't keep a job she won't show up to.

Cam and Leah try to help too, but they're paying off two sets of massive student loans from the private college where they met. I try to do as much as I can so they don't have to, especially because if I hadn't blown through all my Glitter Bats money on pointless bullshit, I'd have plenty to share.

Carrie called me a few months ago when the power was cut off and she couldn't reach Mom. My baby sister was chillingly calm as she asked for help, the soft waver in her voice the only thing betraying her panic. No seventeen-year-old should have to worry about things like that. She acts like it's no big deal, but when Dad left for the third time, I wasn't there for her—I was too busy basking in the worship of the LA music scene. I didn't notice Mom losing all sense of responsibility until it was too late.

I'm not sure if I can handle returning to the industry, but that check could change everything.

Valerie's face softens, and for a heartbeat I glimpse the girl I fell in love with under all her posturing. "Look, the way things went down with the band wasn't right," she says. "This would be an opportunity to end things on our own terms. I know you don't want to come back, but it's just one summer. A month or so of rehearsals to polish the set, and then we do the gig."

I run a hand over my hair. "Valerie—"

"Please, Caleb. I haven't asked you for anything, and you know I wouldn't be here unless this was really important."

The thing is, I really do. If I hadn't left after Valerie hurt me, the band might never have fallen apart. A small part of me still feels like I owe her *something*. And, well . . . I've never been good at saying no to Valerie Quinn, and she knows it.

When we were kids, I always went along with Valerie's convoluted plans. She wanted to start a band, and I came on board without much thought to how it could change my life. At the time, it didn't feel different. I was also there when she needed a cowriter for *Avatar: The Last Airbender* fan fiction (#Zutara for life), or a running buddy when she was training for soccer tryouts, or even a business partner for an Etsy shop to raise money for a theme park trip—turns out I'm pretty damn good at crocheting hats.

It would be so easy to go along with one more scheme. It's not like I expected Valerie to show up on my doorstep, but if I did, it would never have been for a Glitter Bats reunion. This turn of events feels like a fever dream. For just a moment, I fantasize about shoving her out that door and going so off the grid that even Valerie Quinn can never find me again.

But then I think about what this money could do for Carrie's future. I can't fix Mom, but I can make it so my baby sister will never have to worry about paying for her dreams.

And maybe this will give me the closure I never got before.

"Fine. I'm in."

Valerie jolts forward as if she's about to hug me but stops herself.

"Thank you, Caleb." She straightens her spine, as if bracing for impact. "One last summer, and then you'll never hear from me again."

@GlitterbugsUnofficial

Sources close to the band say Caleb left after the
Vegas concert! There was a big blowup with Valerie.

COMMENTS:

@BatsThatGlitter

CALERIE SPLIT CONFIRMED?! 💔 😭

@WanderlustMemes

My friend who works at an LAX Starbucks said she
saw Keeley and Riker this morning. Aren't they
supposed to be heading to Austin?

@YouAreMyGhost

Jane spotted at the Met. Why is she in New York?

@MakeMeMrsSloane

Everyone has been saying there's tension during the
VIP events. Valerie's skipped some of them entirely,
and Caleb had to cover for her. Diva behavior. We
already know the girl is unhinged. Remember
Bonnaroo?

@CalebSloaneDeservesBetter

@MakeMeMrsSloane you are so right. Remember those tacky underwear photos "a source" "accidentally" sent to Gossip Daily? Valerie Quinn is a diva AND a slut. I don't blame Caleb for leaving her.

@BitterSweetGlitterati

Okay but my bestie and I were at the Vegas show and it was incredible! There was a second during "Every Touch" where CalErie were sharing a mic and it seemed like they were about to make out right on stage. No. There's no way they broke up.

@GlitterbugsUnofficial

THE BAND JUST MADE A STATEMENT—ALL REMAINING TOUR DATES ARE CANCELED. [www.glitterbatsmusic.com/tour]

@AllMyFriendsAreVampires

What the hell. Is the band over?

3

+ Valerie +

I hate myself for it, but I've spent the last three weeks thinking about how good Caleb looked on his doorstep: shirtless, dripping wet, and doting on a dog.

Because Jesus Christ.

Caleb was always physically fit, but it was regular-gym-regimen fit, not spends-actual-time-outdoors fit—leaner and more toned than cut and ripped. His tattoos have expanded to full sleeves that ripple and stretch over his biceps and forearms, the kind of arms that can pick you up and throw you on a bed without any effort.

Pretty sure I had a dream like that once. They say you never forget your first, and how could I when he looks like *that*?

I'm embarrassed by the way the memory keeps me going through the sleepless nights leading up to our first gathering as a band in six years. We're staying at the hotel near the rehearsal studio for the duration of the summer, but because security couldn't put everything in place until Monday, Jane offered to put us up at her beach house in Venice for the weekend so we could at least start planning. Because there's so much to do, we decided to meet up as soon as Caleb was off for summer break, despite the extra logistics. We're starting the first night with dinner so we can hammer out details and come up with a set list.

And hopefully clear the air. Caleb isn't the only one I haven't seen in years.

Wade and I split a rideshare after our meeting with my publicity team ran late . . . turns out the big Glitter Bats announcement didn't fix my reputation overnight. He still represents most of the band, although Jane left him (tearfully, I'm told) to sign with a New York agency that specializes in film and TV now that she composes for soundtracks.

Label Records tried to send a few of the higher-ups to meet with us right away, but Wade waved them off for now, knowing their involvement would just make things harder for all of us. I even convinced my mom to stay away—she acted as our manager until the tour for our second album, *Bittersweet*, when we hired Wade, and I'm sure we'll hear from her at some point. But I don't think I could survive this first gathering with her in my ear.

I watch the driver's progress, comparing it to the clock on my phone, and my hands tremble as we get closer to the house. Our arrival time is an hour later than planned thanks to Friday night traffic.

Seeing Caleb in person for the first time should have been the hardest part, but I'm also worried about the reception I'll get from the rest of the band. Wade said everyone agreed without hesitation, but that doesn't mean they're happy about it. Other than Caleb, they all still work in the industry: this is business, a paycheck, good press. They might not have an emotional attachment to Glitter Bats anymore.

And unlike me, none of their careers are hanging on our success.

My stomach churns. When the driver pulls up to the house, I

don't get out of the car. I just stare at the leather headrest and try to gather my courage.

"You good, kiddo?" Wade asks.

I let out a breath after a moment and put on my paparazzi smile. "Ready."

"Atta girl." He pats my shoulder and leads the way.

Wade is kind enough to grab my suitcase while I gather my backpack and guitars to head up the walk. It's a cute place—a white beach house with peachy-pink trim—and there's a neat assortment of plants in lieu of a front yard. Jane, of course, made sure the place was environmentally friendly. The sun is still out, the ocean crashes in the distance, and there's a salty breeze on the early-evening air.

Still, I wonder if I should have just stayed at my place as I press the doorbell. But Wade had suggested we all crash together for "team bonding," and by Keeley's chilly expression when she answers the door, I think I'm going to need all the bonding I can get.

I feel like I'm looking at a stranger. She's chopped her once-long blond hair short so it barely reaches her chin, and now she has the septum piercing she always wanted to go with her ears, which were nearly covered with jewelry the last time I saw her. Instead of drowning herself in an oversized hoodie or flannel like she would have before, she's rocking chic linen pants and a tight black tube top that shows off her muscular arms. Even her eyes are an unfamiliar icicle cold.

"You're late," she says.

I swallow back my defense. "I know. Meeting went late, and then traffic."

Keeley rolls her eyes. "I cannot believe Caleb got a personal invitation to this shindig, and you haven't even called me, asshole," she says, her almost-six-foot frame towering over me even though I'm the one in heels. I flinch, but she pulls me in for a massive hug.

Thank god.

When Keeley releases me, Jane steps out from behind her to usher us inside.

Jane pulls me into a hug of her own. "It really is good to see you," she whispers, and that's that—no guilt trips, no criticisms. As she gives me one last squeeze, I'm comforted by her familiar vanilla scent, from the perfume that Keeley used to complain about on long bus trips. Fortunately, there's no ire in Jane's eyes when she pulls back to look at me. She looks the same, her copper-red curls falling in a ponytail over one shoulder, her makeup so minimal her smudge of freckles is visible, and she's wearing one of her signature flowing minidresses in a sunshine yellow.

She moves to hug Wade, and I take a peek around. The house is so *Jane* I want to cry. The walls are painted a soft sage green above creamy-white wainscotting; maple hardwood floors shine in the spots they're not covered in woven, colorful rugs; and there are plants everywhere, from the monstera in the corner to the pothos on the mantel to the philodendron hanging by a reading nook nestled by two paperback-laden shelves. It's part boho, part cottage-core, and 100 percent comforting. Jane always took care of all of us, and it seems right that this place would feel more like home after less than a minute than my own stark apartment.

Of course Jane notices my curiosity, because she offers Wade and me a tour, but I wave her off as I hear familiar voices in the kitchen. Best not to put this off any longer.

The kitchen is just as inviting as the rest of the house, with potted herbs in the window behind the sink, and Le Creuset in deep blue and sunshine yellow on display above white painted cabinets.

"Hey, Val," Riker says. His back is turned to me, since he's using his considerable height to dig around through clinking bottles in the highest cabinets. Even though it's June, he's wearing a crewneck, and a beanie covers the unruly brown hair that now falls past his shoulders.

"Hi," I say.

Caleb nods in my direction, but that's all the greeting I get as I stand next to him at the counter. His outfit is so familiar it hurts—soft joggers and a faded Blondie tee from his old collection. I lean my elbows against the surface and fold my hands, adopting the most casual pose I can as I smile his way. Maybe if I can just act normal, we can *be* normal.

"Where's Sebastian Bark?" I ask, desperate for him to say something, anything that will indicate normal is possible.

This at least earns me a grin. "I could have brought him down—dude actually loves airplanes—but I didn't think it'd be fair to make him stay at a hotel for the summer. Cameron and Leah have a border collie he's in love with, so I dropped him off at their house this morning. My sister-in-law will spoil him rotten and keep up the Instagram while I'm gone."

I smile. "That's great."

"Least you could have done is brought a *dog*, Caleb. This band always needed a mascot. What are you even contributing?" Keeley says from where she's slipped in behind me. She leans back, one foot against the light blue tiled wall, folding her arms as if she's bored of us already.

I stiffen, worried how he'll react to her jabs after all this time, but Caleb just laughs. "I'm sorry!"

"Fine, I'm ordering pizza," Keeley says, moving on quickly. None of us were ever picky about food, so she orders from her phone without asking anyone what they want, the way she always has. It's like she fell into old habits without thinking. Some things never change.

Maybe that's a good sign, but it gives me a flash of irritation. I would have liked to look at the menu before she put in the order.

"Yes, I found booze!" Riker says, beaming with a huge bottle of wine in one hand.

"You found screw-top rosé, dude. That's not booze, that's a juice box," Keeley says. "Jane, please, I'm begging. Tell me this wine is not yours."

Jane groans from where she's showing Wade the back porch, calling through the screen. "I think it's left over from my cousins. We can find something better or make a grocery run."

Riker holds it high like a trophy. "No way, I love this brand."

Keeley sighs. "You have the palate of a Christian influencer in their 'edgy wine phase.'"

"Laugh all you want, but when I drink, I want it to taste good. But go on pretending to like whiskey or IPAs or whatever fancy shit you're all drinking," Riker says smugly, twisting open the cap and taking a swig right from the bottle. "This is delicious."

"I kind of love IPAs," Caleb says.

"Me too," I admit. Caleb looks over at me, and I expect to share a smile, a laugh, something, but he just looks confused.

And oh, it's too much, being here with everyone, feeling the few feet between me and Caleb like a chasm. Sighing, I head back into the living room to unpack my acoustic.

It's been a while since I used this particular guitar, so I kneel on the hardwood floor next to the cracked imitation-leather case, open the buckles carefully, and begin to run a soft cloth over the lacquered wood body to eliminate any dust and fingerprints. Once I'm satisfied, I try to tune by ear, but the strings are too old to use. So I pull a new pack out of my bag and begin the obnoxious process of replacing them one by one. The familiar routine is therapeutic.

After a couple of minutes, Riker joins me on the nearby couch with two glasses of rosé. He hands one to me, but I just set it on the coffee table.

"Aren't you going to try it?" he asks.

I grimace dramatically and take a small sip. "It tastes like I'm drinking a Malibu Barbie." But then I take another drink. It's not terrible, but it definitely doesn't taste like actual wine. Theo had taken me wine tasting in Paso Robles over the spring, and that was the real stuff . . . and damn it, the bastard turned me into a wine snob.

Riker laughs. "Oh my god, you still have that thing?" he asks, gesturing to the guitar. "I've replaced most of my gear." It's no surprise—Riker was always enamored by a new guitar every few months, especially once he could afford to shop on Sunset Boulevard.

I'd joined him to shop for different models more than once, but I never got rid of my first acoustic—it's the cheap Mitchell I bought at a Guitar Center with my crochet money freshman year of high school. It's not totally useless, but it's scratched, and the neck is just a tiny bit warped from before I knew how to take care of it. I'd never perform with it now, but bringing it along felt right. Like including an old friend in the reunion.

Maybe I need to stop being so sentimental. This summer is just about business.

"Sure do," I say. "How many guitars did you bring?"

"None." He laughs again, so warm it fills the room. "Plus five."

I roll my eyes. "Seriously?"

He shrugs, almost comically. "You *know* it depends on what we're playing. Sometimes you need an extra electric, sometimes acoustic, sometimes I'll play a bass while Caleb jumps on a guitar— and I have different setups based on which songs we're playing."

I do know. I remember arguing about how many guitars we could fit in the Vanagon that Keeley found on Craigslist for our first local "tour." The thing broke down so often it was hardly worth the $1,200 we'd scraped together.

It feels nice, chatting with Riker like everything is normal. At first glance, Riker could be intimidating at a hulking six foot four, but he's always been like this—so natural to talk to, easygoing no matter what's going on. But I can tell he's nervous too. He's chugging the rosé instead of sipping it, and he takes off his beanie, runs a hand through his hair, and shoves it back on his head with too-busy hands.

I wish I knew how to steady them. Riker has always been so unflappable, and I caused this painful rift between us.

I missed him. I missed all of them. Why did I wait so long to make this happen?

"Pizza is an hour out," Keeley says as everyone joins us in the living room.

"My ride is waiting, so I'm going to head back," Wade says.

"You're not going to hang here, Wadie-poo?" Keeley asks.

Wade chuckles but stares at each of us in turn with a mock-sternness that we probably deserve. "I'll leave you with one reminder: your contract with Label Records just happens to expire right after the concert. I guarantee that's why they were so eager to make this happen. Be extremely careful what you say this summer, because they could use any perceived intent to make more music to bind you to a third album."

My jaw clenches. Label Records is footing the bill this summer, and it's obviously because they hope we'll make more music with them. They were so disappointed when the band broke up four years into our ten-year contract.

"That won't be a problem," Caleb says quickly, crossing his arms. My stomach drops. We're not here for a new album, and even if that was remotely a possibility, I didn't need Caleb's protest to know he'd never agree. I'm lucky he's here at all.

"Just try to get to Monday without killing each other. I'm a text away if you need anything," Wade says.

"Right, but we're not going to bother you unless it's an emergency, because you're taking your family to Disney and you should get to enjoy it!" Riker says, glancing around the room pointedly at the rest of us. Keeley raises a brow, but no one argues.

We exchange a quick round of goodbyes with Wade, and then it's just the Glitter Bats. Without a buffer. The sudden awkwardness of our reunion hits me like a bad review, and I'm desperate to fill the silence.

"Well, since we're waiting on the pizza, I think we should start talking set list." I sit on the couch and reach into my bag, pulling out my trusty black Moleskine. "Opening with 'Midnight Road Trip' is the obvious pick for the nostalgia factor. I made a preliminary list."

"Welcome to the Valerie Quinn show, everybody," Keeley says, crossing her arms. "You might be the one who called this little Council of Elrond together, but this is not your decision."

I stiffen. "I never said it was. I was just trying to get us started."

"I think we should all go around and share ideas," Jane says, settling on the love seat adjacent to the couch. At her reasonable tone, everyone else takes places around the living room. Riker joins me again on the couch. Keeley sinks onto the floor next to Jane, leaning against a pile of cushions with one leg propped up, the other stretched out across the rug. Caleb hesitates, staring at the spot in the love seat that would place him right next to me . . . before sinking into the pink beanbag chair across the room.

"Caleb, what do you think we should do?" Riker asks.

He frowns. For a moment, I don't think he's going to have a suggestion, but he surprises me. "'Ghosts' could be a really solid opener since it was our biggest single. It's a crowd-pleaser. I think 'Midnight Road Trip' is a better closer or encore."

"Oh, I like that idea for 'Road Trip,'" Jane says. "We could play around with the arrangement, make it bigger—put Riker on a crunchy pedal, I'll add some synth."

Caleb smiles, eyes brightening with the spark of collaboration. "Exactly. Maybe extend the song and split the vocals up too, give everyone a last feature. The fans will love it."

"That could be cool," I add. "Making new arrangements is going to mean extra work, though, so I want to make sure we're all prepared." This concert will all be for nothing if it's anything less than flawless. "We have to be clean and tight and better than ever."

Caleb narrows his eyes. "We've got almost two months, Valerie. I think we can pull it off. It's not like the fans want to hear us play it exactly like the album."

"Valerie is just worried she'll have to share the spotlight with the rest of us this time," Keeley sneers. "You good with that, princess?"

"What the hell is your problem?" I snap as tension fills my body. Keeley has always been blunt, but she's never been this confrontational. Maybe her career as an in-demand studio drummer is getting to her head. And they say *I'm* the diva. "I'm just trying to make sure we're all on the same page."

"*My* problem is that you always thought this was *your* band, but you don't get to be a dictator anymore. I don't even care that you're using us to clean up your image, but I'm out if you're going to control everything," Keeley says, tossing her hands up in frustration.

Jane puts a hand on Keeley's arm. "I don't think that's what she intended."

"How are we supposed to know? We haven't heard from her in years," Riker says under his breath, just loud enough for everyone to hear. I flinch. *So much for easygoing.* Keeley's anger I expected, but not his. I thought no one wanted to hear from me after what I did.

My throat feels tight, like I'm one step away from losing it. "Well, it's not like any of you reached out to me either," I snap.

I know I messed up all those years ago, but when everything

went down, all of us had participated in the radio silence that fol-lowed the split. I'm not the only one responsible for this estranged awkwardness now, and I don't think I can handle this if they're going to blame me for it all.

Maybe this was a terrible idea.

"Let's take a break until we've all had some food," Jane says, ever trying to keep the peace.

"Fine," I say, abandoning my guitar on the floor. "I'll step out-side and wait for the pizza."

I'm not feeling wanted in here.

4

✦ Caleb ✦

The living room falls silent after Valerie steps outside. We all stay seated, a little stunned, staring at Jane's colorful rug.

I have good reasons to be upset with Valerie. She hurt me and I hurt her, and we both said horrible things we can never take back. But I'm a little taken aback by the anger in the room tonight. Everyone thinks *Valerie* made me leave the Glitter Bats, but they don't know what really happened in Vegas. It's as much my fault as hers.

And sure, after a lot of therapy, I reached out to Jane, then Riker, and finally Keeley a couple of years ago to apologize. Even though each conversation was tough, I thought we'd cleared the air enough that our past wasn't so tortured. We started staying in touch, a little. Sometimes Riker will send me pictures of new gear he's considering, or Jane will text me to ask how I'm doing. Keeley will send me memes out of the blue or demand dog pics. It's all safe, casual conversation, but we're okay.

They've forgiven me for my part in everything, but they're still blaming Valerie for hers. Maybe that's because even after my apologies, I didn't give them the full story. I'll never be ready to reveal everything, but I need them to understand.

"Why are you all so mad at her when *I'm* the one who quit?" I finally say into the silence.

"She cut us all out of her life after that last show." Riker's mouth twists into a sad, wry grin. "And she's the reason you left the band anyway, right? You wouldn't just give up on us."

A lump forms in my throat, and I shift uncomfortably on the giant chair. "It wasn't all her."

If I hadn't forced her hand . . . maybe this wouldn't be a reunion at all. Maybe we'd be on album number five with a few Grammys to our name, the way we always dreamed.

"But it was mostly her, right?" Keeley asks dryly.

"No, it . . ." I swallow thickly, fighting back a lump of *something*. Honestly, I haven't thought about how that night made me feel in a really long time. It's not that it made me cry—I've always been a crier, so that's nothing new—but it made me feel so lost.

Everything that was important to me exploded beyond repair.

But I know that Valerie's not the villain in this story. If anything, we're both antiheroes. My therapist helped me see that there's no clear good and bad side in this scenario, even if that's how it looked to everyone else.

And it's time I told more of the truth. My heart hammers as I try to figure out how to begin.

"It wasn't *mostly* her," I finally say, letting out a sharp breath. Part of what went down isn't my story to tell, but I can at least try to explain what happened. "Things were complicated between us in the weeks before, and I'm sure you all felt it. When we got to Vegas for that final show, we were distracted by an argument and it made us both sloppy onstage. After the concert, we stayed back in the greenroom while you all went to get food. I'm not proud of this, but . . ." I clear my throat. "I gave her an ultimatum, and what happened to the band was because of that decision I forced her to make."

My heart hammers in my ears after I finally admit it out loud, even in vague terms. I'm not some wounded puppy in all this. It was my fault.

I said I would leave if she insisted on hiding our relationship, and she wasn't ready to make things public.

I didn't know what they were at the time, but I was having anxiety attacks too. Trying to keep track of which things between us were secrets and what I could share with the press wrecked my mental health. It felt like living a lie. And I was just so tired of collaborating with Valerie at a safe distance in public and being together in secret. I pushed her to make a decision neither of us was ready for, so of course she pushed back.

So I decided the best thing to do was run. My therapist calls it avoidance.

"Dude," Riker says. "Why didn't you ever tell us?"

"I was embarrassed?" A dry, bitter laugh escapes my chest. "I was twenty-two and heartbroken, and I ran away from everything instead of facing my feelings."

"I had no idea," Riker says. He nudges my shoulder. "That's why you disappeared for so long, huh?"

I swallow hard, nodding. I told myself I wanted a clean break, but really . . . I was such a coward. Apologizing to everyone was both one of the toughest things I've ever done and long overdue.

My eyes fall to the front door. Through the glass, I can just make out Valerie's blond strands from her spot on the porch, like she's standing just outside my view. She's the one person I never apologized to, because I never knew exactly what to say.

How do you repair a connection that's been shattered into a million pieces?

Keeley sighs. "So what? I'm not going to just let Valerie off the hook. Whatever happened between you sucks, but nothing I said was untrue—she *does* have a pathological need to be in charge, and she *is* using this as a last-ditch effort to save her show."

Valerie probably can't hear us from her spot outside, but Jane lowers her voice anyway. "Maybe it's hard for her. The media is eviscerating her reputation, and she probably feels backed into a corner. I heard rumors that The Network won't renew *Epic Theme Song* unless she cleans up her image."

Cleans up her image? Valerie alluded to that at my house, but what is she supposed to do, become a nun? I hate this industry, and that's part of the reason I left, but just because Valerie stayed doesn't mean she deserves this. A wash of some kind of emotion ripples through me, and after a beat, I realize it's indignation. I want to head to The Network offices and yell at everyone who is treating Valerie's private life like it's any of their business.

"How'd you hear that?" Riker asks Jane.

"She knows everyone," Keeley says for her.

"I work on a show for The Network too. I hear lots of things." Jane sighs. "Personally, I think The Network is using this as an excuse. They've been dragging their feet on this show for months, and pinning this on Valerie now is just convenient for them. I'm sure the involvement of another cast member doesn't help. No wonder she's scrambling to find a solution." She clears her throat. "But no matter what started it, I think we all want this to be a good show. Fighting isn't going to get us anywhere."

"That doesn't excuse all the ways Valerie hurt us," Keeley says.

Riker nods. "We didn't hear about the reunion from her. Everything went through Wade. If we're going to pull this off, we're going to need to, like, actually talk to each other the way we used to, figure out our shit."

I'm definitely not talking to Valerie about our fallout in front of the band, but Riker's right. All these pointed jabs and tense silences are not conducive to the creative process. And it also just sucks. The Glitter Bats used to be the only people in the world who really knew me.

The music bonded us, and once, we thought it was for life.

When we started the band, we were just teens at music camp connecting over s'mores and shared big dreams for what could have been only a summer, if we hadn't all been so determined. Valerie and I were best friends from the moment we sat next to each other in kindergarten. The rest of us were strangers, and it was just luck—or fate—that we all lived in the Seattle area. Jane and Keeley went to the same high school, but they were in different grades and social circles. Riker didn't go to school with any of us.

It was tough to coordinate practices, write songs, and find gigs we could actually attend when we were so sprawled out. Only Jane could drive in the beginning, but we were committed to the music, and we made do with Seattle's public transportation system. We played anywhere that would take us: coffee shops, a random assortment of parties, clubs that allowed underage musicians as long as they stayed away from the bar—one time, we even played for Keeley's Aunt Daisy's knitting club. We survived the grind together. In the two and a half years that led to our big break, we became a family.

And we needed one another. With the exception of Keeley, whose family is all sunshine and literal supportive rainbows, the rest of us had a lot of issues at home when we were kids. My parents worked all the time, and Cameron basically raised me and Carrie until she went to nursing school. Valerie's mom, Tonya, was *too* involved in her business but never emotionally available to her daughter. Jane's parents have always been the scary, controlling kind of religious, and Riker's were one disastrous argument away from their inevitable divorce. We kind of saved one another.

I might not want to be around Valerie this summer, but after the part I played in this band's collapse, I owe them this. I can suck it up and play my bass, sing my songs, and smile for the cameras.

Valerie steps inside with a stack of pizza boxes before the conversation can turn any more sour.

"Food's here," she says quietly.

"Great, I'm hungry!" Jane says, a little too eagerly. The energy in the room shifts with Valerie's return.

Keeley ordered a truly unhinged amount of pizza, and we eat it on the floor while passing around the Costco-sized bottle of rosé and talking through Valerie's proposed set list. Once we've gone over it a few times, the time and care she put into it is evident— she's trying to feature everyone's talents and explore our discography as widely as possible. Other than swapping a few songs around for instrument changes and tech requirements, we're all in agreement that it's a good set.

I'm not surprised. Valerie's always been smart about this industry in a way I wasn't. The media calls her calculating, but I think she just knows her shit—and doesn't take any.

I gloss over the acoustic portion that has Valerie and me singing "Every Touch" and "Making Memories" back-to-back. My neck heats, and I wish I could just volunteer Riker to sing those for me. If it were any other concert, we could get away with changing up more parts, but the fans will want to see Valerie and me together. I'm not prepared to sing with her the way we used to, though, sharing one microphone like we were trading secrets.

We're all a lot more relaxed after stuffing ourselves with pepperoni, pineapple, and jalapeño pizza and habanero wings—and plenty of rosé.

"My sinuses haven't been this clear in years. I'm ready to go sing," Valerie says.

"Ugh, after all that dairy?" Keeley asks.

"You're the one who ordered pizza!" Riker adds.

Jane smiles. "We can rehearse more in the morning, but want to play through something? I have a little studio in the basement."

"No time like the present!" Valerie says.

"I vote for 'Making Memories' because I don't have to sing on that one," Keeley says.

I open my mouth to protest, but Riker's already clocked my discomfort. "I can't do a ballad or I'll fall asleep. That yummy wine is making me all warm and fuzzy." Riker's always had a hilariously low tolerance for someone built like Chris Hemsworth.

"Fine. Let's do 'Midnight Road Trip,' then, since we can play it blindfolded," Keeley says.

The others head downstairs, but Riker hangs back with me to tidy up the dishes. "Thanks for that, dude," I murmur, when everyone else is out of earshot.

"I wasn't going to let you clean up on your own. That would make me look like a dick."

I roll my eyes. That's Riker, always deflecting. "I'm talking about the song."

Riker shrugs. "Figured 'Memories' might be a bit heavy for day one. Baby steps," he says.

"Appreciate it."

Once the kitchen is clean, we gather water bottles and head downstairs. I hadn't paid much attention to the space when I lugged my instruments down here earlier, but it's practically a shrine to all of Jane's work—including Glitter Bats.

There are official photos and candids, framed vinyls of each album, even her statuette from the one major award we won: an MTV Video Music Award for "Ghosts." My chest tightens. All of my own Glitter Bats memorabilia sits in plastic storage containers in the back of my closet, packed neatly away where it can't remind me of old dreams.

Very old dreams. I've moved on from all of this. There's no way I'm giving Label another album, and I hope the others are on the same page.

Suddenly, I'm nervous to get started. But even though my hands tremble, I go sit on a stool next to Valerie and pick up my bass. The usual pre-rehearsal ritual begins: Riker hooks a guitar into his amp and starts to fiddle with pedals, Jane plugs a laptop into her Korg and launches her MIDI controller, and Keeley fiddles with her drum kit and cymbal setup. I hum a soft vocal warm-up while I tune my bass, and Valerie joins in like it's second nature.

"Maybe just the original arrangement to warm up?" she asks as everyone finishes their adjustments.

We're all in agreement, and after we turn on the amps, Keeley counts us off, sitting jauntily on her throne.

It's been a while, but the chords come to me like riding a bike. Still, I have to really focus on what my fingers are doing—I play more piano than bass or even guitar these days, and my calluses are gone. It also doesn't help that every inch of me shakes with anxiety.

And when Valerie opens her mouth to sing the first verse, I nearly fumble the bass line.

It's not like I haven't heard her sing in years—Carrie made me watch some episodes of *Epic Theme Song* the last time she visited, but that's different. Valerie has a great voice for the musical theater style, but she was really made for rock. Her warm mezzo-soprano is rich like honey but sharp as a knife. Something about the way she sings our songs has always captivated me, and tonight is no different.

When we get to the chorus, I don't even have to think about it—I jump right in with her.

midnight road trip, windows down
let's go now and leave this town

It feels almost too easy, singing these words. They're cheesy—I mean, what song isn't when you wrote it at eighteen—but hearing our voices together after so long gets my heart racing.

It feels like the first time we all played together at camp twelve years ago. We were doing a cover of "Should I Stay or Should I Go" for the final performance, and we decided to mess with the arrangement to split the vocals between Valerie and me. We'd practiced it a hundred times that week, but on the night of the showcase, something clicked. Even at fifteen, Valerie sang like an angel, and when I jumped in to harmonize with her . . .

It felt like destiny.

Valerie catches my eyes as we sing together, something strange and beautiful and determined crossing her face, and it makes my pulse pound even faster. We're not miked, but the room is small enough that we don't have to be.

our destination's in the sky
we'll chase the stars in our eyes

Despite her earlier reservations about singing, Keeley joins in on the bridge so Val and I can both jump the octave, and it just *works*. Like magic.

After we finish the song, Riker whoops. "Fuck yeah!"

"That was solid," Keeley says. "I knew we could do it in our sleep."

Jane's tearing up. "I'm sorry, I might be a little tipsy from that stupid rosé, but I can't believe it took us so long to play together again. I'm really glad we're doing this."

Valerie is suspiciously silent. I turn to her, expecting to see joy or triumph on her face. Instead, she's frowning at her hands.

"Val?"

"I'm tired. I'm going to go to bed," she says.

And then she leaves the room without another word.

EXCLUSIVE: Glitter Bats to Reunite at Hollywood Stadium

BY MARY KATE HAMPTON, STAFF WRITER, *BUZZWORD*

I got my start covering Glitter Bats when I was a college intern for *Buzzword*. They were a bunch of kids from Seattle with a weird-sounding band name, so no one else wanted to write the story. I jumped at the chance, and as they took off, I was lucky enough to keep following them. It didn't hurt that I fell in love with their music from the first few bars of "Midnight Road Trip."

But I never thought I'd get to say THIS: Glitter Bats are back! I know what you're thinking—it's Valerie Quinn, Riker Maddox, Keeley Cunningham, Jane Mercer, and whatever bass player they're able to find for the event. But nope, it's even better than we could have hoped.

I received an exclusive confirmation from Caleb Sloane's team that the butter-voiced legend himself will be returning to the stage! The official statement from Ortega Management stated, "Caleb Sloane is eager to be back onstage with his friends. He's been working closely with Valerie Quinn to plan some surprises they know fans will love."

Is "working closely" code for "back together"? For years, rumors flew that Sloane and Quinn were more than friends and bandmates, but those rumors were never confirmed. It didn't stop fans from shipping *CalErie* (truly the worst portmanteau, Glitterbugs), drawing art, and writing epic fan fiction. I haven't checked FanficDreamArchive yet, but I'm sure there will be a wealth of new fic inspired by this reunion.

When we reached out to Label Records, they confirmed the concert will be pro-shot in high definition. No news on if this means a livestream or if they're partnering with a streaming service to release a concert film—but my money is on a collaboration with The Network since Mercer is working on a project for the streaming service, and Quinn stars in *Epic Theme Song*. Go stream the show if you haven't already—it's delightful, and we're all hoping for a season three.

Glitter Bats will be playing at the Hollywood Stadium August 15th. For tickets, visit TicketChampion.Live.

Wondering what the rest of the band has been up to since that last concert? Click here for more: **Your Favorite Bands: Where Are They Now?**

5

The next day, I take advantage of the quiet house and sneak in an early-morning shower.

After, I slip back to my room with plans to stash my toiletries and head down to find coffee, but when I hear Riker's always-bouncing footsteps in the hall, my first reaction is to hide. I acted so weird last night.

Cringing, I sink onto the bed. There's no good reason for the way I left rehearsal, but after that first run-through of "Midnight Road Trip," I thought I was about to cry from how *perfect* it felt, playing with the Glitter Bats again. Before anyone could see me lose control, I had to get out of that room.

It might feel like the old days, but this band isn't my family anymore. They can't see me as anything other than poised and ready to bring my all.

And any vulnerability? I have to smother it.

So instead of facing the rest of the Glitter Bats, I wrap up in the fluffy white duvet and google myself, trying to figure out the response to the reunion news. Some sources even say nice things about me. Others complain that reunions are "money grabs" or "desperate attempts to cling to relevance," but a lot of fans are excited to see us again. Every member in the band has fans, but people are excited to see me and Caleb sing together, specifically.

No pressure.

It's exactly the feedback I was hoping for to help my image, but after last night, my stomach twists with shame. Was Keeley right? Am I just using them to try to save my show?

I toss my phone down on the sheets with a huff. It's not like I'm forcing anyone to be here. If they didn't want to do this, they should have said no . . . then we all could have moved on with our lives, former friends growing forever apart.

My motives might have been selfish at first, but I'm glad we're here. All these years, I kept telling myself I didn't need the Glitter Bats, but last night proved just how much I missed this. I just don't think anyone else feels the same.

Running my hands through my hair, I fall face down on the bed, groaning. I have to believe the band is here because they want to be, otherwise I won't be able to shake the guilt churning in my gut.

My phone buzzes softly from where it lies on the bed next to me, and I grasp for it, propping myself up on my elbows to check the notification. We promised not to bug Wade, but he's texted me anyway. I hope he'll have good news . . . because fuck, I wasn't ready for all of the feelings a Glitter Bats reunion would bring up.

Unfortunately, he doesn't have much of an update about *Epic Theme Song*.

Wade: Before we headed to the park this morning, I heard from my contact at The Network. The press is moving in the right direction. They wouldn't say what it's going to take to get the green light, but they said it's not a No yet.

It hasn't been a *no* for the past year, but it hasn't been a *yes* either.

Me: Okay, so what should I do?

Wade: Fans will love the reunion—I know you've seen it, but there's already been positive buzz, and we're expecting to see more as things get closer. Tickets don't go on sale for another week, but our contact at TicketChampion said they have thousands of people signed up for the presale already. The word is getting out. Keep doing what you're doing!

Me: That's it?

Wade: Hang in there, kiddo. We know these things don't happen overnight.

Keep doing what I'm doing? So far I've managed to alienate my band and make everything weird and awkward, but hopefully today's rehearsal will go more smoothly. I know I made a mess of things, but I forgot what it feels like to sing with Caleb.

He sounded so good it hurt.

My mind replays last night as I force myself off the bed. Caleb was always a great bass player, but his real power was in his golden voice, and it's just gotten better in the years since we sang together. Something about this man singing always hits me like lightning— and that's how I fell in love with him the first time.

I blink hard, forcing the thought away. I refuse to fall in love with Caleb Sloane again. There's too much history between us that needs to stay in the past, so many reasons it didn't work that contributed to our breakup. He hurt me too.

I can resist the siren song of his perfect voice for one summer.

Digging through my duffle, I wonder if I should make an effort to look presentable. I could hide out longer, do my hair, and put on the blue romper that makes my eyes pop. Instead, I pull out leggings and an oversized tee, opting for comfort over polish. I have no one to impress.

Like Wade said, I need to keep doing what I'm doing to save my career. No distractions. Just enough nostalgia to get to the fans, but not enough to get to me. I *will* fix my reputation. It's this determination that fuels me enough to face the others downstairs.

All of my anxiety was for nothing, because it's just Jane and Riker eating bagels, and they seem to be the least mad at me. Without a word, Jane hands me a cup of coffee from her Chemex—one fancy coffee apparatus out of four visible on the counter—and it tastes so good I pause on my way to the island to savor it. She obviously buys the good beans.

"Where are the others?"

Riker chuckles. "Keeley and Caleb got up early to go on a 'beach run.' That sounds like pure hell to me, so I abstained."

"Says the gym rat," Jane says with an eye roll. "Don't you have one of the best fitness coaches in town?"

"Yeah, I never thought I'd like weights, but I can't argue with the result," Riker says with a grin, putting down his bagel to flex one of his biceps. "But for cardio, he puts me on the treadmill or elliptical. I'm not going to go run on sand—that's just masochistic."

"Exercise gives you endorphins—happy people don't kill their bandmates," Keeley says as she walks into the kitchen, dropping into the conversation without missing a beat.

Caleb is right behind her, his brow damp with sweat that makes his curls stick to his forehead. His cheeks are flushed and glowing, and he looks the way he always did after a long set.

Sweaty. Exhausted. Grinning.

It still makes my knees weak.

Fuck.

I take a sip from my mug to keep myself from doing something entirely too stupid, like launching at him and getting sweaty myself . . . as if he'd even be receptive to that. I stare down at the coffee, hoping my hair hides my flushing cheeks.

"Well, I just hope you're both planning to shower before we rehearse all day," Riker says.

"No, I'm going to stay really stinky and sit next to you," Keeley says, reaching over him for a bagel. "Of course I'm going to fucking shower."

"You can go first. I'll caffeinate," Caleb says. He steps over to the sink and pulls a mug out of the cabinet.

"You don't want to join me?" Keeley says with a wink.

Caleb rolls his eyes. "I know I'm irresistible, but keep your pants on, Cunningham," he says, and she disappears upstairs with a cackle.

I make an effort to laugh, but it sounds hollow.

Keeley has always been a flirt, and this is obviously a joke, but something about it bothers me now. Logically, I know nothing is going on between Keeley and Caleb. They were instantly like siblings at camp, teasing each other and starting the prank war that nearly got us all kicked out. But even if their relationship has changed, it's not like I have any claim to Caleb. Our love is long gone.

I shift uncomfortably in my seat. After all this time, it still feels wrong to think about him with anyone else. Desperate to do something with my hands, I reach for a bagel and begin slathering it with the open cream cheese on the counter. God, I need to sort out these old feelings before I ruin this for everyone. If I dragged Caleb out here just to revive all of our old drama, I will never forgive myself.

I will be nothing but a goddamn professional, because nothing can ruin this. If I want to save my show (and by extension, my career), I need good press, not bad memories.

I shove a bite into my mouth.

"Would you like some coffee?" Jane asks Caleb, who is still hovering by the counter, empty mug in hand.

"No, thank you—actually, do you have tea?" Caleb says.

"Of course! In the basket next to the fridge."

Caleb rummages around, and Riker snorts around his bagel. "Things really have changed if the king of energy drinks and quadruple espresso switched to tea."

Caleb grins, but there's self-deprecation there. "Yeah, I found out caffeine was bad for my anxiety, so my therapist suggested I cut back."

"Dude, you're in therapy too? I love therapy!" Riker says, and there's not a shred of sarcasm in his voice. He genuinely loves things without reservation, like a six-foot-four puppy.

I set down my own mug. "We all got famous as teenagers. Pretty sure we're all in therapy," I say. Everyone turns to where I've perched at the counter, and instantly, I regret opening my mouth. Do they think I'm making light of mental health?

The four bandmates in this house used to be the only people in the world I could be myself with. Now, I don't know what's safe to joke about and what I need to keep to myself. My cheeks warm.

Caleb breaks the tension, chuckling as he puts the kettle on the stove. "You're absolutely right. Label Records should be paying for it too."

I snort. Their questionable business practices and mind games certainly caused enough damage to all of us.

We finish our breakfast in relative silence, Caleb preparing his tea and leaning against the pantry to savor it, Jane passing out bananas and orange juice, and Riker shooing Jane away so he can start the dishes. Keeley joins us after her shower twenty minutes later, and then Caleb disappears up the stairs.

When we're ready to practice, we head to the basement studio, plug ourselves in, and spend some time tuning and warming up. We start the day with "Ghosts," jumping right in to something complicated and challenging. Today, it's less tight, we're out of sync, and Keeley stops drumming after I miss an entrance. Everyone else crashes to a stop.

"What's going on with the timing?" she demands, gesturing at me with an accusing drumstick. "You're supposed to come in on the *one*."

"I know that," I snap, ears ringing. "I was distracted by Riker messing up the lick—I always use that as my cue." I turn on him. "Dude, you helped us *write* this song! What gives?"

Riker raises his hands placatingly, his Gibson swaying on his favorite studded strap. "I played one wrong note. It's similar to one of the Lime Velvet songs, and I missed it. It'll be right next time."

With our tight rehearsal schedule, *next time* isn't going to cut it. "It better," I hiss, straightening out my cord with a flip of my mic hand. "We have to get this right."

Caleb sighs beside me, but he doesn't say anything.

"Hey, you aren't perfect either! You were a little flat on the verse, babe," Keeley drawls.

"As if you played it perfectly," I say. Arguing with Keeley like this puts a bad taste in my mouth, but I can't stop myself. We're a disaster, and we don't have the luxury of starting from scratch on every song.

Keeley drops her sticks, pointing at herself. "Me? Tell me one thing I did wrong. I'm all ears, Valerie." She laughs dryly as I stare at her, trying to come up with something, but she's right. Not that I'm going to admit it. "Nothing? That's because I did my fucking job and *practiced* before we all got together. Unlike you, clearly."

I did practice. Today is just a mess, and Keeley isn't helping. I roll my eyes. "You could check your attitude, for starters," I mutter.

She gapes at me, rising from the throne. "Say that to my face, I dare you."

"Stop it!" Jane says, rising from her bench, eyes widening. "Arguing isn't going to get us anywhere."

Keeley raises a hand to her neck, chagrined. "Sorry, Jane."

"I'm the one you need to apologize to!" I spit, setting my jaw. "You've been a total bitch since I got here." My throat tightens the moment the words slip out, and I know it was too far.

"*Dude*," Riker says, narrowing his eyes at me.

Keeley reddens, slamming her hands on her thighs and glaring in my direction. "Are you fucking serious right now?"

The room falls silent as we stare each other down. This isn't the Keeley I know. She's snarky, but she was always a great collaborator. Any criticism was constructive.

"Well, this clearly isn't working," Caleb finally says before leaning down to chug from his water bottle. His throat bobs, and I look away.

"We'll figure it out. Maybe we need to try another song," Jane suggests, flipping through her notebook.

Keeley swivels in her throne to look at Jane. "Will another song magically fix Valerie's raging personality issues?" she says. I wince at the sheer hostility in her voice, knowing full well I put it there. Keeley stands. "I didn't sign up for a summer of bullshit. If this is how it's going to be, I'm fucking out."

"Whoa, whoa, whoa," Riker says, eyes wide. He never did like it when tensions rose. "Let's not be hasty. Jane's right, we should try another song."

I clear my throat, neck warming. "No. We need to play 'Ghosts' until we get it right."

Keeley rolls her eyes. "Whatever you say, *boss*." I set my shoulders at the jab. She counts us off without warning, and I hit my entrance for the second verse alright—I hit it so hard it feels like I'm punching the lyrics. Caleb flinches beside me.

But I'll be damned if I miss another note. There's no point in this reunion if we suck. It's a herculean effort to get through the song, and the next one isn't much better.

Our late lunch is a much-needed break, but eating doesn't cool the tension. We come back to our instruments grumpy and sniping, and I'm faced with the overwhelming fear that we can't pull this off. Maybe there's too much rust—or maybe there's too much history between us.

Maybe they can't forgive me enough to get through an entire set.

After another hour of discord, we stop again. "This isn't productive. Let's take a break and come back to it tomorrow," Caleb says.

"We haven't gotten anything done!" I say.

He slips his bass strap off his shoulder, already beginning to stow the instrument away. "Do you really think we're going to get anywhere? We all need to clear our heads."

I open my mouth to argue but stop myself. This practice is miserable, and I'm not at my best. Turns out you can't muscle through music and expect it to feel good. "You're right," I say.

"*Some* of us could benefit from more practice," Keeley says pointedly.

"It's been a while since we played these songs. We're all a little rusty," Jane says kindly, even though she's been note-perfect all rehearsal, throwing in new riffs and filling in harmonies like that last Vegas show was yesterday. "Let's call it for today."

"I'm going to . . . yeah," I say, neck pricking with shame at the way I talked to everyone. I put down my guitar and hurry back up the stairs to go hide in my room . . . again. The walls are thin enough that when everyone has made it back upstairs, I can hear the conversation in the hall, and I worry for a minute that it's about me.

But I quietly put my ear against the door, and . . . it's not. They're talking about evening plans, maybe going out. No one knocks on my door to invite me along. I guess I burned any lingering goodwill between us all.

Fine. I'm perfectly fine staying here alone and wallowing. Did I really beg the band to reunite for this disaster?

The front door opens and closes, and for a few minutes, I think I'm alone, but I hear someone shuffling outside. A soft knock follows. The last thing I want to do is face any of my former bandmates right now.

"Valerie?" Jane calls. "I know you're in there."

I sag a little, knowing this at least won't be a fight. "Come in," I say. She slips into the room with a reusable grocery sack on her arm.

"Today was rough. You doing okay?" she asks.

"I . . . may be a little on edge with all the pressure of this show," I say, sighing.

She nods, leaning against the doorframe. "I can tell."

I bite my lip as the shame washes over me. "I thought things would feel the same as soon as we picked up our instruments. Instead, everything is such a disaster."

"It just might take a few days to get back into the swing of things," she says, too kindly. Jane was always the best of us. Honestly, in the few years we were making music, I felt more cared for by her than I ever was by my mom. Jane kept us hydrated, mediated arguments between me and, well . . . everyone else, and always just assumed the best in me.

Even when my best was lacking. Like today.

I grimace. "Thank you, but I know I fucked everything up."

She does me the courtesy of holding back a response. "Well, I have something that might make you feel better." She digs into the sack. "I went to grab snacks last night before you got out here, and I couldn't resist picking up a bottle."

In her hand is a container of Pink Crush, the shade I used to dye my hair back in the day. Even when we could afford a stylist, I still used the cheap stuff because I liked being able to touch it up constantly. I can't help it—I grin at her through watery eyes, and it's the first real smile I've had all day.

God bless Jane Mercer for just existing in this world like the angel she is.

My blond hair is already platinum, so it won't take much prep. This could be the first normal thing that's happened all weekend. Whatever stylist we end up hiring will bemoan my choice of drugstore dye, but at least it's vegan. Can't do too much damage.

"Thank you—seriously," I say, hugging the bottle to my chest.

"When I bought it, I wasn't sure if I was going to give it to you or not. But after this afternoon . . . well, I thought it might help if you feel more like the old Valerie," she says. "You're welcome to use my shower. It scrubs clean easily."

Jane has given me an out for the solitary evening I thought I wanted, and I'm grateful—but then I recognize an opportunity to mend another fence. Caleb and I were thick as thieves and used to tell each other everything, but I had special relationships with each of the others too. In Jane's case, I used to go to her for the advice I could never get from my family, and she used to vent to me in private when her parents were being too much.

And Jane may not be outwardly upset with me like the others, but we've grown apart and it makes my heart ache. I *want* to be her friend again.

"Want to help me?" I ask, gesturing with the bottle. "Like old times?" Jane was always the one who was patient enough to help me keep my head pink, and we spent long afternoons with hair dye and nail polish in hotel bathrooms. "You know I suck at getting the back."

Jane grins. "Yeah, I'd love to help. I'll go make us some lattes first?"

"Perfect."

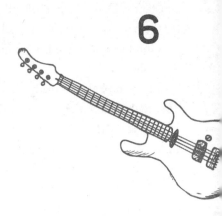

6

Caleb

Riker's superpower is finding a hidden gem in every neighborhood. He used to make it a challenge when we were touring from city to city, and he's clearly held on to the magic.

Twenty minutes online, and we're heading to karaoke a solid walk from Jane's house. Keeley wouldn't allow me out of the house in my usual summer uniform of a T-shirt and shorts, so I've changed into a different T-shirt and faded black jeans, which is about the best I can do at the moment.

At least I'm comfortable on the breezy two-mile walk.

Most of my stage wardrobe is gone, but the others have that effortless rock star look down. Riker's wearing a muscle tank and pale jeans with a flannel tied around his waist, and Keeley changed into a cropped Pearl T-shirt, a denim jacket, and ripped white shorts that make her look even taller. Between my two towering friends, I'm sure I look like a hobbit, but being on the shorter side never bothered me.

We're quiet at first as we walk, but quickly default to the worst kind of small talk.

"Siren Karaoke Bar—don't they know sirens sing sailors to their deaths?" Keeley says, gesturing at the sign. "It's kind of a weird metaphor."

She's acting a little too normal after what went down in practice, but I don't say anything about it. We all know Keeley doesn't stay mad for long. And, well, Valerie was kind of being awful to her. I wish I knew how to fix it.

I blink. That's not my job anymore.

With a sigh, I follow the others inside the shabby-looking bar, which is surprisingly bright and eclectic within. The place really plays up the theme, making it look more like a seafood joint than a karaoke bar. There are kitschy seashells and anchors in all the decor, and the stage has an under-the-sea backdrop. There's even a silhouette of a mermaid on the rocks on one of the walls.

Total tourist trap.

"Yikes," Keeley mutters.

"It's . . . a lot," I say.

"Well, the reviews are good." Riker laughs, gently punching my shoulder. "So they have a huge selection on tap for you beer snobs, but they also have a full bar, and I'm thinking we need shots. Desperately."

We find an open table close to the stage. As soon as we're seated, we start scanning the sticky drink menu.

"I will do exactly one round of shots, Riker. I do not bounce back the way I did in my early twenties, and I'm not about to suffer one of those hellish practices with a hangover," Keeley says.

I nod, thinking about the last time I got drunk at Cam and Leah's and crashed on their couch for a good twelve hours afterward. "One round is about my max too."

"Will that be enough to convince you to sing?" Riker asks, tilting his head at the stage, twisting his mouth into a wry smirk.

"Absolutely not," Keeley says. "With all the press about the reunion, that's just asking to go viral. No thank you."

I open my mouth to agree with her, because we both know Riker isn't serious.

But then I remember the pressure on Valerie's public image— the whole band's image. The thing is, I do still know Valerie. She was stressed out today, which is why she lashed out. It's not okay, but maybe if there were less pressure, she wouldn't be so wound up.

And I think I can help with that.

"Maybe it's not the worst idea to be . . . seen," I say. "Out in public . . . having fun together. It'll be good press for the reunion." The idea makes my stomach churn, but we might as well dive in headfirst.

Riker's eyes widen. "Hey, if you're serious, I can see if MK is around. I'm sure she'd love to get a quick sound bite."

My mind reels, and I clutch the tabletop, immediately regretting everything. I don't know if I'm ready for publicity. The familiar buzz of anxiety hums in the back of my brain, and I close my eyes for a second, trying to ease out of the mental spiral.

"You just want an excuse to see your little crush," Keeley says.

"I do not have a little crush!" Riker insists, gaping. Which is hilarious, because he's been watching her with puppy-dog eyes from afar since that first interview. "We've just . . . stayed in touch is all. She texted me a congratulations when the announcement dropped."

Mary Kate Hampton is a journalist who's been covering the Glitter Bats from the start. It was kind of random at the time—no one wanted to write another story about viral teenagers with no record deal, so they gave the story to the college intern. But as we took off, so did Mary Kate's career. Her Glitter Bats coverage earned her a permanent staff writing job on the entertainment beat for *Buzzword*.

I've always liked Mary Kate. Even with the constant speculation about me and Valerie in the media, Mary Kate did her best to take a wider approach, focusing on the band as a whole. She never tried to trick us into saying something embarrassing or sensational—she just did her job. The same can't be said for a lot of her peers.

If we're going to do this, I trust Mary Kate to do it right.

"You should text her," I say, heart hammering at the thought of inviting the attention. But it's going to happen sooner or later.

"You can't be serious," Keeley says. "Dude, you can ease into it. I know this is going to be a lot for you."

I shoot her a grateful glance. "It's better than being spotted by someone we don't trust. You all wanted to go out, but we know the risks of that. Inviting Mary Kate ensures at least a balanced report."

Riker nods, looking at his phone. "Well, that's good, because she's already on her way. I'll text Jane too, see if she can get Valerie out."

That makes sense for the optics, but my shoulders tense at the idea of playing nice with Valerie for the press, especially after this afternoon. I know we're going to have to do it eventually, but today felt so *off*. Faking it isn't going to be fun, especially since all it does is bring back the memories of how easy it used to be.

Back in the Glitter Bats heyday, a tough rehearsal rarely made us snipe at one another. We were a cohesive unit, able to get past our issues and focus on the music. And with Valerie, it was like I could read her mind. I could tell where she was headed during a song, when she wanted to take things in a different direction, even when she wanted to improvise—I just knew implicitly what made her tick, both as a musician and as a partner.

Until I got it all wrong.

"What, so we can be seen as the big happy family we used to be?" Keeley drawls, practically reading my mind.

But I need Keeley to chill out.

I sigh. "You know, we might be able to get through a rehearsal if you didn't keep antagonizing her."

"She was antagonizing me back!" Keeley says.

I lower my voice, trying to keep my tone soft despite the general noise of a bar on Saturday night. "Does that really make it better? I'm not talking about Valerie right now—we need to hold her accountable too—but you really didn't help by dishing it back."

Keeley raises her hands, but she looks a little sheepish. "Did I say anything untrue today?"

"It's not what you said, it's how you said it," Riker says.

"That's all I'm saying," I say. By the way Val played last night, it's clear she can still do this. Today wasn't about skill—it was about old wounds. It doesn't help that there's a lot riding on this for Valerie. Even I can see past my hurt feelings enough to know that.

If nothing else, we'll have to be civil to get through this.

"It's not like any of us have had a chance to play together recently," Riker continues, rubbing his temples. "We're all out of sync—and it's not all on Valerie. I forgot the chords on the bridge to 'Fallout,' and she was right about that 'Ghosts' riff—there was no excuse for screwing it up."

He's being generous—I don't think he messed up on "Fallout"— but I appreciate him backing me up. Riker has always been a peacemaker, sometimes to a fault. But I get why Keeley's upset. When my relationship with Valerie imploded, it tore the band apart. We all sacrificed a lot to pursue our music in the first place, but Keeley said no to some prestigious college offers that would have led her down a very different path. Her career has been solid, but she must have felt abandoned and hurt when the band collapsed.

I squeeze her shoulder, and she sighs, playfully shrugging me off.

"*Fine*," Keeley says. "I'll try to play nice—but Valerie's going to take it down a notch. We also need her to remember her entrances without Jane directing everything into the talkback. Jane needs to sing."

Jane is a fantastic harmonizer, but as our keys player, she also took on the role of cueing us onstage when we wanted to vamp or improvise. It meant juggling two mics: one that only played into the monitors, and another that played in the actual mix, but Jane is just that good. Our sets have always been tight with her keeping us in line—but it's not something we want to rely on.

"I think Valerie will be receptive to *constructive* feedback," I say. Valerie has always cared about the music. "She always wants to be better."

Keeley throws up her hands. "That's true enough. It doesn't mean I don't need a drink, though."

Fortunately, a server shows up and takes our orders. I agree to a single shot of tequila, after which I intend to nurse a beer for the rest of the night. We also order food because the menu looks incredible—a chimichanga, quesadilla, and taquito sampler with fresh guacamole and queso. This is so much better than the seafood I expected.

Mary Kate waves at us from the entrance less than an hour later, so I suspect Riker texted her before he even *suggested* we go out, but I don't have the heart to call him on it. Maybe we're all hoping to drum up good press.

I've never been comfortable with the media, but Mary Kate is about as low-pressure as it gets. Hell, she covered us so often and for so long that she's basically an honorary Glitter Bat at this point. I also strongly suspect she ran one of our old fan accounts, because @GlitterbugsUnofficial always knew just a little *too* much, too soon, but she always refused to confirm—or deny—my theory. Still, my hands sweat as she approaches our table.

Mary Kate is almost as tall as Keeley in her towering heels, with shiny brown hair cascading past her shoulders and a rosy blush on her pale cheeks. She wears a crisp white button-down over black pants that make her look more like a lawyer than a journalist, but she greets each of us with a dimpled smile and a hug.

Even me.

"It's so great to see my favorite band back together!" she says as she pulls away. "Damn, Caleb, you look great. Where have you been hiding?"

I grin. "On or off the record?"

Mary Kate laughs. "That's up to you. Riker just invited me to hang out."

"I wasn't aware you were *hanging-out* kind of friends," Keeley says.

Riker flushes, and Mary Kate shrugs. "Why not?" she asks. "I've known you all as long as anyone in this town."

Her ease calms my nerves a bit. "Well, you're welcome to say on the record that I've been exploring a new career as a music educator."

Mary Kate makes a note in her phone, then bites her lip. "I did want to ask a quick business question before we have fun. I'd really love to get an exclusive opportunity to cover the reunion for *Buzzword*: visit a couple rehearsals, hang out backstage, film some interviews. You'd all have a final say in what you want to share, and I'd just be privileged to be a small part of it. What do you think?"

Riker nods. "That would be rad!" Keeley shoots him a look, so he quickly backpedals. "*But* we should probably make sure the rest of the band is on board, so I think it's best if you formally run it past Wade. But I'll tell him I'm in."

I swallow—filmed interviews?—but I nod. "Me too."

We turn to Keeley, who runs a hand through her bob. "Fine, but I'm not talking about my feelings regarding the reunion on the record."

Mary Kate's eyes widen, and I know she wants to ask about the tension, but thankfully she holds back. "So are any of you going to go up there, or is this just observing for fun?"

Keeley grins. "Oh, I already signed Caleb up."

All the blood drains from my face. "What?" When the hell did she even have time to do that? She hasn't left the table. I know I agreed to this, but I thought I had more time to gather my nerves.

"Oh yeah. Cheap Trick. Get ready, 'cause you're tenth on the list." She pulls an eyeliner stick and a small tub of pomade out of her bag and hands them to me.

"No way, I'm not doing that," I say, understanding *exactly* where she is going with this. Keeley always pushed me out of my comfort zone, and I used to love her for it when it got me out of my own head.

But this . . . this isn't going to feel right. Not yet.

She raises her brows. "You need to get your stage presence back. The stakes could not be lower tonight. So go make yourself hot, and get up there."

I turn to Riker for the usual backup, but he just shrugs, betraying me. "Keeley's right. Go make yourself hot."

Damn him for always going with the flow. I sigh but grab the supplies and head into the stuffy bathroom. Keeley has a remarkable memory—this is the Perversion eyeliner stick from Urban Decay, the exact shade I'd used once I could afford more than the cheap drugstore pencils. I inhale sharply, staring at my blank face in the mirror, my normal hair.

It's the face I'm used to seeing.

Putting on the makeup feels oddly symbolic. Carefully, I line my eyes with Perversion, then smudge it with my pinky to cover up my shaky application. Once I'm satisfied that it doesn't look terrible, I get my hair a little damp in the sink, then slowly, methodically, scrunch it with the pomade over the basin, defining my natural almost-curls.

Glancing up at myself, I freeze. My hair isn't the same length I'd rock on tour, but I look like him again: Caleb Sloane, rock star. I didn't realize how easily he'd return until he was staring back at me in the mirror.

Huh.

By the time I emerge, there's an emcee introducing the next person on the stage—by the sash, it looks like a bride-to-be on the first leg of a bachelorette party singing an off-key but enthusiastic rendition of "Still Into You" by Paramore. A lot of Paramore fans were kind enough to like our stuff too, even though we entered the scene much later, and I wouldn't dream of comparing us in any way—except to say we deeply admire their music. Still, we've shared space on plenty of playlists over the years.

Maybe the eyeliner was a mistake. If any of the people in the bride's entourage are Glitterbugs and post this online, I might just go viral as planned. I'm not ready.

But I square my shoulders, steeling myself.

"There he is!" Keeley calls, and I hurry over, shading my face with my hand. "You sexy motherfucker."

"This was a terrible idea," I mutter.

"You look so good, holy shit," Riker says. "It's like you went in the bathroom as Teacher Caleb and came back as Heartthrob Caleb."

"Maybe *you* should put on eyeliner and parade around onstage," I say, trying to shove my shoulders down from where they're hunched to my ears.

"Dude, *please* let me record this," Mary Kate says, pressing her palms together at her chin in a pleading gesture.

"Only if he's comfortable," Riker says instantly. I soften at his defense. Even though he invited MK here, Riker's got my back, and I know Keeley does too. It helps me breathe a little easier knowing I have friends I can rely on. I forgot how nice it was to have them in my corner . . . even as they're literally pushing me onstage.

The emcee is calling next up, and it's my number. I sigh, knowing full well I've lost control of the situation. "Record it, stream it, I don't care. I'm going to go get this over with."

I weave around the tables to the stage, trying to ignore the murmurs of the room. There's no way anyone knows I'm here—or, at least, no way *everyone* knows who I am—but if they do, I don't want to know. Before he presses play, the emcee shows me where to see the screen, but I could sing the lyrics to "I Want You to Want Me" in my sleep.

Because *10 Things I Hate About You* is Valerie's favorite movie.

My heart races, and my hands shake on the mic, but I do my best to relax as I wait for the cue, jumping in with a clear voice. After the first line, the bar falls quiet. Phones come out to record. Someone in the bachelorette party squeals. But instead of freezing up, I feel an electric spark running through my veins with each beat of my hammering heart. I croon, I smirk, I swagger across the tiny stage. It feels so good to just be up here making people happy again. The excitement in the room is so thick you could cut it with a knife.

And when I get to the chorus, I see her across the bar, leaning with a casual ease against the back wall.

Straight out of a dream, hazy and dim in the lights of the room—she looks like she did *then*. It catapults me six years back. Valerie's eyeliner is thick, she's rocking ripped black jeans and an old The Clash T-shirt that I could swear she stole from me during the *Wanderlust* tour, and . . . and her hair is bright pink.

God, that hair. I can't help but think of all those times I buried my fingers in those gorgeous locks. I'm not proud of it, but that pink hair has continued to star in so many of my fantasies. I even remember what that damn color is called—Pink Crush, as if it could ever be so innocent. But it's seared into my memory, formative and life-changing. An instant turn-on.

And seeing her here, like this, makes all of my remaining nerves melt away.

Before I can stop myself, I wave her up to join me onstage.

@GlitterbugsUnofficial

SPOTTED: The Glitter Bats entering Siren Karaoke
Bar in Venice! Our source confirmed Riker, Keeley,
and CALEB FUCKING SLOANE entered the building
tonight about ten minutes ago. No idea if they're
singing, but if you're local, you should get
there ASAP!
We're back, babes!

7

If the song choice hadn't surprised me enough, the eyeliner stops me in my tracks.

Urban Decay Perversion, on top of tousled waves, and that electric presence that casts the whole room in neon—Caleb looks and sounds incredible. The original key of this song is at the top of his range, but his voice is sinfully sweet on the highest notes. I've missed every version of Caleb, but especially this one—free, fun, having the time of his life and making you feel like it's the time of yours just because you're witnessing his joy.

Now he's waving me up there in the middle of a song.

It's like I'm time traveling six years in the past—or hell, *ten*—to become the girl I was back then, the girl who sang with him. I'm even wearing a vintage T-shirt I stole from him years ago, and it's become so integrated into my own wardrobe that I forgot where it came from until this very moment. The room is full of people recording, and this is going to get out . . . which I remember is exactly what I wanted. Caleb is throwing me a lifeline. The gesture feels intimate, the first connection we've had in years, and I almost don't want to let all of these people back in.

But performing is like improv—the only response to your partner can be "Yes, and . . ."

So I say yes. Jane's already urging me up with a gentle push, and as I weave around the tables, the buzz of the crowd intensifies. The bar is hot, almost humid, and my feet keep sticking to the floor where beer has spilled, but I don't let anything stop me until I reach him.

I smile shyly at Caleb from the base of the stage, but I'm not sure what to do. The chorus is almost over and I don't see another microphone—are we supposed to share one shitty karaoke mic? But the emcee is paying close attention, and with a light of recognition in his eyes, he hurries up to plug in the second microphone, offering it to me like a gift.

Here we go. I climb up the steps to the stage and grab the mic for dear life. It's cold and rough in my hands, the grille dented and scraped from years of misuse.

Caleb points to me and points up. Immediately recognizing the signal, I take melody on the next verse. Caleb layers an earnest harmony on top of my line, his eyes never leaving mine, and his voice is a delicious embrace, even on this cheap sound system in an unremarkable bar in Venice.

And then I remember it all over again.

No matter when or where we play together, it happens every time, this spark. The music we make is lightning across my skin, burning through my veins, igniting me from head to toe. Our hearts set the beat.

I don't know if I can't look away or if I just don't want to.

But a whoop from the crowd shocks me back to my senses, and I tear my gaze from him. I face the room and wink; I toss my hair and sway my hips and lean into the high notes. I make it a show.

Because that's all this is, for show. No matter how good this feels, I won't fall for him again—on- or offstage.

This synchronicity is what was missing during rehearsal today. I couldn't separate the intensity of it from my connection to Caleb offstage, but if we can just connect as musicians like this, that will be enough to make this work. Too quickly, the song ends, and as we each take a little bow, the crowd demands an encore.

The emcee comes up, begging us to honor that request. I squint at him through the harsh spotlight that's hooked up too close to the stage, trying to survey the packed room. Where did all these people come from?

"What do you think?" Caleb murmurs. He's all sweaty, face flushed, looking the way he did after his run this morning. But he's also having fun. And still, he's asking me what I want to do, the way he always did. Making sure we're on the same page. Deferring to my comfort.

There's so much hope in Caleb's eyes that it just might break me. Something deep in my chest twists. Things have to be different this time—*I* have to be different. So I just nod, almost violently, and he leans into the microphone. "Do we have any *Grease* fans in the house?"

I laugh. Fine, Caleb. We can play.

"You're the One That I Want" cues up on the screen, but we don't need the lyrics. This was our go-to karaoke song back in high school, when we were playing smelly pubs and crappy time slots and would find a random place to unwind after a show—usually the pizza joint near Riker's house that was open super late. The arcade was full of broken games, but somehow the karaoke machine always worked.

As the tinny, generic version of the opening bars plays, I flip my hair and smirk, mouthing *Tell me about it, stud* to Caleb. He grins, then literally gyrates his hips, and I cackle as he turns to the audience, channeling Travolta.

But damn, my throat catches when he sings the first line. I always thought Caleb should have done Broadway, and I believe it even more tonight. He's got the chops. Caleb slides up to the high notes like they were made for him, and I enjoy getting to hang out in my low register after singing all day. Still, my voice aches a little from fatigue, and I pull back, letting Caleb steal the show this time.

As I finish the second verse, he gestures up with his chin, urging me to join him on his microphone. Heat creeps up the back of my neck. Too many feelings are swirling in my gut and I'm afraid that if I get any closer to him, I'll fall back into old habits entirely.

So instead, I turn to face the room and grip my microphone tighter as I belt the chorus out to everyone. To make it look intentional, I use the mic stand as a prop, making it sway with my body as I serenade the tableful of bachelorettes near the stage. They whoop at my efforts, and I blow them a kiss. I avoid looking at Caleb as we finish the song, but it doesn't matter—the crowd is going completely bananas.

A crowd that has clearly doubled since I joined the stage. It's standing room only now.

Breathless from the performance, I finally look at Caleb. My chest heaves, but I'm grinning—and his smile is completely gone. Instead of looking happy, his face has lost all color. He swallows thickly, glancing around the room.

Shit, he mouths to me, indicating the crowd with his eyes in a subtle way only I can understand, even after all this time. I can see by his wide eyes that he's panicking, which is strange.

Caleb was always so great with fans. He could hang out for hours after shows, signing merch and taking selfies and just getting to know the people who loved our music. Hell, he used to lecture the rest of us when we'd get tired, reminding us to honor the fans who made all of our success possible. And I'd sign tickets and posters and pose for photo after photo, no matter how my feet hurt, because he was right. We owed it to them.

Something is wrong.

"Thanks, everyone, have a good night," I say quickly into the microphone. People rush up to the stage.

"Keep your pants on, kids," Keeley shouts from her place near the stage, where she must have shouldered through the crowd, but her voice is drowned out by the commotion in the room. We've really done it now. People aren't just pointing at us—they're taking not-at-all-subtle photos of the rest of the band too. I blink when I notice Mary Kate Hampton from *Buzzword* next to Riker. When did the press figure out we were here?

Glancing around frantically, my pulse steadies when I don't recognize anyone else. And maybe MK's presence is totally innocent—I know she and Riker are friends. Still, as much as I wouldn't mind some decent headlines, I can tell Caleb needs to get out of this room.

Setting my jaw, I square my shoulders and turn to the emcee. The guy is broad-shouldered, maybe late fifties, wearing a black bar T-shirt, black jeans, and an LA Kings cap. He looks like every reliable sound technician I've ever worked with, and it makes my muscles soften a little. "I'm so sorry about all the fuss."

He shrugs. "It's good for business. But I do have to get to the rest of the karaoke list at some point."

"Do you have another exit?" I ask. I don't blame him for wanting to get on with his night. We made a spectacle of ourselves.

He turns to us, grimacing. "We do, if you can make a run for it. Head left past the bathrooms through the door that says STAFF ONLY."

"Thank you," Caleb says.

I shoot a desperate look at Keeley behind the fans, and instead of ignoring me the way I deserve after rehearsal today, her eyes fall to Caleb and light up in understanding.

I got you, she mouths, and I want to cry as she makes a beeline for our table.

"Hey, who wants a picture with *Riker Maddox*?" she shouts. "If you're really polite, he'll sign your tits!"

"No, I won't!" Riker squeaks, but the crowd starts to shift toward their table in the back. The commotion pulls enough attention away from us that we're able to escape into the hall.

We turn the corner past the bathrooms, which leads us into a concrete storage room with a dull green EXIT sign out the back. There are boxes stacked haphazardly, and several are open to reveal napkins and condiments and bottles of alcohol. If anyone followed us, the last thing I'd want to do is hang out back here, but Caleb doesn't hurry for the exit. No, he's leaning against the brick wall, panting.

"Caleb? We should really get out of here."

He nods but keeps his eyes closed. "Yeah, just . . . give me a second to catch my breath. God, I forgot how much I hate this."

I blink, confused by this revelation. "What do you mean?"

Caleb opens his eyes, and he glances over at me, something guarded in his gaze. "I didn't just leave the band because of you, you know."

I flinch. "Wow, okay."

He shakes his head. "Sorry, it was just . . . things were fine when we were onstage, but then when I saw the crowd at the end, I felt trapped."

"You were always so good with fans," I say carefully.

"You're not the only one who can act," Caleb says, laughing dryly. "I have anxiety attacks. It's been a while, and they're mostly under control, but . . . between school ending and planning to be down here for the summer, I forgot to refill my prescription. Just give me a minute."

"Do you need me to . . ." I trail off, because I don't know how I can help him. In the dim lighting, he's ghostly pale. I mirror his posture and rest against the opposite wall, the rough brick clinging to my damp T-shirt.

He clears his throat. "No, I just need to do a couple breathing exercises." He pulls out his phone, and for a moment I think he's texting, but we're close enough for me to see he's watching the clock. Counting his breaths.

Jesus. He wasn't ready for this. I brace myself, unsure of what to expect, but after a few minutes, color returns to his face.

"Okay, I'm good now." He still looks a little shaky, but I don't want to push it. Almost of its own accord, my hand reaches out to comfort him, but I think better of it. Instead, I wipe pretend dust off my jeans.

"I'm sorry," I say. "I didn't realize . . . you were always so natural at all of this. It always seemed like you *liked* the promo stuff." I thought we were close, once upon a time. If I didn't know he had panic attacks, what else was I missing? We were supposed to take care of each other. I can't believe I was that wrapped up in my own shit.

He shrugs. "I was good at hiding it. I might know how to socialize, but I only ever wanted to make music that meant something to people. I never really felt comfortable with the attention."

"Oh." This surprises me. Maybe I really don't know Caleb at all. When I asked him to do this, I didn't even ask how he might feel about it. I asked him to jump in headfirst.

"Don't worry. We made a deal, and I won't go back on it. I'll do whatever you need as long as I'm off the hook after the concert," he mutters, running a hand through his damp waves.

My face warms. "That's not . . . I just want to make sure you're okay."

"You don't have to make sure I'm okay anymore, Valerie."

My jaw tenses. There isn't exactly venom in those words, but it's enough of a stark reminder that this isn't some happy reunion. "Right."

"There's a reason I left this life behind. It wasn't so bad being onstage, but . . . I forgot how much I hated feeling like a commodity after. I'll do the show, but you don't have to pretend in private that you care how I feel."

Maybe there is some venom after all. The coldness in his voice reminds me of that night we fought in Vegas, and something about it shocks me back to reality. We were having fun onstage tonight, but that doesn't mean anything. It was just for the crowd.

Still, he's here, and I'll take what I can get.

"Okay," I say, nodding sharply. "I'll let it be."

"Thank you," he says. It's the least I can do for putting him through this. Suddenly, I realize that while Caleb might *look* like he did six years ago with a little makeup and styling, he's a complete stranger to me now. So I just let the silence grow between us until it's unbearable.

"Are you ready to sneak out?" I ask.

"Yeah," Caleb says. "Should we call a car or something?"

"That could take ages. Let's just make a run for it."

"Deal," he agrees. When we slip through the exit, there isn't the crowd of fans I was dreading under the starlit sky—but there is one reporter waiting for us in the loading zone. It's not Mary Kate Hampton—she must still be inside with the rest of the band—but Ryan Tate from *Gossip Daily*, someone I know all too well from years of bad press.

My stomach drops. How the hell did this jerk get here so fast? *Gossip Daily* is a lot more inflammatory than *Buzzword*, and they've been giving me a hard time since the first Glitter Bats album dropped. Ryan loves to paint me in a bad light, and he even wrote one of the worst articles about me and Roxanne. He's made plenty of money off me. His eyes light up when he sees us.

I ball my fists so tight my freshly painted nails dig into my palms.

"Valerie, Caleb, how does it feel to be back onstage together?" Ryan asks with a swagger. He's white and super tanned in a weathered way from too many sun beds, and his brown hair has that frat boy swoop. He's wearing a too-tight, deep V-neck tee, and the Ralph Lauren Polo is wafting so strongly I want to cough.

But "no comment" won't be good enough to get him to leave, and it won't drum up the good buzz I so desperately need. I force my shoulders back and smile sweetly at him.

"It's nice to sing together again," I say. "Now please excuse us, we need to get going."

He turns to Caleb, whose jaw is set with determination. "I want to hear what Caleb thinks. It's good to see you, man. It's been a while."

Despite what just happened in the stockroom, Caleb flips a switch. Charisma shines off of him in waves, and he looks like a completely different person from the guy I watched fight off a panic attack moments ago. He turns a megawatt smile on Ryan. "It's good to see you too. Honestly, it's great to be working with the Glitter Bats again. We're excited to give the fans a concert to remember. It's been too long since I've gotten to work with Valerie, and sharing the stage with her again is an honor and a privilege. She's as beautiful and talented as ever."

My heart flutters, and I try to remind myself he's just acting. Like he said. I force my own calm and put on my best media face.

Ryan smirks. "Any truth to the rumors that the two of you have been carrying on in secret for years, despite Valerie's parade of partners?"

I open my mouth to shoot the rumor down, but then an idea

sparks: it might be better to spin this. Maybe a connection to Caleb—or even the slightest hint of one—could be enough to shine up my reputation. And hey, he just agreed to do whatever I need.

I need a miracle, and this might be it.

Before I can stop myself, I open my stupid mouth. "Oh, Ryan, our personal life is just that—personal," I say coyly. "I don't kiss and tell."

The moment I say it, I want to pull the words back, worried I've gone too far. But when I turn to Caleb, he winks.

"Neither do I." He turns to Ryan with a smirk. "If you think for a moment that Valerie Quinn would cheat on a partner, you're clearly just reaching for headlines. But Valerie is right—what we do *offstage* is our business."

He says that last part with such innuendo it makes a shiver run down my spine.

"Come on, we're old friends here. Can't you give me anything?" Ryan asks, like Caleb is his frat bro or something.

Caleb shakes his head. "Sorry, *bro*. Any interview requests about the concert can be fielded by Ortega Management."

And then Caleb kisses my cheek, reaches an arm around my shoulders, and marches me into the night. I know it's all for the media, but the gesture makes my stomach flip.

It's a lie, it's a lie, it's a lie.

But the tiniest part of me wants to believe it's not.

8

✦ Caleb ✦

A part of me knew that coming back meant giving Valerie the power to hurt me again—I just didn't realize how vulnerable I'd feel until last night.

How can she think it's a good idea to pretend we're *together* on top of everything? Valerie may be desperate for good press, but I don't like this at all.

I played along just to get Ryan Tate off our backs, because I can't stand that douchebag. But as soon as we got back from the bar, I hurried to my room without another word. Faking it or not, the motions felt a little too familiar for comfort, and it threw my thoughts into chaos. I could almost believe there was still something between us if my heart hadn't been so shattered that night in Vegas all those years ago.

We need to set some boundaries.

I spent the night tossing and turning, and this morning, I skipped my jog in favor of scouring the internet. Nausea roils my stomach, and I know I need to put my phone away, but it's hard to stop scrolling. Seeing my name everywhere triggers my instinct to run the hell away from all of this.

My chest tightens when I discover #CalErie isn't just back—it's trending. I loathe the portmanteau as much as I loathe how invasive it feels to have my private life speculated about all over the internet. It's one thing when they're talking about the reunion, or even the dynamics between the band, but I wish my relationship status was off-limits. It doesn't help that Ryan took our statements and ran with them.

Or that there's proof.

One camera caught me gazing across the stage at Valerie like I was completely in love with her. The caption says as much, and the old fan accounts are spinning wild theories in the comments about our supposed "rekindled romance." The image is so startling that I stare at it for a solid minute before I come to my senses and delete the app, as if that could erase the evidence.

I was *pretending*, damn it.

We're getting into the hotel a day early to increase security, so I busy myself by repacking my bag, gathering the shirts I scattered while trying to meet Keeley's "minimum professional standards" last night.

The headlines flash through my mind as I fold each one. My reaction to all of this is ridiculous: I knew this was coming. We're all over social media, just like Valerie wanted. We probably should have planned our first public appearance better, but the damage is done.

I just start to wonder if we should issue a statement when I hear a knock on the bedroom door.

"Come in," I call.

"We're *trending*!" Valerie squeals. This morning, she's still got some of last night's eye makeup on her face, and she's wearing an old T-shirt and gym shorts, but she still looks like the girl I loved with that pink hair, and a visceral jolt runs through my veins. There are pieces of our old selves I'd rather not revisit.

I swallow thickly, settling on the bed. "I saw. I wish you hadn't made up that stuff for Ryan. You knew he'd sensationalize it."

She bites her lip. "I'm sorry. I just got the idea in the moment." That's her problem. She doesn't think things through, and now the internet believes we've rekindled a relationship we'd never even confirmed in the first place.

"That's fine, but we should probably issue a statement before fans get the wrong idea."

"Actually . . ." she trails off, biting her lip.

Dread curls in my stomach. "What?"

She shakes her head. "No, it's a terrible idea."

I cross my arms, narrowing my eyes at her. "You could argue this entire concert is a terrible idea. What do you want?"

It's obvious when Valerie Quinn wants something. She breathes a little shallower, fidgets with her jewelry, purses her lips—and I check each action off one by one as I watch her from where she leans against the wall of the bedroom. Still, there's something almost shy in the hunch of her shoulders that makes me want to know more.

"I think we should consider playing into it," she says, not quite meeting my gaze. "Letting them think we're together."

Heat flushes the back of my neck. This is too far, even for her. "Are you serious right now? How's that going to help your image?"

She clears her throat, looking anxiously over at me. "I know, it's a huge ask, and maybe it's a terrible idea. But I've been thinking about this all morning. I . . ." she trails off, running a hand through her hair. "I don't think the reunion alone is going to be enough to fix my image—not in one summer. And, well . . . the press always liked me better when I was with you."

"We never confirmed our relationship," I blurt, because that was the whole problem, wasn't it?

Valerie reddens. "Sorry, when they *thought* I was with you. I'm not saying we confirm anything now. That would be . . ." she trails off, chastened. "We can just drop some vague hints. If everyone starts to, I don't know, assume that we're together, it can only help my image even more. Plus it'll sell more tickets, and we get that bonus if we sell out."

I let out a breath. "Do you really think this is a good idea? Did you talk to Wade?"

She snaps her gaze to mine. "No, but I spoke to my publicist. She agrees that we could benefit from a showmance—but I'll only do it if you're comfortable."

A lump forms in the back of my throat as emotion threatens to overwhelm me. After everything that happened between us, I really can't believe she's asking me to do this.

Then again, maybe I can. Valerie has never been afraid to ask for things. And besides, she knows this business better than I do these days. Last night I might have looked the part, but I don't even know how to be rock star Caleb anymore. The last thing I want to do is complicate that further by pretending we're some happy couple, but . . . damn it.

Her eyes are filled with so much hope it makes my heart twist. Despite everything, I just can't say no to her. And hell, I'm already here. What's one more thing outside of my comfort zone?

"Fine, we can play it up for the cameras. Now can I finish packing?"

"Thank you!" she says. She presses a quick kiss to my cheek before darting back through the door.

My skin burns from the touch of her lips.

When the door clicks shut, I don't resume packing. I just stand there for a minute, stunned. Did I really just say yes to fake dating my ex, who flat-out refused to confirm we were dating back when we were *actually* together?

Oh god.

I guess if it helps Valerie renew her show, then fine. That's what she wanted. I'm already here anyway, so I'll do it, even if seeing my name all over social media makes me want to throw up. And yeah, I can see how generating more interest might help us make that bonus. The more money I can put in the bank for my little sister, Carrie, the better.

And maybe . . . I need to give Valerie this. I broke up the band because I was wounded enough to leave the industry without looking back at the friends I left behind. If we'd continued making music, Valerie might not be scrambling to save her career. Maybe she'd have that Grammy by now.

Her desperation is my fault.

Still, I don't love this idea. I knew there'd be some press when I agreed to the reunion. I just wasn't planning to add our complicated relationship to the mix any more than we had to. I laugh dryly to myself. At least the fans will be excited.

A few minutes later, I get a text from Carrie.

Carrie: OH MY GOD. Are you and Val back together?

God, seriously? Now I have to lie to my sister.

Me: None of your business.

Carrie: That's not a NO.

Me: We haven't seen each other in years, do you really think we're back together?

Carrie: Fuck, I don't know. I always shipped you.

Me: Don't say fuck.

Carrie: What, like you didn't say fuck when you were in high school? I know every word on Wanderlust, you know. But seriously, you haaaaave to tell me—are you and Val back together? That would rock. I always liked her better than Morgan.

The last thing I need to do is get her hopes up.

Me: You met Morgan ONCE before we broke up. That's hardly a fair comparison.

Me: The media is going to speculate about Valerie and me, but that doesn't mean it's true. Just part of being back in the industry.

Being vague with my sister isn't much better than lying, and I feel ashamed, but it's too late now. Still, I want her to stop reading into all the headlines.

Carrie: Whatever you say.

Me: Why are you reading all that garbage, anyways? You know half of it is completely made-up. Have you even practiced your audition piece today?

Carrie: RUDE

Me: Go practice.

Carrie: . . . fine. 😐

I worry I'm going to get a call from my mom next, but she doesn't reach out. Fortunately. She didn't really react much when I texted her to tell her about the reunion—but I guess she's distracted by this new boyfriend of hers. Apparently he has a boat, so she's out of cell service.

Same old story.

If I could wish for anything in the world, I'd wish my mom was more responsible. It's a good thing my baby sister has such a good head on her shoulders, because she's certainly not getting the structure she needs from Mom.

Maybe it'd be best if I looked for a job in Seattle for her senior year, but that wouldn't be smart for my teaching career. Carrie has only one year left of high school, and then she'll be headed to college—probably the East Coast, since she still has her heart set on a music conservatory.

I'd still be proud of her if she didn't want to go to college, but it's cool to see her taking such an interest in music. With all her classical prowess, she's definitely more driven than I ever was. Not like her brother, who tried to run away when a few fans wanted to see him perform after years of nothing.

I really need to refill my medication. I pull up the portal for my health insurance and start researching pharmacies near our hotel, then click through to order. Repeating last night is not an option.

"No more karaoke," I promise to myself. I just need to be better prepared for our next appearance. And apparently, Valerie and I have a reunion story to get straight.

By the time we get to the hotel Sunday afternoon, I'm exhausted. They've got us all on the same floor, which is to be expected, but what I don't expect is that there's an adjoining door between my room and Valerie's.

Neither of us asked for it, and we don't discuss the implications.

The silence of that closed door feels unnecessarily loud. There's something intimate about being able to get to each other without heading into the hallway, but we don't have to use the door. No, we can just act like it's not there.

More pretending.

Full of restless energy, I wander around, checking out all of the accommodations. There's definitely enough in the room to distract from that door. It's a nice, trendy hotel, all Art Deco chic with vibrant colors and modern fixtures. There's both a shower and a separate bathtub, and all of the soaps are small samples from Kiehl's. They've left complimentary bottled water and chocolate truffles on the desk, and there's an elaborate room service menu . . . the kind without prices. For a moment, I freeze, worrying about the bill. But then I remember Label Records is paying, and my shoulders relax.

Since I usually have a Holiday Inn Express budget, I forgot how nice it is to stay in a fancy hotel. Before I change to head down for rehearsal, I sink into the king-sized memory foam mattress, deliciously stretching out my limbs. Jane's house was super nice, but I had to sleep on a twin bed, and even with my limited height, my legs cramped up in the middle of the night.

As I'm tugging on a fresh shirt, my phone rings. Maybe my mom is finally calling.

Without looking at the screen, I answer it.

"Hey, Caleb, it's Gina Choi from Label Records. Is this a good time?"

My stomach tightens. I haven't spoken to the VP in a long time, but she always made me nervous. "Gina, hello."

"Look, I know it's a Sunday, but we just wanted to reach out. We're all so excited you're returning to the Glitter Bats."

"It's just for one night," I say.

"Right, right. Just one concert. Still, I wanted to float something by you. Technically, you all signed a contract for ten years.

Since you're obligated to give us any new music you produce until that expiration date, and we know how prolific you all are together, it might be a lot cleaner if you all just come in to record a few tracks now. A comeback EP. Valerie has already said she's up for it."

I groan. Would Valerie really hide this from me after the conversation we had with Wade on Friday, or is Gina just trying to trick me? The start of a panic spiral tugs at the back of my mind. I don't know this version of Valerie well enough to know how far she'd go without checking with the rest of us, but I think it's possible she'd make some moves. This is a shitty way to find out. Implying a romance is one thing—I'm not happy about it, but I'll do it—but I did *not* sign up for more music.

I'm giving more than I bargained for already.

I want to snap at Gina, but I stop myself. There's one easy way to stop this line of questioning. "You'll need to run all professional inquiries through my manager."

"Oh? I heard you no longer had representation."

There's no way she heard that, because Label has been working closely with Wade on this reunion. "Nope, I'm still represented by Ortega Management."

"Well, this is just a friendly chat, no need to involve them yet."

I grit my teeth. "Everything needs to go through Wade. Have a great afternoon, Gina."

She immediately calls me again as soon as I hang up, but I put my phone on silent and sink into the oversized yellow chair by the razor-thin TV. This is what I was afraid of—that one concert wouldn't be enough for anyone, and I'd be obligated to pick my old life back up again.

Everything swims in my vision, and I move from the chair to the floor, taking a minute to complete a grounding exercise.

I desperately need that prescription.

The exercise helps, but my shoulders are still tense as I head to rehearsal. Because the studio is just down the block from our hotel, it doesn't take long to set up our instruments and get to work for the afternoon. The sound technician hired for the concert is working with us in rehearsals, and it's a nice change from a basement practice session or a karaoke machine. Despite the lingering tension between Keeley and Valerie, we get right to work without any issues, and everyone sounds great.

Except me. I screw up the chords on "Ghosts," forget my harmony on "All My Friends Are Vampires," and overall just make the rehearsal unpleasant for everyone. I can't focus. My mind is reeling as I wonder if all of this has been a setup from the start. I even forget to come in on "Midnight Road Trip," and everyone stares at me as the rehearsal crashes to a halt.

"Okay, that's it. What's wrong?" Valerie says to me. "You're in a completely different place today."

"Yeah, well, I'm just not sure this is worth it," I say, trying to catch my breath.

"Uh, what's this about?" Riker asks, frowning at me across the space.

Warmth flushes the back of my neck, and I don't look away from Valerie. "You know, I agreed to this because you needed it, but it's not just the one show, is it? You're *all* hoping to record again, aren't you?" I ask, heart pounding.

"Pretty sure we're all too busy for that," Keeley says, but it lacks bite.

Jane frowns at me from behind the keyboard setup. "Caleb, where is this coming from? Let's talk."

"Are you really all okay just exposing yourselves to all of this nonsense again, for *her*?" I say, pointing at Valerie. I know I'm not being fair, but my pulse won't stop racing from the adrenaline as I prepare for yet another fight. "I got a call from Gina at Label Records, and she said Valerie agreed to another record."

Valerie gapes. "That's not true! I'd never do that without talking to you."

I feel disoriented. I'm not sure what to believe, but I won't fall for her wide-eyed denial so easily. "You set up this reunion without discussing it as a band first. Why should this be any different?"

Valerie unplugs her guitar. "You know what? Forget it. I'm not going to stand here and let you accuse me of something I didn't do." She storms out of the studio. The others just stare at me.

"Can you believe her, going behind our back like that?" I ask, pacing the distance between my amp and Valerie's pedalboard. "She just expects us to go along with everything."

No one agrees, but I know they want to. They *have* to. I can't be the only one who feels like I got suckered back into the whole damn thing.

Finally, Keeley breaks the silence.

"Dude, you're being a dick," she says. "You know Label is super fucking sketchy. Of course they're trying every tactic in the book to get us to agree to a third album—this is their last chance to get more money out of us."

Jane nods, tucking her hair behind her ears. "She's right. They reached out to my agent too, but we're not going to respond." Her words are slow, measured, like she's trying not to spook a wild animal.

Do I really look that out of control? I stop pacing and close my eyes, trying to catch a breath.

Riker grunts. "I'm sure if Wade wasn't literally at Galaxy's Edge right now, he'd be calling us with the same news." He gestures toward his phone, where Wade's private account shows him with his daughter in matching mouse ears.

All the fight leaves me in a rush.

"You're right. I can't believe I fell for that so easily." I jumped to conclusions, because even for all my talk about trying to make peace, I wanted to believe the worst in Valerie. It wasn't fair.

And my anxiety brain lies to me. My therapist said that a hundred times, and it's like I've forgotten all that work I've done in the span of a few days.

God, I messed up.

"You just forgot what it's like in this industry," Riker says generously.

"Shit," I sigh, swallowing thickly. "I just . . . I don't know how to navigate this anymore." The fans, the label . . . I forgot how overwhelming this life could be. I'm not at my best. Throw in all my complicated feelings about Valerie, and of course I'm all over the place. But my anxiety is no excuse for attacking her. I didn't even give her a chance.

"That's why you're in a band, dumbass," Keeley says. "You don't have to figure it all out alone."

Is a New Glitter Bats Album in the Works?

RYAN TATE FOR *GOSSIP DAILY*

The Glitter Bats are back! I was lucky enough to spot Valerie Quinn and Caleb Sloane getting cozy both on- and offstage at a karaoke joint in Venice this weekend. They're clearly shaking off the rust, but they're still the most watchable duet partners I've ever seen, even after all those years apart. They didn't share a microphone in their iconic fashion, but it sure felt like there was some lingering tension when they sang together—twice! Click this *link* to view a clip from their HOT rendition of "I Want You to Want Me."

But the real coup here is that things might be heating up in the sound booth again. For years, rumors have circulated about the announced-but-never-released third album from the Glitter Bats. A representative for Label Records said they're "hopeful" that we'll see new music soon.

It sounds like this reunion might be for more than just a concert—if Quinn stays interested long enough to remain with the project. But if The Network decides to renew *Epic Theme Song*, they'll likely start filming right away, and the reportedly demanding schedule won't leave room for side projects. If I were one of her bandmates, I'd lock down an album before she can make other plans. We all know Quinn is flighty.

Only time will tell if the Glitter Bats will keep flying, but stay tuned to our feed for updates!

9

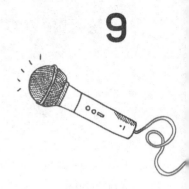

Valerie

What happened at rehearsal is my fault.

I should have gone anywhere but back to the hotel room, but I left in such a rush of sadness and shame that I wasn't thinking clearly. I could have called some friends, gone to a bar, let off steam. Instead, I'm watching cars slog through early-evening traffic out the window.

But if I'd gone out, I would have just spent the whole night thinking about Caleb. Guilt churns in my stomach as I remember the sheer panic on his face today. I haven't given him a single reason to believe me over the label—I just threw him into all of this and expected him to read my mind. No strategy, no boundaries, not even a real apology. I've made such a mess and it's only been two days.

Maybe, if things were different, we *could* be talking about a new album. I'd love to write music together again—but I'd never force Caleb into something he doesn't want . . . at least, not more than I already have. A new album only exists in my wildest dreams.

I wish it didn't. In another life, this summer could be a relaunch instead of a reunion. Even in one weekend of messy rehearsals, I've felt more creative than I've been in years. But the Glitter Bats are back for one final bow, and that's it.

All of my focus needs to be on *Epic Theme Song*.

I should have warned Caleb. Label likes to call Wade every six months or so, to try to convince us to bring the band back together. Last year, they even had a truly terrible plan to bring in a new bass player, and we made it very clear that replacing Caleb wasn't on the table.

Label can be manipulative. They're a big-enough company, but when we were all just kids, they had us sign a truly heinous record deal. But it was legal enough. That was the steep cost of my mom's mismanagement—before Wade signed on and taught us we deserved better.

They're footing the bill for everything leading up to the concert, because all this press increases merch and record sales, and they'll get the bulk of the concert revenue (after our checks). But they also want more Glitter Bats, and they don't care if it means pitting us against one another.

A knock on my door shakes me out of my pity party. At first, I think it might be Caleb, but Keeley's the one leaning against the doorframe. She rubs her neck sheepishly.

"Can we talk?"

I swallow, unsure what to expect. Keeley and I also need to clear the air. Yeah, she was awful to me in that first rehearsal . . . but I made it worse. We've been tiptoeing around the tension ever since.

"Yeah, of course. Come in," I say.

She runs a hand through her short hair but doesn't move to come inside. "Look, I can't stay. I have a call in five minutes to talk about a potential gig—but I need to apologize."

I blink, taken aback. "What? No, I'm the one who needs to apologize."

"Oh, I'll take it, but let me get this out," she says, grinning sheepishly. "I've, uh, been super bitter about how everything went down with Glitter Bats. When you left, Jane, Riker, and I tried to stick together, but our careers took us all in such different directions. The three of us have gotten together a few times over the years, but it was never the same. I think I've held you responsible for it all."

That explains a few things, and it's entirely fair. This weekend has felt so tense and awful. The Keeley I knew was blunt, and would hold a fierce grudge for a few days, but then got over it pretty fast. She's a firecracker who will explode, then fizzle out.

But she's been holding this in for *years*, and that just shows how much I hurt her when I left. My chest tightens, and I lean against the doorframe to steady myself. It's always my instinct to defend myself at the slightest provocation, but I know I have to take responsibility for this . . . and not just for the sake of the concert. I miss my friend.

"Look, I'm really sorry for how I spoke to you yesterday." I pause, swallowing thickly. "And for the way I left you all in Vegas and never looked back. I was selfish and careless, and you deserved better." If I'd thought of everyone else instead of my own rise to the top for just one moment . . . we really could be on album number five by now. "I'm responsible for tearing us all apart."

The Glitter Bats could still be rocking, and maybe Caleb and I could have had a chance.

"No, you're not." She puts her hands on her hips, laughing nervously. "Okay, yeah, you kind of are, but it took seeing just how unfair Caleb was to you today for me to reflect on my own behavior. So I went for a walk after rehearsal and figured out my shit. I'm sorry I never bothered to reach out to you after Vegas. It's not like you changed your number. I could have called you, checked in."

I shake my head. "You shouldn't have had to."

She smiles sadly at me. "Yeah, I should. Your friendship still matters to me, even if I'm still a little mad at you."

"Keels—"

She interrupts me, her voice going dry. "No. I know I can never fully understand what happened between you two, or why you left. For what it's worth, I forgive you for all of it. I know you're trying to make this work, so I'll try to have an open mind going forward instead of dwelling on ancient history that doesn't help anyone."

My eyes sting, and I blink quickly, trying to recover. "Wow, thank you for saying that."

She smirks. "You forgive me too, right?"

I laugh, and all the tension between us snaps. "Of course I forgive you. We're still family."

"You bet your ass we are." She shakes her head but pulls me into a tight hug. I forgot how great Keeley's hugs are, like she's holding on with her whole body—probably the product of her being in a close, loving family.

She draws back and glares at me. "You be careful with Caleb, though. He's still so soft, and I think this whole pretend romance thing is a bad idea."

"He told you about that?"

She rolls her eyes. "He didn't have to. I've been online. But I think it's just going to complicate all of this, and we have enough old wounds."

I bite my lip, heaviness sinking into my chest. "Well, I doubt he'll be on board now."

She raises a brow. "You know that man would do literally anything for you, right? He'll get over today and play along. Just . . . don't break his heart again."

Who's going to stop him from breaking mine? I want to ask, but Keeley's phone rings, and she waves and hurries down the hall to her own room.

The thing is, I don't want to break Caleb's heart. I also don't know how to convince Caleb that I'm not scheming to make him record an album. But maybe if I just apologize for the way this all started, that'll be enough to get him to trust me again.

Hell, it's worth a try. So I listen at the door connecting our rooms until I hear him shuffling next door, and I knock.

It's loud enough that I'm sure he'll hear it but soft enough that he can ignore me if he'd rather just pretend he didn't. I don't want to push him, especially if he's already feeling vulnerable.

But after a couple of heartbeats, he opens the door a crack. His hair is damp and his face is flushed, like he's just taken a shower, and his white T-shirt clings to his pecs in a distracting way.

A way I can't think about if I'm going to get all of this out.

"Can I come in?" I ask. And forget butterflies—my nerves are swarming in my stomach like agitated bees.

"Sure," he says quietly, eyes downcast.

His room is identical to mine but flipped, like stepping into a mirror dimension. It's weird to know our beds are only separated by a thin wall. For a few precious years, nothing separated us at all. But I shove those memories away and turn to face him. His eyes are tired, but there's no ice left in his gaze.

"I'm sorry," we both say at once. We stare at each other for a second, and then laugh.

"Me first," I say. "I really should have warned you about Label. They've been on our case about GB3 for years, since our contract is still valid, but I didn't think they'd try to sink their claws back into you so quickly."

He sighs, running a hand over his hair. "I should have seen it coming—Wade warned us, and I knew they were involved."

"Yeah, but still. I should have warned you too."

He grins ruefully. "I should have heard you out instead of

assuming the worst. Anxiety got the best of me, but that's never an excuse. I'm truly sorry for my behavior."

"I really don't blame you." I hate that I made him anxious, and I kind of wish he'd yell at me more. I deserve it. I ruined everything back then, and it's up to me to prove I won't repeat past mistakes now.

"Well, if it makes you feel any better, Keeley called me a dick for how I acted."

"Of course she did." I laugh. "Still, you have every right to assume the worst in me. You're right that I have selfish reasons to do the concert—but now that we're all together, it also feels right, doesn't it? Like after all those years of rumors and distance we can finally come together and send Glitter Bats off in style." I don't voice my hope that things could continue after this concert, because he'll never want that. It would just drive him away even faster.

He nods, sinking onto the bed. "Yeah, it's been too long since we were all together. It'd be a shame to leave this all behind without seeing it through."

My stomach unclenches a little, and I let out a long breath. "Good. I'm glad to hear it."

He clears his throat. "So . . . do you want to go grab dinner and talk through some things? Just the two of us?"

I flush. "Are you sure? If we're seen, that'll start more rumors."

He rolls his shoulders, then nods. "Don't we want to encourage those anyway?"

It's more than I'd hoped for. I sink onto his chair and tuck my feet under me, still anxious. "We should talk about it more before we decide to do anything. I know you're already uncomfortable with this reunion, and it wasn't fair of me to throw this at you. I feel like I forced you into it."

He smiles, and it makes my knees a little weak. God, I need

to keep it together. "We should talk about it. You can tell me everything your publicist said, and I'll make an informed decision after that. Besides, I'm already here for the reunion and, well . . . it's not like the fans aren't talking about us anyway. What's a little acting for the cameras?"

Acting. Right. "I'd love to grab dinner and tell you all about it. What did you have in mind?"

"Thai?"

"Oh my gosh, yes. There's a great place a couple blocks from here."

"Sounds perfect. Meet back here in ten?"

"Fifteen," I say. I really should shower, but at least I can change into fresh clothes and touch up my makeup.

"Of course," he laughs as I slip into my own room.

After I've changed and popped back over to meet him, I feel less anxious about invading his space—it's more like we're our old selves, constantly in each other's orbit. Jane texts us that the rest of the band went to get sushi, so we feel fine going to do our own thing. We decide it's best to call a car this time, and it's not long before we're on our way to Thai food.

The restaurant is quiet since it's on the early side for dinner, but hopefully that means we can escape without incident. Soft overhead lights cast a warm glow around the dining room, and we tuck ourselves away in a green vinyl booth in the back. I order the spiciest noodle dish on the menu, while Caleb sticks to a milder curry.

"Come on, the spice is good for your sinuses," I joke as we hand menus off to the waiter.

"And terrible for my stomach, thank you," he says.

"Fine, fine. I respect that."

We make small talk as we wait for our food to arrive, which happens in record time. But we stay carefully away from talk about the industry as we start to eat. He tells me more about teaching, and his family, and I learn all about the trials and tribulations of running a social media strategy for a dog. Once he's relaxed, leaning against the back of the pleather seat and smiling across the table at me, I tell him what my publicist said: that my bad reputation has a lot to do with who I date, but just the appearance of being with someone as well-liked as Caleb could go a long way to improving my status in the public eye.

"Okay. Let's do it," he says, before leaning in for another bite of curry, like he's agreeing to the most innocuous thing in the world. I'm so surprised that I stutter, and I have to take a sip of my iced tea to steel myself.

"Okay, so ground rules," I say, clearing my throat. "We'll let the media speculate about our relationship, but we're not going to do anything either of us is uncomfortable with. Holding hands should be fine? Probably no kissing."

"Right," he says, flushing a little. But maybe that's just because it's warm in the restaurant.

My mouth goes dry, but I know we need to set this next boundary, even if it hurts. "We'll send any serious band-related inquiries through Wade, but we won't even hint at a new album—or any future for the band after the concert."

"Yes, I won't budge on that. No tours, no albums, nothing after August 15," Caleb says, and my heart sinks. But I know it's for the best. "We'll make sure the others are in at brunch tomorrow."

It's best if we all make this decision as a group. We might not be a family anymore, but we used to be. This was never just about me and Caleb.

"Agreed," I say. "And now I need dessert."

There's an incredible cupcake place just down the block, so I pay the bill before Caleb can protest.

"You know I'm not destitute, right? I can pay for my own dinner," he grumbles, but I don't miss the relief in his eyes. The check wasn't an insignificant factor in getting him to agree to the reunion.

But I also know Caleb has a little pride. His family always struggled a bit, and he took a lot of responsibility for making his own money and contributing when he could, even before the Glitter Bats. I wonder if he still does that, or if his mom has stepped up and actually takes care of Carrie.

"Think of it as an apology dinner," I say. "And if you're really bothered by it, you can buy my cupcakes."

Once the server comes back with my card, I leave a tip and lead the way out of the restaurant and down to Magic Cupcake.

"Okay, this place looks incredible," Caleb says. "You were right."

"I know that," I say, grinning at him. It's a rainbow of colors, both on the walls and behind the pastry counter. The cupcakes are huge and they serve every flavor you can imagine, so I order myself a single caramel bourbon one while he chooses a vanilla Earl Grey. Just like at the Thai restaurant, we tuck ourselves into a booth in the back of the shop.

"Oh my god," Caleb moans after his first taste, the sound practically pornographic. Heat runs down my spine. I've heard that moan too many times before to be left completely unaffected, but I try to remember it's just a really good cupcake. I play it cool as I take my own bite.

"Good, right?" I ask.

"Amazing," he says around a mouthful.

"I discovered this place when I was doing callbacks for *Epic Theme Song*, and I always try to stop by when I'm in the city," I say. It became my treat for getting through long rehearsals—something my therapist insisted I try to fight burnout.

"I can see why," he says. "Do you like it? Doing TV?"

I take another bite, considering his question for a moment. There are parts of TV I really hate, but I don't want to share that with him. Even being jaded, I don't want to discount the meaningful parts of the work. Hell, it's why I'm still fighting for the show.

"I didn't think I would—and it's really different from playing music—but there's something really special about storytelling for an audience. I know we do that with our songs, but the fans really adore this show. It's an honor to play a bisexual character who's allowed to have love interests of different genders, and I've had so many fans reach out to tell me how they feel *seen*."

He smiles. "That's really cool. And you're fantastic in the role, so it totally makes sense that people would connect in that way."

I blush, suddenly feeling shy. "You've seen the show?"

Caleb nods, his own cheeks reddening. "I mean, I haven't watched every episode, but Carrie always puts it on when she visits. She really looks up to you."

"I know," I admit, folding my cupcake wrapper into careful triangles. "We've . . . stayed in touch. She's actually how I found you."

"She never told me that," he says ruefully, folding his hands on the table and leaning forward. "Then again, I'm not surprised. She probably wasn't sure how I'd react."

"You're not mad, are you? We don't talk about you," I say quickly. "We mostly just chat about music. She sends me recordings of her playing, and I offered to write her a letter of recommendation for college applications."

His eyes widen. "You don't have to do that."

"I want to, and that's why I offered," I say. "She's incredibly talented. I may not be a classical musician or anything, so my recommendation might not hold much weight, but I want to support her. She deserves every opportunity to pursue her art."

Caleb leans back, smiling. "Thank you. That really means a lot."

"Your family has always felt like mine. I know I don't get to, like, claim that anymore, but I can do this," I admit.

He opens his mouth to say something, but we're interrupted by soft voices.

"Excuse me?" they say. We turn to see a group of kids hanging nervously back. They look like they're about college age, and they're dressed like . . . well, us. Band tees, black jeans, flannel. They look like Glitterbugs, but they're not in our face about it.

They're so nervous, I want to offer them a hug. But since Caleb is the one who hasn't been in the spotlight for years, I follow his lead.

"Hi, I'm Caleb," he says.

"Oh my god, we know," one of them says. She's Black with long braids and a wrist full of rainbow bracelets, and she can't be much older than we were when Glitter Bats took off. "I'm Sophie! We're all so excited for the reunion!"

"Thank you so much. What are your names?" Caleb asks, gesturing to the others.

"I—" the one on Sophie's right starts, then stops, staring at Caleb's shoes.

"They're Whit, and they're totally obsessed with you," Sophie says brightly to him.

Whit—a white kid with freckles and a blue shag cut—blushes. "Shut up. As if you didn't have Valerie as your lock screen all last year."

"That was fan art of Wendy the Wonder kissing Shadowgirl!" Sophie says, but she doesn't look embarrassed.

The guy on her left—a taller Asian boy with short hair and gauged ears—rolls his eyes. "I'm Aiden, and I'll get my friends out of your hair."

Caleb and I share a look, and understanding passes between us. This is the good stuff, as far as fan interactions go. It's low pressure, and even though we just met them, they all seem like genuinely nice kids.

"We're not in any hurry. Do you want to take a seat for a minute?" Caleb asks them gently.

Something about Caleb puts them at ease, and they join us in the booth and start to talk—not about our relationship but about songwriting. We learn they're all second-year music students at a nearby university, and after some prompting, they have a few polite questions about the industry. Eventually, Aiden is the one to ask us for a group photo.

"If it's okay with Valerie," Caleb says.

"Absolutely," I say, smiling at him. We flag down a staff member, who happily takes a photo with the promise the trio will tag the store.

"Can you wait, like, ten minutes to post that?" Caleb asks, lowering his voice as if to share a secret. "Valerie and I need a little time to make our escape."

"Of course! We completely understand," Sophie promises. "You don't want to get mobbed."

"I mean, we're not Beyoncé-famous, but we've found it's usually safest to post where we've *been*, not where we *are*," he says. And then his posture changes. "Actually, you should all do that. You know it's safer not to share your exact location on social media."

I laugh. This must be Caleb's teacher mode, and it's kind of adorable. And then I remember something.

"Let me get your full names, though, if that's okay," I say, pulling out my own phone and opening my Notes app. "VIP sales aren't up yet, but we should be able to get you on the list."

"Oh my gosh, are you serious?" Whit asks, raising their hands to their mouth in excitement.

"Absolutely." I fish one of Wade's cards out of my purse with my free hand. "If you have any trouble, call this guy."

After a chorus of thank-yous, the group leaves.

"That's the part I always loved," Caleb says quietly. "Talking to fans about the music, knowing it made a difference to them." Suddenly, I'm filled with memories of all the things we shared. Back when it was just about the music and nothing else. I was so creatively fulfilled when we wrote together, and Caleb challenged me artistically in a way I haven't felt since.

I wish I could have that back.

"I didn't realize how much I've missed this," I admit.

"Same," he says, and those devastating green eyes lock onto mine. I almost think he's talking about more than fans and cupcakes. For the first time all summer, I feel like we're on the same page, and I want nothing more than to make this night last.

But I know I can't.

I clear my throat. "Uh, we should get back to the hotel before that photo goes up."

He blinks, startling out of our staring contest. "Right. Let's go."

10

+ *Caleb* +

Something transforms in rehearsals over the next few weeks. Valerie and I are on the same team again, and it makes all of this feel possible. The tense practices turn into hours of laser focus and joyful collaboration. After a few painful days of playing bass nonstop, my calluses start building up again too, and it makes it easier and easier to pick my instrument.

One morning, during our last run-through before some Label executives come in to watch us, I realize I'm excited to perform for an audience . . . despite who it is.

As we run through "Fallout," I glance around the rehearsal space. Jane winks across her multi-keyboard setup at me, throwing a new synth pad into the mix on a whim. It makes the vibe gritty and fresh. Keeley laughs delightedly at the new sound but doesn't miss a beat, our strong, ever-steady presence. On the build to the bridge, Riker grins and bounces on his Converse as he takes over Valerie's lead line.

With a toss of her hair—and another of her guitar over her shoulder—Valerie leans into her mic and sings the high notes with her whole chest. She's effervescent. My pulse rushes in my ears as I try to focus on harmonizing, but I can't stop staring at the god-damn rock legend in the making beside me.

She was made for this.

It's like a switch has flipped over the past few weeks, and I'm seeing both the girl she used to be and someone new entirely. When we're not rehearsing, she's been reserved, almost timid, but she's confidence incarnate every time she steps onto this practice stage. Today, her guitar riffs are crisper than ever, her vocals are crystal clear, and her energy is electric. It doesn't matter that the floor is dusty and the walls are scuffed—her presence fills the room with light.

And I feel my own confidence returning alongside my longtime collaborator. It's undeniable—the Glitter Bats are back. The label coming in to scrutinize our progress can't take this joy of making music away.

Keeley whoops as the final chord rings through the studio. Even with the shitty acoustics of the rehearsal space, I have goose bumps.

Riker pumps his fist. "That's the best we've ever played this song, I swear to god!"

He's right. It's like now that we've truly made amends, there was space to recapture this lightning in a bottle.

Valerie unshoulders her guitar before walking over to me. "You ready?" she asks. There's no judgment in those words, no frustration. She just wants to know if I'm okay. She's made a habit of this, checking in on me, and I don't mind.

I nod. "I had a session with my therapist yesterday. I'm as pre-pared as I can be for anything they might throw at us."

Valerie nods. "Good. I'm glad." Her hand jerks to the phone outline in her pocket, and then she hesitates, thinking better of it.

I chuckle. "What are they saying?" There have been more

rumors about our relationship every day—but this time, it feels like we're in on the secret. It only sometimes makes my anxiety stronger, but I know I owe her this, especially because I'm only coming back for the concert. I want to do as much for her as I can.

Maybe this will make up for walking away on the *Bittersweet* tour.

She shrugs. "I don't know! I haven't checked today."

I raise a brow. "Really?"

Valerie pouts. "Okay, fine, I haven't checked since we started rehearsal. But . . . I think it's working. They're saying nice things about us."

"Good," I say, and I mean it.

Suddenly, Valerie freezes. "Oh my god. What about your students?"

I pause. "What about them?"

"Is it weird that they'll be reading about us in the media?"

I shrug. "If they even pay attention, maybe. But it's fine. I knew some of them would figure it out eventually."

Valerie raises her hands like the shrugging emoji. "Maybe they'll be inspired to keep making music if they see us out here."

My jaw falls open as the idea hits. "You're a genius."

She laughs, twirling a finger in her pink waves almost flirtatiously. "I know, but why do you say so?"

"Bear with me," I say, trying to ignore the way that tiny motion affects me, because this is important.

I'd love for my students to learn from the Glitter Bats—they're some of the best musicians I know. Mind spinning, I turn to the rest of the group, who are sitting in a semicircle on the tiny stage with water bottles and snacks. "I have a wild ask."

"We like wild," Riker says, voice muffled by the carrot stick he's chomping on.

I plop down next to him.

"Would you all be willing to film a couple of tutorials for my students? I could pay you, of course—not much, but I think they would really get into learning from some real musicians."

Keeley finishes taking a sip of her water, then laughs. "You're about as fucking real as it gets, dude."

I roll my eyes. "You know what I mean. It'd be a way to share this with them, and they might take you all a little more seriously than their boring old teacher."

"Uh, why haven't we done anything like that already? Let's do it," Riker says. Jane and Keeley nod in assent, and we all turn to look up at Valerie, who is pursing her lips in thought.

"Only if we're all on board," I say carefully, trying to gauge her reaction.

"It's not that," Valerie says quickly. "It's a really great idea, but would you be willing to think a little bigger?" she asks, almost like she's nervous to ask.

"Go on," I say, trying to encourage her with a smile. She catches my eye and bites her lip shyly as she steps over to join the circle.

"Okay, so you know how we were talking to those music students a few weeks ago? We could totally do a series of mini master classes on social media or something," Valerie says, folding into a seat on the floor next to Riker. "We could do a lot—who knows, maybe we'll inspire some kids to pursue music."

"That could be super cool," I agree. "For my students, I'd like to talk about how we take care of our voices during long weeks of rehearsal, how we use the techniques I'm teaching them in a real, practical way. We could get into finding harmonies, listening for blend, and then expand into other instruments and some industry info."

"I'd love to talk about some of the composition work I do for film and TV too," Jane adds. "It could be like Crash Course, but specifically focused on music. We could film everything this summer and then release them on a set schedule this fall. I know we said we'd stop the content after the concert, but this could be a way to give back."

This is so much better than I anticipated. Not only is the band willing to do this, but they're running with it. Valerie's right—it reminds me of how it felt talking to those music students. But something makes me pause.

"Do you think we need the label's permission?"

"Absolutely not. This has nothing to do with them," Keeley says, flipping her honey-blond hair out of her face. "Fuck the label."

Not a minute later, a knock sounds on the door. Wade slips in, followed by a couple people I vaguely recognize from the label—including Gina, unfortunately, who gives me a sharklike grin as she enters the room in towering heels and a power suit. Fortunately, these walls are pretty dang soundproof, but Keeley is still on her best behavior, rising quickly to greet everyone with a handshake and a polite smile in case they overheard.

I try to follow her lead. It's been way too long since I've done any of this, and I'm really rusty, but I know how to be professional. So I keep my shoulders back and smile at the group, jaw so tight I can barely breathe. Once we've all exchanged pleasantries, the executives and Wade sit in the folding chairs we set out in front of the practice stage.

"Do you have any new music to share with us?" Gina asks as we step onto the stage.

"Absolutely not," I blurt, shoulders tensing.

Riker coughs. We're supposed to let Wade be the bad guy—that's his job.

"This is a reunion only, and as such, the band will be focusing on old favorites. There are no plans to release new music," Wade says quickly.

"Well, that's going to disappoint a lot of people," Gina says.

Anxiety starts to flutter in my chest, but I'm grounded by the soft-est of touches. It's Valerie, brushing my pinkie with her own—reminding me I'm not alone in this.

Just one rehearsal. I can get through one rehearsal with these people, and then one more. One thing at a time.

"Take it away, kiddos," Wade says.

Valerie swaggers over to her mic. "Good afternoon! We've only been rehearsing together for a few weeks, but we hope you're ex-cited to get a small peek at our concert set. We'll start with 'Ghosts,'" she says, reaching down to shoulder her guitar.

Keeley counts us off, and we all jump in on cue. Maybe I am anxious, because my mouth goes dry, and I have to blink hard to focus on the verse. Then I make eye contact with Valerie, who winks as she sings her line. All my nerves melt away into warm focus, because deep in my heart, I know I'm okay—as long as I'm looking at her.

And even with this audience, we're on fire. Keeley's beat is im-peccable, Jane's sound is spot-on, and Riker and Valerie play on top of it all while I keep the bass line strong. Valerie and I each take a verse on this song, and she jumps in harmony on my chorus, but it's the bridge that's really special, and you can feel the anticipation in the room as we build up to it.

We always wrote it so I would jump up the octave and she'd layer in a perfect belting harmony, but that doesn't feel right in the moment. So instead, I jerk my chin up, inviting her to share my mic the way we did so many times in the past.

I don't think she's going to do it—she could just turn back to the room the way she did at karaoke a few weeks ago and no one would know the difference. But this new, confident Valerie strides over to my microphone with purpose.

Jane nods at us and adds the bass line on her keyboard, so I swing the bass over my shoulder. Valerie keeps playing her guitar part, but I point to her and then to me, and she nods.

And just like that, we're alternating lines in the bridge over the mic, like two people having a conversation about a past life. We somehow just *know* that in the last lines of the bridge, she sings the harmony, and I jump in up high.

And it's in that moment that I remember something I'd said to her late one night years ago, when we were both exhausted after a long rehearsal, tangled together in hotel sheets.

Sharing a microphone makes me want you.

And fuck.

Maybe that's still true.

SET LIST

Final Glitter Bats Concert:
Las Vegas—August 1, Six Years Ago

MIDNIGHT ROAD TRIP

ALL MY FRIENDS ARE VAMPIRES

EVERY TOUCH

GHOSTS

ALL THE LIPS YOU KISS

SPARKS

OVER THE BULLSHIT

CAFFEINE DREAMS

NEVER WALK AWAY

SUMMER SUNSET

FALLOUT

MAKING MEMORIES

STILL DANCING

11

⋆ Valerie ⋆

I can't tell what's louder—Keeley's drumming or my heartbeat.

As we're singing perfectly alternate lines of the bridge on "Ghosts," every nerve in my body is alight with tension. This is what I was afraid of back at karaoke—that we'd sing together and it would feel like this.

Like fucking foreplay.

It would be so easy to fall for Caleb again. We're not alone, but I only have eyes for him, and his are sparkling back at me across the microphone.

Sharing a microphone makes me want you.

I remember him whispering that in my ear in the middle of the night all those years ago. But no, that's not what this means. He's playing a part.

We both are.

We'll let everyone think we're *something* so the buzz around this reunion gets even hotter, and then The Network won't be able to do anything except renew *Epic Theme Song* on my coattails. That's the goal here, and I need to focus on it. Not the sweet nothings of the past.

I'm sure Caleb forgot he ever said those words to me.

He agreed to help me, so he's playing it up for the people footing the bill. But when we're in the cramped studio singing like this, so tightly in sync we're practically reading each other's minds, it's hard not to wonder if there's still a spark there.

But it's probably just old feelings. Residual static. A sense memory in my body that will pass.

I gasp as I lose focus, trying to keep enough air flowing through my vocal cords for the high notes. Caleb made it very clear that he's done after the concert. He has an entire life he's built away from the industry. In what world could we make it work, even if this thing between us still lingers? It wouldn't be fair to him to act on it.

Not that it's there. Obviously. I'm just horny and reacting to old feelings.

Once we finish the bridge, I tear my gaze away from his, rushing back to my own microphone. This last chorus is subdued, like I'm telling the audience a secret, and I do everything I can to really sell it. Caleb layers in a harmony, so sweet and soft and full of longing that it almost makes me look back at him, but I don't. I focus on the music, remind myself why I'm here.

Wade flashes a covert thumbs-up as we finish the last line, and the notes ring out despite the terrible acoustics. The executives give us a polite round of applause, but there's something on Gina Choi's face that I really don't like.

She's calculating.

"That was really nice work, kids," she says. It's fine when Wade calls us kids, but from Gina it feels condescending—especially since she's not much older than we are. From Wade, it's affectionate. But from Gina, it's like we're children to be managed instead of adults who have something of value to offer.

How Label Records has always treated us.

If I could go back and do anything over, I'd only sign on for

Wanderlust, our first album. But when Label Records flew us down to LA, they offered us what was essentially a ten-year 360 deal—which means they pay for all Glitter Bats touring, merchandising, and promo, and in return, they get an offensively large cut of every stream of revenue. We didn't know we were signing our lives away; we just couldn't believe someone wanted us to make albums.

After scrimping and saving in those early years just to make it to gigs within driving distance, the idea of them paying for everything was too good to resist. By the time we thought to hire an entertainment lawyer, it was too late. It doesn't help that my mom knew absolutely nothing about contracts. She's a boutique hotel manager, not a contract expert.

Or, at least, she was a boutique hotel manager.

I don't know how she managed to swing it, but she got paid quite a bit during the early Glitter Bats days. Now, she's always on a plane to a different vacation, and I never know what time zone she'll be in. Not that I mind. My mom and I don't exactly talk unless she needs something—usually once or twice a year.

Which is why everything in me goes cold as Tonya Quinn walks into the studio. She's wearing a Dolce & Gabbana sweat suit that makes her look like a wannabe Kardashian, and because of this cosplay she feels the need to wear her Prada sunglasses inside.

My mother, the picture of class.

"Mom. Who told you where we were?" I ask, obnoxiously using the mic instead of speaking into the room. An old bad habit.

"That's no way to greet your mother. Come here!" she says, arms wide.

I feel a brush of fingers against my elbow, and it's Caleb, reminding me I'm not alone.

He knows more than anyone how stressful her presence is for me. One of the things Caleb and I bonded over was having difficult mothers. His mom is actually really sweet; she's just unreliable and bad at making decisions. With Tonya, it's all so calculated. She doesn't care that she's hurting me over and over again; she just cares that she can get something from me. We were the famous ones, but the Glitter Bats' success was always about her. She took credit for every single win.

And now she's here.

"My assistant invited her," Gina says, as if reading my expression. "She's still a party to this contract, and it was only right to involve her."

"Frankly, I'm appalled you didn't call me yourself, Valerie. I had to hear about this from an *assistant*!" Mom says—then she laughs, fake and brittle, like she's just made the funniest joke. As if an assistant is beneath her level.

My stomach drops.

"Hilarious," Keeley says dryly. She's never hidden her disdain for my mom, especially not after everything we went through with her as our manager. Because of the nature of our contract, Mom sided with the label on every request, no matter how demeaning or offensive it was. Once, we were even forced to do an ad for "rockin' deals" at a furniture store.

She's never on my side. If she's here, it's for her.

I grit my teeth, turn off my mic, and shuffle over to my mother like I'm walking the plank. She envelops me in a stiff hug that smells like cigarettes and Chanel No. 9, and I try not to cough.

"We really do need to get back," I say.

"You are such a little workaholic, just like you were in high school! You can take a break," she says, giving my shoulder a sharp squeeze with her manicure. "Breaks are good for you."

Says the woman who has been *taking a break* ever since she got that first Glitter Bats check. Sure, she technically manages a few bands now, but I'm not sure I've ever seen her do any real work. (Then again, I try to keep as much distance between us as possible.)

Still, she's raking it in enough to fund her lifestyle of designer clothing, luxury hotels, and fabulous vacations.

"We literally just got started," I say, backing away from her clutch.

Caleb hurries to my side. "Hi, Ms. Quinn. What if you take a seat next to Wade—he can fill you in on all of the details we've worked out so far. We wanted to show everyone a few more songs, and then we'd be more than happy to catch up over dinner? You choose the place."

"Oh, Caleb, sweetie, you're always such a good boy, but I can't stay," she croons. Of course she can't. "I'm just dropping in for a bit. Think of me like a fly on the wall."

Yeah, one I want to swat.

But I don't say that. I just head back to the stage and try to relax the tension in my shoulders. Of course my mother would show up just when things are feeling solid. Just my rotten luck. I get why Label invited her, but I don't understand why she's here.

What the hell does she *want*?

"I think this is a good time for 'Vampires,' don't you?" Keeley asks, quiet enough so no one else can hear. We wrote the song about what our fame did to some of the people in our lives, always expecting some perk because of us.

"Perfect," I say, pushing my shoulders back.

With a scowl disguised as deep focus, Caleb begins the thrumming bass line, the tick in his jaw the only clue to his true feelings. I sing the first verse solo, staring right at my mom as I lean into the pre-chorus.

> *but they take, take, take*
> *'til there's nothing left*

My mother's facial expression doesn't change, even as I launch into the chorus with a growl.

everybody wants something
I just wanna be free
when I think they have enough
they drain more from me
no matter how I beg
they won't stop making me bleed
'cause all my friends are vampires

It's funny how I wrote this song eight years ago, and it's a self-fulfilling prophecy. Nearly everyone in this room wants to sink their claws back into my flesh. The song is a little cheesy, a little angry, and a lot of loud, but I sing every word like I mean it more than ever before. Caleb duplicates my melody on the bridge so it sounds like we're well and truly shouting:

I'm not a commodity
so fuck you for consuming me
with ink and blood like puppet strings
you exploit my life to live like kings

you crossed my lines, I cross my heart
and hope you cry when I depart
I'm tearing free from all your fangs
staking claim on my own damn name

"Vampires" is always a crowd favorite, and the adrenaline rush I get from the lyrics helps me channel my energy until the final notes ring out. When it's time to transition into "Making Memories," I swap out my electric for an acoustic while Caleb takes a sip of water.

Our ballads are too personal and they still don't feel right yet, but we've been working on this one a lot, and it felt like a good chance to show some range. I swallow thickly as I pop on a capo and begin the opening chords.

My heart twists as Caleb starts singing the verse. "Making Memories" is a song we wrote about falling in love with your best friend. It's vague. We never confirmed our relationship. But that doesn't mean it doesn't *feel* intimate. I have to dissociate myself from the lyrics and just sing like it's my job, because we have to finish this afternoon in one piece.

When the ballad ends, we turn to address any questions from the room. At least Wade is here, but I can tell by the set of his jaw that he's concerned about my mom's surprise visit. He took over our management for a reason, and we all know it. There's a round of compliments and some questions from the suits, and then my mother opens her damn mouth.

"I heard you all are refusing to make another album. It just doesn't make sense!" she blurts.

"We're not refusing to make the album—there's no album to make. The band broke up," I say, clenching my shaking fists.

She places a hand on her chest. "Well, you don't look very broken up to me. In fact, you all looked pretty cozy on that stage. Very . . . strategic."

She's glancing between me and Caleb like she knows a secret, and it makes me want to scream. I don't want her making this thing between Caleb and me dirty, like I'm using him for my image. Even if I am, a little.

"We're just here to thank the fans for supporting us after all these years," Caleb says diplomatically, but his brow's a little furrowed. He's not happy.

"Yes, and I unfortunately couldn't commit to another album given my current schedule," Jane says. "We've all moved on to other projects."

Keeley grins like a lion circling her prey. "Yeah, everyone wants a piece of me, I'm sorry to say."

Riker laughs. "My next year is packed too."

"We can work with your schedule, if that's the problem," Gina says, eyes lighting up like she's caught us.

"No problem here." Wade clears his throat. "We've already said there will be no album."

"But if there were, you'd record it at Label, right?" Mom asks.

The color is draining from Caleb's face, and my stomach starts to twist. This isn't what he wants. It's not what any of us wants. We need to do this concert and move on with our lives.

"Alright, you've made your request. Everyone out. I need to talk to my band," Wade says.

There are a few protests—the loudest of which comes from my mom—but finally Wade manages to clear the room.

"Fuck them," Keeley says, as soon as we're all alone.

"They're very pushy. Do you think they called in your mom to influence us?" Jane asks.

"Absolutely. She gets a cut from that first contract, so I'm sure she's hoping that we make another album so she can book a trip to Fiji," I say. "Sometimes it feels like she signed those contracts in my blood."

Wade winces sympathetically. "Our legal department checked out the contracts Tonya delivered when you signed with me. The royalty rate is criminal—any real manager would have steered you far away from a 360—but it's all aboveboard." Something about that doesn't settle. I never realized it was my mom who sent the contracts to Ortega Management. I always assumed they would have gotten anything they needed from Label directly.

I'm probably just paranoid. I shake my head and tune back in to Wade's pep talk.

"Regardless, I want to make it clear to all of you that I won't allow Label or anyone else to pressure you into a third album. You showed really incredible work today, Glitter Bats. I'm so proud to return for your final bows."

And with that, my eyes sting. At least Wade has our backs. If he didn't, I'd have fallen apart by now. Even after all this time, I'm surer than ever that the only people I can trust are standing in this room.

12

+ *Caleb* +

When I head back to my room after the showcase, there's an idea I can't shake.

I have no desire to record a new album. That hasn't changed. But the moment I'm alone, I start to rifle through my songwriting journals, knowing it's here somewhere. Originally, I wasn't going to bring them all to LA, but I tossed them in my suitcase last minute.

They're so full of ink that it bleeds through the pages. Some are discarded or unfinished drafts from old writing sessions with the band, and some are my own two a.m. thoughts about almosts and could-have-beens. In one of the most battered books, I find the old collaborations, Valerie's messy scrawl in her favorite purple ink mingled with my neater hand in blue.

I can't stop thinking about them as I shower and change. Once I've cleaned up, I knock on the adjoining door to Valerie's room.

After what feels like an eternity, it opens. She's changed into an oversized white T-shirt and barely-there shorts. Her eyes are soft, her fading pink hair mussed, and I laugh.

"Were you asleep?"

She covers a yawn with her fist. "Just a power nap. Had to re-cover from today. What's up?"

I wanted to present this in a very specific way, but I just blurt it out. "'Daydreams Like This.'"

Her eyes widen, and she straightens a little, as if that woke her up. "What?"

"We should finish it."

"Are you serious?" I know what she's thinking—that's the song we were working on right before we broke up. It's not the reason for the breakup, and it didn't ruin the band, but it's part of all those tangled-up emotions surrounding our past.

And it's also something I never forgave myself for leaving un-finished.

"We could see what happens, finish it just for us," I say. "It's a great melody."

Valerie bites her lip, frowning. "Caleb. It's a love song."

I clear my throat. "I'm very aware of that."

"About us."

"Yup. But we have a little time, and . . ." I brace myself, resisting the urge to tear my gaze away from hers. "I miss writing with you. This could be our chance to do it again."

Valerie bites her lip, tucking a stray lock behind her ear. "I miss writing with you too."

This was the thing that always came easiest to us: the juncture of friendship and music, this thing we both loved. The industry, the media, even our feelings—they complicated all the reasons we started the band in the first place. But maybe I can give her this: a reminder of why we started. A space to be creative. Closure that's more than bitter memories.

God knows we need it.

"Maybe it's not a terrible idea . . ." she says slowly, eyes spar-kling. "Okay, Sloane. Let's see if we have one more song in us."

I grin, triumphant. "Let me grab my guitar."

"I have, like, three in here. Come on," she says, as if deciding something. She grabs me by the wrist and drags me into the room, and damn it if my pulse doesn't beat a little faster at the urgent press of her fingerprints on my skin. Somehow, after all this time, her touch still sends a thrill through my veins.

But it's only the ghost of old feelings come to haunt me—and I'll keep reminding myself this is strictly professional. I can get through one writing session without wanting to shove Valerie up against a wall and kiss her breathless.

Problem is, that's how the night ended the last time we wrote together.

Shit, I need to get it together.

While Valerie rummages around in her bag, I take a few deep breaths, trying to ground myself the way my therapist taught me.

Okay, so we're doing this.

I only thought of presenting the idea to Valerie, but I didn't think of what would happen if she agreed: Us. Alone. In her hotel room. Now.

Writing a love song.

"Text the others—we'll order in," she says.

Relief floods through my chest. If we don't do this alone, it'll be easier. "You want to invite them to collaborate?"

"No," she says quickly. "I mean, we're technically making new music together, even if we have no intent to share it with anyone. It can't be Glitter Bats music. Label will want it if they ever find out, and that's not what we're here to do."

"Right," I say. "Okay, so we'll skip dinner with the others. Want to do room service whenever we get hungry?"

"Perfect. I made a TJ's run so my little kitchenette is pretty stocked."

I smile, because some things never change. Valerie might be

famous, but she still loves her cheap Trader Joe's goodies. I mean, she's not wrong—they have great snacks. I grab the mini chocolate chip cookies and olive oil popcorn from the counter and bring them over to where she's spread out her guitar and a blank notebook.

On her bed.

How am I supposed to focus when the scent of her is everywhere? She's always used shampoo that leaves an unmistakable scent of sugar in her wake. Now there's something new in the mix, warm and citrusy, and the combination is like she spent the day baking lemon bars.

It makes me wonder how her soft skin might taste.

Clearing my throat to banish the thought, I grab the guitar from Valerie's floor and sink onto the far corner of her bed with my journal, trying to keep enough space between us to chill out but not make the distance obvious.

We're just writing. Nothing more. It's hard enough to work together again—I don't need to make it weird by smelling her, even if she's intoxicating as hell.

God, if I keep this up, my sweatpants are going to betray my thoughts.

Swallowing thickly, I close my eyes and try to center myself. Instead of thinking about how good Valerie would look naked on the soft white comforter, I try to remember this song. We only really ever had a chorus.

I lightly strum through the chord progressions and look at her as I sing the lines, remembering the words as if we just wrote the song yesterday.

we had so many daydreams just like this
seeing our name in lights from Seattle to Paris
don't care how far this old Fender goes
no matter where we are, you're still my home

Valerie doesn't sing the words, but she hums a low harmony. "You remember it all."

"Yeah," I say, tearing my gaze away from hers, trying not to be too overcome. These lyrics have haunted me for six years, this last connection between us that never resolved. Of course I remember every single word of it.

So many sleepless nights have featured this song.

"This really could have been something, I just know it," she says. She gestures for the guitar, and I hand it over to her. She starts noodling with the scraps of an unfinished verse.

We were working on "Daydreams" for our third album, the one that never existed. A slow, intimate love song isn't exactly our brand of pop-punk-inspired rock—and honestly the song has more folk vibes than anything else—but this album still would have included plenty of what our fans expected. The band agreed the two of us could include something a little more personal on this one. Valerie and I were finally ready to let the world in on our not-so-secret love story.

Or at least that's what I thought, until I took it too far and it all fell apart.

"I still haven't apologized to you for that night," she says, playing the chord progression over and over, like she's reaching for a feeling.

"No, please don't apologize." I sigh. "We were kids. I was asking you to commit to something you weren't ready for, and it wasn't fair." I can't help but feel like if I'd just been paying attention, I'd have realized the timing was all off.

She huffs. "It's not like it was a surprise. We were serious about each other. I was on a high after the concert. And when you proposed . . . for a moment, I was on top of the world. But then the panic set in."

My mouth goes dry as the shame comes back to me in full force. The two of us alone in that greenroom after the show, me holding her back while the others went ahead to the hotel. The ringing silence when I asked a question she wouldn't answer. "It was too much. I scared you away."

"It's just . . . making any plans for my future outside of music scared the hell out of me. There was all this pressure to get a new record out and capitalize on our success, and I couldn't think about anything else. Instead of telling you how I was feeling, I asked for space." Her hand stills on the frets, and I think about the phantom ring that might be there if things had turned out differently. That big flashy diamond I'm not even sure she liked, but I spent an unbelievable amount of money on anyway.

The reverberation of the guitar stops, muffled, until there's nothing but silence between us. Finally, Valerie breaks it. "And we couldn't continue, not after I hurt you like that. It's my fault the band fell apart."

"I thought . . ." I swallow thickly as the emotions start to stir in my chest again. Trying to clear my head, I resettle on the bed, crossing my legs. "I thought when you wanted to keep our relationship a secret, it meant that you weren't happy. I was convinced you only stayed with me because of some obligation, an old friendship, a fear of breaking up the band and publicly ruining everything." I sigh, gathering my nerve. "Don't get me wrong—I proposed because of how I felt about you. But I think it was also about me trying to hold on to you tighter, instead of really thinking about what it would mean for us. I mean, we were so young. And then when you asked me for some time to think about it, it felt like you were letting me down easy. So I cut and left before my heart could break any more." I didn't just lose the person I thought was the love of my life that night. I lost the best friends I've ever had.

I broke up the band, not Valerie.

Her eyes widen, and if I didn't know better I'd think she was holding back tears. "Why didn't you tell me how you were feeling?"

"Because I was twenty-two and an idiot. That ultimatum was really just self-sabotage." My shoulders tense as I remember that night, shame flooding my bones. I really said I was done waiting for her to put us first. That if she really wanted me, she had to decide then and there if she was all in.

I gave her a *now or never* and walked away with empty hands.

All at once, the pain of that moment comes rushing back. The greenroom was dusty, the scents of hair spray, coffee, and sweat permeating the air, but I had so much hope. And then there was the shouting, the tears, the weight in my chest as I walked away from the best thing that ever happened to me.

Because it was always the Glitter Bats. It was always *her*.

"I wish you'd told me," Valerie says. "Because then you'd know I didn't want to keep you a secret out of obligation or regret, but to protect us from the world."

I freeze. This is news to me. "What do you mean?"

She glances up at me through those long lashes, then stares at the duvet. "You know what fame does, how this industry can be. There was already tension in the band, and the media was getting worse, calling me a loose cannon and a hack . . . and a slut, after those photos leaked. I was living every day in survival mode. We'd get back from long hours of rehearsal and there my mom would be, waiting in my room, ready to read through all the headlines—good and very bad—and tally the engagement like I was a show pony."

"Valerie, I . . ." I can't believe I didn't see it back then. She must have been barely holding it together. Her mom, the label, the media—she wrote a song about it, and I still didn't see. Everyone wanted something from her, and then I added the ultimate pressure. That ring probably felt like a chain.

"But when you and I were together, everything was perfect. Some days, you were the only thing that could make me smile, and all I wanted was to get you alone where I felt safe. If we were alone, no one could touch us. And then you were on one knee with that massive diamond, and after my heart stopped racing, I had this vision of me ruining it and landing us on some list of failed celebrity marriages in ten years. I couldn't take losing you like that."

My jaw drops. "I had no idea," I say as I suddenly realize something. "I was doing what everyone else was doing, wasn't I? I was telling you how to live your life when you needed space to decide for yourself. Hell, I was practically *handling* you when I delivered that ultimatum. I'm so sorry I didn't see it before."

Valerie gives me a watery smile. "I mean, you poured your heart out and I rejected you, so don't be too hard on yourself. Besides, we both said vicious things that night." She sets the guitar down and reaches for my hand, sending warmth across my skin. "And I'm really, really sorry too. I'm sorry I hurt you then, and now."

I squeeze her hand. "You didn't hurt me now."

She groans. "No, don't lie. I'm sorry for the way I approached you about the reunion. And then . . . asking you to pretend we're together? It was so wrong of me, and we really can drop it."

I thought that's what I wanted, but when she says it out loud, I really hate the sound. My life might be comfortable, simple, but I forgot how much making my own music—with the Glitter Bats—made me come alive.

I don't know what that means, but the least I can do is help Valerie.

Suddenly, this feels too important to drop. "Has The Network renewed *Epic Theme Song* yet?"

She closes her eyes and lets out a long sigh. "No. Wade thinks we're off to a good start, but we haven't convinced the higher-ups that my reputation has been redeemed enough to repair the damage from Roxanne dropping out."

This whole thing is bullshit. The Network expected the cast to do all this free work promoting the show, and now they're blaming

Valerie for its fate. Because fine, after that first night at Jane's house, I might've done some digging into the scandal that brought us all here. Theo Blake is obviously full of it.

And if I understand correctly, Roxanne made a snap judgment without asking Valerie for her side of the story. It was probably to protect herself from the vicious press, so I can't blame her without knowing more about her situation, but that doesn't make this Valerie's fault.

She needs this.

"We're just going to have to make more headlines," I say, a little suggestively, just to make her smile.

She does, but she also shakes her head. "This is too much. You shouldn't."

"I already told you—I'm offering. Friends help friends save their TV shows."

Valerie grimaces. "It's way too much to ask of you. I can't believe I ever brought it up."

"It's fine. We'll play up the romance, make sure we're seen out in public. Then when the concert comes around and we break out this duet, everyone will be talking about it. If *Valerie Quinn* is a trending topic, they won't be able to deny you another season."

She looks up to the ceiling, like she's praying to God or Kurt Cobain, and then she locks those blue eyes onto mine.

"Alright, rock star. Let's write this song."

It Was Always You by GlitterBugForever
(posted five years ago)

Rating: [Mature]
Fandom: Glitter Bats (musician/band)
Tags: Caleb Sloane/Valerie Quinn, CalErie, SloaneQuinn, Glitter Bats, Yes I Ship Real People, If You've Seen These Two Share a Microphone You Won't Judge Me, Riker Maddox, Keeley Cunningham, Jane Mercer, Original Character(s), CalErie Never Confirmed They Were Dating So I'll Make It Happen Here, Coffee Shop AU, Food Porn, Maybe Other Porn Too, Baking Together as Foreplay, We May Never Get a Glitter Bats Reunion but We'll Always Have Fic, Slice of Life, Slice of Pie

Synopsis: Barista Valerie Quinn gets a new job managing Glitter Coffee. Caleb Sloane owns the bakery next door and delivers fresh pastries to her shop every morning. Valerie isn't sure what's more delicious, him or his cinnamon rolls, but she's too focused on doing her job well to act on it. But when Caleb learns Valerie is a singer-songwriter and invites her to jam with his band, sparks really fly.

Words: 42,013	**Likes:** 7,217
Chapters: 8/8	**Comments:** 2,319
Hits: 69,701	**Bookmarks:** 336

13

✦ Valerie ✦

I forgot how much I love writing with Caleb.

By one a.m., we're both hoarse from singing the same lines over and over, but it's obvious we're pleased with the progress on "Daydreams Like This" as we pack away guitars and notebooks until our next session. For a heartbeat, I wonder if he'll crash on my bed like old times.

It really wasn't sexual at first, the bed sharing. We'd work on songs until we were exhausted, so we'd fall asleep, so comfortable sharing a space that we didn't give it that much thought. And then we were *together* and so tangled up in each other that we didn't sleep apart for years, even though we kept our relationship as private as we could. We were always good at keeping secrets, even if people assumed they knew what was going on.

And sleeping next to each other always made sense. Even now, I probably wouldn't stop him if he started to doze.

But he doesn't. Ever the gentleman, Caleb treads sleepily into his own room once we're finally done for the night. Because he was here for hours, the blankets are mussed from his spot at the foot of my bed, and I want to curl up in his phantom warmth.

Hurriedly, I smooth out the duvet, but Caleb's presence in the room is still so palpable I can't bear it. Every inch of my skin is buzzing with awareness, and the idea of sleep suddenly feels like nothing more than a distant possibility. As I brush my teeth, I can't imagine how I'm supposed to just go to bed. I don't know if I should eat a snack or get myself off or just take a fucking sleep aid, but I don't do any of that.

Just like my therapist taught me, I make a list in my Notes app of everything on my mind:

- working with Caleb again
- finally talking about The Proposal ☹
- pretending I'm not still attracted to Caleb (because *damn*)
- reuniting with the Glitter Bats and fixing those friendships
- the fate of *Epic Theme Song*
- hundreds of jobs on *Epic Theme Song* depending on my reputation
- dealing with Label Records and their bullshit
- the weirdness of Mom's visit today

My mind tumbles as I stare at that last one, remembering what Wade said after rehearsal this afternoon. *Mom* sent the contracts to Ortega Management. I trust Wade's legal team reviewing the contracts, but I don't trust Tonya. If she had a chance to do something shady . . . well, I think she might have.

It's just a feeling. But living with Mom taught me to never ignore my feelings.

Padding over the thick carpet to my bag, I pull out my laptop, then settle over at the desk. I'm not quite sure what I'm looking for, but I know where to start. Before I revealed I'd hired a real manager, I snuck into my mom's home office and scanned all of her Glitter Bats records to the cloud. It's not like seventeen-year-old me knew to keep track of my own legal documents, and by the time I wanted them a few years later, it was almost too late.

Mom acted so altruistic when she took care of everything. *I just don't want you kids to worry about the boring part. Just enjoy the fame!* I had this strange hunch that she'd take it personally if I just asked for copies, even refuse to give me everything I needed.

Although I should never have had to outwit my own mother, that was just childhood at the Quinn house. She was so determined to show everyone how well she could raise me alone that she never actually did. I raised myself, with a little teenage guidance from Cameron Sloane when she was around, and the one thing I learned from Tonya was to always think ahead.

Good thing.

I pull up the digital storage, enter my password, and thank past Valerie for her efficiency. There are so many documents in this file, all those different contracts and press releases and financial statements without any recognizable organizational scheme. But I don't care about the episode of *Riverwood* that featured "Midnight Road Trip," or our first magazine shoot. I sort by date and there it is: the contract we signed before recording our first album, promising Label Records anything we produced for ten years.

For a moment, I think I'm seeing double.

My hand stills on the track pad. There are *two* of them. I blink, unable to make much sense of what's on my screen. With different naming conventions, I didn't notice the duplicate in my rush to copy everything and get out of the office unnoticed all those years ago.

It doesn't add up. Why would Mom have two copies of the same document? Maybe it's just her not being the greatest with technology, but . . . I doubt it. The contracts are long, and there's no way I'm making any sense of them tonight, so I dash off an email to Wade with both files.

My heart pounds as I click send. There's no way I can sleep now. Tonight's as good of a time as any to check social media.

With a yawn, I pull on a hoodie, tuck up my legs, and dive in.

Wade would update me if there were positive changes on the *Epic Theme Song* front, but I scroll the tag anyway. My costar Lola Martinez just did a livestream, so most of the recent posts are about her. She's promoting her new film, but fans ask her about playing Shadowgirl on *Epic Theme Song*, and there's a nice sound bite I catch about my own side project: "Of course I heard about the Glitter Bats reunion—it's super exciting! Valerie's so talented— the whole band is—and I was a bit of a Glitterbug before I even worked with her. It's going to be great to see them all together again."

I send Lola a quick thank-you via DM, because she really didn't even have to respond to that question. It was kind. We're not super close, but we're friendly. It certainly made the half a season we spent making out in front of the cameras more bearable. She smells good, she's a respectful kisser, and she always has Altoids. Best partner for a romantic scene I've ever had on a set.

Not like Tyler Rowe, who tried to stick his tongue in my mouth without warning and got yelled at by our intimacy coordinator.

If we get renewed, I hope they write Tyler's character off the show.

Despite all of my scrolling, I can't find any clues that lead to the fate of *Epic Theme Song*. In the hashtag, though, my heart breaks at the determination of our fans:

Hey, Wonderfans! Let's all stream **#EpicThemeSong** on repeat on July 30th to get it back in the top 10! The Network will have NO CHOICE but to #RenewETS. Tell your friends!

—56,192 LIKES —11,333 REPOSTS

I JUST FINISHED **#EpicThemeSong** AND I NEED ANOTHER SEASON #RenewETS

—1,230 LIKES —428 REPOSTS

#EpicThemeSong is the best show of all time and if @TheNetwork doesn't #RenewETS I will show up at their corporate offices and demand an explanation. I'm not even joking.

—99 LIKES —12 REPOSTS

HOW DO WE KNOW NOTHING ABOUT SEASON 3 of **#EpicThemeSong** YET?! #RenewETS YOU COWARDS @TheNetwork

—702 LIKES —258 REPOSTS

My friend started a petition to #RenewETS so come on Wonderfans! If you want more **#EpicThemeSong**, help us get to 100,000 signatures!

—27,908 LIKES —8,992 REPOSTS

Eyes stinging, I slam my laptop shut. They're trying so hard, and it's not enough. The fate of this show rests on my shoulders. Scrolling to watch them beg for something only I can give isn't going to make any progress, but it's sure as hell a good reminder of why I'm in this hotel.

I've been so distracted since we started rehearsing, but I need to focus on the prize: getting enough good press to renew this show. The fans deserve better than a fickle network and a messy lead.

"Fuck, fuck, fuck!" I shriek, way too loud this late at night. Sure enough, Caleb busts through the door connecting our two rooms that neither of us bothers to lock anymore. He's shirtless, which is distracting enough without seeing his hair all rumpled from sleep. Because it's two a.m. and I clearly woke him up with my outburst.

"Oh my god, I'm so sorry. Please go back to sleep," I say.

He opens his mouth to say something, then closes it. Finally, he asks, "You okay?"

"Yeah," I say. "I just . . . couldn't sleep, so I was torturing myself with social media."

"Did that help?" he asks, his voice soft and rough.

I groan. "No." I sink back against the chair and groan. "Ugh!"

Caleb blinks, obviously half-awake. "Want me to stay?"

Always, I think, and then I'm jolted back to reality. Starting this up again is a terrible idea. But god, why the hell not? It's two a.m. What's really going to happen?

Nothing.

Anything.

Everything.

Clearly I'm gaping, because he grins sleepily at me. "This would seriously be the weirdest booty call ever. I want to know if you want me to sleep with you. Literally. God, you know what I mean. We used to do this all the time." His eyes widen, and I watch as the realization sets in. "And now by your deer-in-the-headlights look, I realize how inappropriate that suggestion was, so I'm going to go back and crawl into my own bed now and pretend this conversation never happened."

He's cute when he talks too much. It doesn't happen often, because he's usually so careful and reserved. But when he's tired like this, I'm seeing past all of his walls.

"Honestly, I'd like it if you stayed. Being around you . . . it helps make all this feel somewhat normal," I admit.

His lips twist. "Helps me too. Probably would never fess up to that in the morning, but here we are."

I clear my throat, suddenly shy. "Right, well . . . I should probably wash my face."

He nods. "I can set up the bed."

Before I can tell him to forget all of it, I hurry over to the bathroom and stare at my greasy, day-old foundation in the mirror. As this impossibly long day hits me all over again, I scrub my face and moisturize, then brush my teeth again, forgoing a longer routine for the promise of sleep. When I get back to the room, Caleb is already in my bed like it's no big deal.

Maybe it's not.

As gently as possible, I slip into the sheets and turn off the lamp. I sink in next to him, letting that minty scent of his body-wash fill my lungs. For a moment, I don't know how this is supposed to go—do I lie flat on my back? Shove a pillow between us? Surely he can hear my pulse thrumming in my ears, sense the heat of me between the sheets the way I can feel him.

"Want to stop freaking out and come cuddle?" he murmurs, touching my shoulder softly in a way that will guide me to him if I let it but isn't forcing me to do anything. As always, he's respecting my boundaries even without words.

But this isn't a boundary I want to keep between us anymore. I'm craving the familiarity of his touch. Without it, I've been un-moored. Adrift on the sea of all the things I thought I wanted, floating helplessly on the things that pushed him away.

I need this.

So I let Caleb slip an arm around my waist and pull me to him, and I sink into the softness of his T-shirt. Because even though he's exhausted, while I was getting ready to sleep, he grabbed a shirt. Probably to make me more comfortable.

I could live a hundred lifetimes and never deserve Caleb Sloane.

Despite the T-shirt, my body remembers just how to fold into his. I know where my head fits on his shoulder, where my arm rests on his chest, where to hook my leg around his so I'm flush against his side but not on top of him. Maybe I've been touch starved, but I'm overcome with relief as the warmth of him envelops me. All at once, I remember what it was like to be in love with Caleb, falling into those thoughts like a dream.

Did those feelings ever go away?

My memories are like a photo album of emotions I'm revisiting one by one, but I can't tell if they're snapshots in time or places I can return to again and again. I'm too tired to decipher if it's just all of this nostalgia getting the best of me. Or maybe he's still got that soft, gentle grip on my heart, safe in his careful hands.

But maybe, just at two a.m. as I fall asleep, I can admit that my foolish heart never stopped wanting him.

14

Caleb

I've made a lot of stupid decisions this summer, but the worst by far is inviting myself into Valerie's bed.

Nothing happened, but I'm still high on *her* when I slip back into my own room the next morning, giving her a few minutes to hit snooze. As soon as I'm alone, I sink against the door between our rooms and lean my head back, trying to catch my breath. Even with a wall between us, I can feel her effect on me.

Her sugar and lemon scent. The tousled pink waves tickling my shoulder. Sheets pulled taut because they're wrapped around curves.

I am definitely not over Valerie Quinn.

She makes me feel like I'm eighteen again, nervous and jumpy and flushed, desperate to kiss my best friend. There's no way I'm going to get through another day all jittery like this without doing something to burn off the energy.

Hating myself for it, I stumble into the shower, turn the water to scalding, and try to get off as efficiently as I can. Like I've done so many times over the years, I embrace my guiltiest fantasy. I imagine it's her hand instead of my own grasping my cock, water trailing down every delicious curve of her bare skin. I come embarrassingly fast.

God, if she knew what I was up to on the other side of her wall, she'd never let me back into her room.

There were a few times last night when I thought she might want me back, even before we shared the bed. Her eyes would linger on me too long, or her fingers would casually brush against my arm as we were scratching out lyrics and trying new melodies.

But there's no way she actually still wants me.

After we cleared the air, I was reminded all too well that I hurt her just as much as she hurt me. Even if there was a future for us, I couldn't expect her to try again. She's obviously moved on. Hell, she might have only shared the bed last night because she pitied me, pining away for her from afar after she rejected my proposal.

But even though all we did was lie next to each other, something about it felt safe. Right. Like it's something that never should have stopped.

My heart races as I try to make sense of that.

As I finish getting dressed and ready for the day, I think about how easy it would be to walk back into this life for good. The others are all still working in the industry, and they might be open to talking about a new album, no matter what they told Label. I don't think a real Glitter Bats return is out of the realm of possibility, if I was on board.

I'm starting to wonder if leaving this life behind is really what I wanted, or if I was just running away from my problems.

But then my phone buzzes, and I shake off the thoughts. I need to get a grip. The text on my phone is from my older sister, Cameron, and I practically roll my eyes at the universe for the timing of her message.

Cameron: Hey! Hope the rock star life isn't too terrible 😌 We miss you!

The text includes a selfie of her with Sebastian Bark laying his head on her shoulder. My dog is smiling, and Cam is making a pouty face.

My heart twists. God, I miss them.

She follows up almost immediately with a second text.

Cameron: Are you still planning to fly back in the middle of August? Carrie wants to pop down for a visit.

These past few weeks have felt like less of a brief visit to the musician life and more like an inevitable return, but I can't believe she's even asking. Of course I'm coming back after the concert. Cam's text is a sharp, timely reminder that I can't let Valerie lure me back to the industry. I need to focus on getting through the reunion so I can return to my life. My *actual* life in the real world. Reuniting with Glitter Bats is a fantasy, a temporary escape from reality.

Returning for good was never the plan. I have to be practical. I shoot off a text to Cam:

Me: Yes! Maybe we can take Carrie to the coast if you can get the time off?

Cameron: Sounds perfect. I also wanted to let you know—Carrie mentioned these music schools like it when prospective students show up for in-person auditions in the fall. Did you know anything about that?

My stomach drops. Mom can't afford to send Carrie to New York, and I absolutely can't see her remembering to go with her even if she charged it all on another credit card.

I swallow thickly.

Me: No, but I'm happy to buy her plane tickets. I'll take my personal days and go with her.

Cameron: I have some personal days too, and we can *split* the tickets.

I don't want Cam using her money for this, not with what I'm doing this summer.

Me: No, I got this. I'm getting paid really well for this concert, you know.

Cameron: 😑 I'm sure you are, but this isn't just your responsibility. Hell, it should be Mom's responsibility.

It should be, but we both know Mom can't do it. I'm sure these auditions could be taped instead of in person, but I want Carrie to have every edge she can get.

That's why I'm here—so my baby sister can pursue her dreams.

Me: Okay. We'll talk more when I get home.

I run a hand through my hair. Cam and Leah shouldn't have to help. I never should have run through all my Glitter Bats money. God, if I'd hired a financial advisor like Keeley did, maybe none of my family would have to work now, even with those criminal royalty rates.

Cameron: Sounds good. Love you.

Me: I love you too. Kiss Sebastian Bark for me.

I let out a long, slow breath, trying to focus on the day ahead. So I brush my teeth and style my hair and try to remind myself this is all an act. Just as I'm finishing getting ready, there's a soft knock on the door between rooms.

"Come in," I call.

Valerie slips inside. "Good morning," she murmurs, her hands wrapped around a water bottle.

"Good morning," I say back. And *damn*, the way she's smiling shyly at me almost knocks me off my feet.

At practice yesterday she was just wearing a hoodie and leggings, but we're back to the rock star look—she's in an oversized white tee, ripped black jeans, and combat boots, with a bunch of leather bracelets on her wrists. She's playing up her eyeliner with a knife-sharp cat eye, and it makes her look a little mischievous and a whole lot sexy.

When she was on the other side of this door, I could almost believe those feelings weren't real. Now, with her looking like a dream right in front of me, I don't know what to think. So I just try to act casual. Valerie's got enough going on—she doesn't need to deal with all of my feelings.

"Ready to head down to brunch? Wade's coming by so we can all talk," she says.

I blink. "Oh. What about?"

She bites her lip, frowning. "Business."

That's ominous, but I know I'll find out soon enough. "Okay. Let's go."

"Wait. Is that all you're wearing?" Valerie strides over to my chair and grabs the leather jacket I draped over the back. She offers it to me. "Wear this too."

I roll my eyes. "It's like eighty degrees out."

She pouts, fluttering her lashes dramatically as she looks at me with doe eyes. "For the aesthetic? Please?"

And damn it if that *please* doesn't turn me on all over again. I definitely still can't say no to Valerie, especially when she begs. Utterly powerless to resist, I reach out to take the jacket from her. Our fingers brush. My hands ache with the need to touch her again.

So I hurry to put the damn jacket on before I can do anything stupid. I clear my throat. "Fine, you win."

Valerie puts her hands on her hips, stepping back. She assesses me, eyes slowly considering every piece of my haphazard outfit: Docs, jeans, a too-tight T-shirt. I warm under her scrutinizing gaze.

"You checking me out?" I ask, trying to sound casual despite the hoarseness in my voice.

"Do you have a problem with that?" she asks, eyes sparkling.

I reach a hand to my neck. "No."

"Good. Had to make sure you're pretty for any cameras. Let's go." And with that, she leads the way out of my room.

Dazed, I follow her through the door and down to breakfast.

There's something public about brunch at a fancy restaurant in LA, and the hotel restaurant is one of the fanciest. Even the wrap I ordered from room service last week was decadent. The dining room is buzzing when we arrive, but I'm grateful when the host leads us to a private room.

But I'm a little confused. I thought the whole point was generating press—so why are we being secreted away?

The table is set with white linens and dishes, polished flatware, and carafes of coffee, hot water, and several kinds of juice. Two ice buckets hold champagne for mimosas, but I decide to abstain in favor of tea.

It's just Wade, Keeley, and Jane so far, which means Riker is no doubt still making his way downstairs. Back when we were broke and splitting shitty hotel rooms, I learned just how impossible it was to wake him up. Once, in Nashville, I literally had to throw a glass of ice-cold water in his face. Good thing he's such a good guitar player, because dude can't show up on time even when he's getting paid.

"Did anyone check on Riker?" Valerie asks.

"Oh yeah, I made him give me his second key so I could wake him up. He's on his way down," Jane says.

A shadow crosses over Keeley's face, but she takes a sip of coffee and it disappears. Is she jealous of Jane—or of Riker? I always wondered if there was *something* going on there, some kind of attraction, but Keeley flirts with Val and me too. It was always hard to tell, especially because Jane is so private about her dating life. I don't think any of us ever knew the kind of people she's attracted to.

And it's none of my business. The last thing I need to do is get involved in the romantic entanglements of my band, especially when I can't make sense of my own. I busy myself making my tea, forcing all those old feelings away. Now is not the time.

Finally, Riker arrives, we all put in our orders, and the server leaves us to chat. As soon as the door to our private room clicks shut, Valerie clears her throat.

"We need to talk," she says, and the look on her face is so vindicated that I wonder if we pulled it off.

Are they renewing *Epic Theme Song*? Warmth fills my chest as I think that yes, we did it, and the media has finally been convinced that she's not the villain. That's the news I'm expecting.

The news she shares pulls the world out from under my feet.

"Our record deal wasn't as bad as we thought." She sighs, folding her hands on the table. "That is, our real deal. I found two copies in the files I scanned from my mom's computer years ago—one real contract, and the doctored version she sent to Ortega Management."

My stomach drops. I suspect I know where this is going.

"What?" Keeley says, almost dropping her coffee.

Wade sighs, scrubbing a hand over his face. "It's true. I had an emergency meeting with legal this morning, and we combed over every line—the version we received from Tonya Quinn hid the real royalty rate. In fact, we just received the original after contacting Label, and it confirms it."

"The fuck?" Riker demands.

Valerie's eyes flash. "The true contract gives us double the royalties we've been seeing—but *half* is all going to Tonya. It explains why she showed up yesterday. She wants us to make another album so we're still attached to Label. She's a part of that original deal."

"And Label thinks she can convince us to do it," I say to Valerie.

"Yeah, I don't think Label knows what my mom did." Valerie clears her throat. "She really got herself the best deal out of anyone." I'm not surprised, but it still makes me sick. Tonya has always been sneaky, and *damn*, I could have used my part of that money.

Double our royalties. Jeez. It would still be a bad record deal, but it would have made a difference.

"Oh, you've got to be fucking kidding me," Keeley says.

"I wish I was," Valerie says. "She's contracted as our manager, but we aren't seeing anywhere near the royalties we should be—because she finagled everything so she's getting 50 percent commission from each of us in addition to her cut from the band as a whole. Everyone in accounting at Ortega did the math. We just never caught it before because our royalty statements are net, not gross."

I wince. My relationship with my mom is tough, but she's never taken advantage of me the way Tonya does with Valerie. Tonya has always acted like her daughter is her meal ticket. She'll do literally anything for a paycheck. Right before we released *Bittersweet*, some private photos Valerie took got leaked to the press, and I always suspected Tonya had something to do with it. I can't imagine what that kind of relationship feels like.

To top it all off, she manipulated things from the start.

Yeah, I've paid for Mom's groceries and utilities, and even fronted her rent a couple of times, but that was always initiated by me. Maybe I feel obligated to help take care of my sister, but it's not like she's taking money that belongs to me behind my back—or taking even more.

"Do we have any legal recourse?" Jane asks.

Wade sighs, running a hand over his face. "I have no idea. Our lawyers are on it."

"I also know somebody who knows a PI, if we need one," Riker says.

Wade opens his mouth to protest, then pauses. "That's certainly one route, but I can't *legally* advise you to do that."

Riker shrugs, then fires off a text.

"So if we wait Label out, we could make another album in, say, December and actually *earn our damn royalties*," Keeley says. "Fuck, I want to get what we deserve. We're damn good at making music. This is such bullshit!"

"But we're not going to record again," I say quickly.

Riker takes a slow sip of his coffee. "I know we told Gina that, but I don't think we should rule it out." His words are casual, measured, and I know what he's doing: hedging his bets. I love Riker, but I can't count on him to be a decision-maker. He'll do what everyone else decides.

"We should only consider it if we all agree that's something we want," Jane says, catching my eye. "I'm interested, but it has to be unanimous."

I give Jane a grateful glance, and she nods. Even now, she's still trying her best to take care of all of us, the way she's done so many times before. My eyes fall to Valerie, desperate to know what she's thinking.

"I'm still processing the part about my mom stealing from us." Valerie reddens, tearing her gaze from mine. "It would be great to make something she can't touch. And I mean, there are songs we never recorded—hell, Caleb and I just worked on another last night. We could surprise the fans with it at the concert, and it could easily be a sneak peek to a new album."

New album. My palms go damp with sweat, and I have to set down my mug of tea for fear of dropping it. This is happening so fast.

Wade raises a finger to interrupt. "Your contract is still crystal clear that if you express any *intent* to record additional music before expiration, it goes to Label. Watch what you say on that stage. Every word matters."

I shake my head, trying to make sense of what's happening. These plans are spinning so far out of what we agreed to that I have whiplash. I grab my napkin and ball it into my fist, trying to ground myself.

"Oh my god yes, I can't wait to hear it!" Keeley says. "Everything the two of you write together is pure gold. Maybe it could even be a lead single."

I clear my throat. "No. This concert is a one-time thing." I try to say this with as much certainty as I can, but something twinges in my chest. Because after playing with everyone over the past few weeks, I do miss these people. I miss feeling like a family, and making *our* music together. There's something so rewarding about all of it.

The money would have been rewarding too, if we'd gotten our fair share.

I miss writing with Valerie the most, but I have obligations back at home. Still, after this concert, will I really be ready to go back to my own life? To leave her behind for good this time?

I'm not sure. But there's a twinge of a headache threatening at my temples, no doubt from the tension creeping up my shoulders. Part of me is tempted to pour coffee instead of the tea, but I know that'll just affect my blood pressure.

Really, I should probably eat, but suddenly my stomach is twisting with anxiety and I can't imagine taking a single bite of even the driest toast. As much as I would love to make everyone happy and jump on board the Glitter Bats 3 train, I know I can't do it. Not yet.

Maybe not ever.

"I'm going to go on a run. I need to clear my head," I say.

"Caleb, wait—" Valerie starts, but I cut her off with a hand, rising out of my seat.

"No, I really can't talk about this right now. I'm happy we're almost free of Label and I'm happy to discuss playing 'Daydreams' at the concert. But I'm not ready to make any decisions beyond that—even doing this concert was hard enough."

And then I leave the restaurant before anyone can try to stop me.

GOSSIP DAILY LIVE INTERVIEW:
THEO BLAKE AND RYAN TATE

[transcript]

RYAN TATE: Theo! Thank you for taking the time to meet with us today. I know you have a busy schedule. What have you been up to?

THEO BLAKE: I'm currently filming *Fantastical Mysts* in Spain.

RT: Isn't Spain stunning?

TB: Yes! As an actor, you're always just grateful to keep working. Working in a place like this is such a blessing.

RT: You still have three more months filming *Fantastical Mysts*. Have you read the book by Reina Johannsen?

TB: Yes, and I was a fan of the book before I even got to the audition stage. I'm actually a huge nerd, if you can believe it. I'm so lucky to be playing Heath Firekiller.

RT: It's a great role, and we're all excited to see what you do with it. But let's talk about your personal life for a minute, if you don't mind?

TB: [*smirks*] That's what you do, isn't it?

RT: Well, there's been a lot of speculation about your relationship with Valerie Quinn.

TB: [*face sobers*] Valerie is a . . . complicated girl. I've said all I need to say about our past relationship.

RT: You previously implied she cheated on you with Roxanne Leigh, but sources close to Ms. Quinn say that's impossible. Do you stand by that statement?

TB: All I can do is share my own perspective. I should have known how she'd act. I learned a lot from that relationship, and I'm just doing my best to move forward. I'm going to be a lot more protective of my heart.

RT: What are your thoughts on the rumors about her and Caleb Sloane?

TB: [*chuckles dryly*] Good luck to him.

RT: What do you mean by that?

TB: The thing about Valerie is that she always needs to be in a relationship to feel validated, but she's also incredibly calculated about how she chooses her romantic partners.

RT: Are you saying she uses people?

TB: I'm saying she's very aware of optics and how they'll benefit her career, which we all know is hanging on by a thread with the fate of *Epic Theme Song*. I don't know Caleb personally, but I'd imagine their history makes him vulnerable to . . . well, I'd hate to speculate. But if he is getting involved with Valerie, I just hope he knows what he signed up for.

RT: I guess we'll all find out at that concert.

15

✦ Valerie ✦

Today sucks.

After Caleb left, we all dispersed to our rooms, the mood significantly dampened. Keeley asked if I wanted to hang out, but I lied and said I needed to shave my legs. Instead, I'm hiding out in my hotel room, curtains closed against the too-bright sun, pacing a line into the plush carpet.

My mom *stole from us*. It might have been legal, but that doesn't make it right. Part of me wants to wait out the contract and make another album just to spite her. Getting that news from Wade should have made me sick—but it felt like my first glimpse at true freedom.

I refuse to owe Tonya Quinn another damn thing.

If I could make a new album with full creative control, I wouldn't feel so much pressure to survive in TV. *Epic Theme Song* taught me to enjoy acting, at least a little, but all of this desperation to save the show? It's because I feel like I have no other options. I didn't go to college. I have money in savings, but I don't want to be a washed-up has-been before I even turn thirty, living off conventions or begging for a spot on one of those dancing competitions for former stars losing their shine.

I want to keep making art that matters to people.

Returning to *Epic Theme Song* wouldn't feel so dire if we could be the Glitter Bats again for good—but better, because Label wouldn't be trying to mold us into these people we weren't. We could start fresh. I'd have a direction for my future I could get excited about. The problem is, I presented this all wrong, again, and I scared Caleb off.

Just like I did when I rejected his proposal all those years ago.

At least today was a scheduled day off from practicing, because none of us are up for it, even with the concert a month out. The mood soured even more at brunch after Caleb left. Jane called her agent. Keeley ran down to the gym. Riker just started pouring a mimosa that was all champagne. It was clear we'd get nothing done today. We've all been going nonstop, and Caleb's not in the right headspace. When I pace over by his door, I can't hear him shuffling around, so he must still be out on a run. I hope he doesn't hate me now.

Last night, it felt like everything between us could be right again.

I don't know how I survived so long without his friendship. It's not like I expect him to rekindle our romantic relationship—I know I hurt him too much for that to ever be a real possibility again—but it felt like we were friends, at least.

The other feelings are there too. Even totally exhausted, being wrapped up in his arms again was almost too much. My skin melted at his touch, just the way it did all those years ago. Maybe I never stopped loving him, but that's okay. I can love him like this too.

I'd happily pine after him for the rest of my life if it meant hanging on to our friendship.

I sink to the floor and groan, pulling up the article that's been hanging over my head . . . again. As if any of this wasn't difficult enough, of course, Theo opened his big mouth—I'm starting to think he has *Gossip Daily* on retainer. Ryan Tate has always been a problem, and when I watch the two of them together all I can see is obnoxious trust fund–boy energy. Like they're entitled to the world.

They know they can say whatever they want, and screw the consequences to other people's lives. I wish I understood what I did to make Theo want to destroy me. Hell, *he's* the one who said long distance wouldn't work.

We were together for only six months, and it was mostly to be each other's dates to award shows and premieres. I mean, I guess we had fun. The sex was mediocre (he thinks foreplay is optional and rarely reciprocated oral), and he was always a little *too* excited about the fact that I'm bisexual (almost as if my attraction to people is a reason to objectify me). But we laughed enough that it was worth playing out. Or so I thought.

He's doing what he accused me of in the latest article: using the media to further his career. If anything, it should be obvious to the public that he's just another loud person trying to cling to relevance as the *Fantastical Mysts* hype wanes. He doesn't care who he hurts in the process.

No matter. I'll just have to strategize with Wade to figure out how to reset the narrative. I know the publicity team has already been working overtime on my reputation.

But Theo Blake isn't my biggest villain today. No, that honor rests solely on my mother's shoulders. I try to spend the rest of the morning taking care of myself. I tidy my suitcase; try to meditate; take a long, luxurious bubble bath; meticulously rewash my face and hair—none of it works. I still feel dirty, tainted.

Used.

Because what kind of mother steals from her own kid? Those royalties belong to the band. Tonya isn't really much of a mother at all—she's just one more vampire trying to take something from me, and I'm tired of it. Once I've dried and styled my hair and put on a new face full of makeup, I swallow down my nerves, pop in my AirPods, and call her.

"Valerie, good, I was hoping you'd come to your senses."

That's just like Tonya. No greeting, no recognition. Just straight to the topic that interests her today.

Pulse racing at the impending confrontation, I swallow, sinking onto the bed. "Hi, Mom."

"Have you already called Gina about writing and recording your next album, or should I? I know studio space is at a premium right now, but I'm sure she can bump someone, get this out before the concert."

My stomach twists. "We're not recording an album we haven't written yet in less than four weeks. That's impossible." We're not recording an album *at all*.

Mom huffs, as if my objection is ridiculous. "If you just buckled down and focused, it wouldn't be that difficult. I'm telling you— you need to work as hard as Taylor Swift if you want to survive in this industry."

This is what my mom expects—unattainable levels of productivity. She wants me to meet impossible standards when it benefits her.

"Taylor Swift is one of the most prolific songwriters in our generation, and . . ." I clench my fists. "You know what? No. I'm not going to try to reason with you. We need to talk about that contract with Label Records."

She lets out an audible breath. "Absolutely. You owe them an album, and you need to meet your obligations."

Wow. My head swims at her audacity. "No, I don't." My jaw clenches, and I pop up from my seat on the floor to resume pacing.

"That contract expires the day after the concert—but you only want us to make an album because it's your last chance to squeeze money out of us." Blood rushes in my ears. "What the hell did you do with all those royalties?"

My voice shakes as I say it. I know she never wanted me to find out. She wanted to just coast on my success for the rest of her life.

"Excuse me? You think it's unreasonable that I want to get paid for my work? I quit my job for your band! How was I supposed to put food on the table if I wasn't getting a steady paycheck?"

And here she is, making herself a martyr. I ball my fists. "No one asked you to quit your job! You inserted yourself into the Glitter Bats and started trying to control everything."

She lets out a humph. "You were *children*. Someone had to make sure you weren't completely taken advantage of."

"By someone else," I say, my hands trembling as the adrenaline hits.

"What?"

Blood rushes in my ears. "You made sure we weren't taken advantage of *by someone else*, because you were doing it already. I don't care if the contract was legal—it's wrong!"

"Oh, Valerie, you sound hysterical. Do you need to go refill your prescription? At least take a drink, honey."

I slam my fist down on the comforter. I cannot believe her. "I read the contract. You can't pretend you're innocent here. Stop gaslighting me."

"Gaslighting? Your generation is so paranoid." She laughs. "You just need to fulfill your obligations, sweetheart. Someone needed to take care of you back then. You were so impressionable. And who better than your own flesh and blood to protect you? I put so much time into your career. You owe me another album."

My throat tightens, but I refuse to cry. She'll be able to hear it in my voice and then she'll just call me weak. "I don't owe you *shit*."

She huffs so loudly I can hear it through the speaker. Her voice turns sharp. "You know, you're lucky I've only taken a few of the many talent management jobs I've been offered over the years. I could easily be working with your competition."

Not sure who she means by my competition, but I don't even care. I wish I knew how to hurt her the way she's hurt me.

But she still somehow holds all the power.

"What do I care? You're not my manager anymore."

She sighs. "Call me when you've calmed down—you're being so goddamn emotional right now, it's embarrassing."

I hang up before she can do the honors. Sometimes, I wonder what it's like to have a mother who isn't like this: selfish, controlling, emotionally manipulative. But wondering won't fix all the broken things between us—she shattered any last trust between us years ago.

That contract, though—it just proves everything I already knew. I'm not a daughter to her—I'm an opportunity.

I fire off a quick text to Wade:

> **Me:** Can you please tell security my mother is persona non grata? Probably best to tell the hotel too.

Our security is pretty minimal, but we do usually have someone posted to this floor. The last thing I need is Mom sneaking into my room.

Wade takes a few minutes to reply, and I hope it means he's spending time with his family. Or god, taking care of other clients. I'm sure I take more time than he bargained for when we first signed with him.

> **Wade:** Consider it done. You okay, kid?

Me: No, but I will be.

I've been letting other people control me—and the narrative—for so long, and I'm done being told what I can and can't do. Before I can think better of it, I send another text.

Me: You wanted some exclusives, right? How about one-on-one with me?

This response comes right away.

Mary Kate Hampton: YES! Name the time and place. Hell, I'm free today.

My palms go damp—because really, today?—but I'd rather get this over with.

Me: That's perfect. What about my hotel bar, 4pm? I'll send you the info.

Mary Kate Hampton: Riker already let slip where you're staying. I've got you in my calendar.

As soon as I have a plan, I do finally hear shuffling next door. Really, for such a fancy hotel, you'd think the insulation would be better, but maybe it's just because our rooms share a door. My stomach twists, and I worry maybe I was trying to control Caleb the same way my mother was controlling me. But I don't go bother him right away. Instead, I listen for the shower, and try not to listen *too* hard, or think about hot water dripping down his muscled torso . . .

Nope. Not going there.

But finally, I hear the shower turn off. I give Caleb a few minutes to get dressed, and then I head to the door connecting our two rooms. He knocks before I get the chance.

I swing the door open immediately. Caleb's waves are damp, and the scent of herbal bodywash radiates off his skin, like a sweater I want to wrap myself up in. But instead of moving closer to him the way every part of me craves, I hang back.

"Hi," I say.

"I'm sorry," he says.

I blink, stunned. "What? I'm the one who owes you an apology."

He runs a hand over his hair. "No, you don't. You were just trying to share information this morning, and I panicked. It's not fair of me to shut down any conversations about the future of this band without hearing you all out. I need to . . . stop running away whenever we talk about hard things." He clears his throat. "And, uh, singing 'Daydreams' at the concert is a really good idea. It would be really special for the fans. We'll just follow Wade's instructions and be careful."

I bite my lip, bracing against the guilt. I can't believe I put him in this situation. "You said you were done, and that means I need to respect your boundaries."

He frowns, crossing his arms. "Well, I thought I was done, but something about being back in the city, making music with the band again, writing with *you* . . . I don't think I realized how much I wanted it."

"Oh," I say, because I don't know what else there is to say. I'm too scared to hope for more, but my chest warms at the thought. "So what are you saying?"

He shrugs. "I don't know. But I'm going to try to be more open instead of so bitter and wounded all of the time. No matter what we decide, we should all decide it together."

"Right, that sounds good," I say, trying to swallow the lump in my throat. This is better news than I ever thought I'd get, but my mind is a mess. I don't want to pressure Caleb the way my mom is trying to pressure me.

His arms fall back to his sides, and he steps just a bit closer to me. "Are you okay?" he asks.

"No," I admit. And then the hell of today all comes out in a rush. "I tried to confront my mom just now, and she totally dismissed me. But even before that, Theo was running his mouth in front of the media again, and I'm so tired of him controlling the narrative. I texted Mary Kate to do an exclusive tonight. I'm meeting her down at the hotel bar in an hour."

"Holy shit. That's a big step," he says.

"Yeah, I just think it's time I stopped trying to give them something to say about me. I need to use my own voice."

He grins. "That's the Valerie I used to know."

Warmth radiates through my chest at the fondness in his gaze. "She never left, just lost her way a bit."

"Do you want some backup?"

EXCLUSIVE PROFILE:
Valerie Quinn and Caleb Sloane

BY MARY KATE HAMPTON, STAFF WRITER, *BUZZWORD*

Valerie Quinn sits at a hotel bar sipping a Moscow mule. (I'm not going to tell you the name of the place, because it's where the Glitter Bats are staying as they rehearse for their reunion at the Hollywood Stadium on August 15th. I have too much respect for these musicians to betray their privacy.) Quinn's hair is back to bubblegum pink, and she's wearing a cropped tank, high-waisted shorts, and a denim shirt—she looks every bit the pop punk queen she was years ago, and she's not alone. Caleb Sloane sits next to her, back in that famous eyeliner. (He tells me it's Perversion by Urban Decay, for anyone curious, and the name is too perfect for those bedroom eyes.) He's drinking a glass of rosé, which seems to be some kind of inside joke between the two, and he's fiddling with the leather bracelets along his wrists.

Sloane's wearing tight black jeans and a throwback Foo Fighters T-shirt with the sleeves cut off. He's embodying the rock star look the way he always did, but there's something different about him. Maybe he's more guarded than he used to be, but to Sloane's credit, he's trying to keep his new private life private, and I'm going to do my best to respect that. But when these two offered *Buzzword* an exclusive interview, I couldn't turn it down. We're all desperate to know what's going on behind the scenes as things ramp up for the concert.

MARY KATE HAMPTON: Thank you both for meeting me today. We didn't have a chance to catch up the last time we saw each other.

VALERIE QUINN: [*laughs*] Yeah, that was a wild night.

We're referring to the performance at the karaoke bar in Venice, which I'm sure you've seen as it's been all over the internet. I was lucky enough to witness that night unfold firsthand. If you haven't seen a clip of their fabulous rendition of "You're the One That I Want," visit our Glitter Bats page: buzzword.com/tag_glitterbats.

MKH: Was that the first time the two of you shared a stage since Glitter Bats broke up?

CALEB SLOANE: Yes. I've been working outside of the industry for the past six years, so that spontaneous karaoke night was the first time I'd performed in a while.

MKH: Well, you sounded fantastic.

CS: Thank you, that's very kind.

VQ: If anything, being away from the industry has made Caleb better than he ever was. Wait until you hear him play our stuff again.

MKH: We're all excited to see the Glitter Bats perform together again. Can I ask you something I've always wondered?

CS: [*grins*] You can ask.

MKH: Where'd you get the idea for the band name? It's so unique.

Quinn and Sloane lock eyes with a grin, and something that I have no words for other than intimate *passes between them. These two have always seemed to communicate on-stage without words, but it's a sight to behold in person.*

VQ: Caleb was high off his ass.
CS: [*flushes*] You make it sound like I have a drug problem—I was on painkillers!

He turns to me hurriedly, clearly wanting to set the record straight.

CS: I'd just gotten my wisdom teeth out! Valerie came over to keep me company because my mom had to work, and my little sister was too young to take care of me.
VQ: But he was *very* high. They don't mess around when they give you painkillers after surgery, and Caleb was trying to entertain me, since I was "the guest."

She uses actual air quotes for that.

MKH: That sounds very sweet.
VQ: [*bites her lip*] That's Caleb for you. But I was trying to force him to rest, and he made me pick a movie. I put on *Twilight* since neither of us had seen it. When we got to the part where Edward Cullen becomes a sparkly vampire, Caleb asked if the vampires in the movie turned into glitter bats.

cs: I have no memory of this, but I still think it's a valid question.

vq: When I was relaying the story to the rest of the band, Keeley said Glitter Bats would be a great band name, and the rest was history.

cs: I kept trying to come up with alternatives, but they wouldn't have it.

mkh: So this whole time, it's just been an inside joke?
cs: [*nods*] At my expense, of course.

Sloane and Quinn share another of those secret smiles, and I nearly feel like I'm intruding. So many people have suggested the chemistry between them was manufactured for the stage, but there's nothing fake about this ease they have with each other. Forget music—someone should cast these two in a romantic comedy.

mkh: It seems you have a lot of stories like this.
vq: [*smiles*] That's what happens when you start a band with your best friend.

mkh: And that's all it's been between the two of you? Just friends?
cs: [*clears his throat*] No comment.
vq: [*blushes*] What he said.

mkh: Fair enough. There's been a lot of speculation about you two, though, both before and after the Glitter Bats broke up. People have also made a lot of accusations about you specifically, Valerie. Do you want to discuss any of that?

VQ: Yes.

Sloane squeezes her hand under the bar. It's subtle but impossible to miss. Quinn squares her shoulders and turns to me.

VQ: I know certain people have made allegations about my behavior. I'll call it what it is—misogyny and biphobia. I've done a lot of things wrong, but I've never cheated on anyone in my life.

CS: The media hasn't been fair to Valerie, and the way they've framed her love life is a thinly veiled commentary on her sexuality. It's beyond problematic.

VQ: [*mouths* thank you *to Sloane*] I hate to name names, but I want to make it clear that I was no longer in a relationship with Theo Blake when I was spotted with Roxanne Leigh. When Theo booked the *Fantastical Mysts* gig, we ended our relationship amicably. F-ck, it was his idea to break up. If he was hurt by the way things ended, it was news to me, but we had broken up more than a month before I went out with Roxanne. And nothing really happened that night.

MKH: So you didn't do anything wrong, but your reputation was still put through the wringer. It seems like that's happened to you more than once.

VQ: It has, but I'll also be the first to admit I haven't always made the best decisions in the past. We got a record deal ten years ago, when I was just seventeen . . . I had a lot of growing up to do. Going viral, finding that instant success . . . it's hard for anyone to navigate, and even worse when you're still a kid. I was cocky and immature and sometimes careless. I made plenty of mistakes.

MKH: But you've grown up a lot, haven't you?

VQ: I hope so. I know I'm not perfect, but that has nothing to do with the specific night we're discussing—even if the media tried to spin it as yet another of my so-called wild escapades. My only regret was the negative attention that landed on Roxanne as a result. She's an incredibly talented, intelligent woman, and it was never my intent to put her in a position that could harm her image or career.

Quinn is selling herself short—she's definitely grown up since our first interview. She handles herself with the grace and poise of a star twice her age. It's clear by the look in her eyes that this whole experience has caused her pain, but she's trying to protect other people—Leigh, and maybe even Sloane.

CS: I know I said no comment, but I will say this about my relationship with Valerie: the two of us have known each other since we were kids, and there's a complicated history there. If we are together . . . [*pauses suggestively*] . . . or *back* together, as has been implied, it's not a rebound, and people should stop treating it that way. We have a lot of love and respect for each other.

VQ: I think Caleb summed it up.

It's clear they're still being coy, but these two have been involved in too many headlines for me to add to the noise. We'll leave any speculation up to the fans. But I can attest that the warmth and respect between these two is palpable.

MKH: What can fans expect during the concert?

Sloane and Quinn share yet another private glance.

VQ: Of course we're planning to play songs we love, that we hope the fans love, but it's not just going to be a blast from the past. We have a surprise up our sleeve.

CS: I'm just excited to get back out there and give the fans the closure they deserve.

I wouldn't miss the concert for the world—I got my ticket when they first went on sale, and they're nearly sold out. If you want to try your luck at nabbing one of the remaining seats, or if you're interested in the livestream, visit Ticket Champion.Live for details.

Sloane and Quinn invited me to a closed practice next week, and I can't wait to share what I can with readers. Keep following *Buzzword* for more exclusive Glitter Bats content.

16

+ *Caleb* +

After Mary Kate leaves the bar, I can feel Valerie's anxiety sharp in the air, like static before a storm. I've always been attuned to her emotions, but something about sharing a bed last night made our connection so much stronger, like I can once again read her mind.

I also want her so bad it hurts.

She stares down at her unfinished drink, and I know she needs reassurance right now, not more flirting. "That was brave," I say softly.

She scoffs, glancing up at me with a stubborn tip of her chin, but there's uncertainty in her eyes. "Was it? I barely said anything."

"We could have played up our relationship more, you know," I say with a wry grin, elbowing her in the side.

I hoped for a laugh, but this at least gets me a smile. "I think keeping it vague is better. Besides, you said you didn't want to lie to anyone."

Is it a lie? I want to ask, but I hold my tongue. She's in no mood for teasing, or trying to get to the heart of whatever might be going on between us. "Fair enough. But speaking up for Roxanne, refuting Theo's lies—that took guts."

She sighs, stirring her drink. "I don't know if it'll work. All of my media training says not to respond to rumors, but it's gotten to the point that I couldn't just stay silent anymore. Everyone loves Theo—I'm not sure if they have enough reason to believe me instead. At least Mary Kate is one of the good ones, and she gave me a chance to try."

Even knowing how much Valerie needed this, it was hard to go into the interview—but Mary Kate made it almost painless. A warm feeling spreads in my chest, and I know it's more than just the wine. I'm starting to believe this industry isn't *all* that bad.

At least, not when I get to be next to Valerie.

I nod. "I think it'll be a great piece."

Valerie bites her lip. "Are you still feeling anxious about all of this?"

And there she is, caring about me even when she's the one having the worst day. I want to lie—I want to protect her from the guilt I know it will bring, but enough people in Valerie's life have lied to her lately. She deserves truth from me, at least.

"How could I not be anxious? I thought I closed this chapter a long time ago," I admit.

Valerie takes a long sip of her drink. "Do you regret coming back?"

"No," I say quickly. She looks up, and there's so much damn hope in her eyes I can't look away. But this is also the truth, and I can't do anything but be honest with her. "I thought I would, but I don't regret it. Not for a second."

"That's good," she says. "I'm . . . I'm really glad you came."

"Me too."

We sit in silence for a bit, me drinking the last sips of my fruity rosé, her finishing the dregs of her cocktail.

"Do you want to go out on a date with me?" I ask in a rush, and nearly want to laugh because I sound so damn earnest, like I'm sixteen again and asking her to the homecoming dance. All of that tenuous pretense before our first real kiss.

Valerie gapes. "What?"

I rub the back of my neck, shifting awkwardly on my barstool. "We've talked about feeding our relationship to the media, but we haven't actually gone out very much. We should go somewhere we'll get photographed."

She purses her lips, clearly not convinced, using her straw to stir the ice in her empty mug. "You said you didn't want to lie to anyone."

I swallow, getting as close to the truth as I dare. "We haven't hung out in years, and I want to spend as much time as I can with you before the summer is over." I lean closer to her, lowering my voice. "Since we have nothing scheduled tonight, we should take advantage of our free time and catch up. That's not a lie."

My blood rushes to my head. Maybe this is too honest, but the words are out there, hanging between us. No going back.

Valerie's cheeks turn the prettiest shade of pink. She opens her mouth as if to argue, then closes it again. "Okay, fine. Where are you going to take me on this date? And it better not be at this hotel because the food is great but I'm tired of this menu."

Other than Valerie's dwindling stash of Trader Joe's snacks, we really have been eating hotel food almost nonstop for weeks. I shouldn't have an idea already, but I do, because I've known Valerie for years and I can't help but notice things that she'd like.

Or maybe it's just because I'm still completely gone for her.

My heart swells, and I hurry to tell her my plan before she can change her mind. "There's this company playing outdoor movies down at the pier, and I know the press have been hanging out because Lola Martinez was spotted a couple of weeks ago. A bunch of food trucks have signed on too, so there's anything you could possibly want." And then I bring it on home. "They're showing *10 Things I Hate About You* tonight."

She laughs happily, placing a hand on my arm. That tiny touch makes me grin like a fool right back at her. "Oh my god, what? That's my favorite movie!"

The surprise in her eyes is so funny I want to laugh. Our lives were so intertwined that her details became mine, that everything she loved was imprinted into my memory. And I remember everything.

I remember everything almost embarrassingly well. My neck warms. "How could I forget?"

Valerie beams. "Okay, you got me. I'm in."

Her face lights up so brightly it almost brings me to my knees. Every time she smiles it hits me, how lucky I am to be in her orbit. But it's never just been an orbit. We collide, again and again, like two stars in an explosion of light and color. I used to be so afraid of the damage in our wake.

The only thing at risk this time is my heart.

After all these years apart, the connection between us is undeniable. Maybe she's not a star at all. Maybe she's my gravity—the unstoppable force holding down my universe.

It doesn't have to be romantic if she doesn't want it to be, but I'll be damned if anything stops me from making this night perfect. I can give her that.

We're both dressed comfortably enough for a night out, so I buy tickets on my phone while Valerie orders a car. LA traffic is always ridiculous, especially on a Saturday night, so we talk about everything and nothing on the trip. I tell her about teaching choir kids, including one particularly awkward moment when the dad of two of my students recognized me in the middle of a booster meeting and asked me to sign a dollar bill, and she tells me about life in the industry for the past six years. Before she started working on *Epic Theme Song*, she recorded a solo EP and opened for Holly Harper on her tour.

"I wish I could say I've heard the EP, but I haven't," I admit.

Valerie, to her credit, doesn't look upset, just curious. "Why's that?"

"Carrie said it was good, but I never could bring myself to listen to your solo music. It was almost like if I didn't listen to it, I could pretend things hadn't fallen apart."

"And . . ." she trails off, fiddling with a bracelet. "Why would you want to do that?"

Because it hurt? Because I missed you? I shake my head. "Because every day, I wondered what would have happened if I'd stayed."

Her lips twist. "Well, you're here now." She reaches across the seat to squeeze my hand, and my heart skips a beat. I can't tell if it's a friendly gesture or something more. "And besides, the EP was a flop. Didn't have the same magic as our Glitter Bats stuff."

I think about Valerie at twenty-one, on her own for the first time without the Glitter Bats and trying to go solo. Even when she doesn't have her safety net around her, she always shines. "I'm sure you were great."

"Thank you," she says, flushing. "Oh look!" She points out the window, leaving my hand to sit on the seat, burning from her touch. But I lean forward and smile when I see what she's gesturing at.

It's a billboard advertising our concert. They're using an old album image from *Bittersweet*, since we haven't done any official new photos yet—that's still a couple weeks out. Before that, though, we have tickets to the premiere of Jane's newest animated series, which means coming up with red-carpet *looks*. Fortunately, Keeley knows a stylist willing to drop everything and help us, because I definitely need help after all this time.

The last thing I expected this summer was to walk a red carpet, but I guess we're doing this all the way. Billboards and all.

"It looks good," I say, because what else do you say when there's a sign above the road with your face on it?

Valerie laughs as the car moves forward, and we both settle back into our seats. "People will be disappointed when we don't look like kids anymore." She gestures at her face, and I take a moment to really look. It's not like she's gotten *old*—twenty-seven is plenty young, even by the industry's standards—but her cheeks are less round, and there are a couple of fine lines under her eyes. She looks every bit her age, and it stops my heart more than ever.

"You look better," I say, unable to stop staring at the woman next to me. I don't know how it's possible, but Val's gotten prettier every day we've been apart. Now, it's hard to look away.

She catches me staring, and flushes. "I'll say, Mr. 'I Work Out but Not at a Gym So It Looks Even More Impressive.'"

My skin tingles at her appraising gaze. "What?"

"The first time I saw you in six years, you were shirtless looking like you just got off a mountain."

I gape, trying to make sense of this admission that she'd been checking me out that day too. "I did just get off a mountain. I was hiking."

"Like holy fuck, Caleb," she swallows, like maybe she's serious. "That was . . . a lot to take in. You were like a walking thirst trap."

I laugh, because what is going on? "I'm sorry?"

"Don't be," she says, and *there*. It's just a hint, but her tone is suggestive.

Oh hell.

"Alright, then I'll just be over here trying not to blush," I admit.

"I like it when you blush."

"Well, you're the only one who makes me." I don't know why I said it, because suddenly the back of the car is flooded with subtext and history and pure longing. God, I want her.

"Caleb, I—" she begins, but the car comes to a halt.

"Is this it?" the driver asks. I want to curse them for interrupting, but it's a good thing they did, because I forgot the two of us weren't alone in this car. It's this thing Valerie does, like she draws all the light in a space to her and everyone else fades to black.

And I'm like a moth, powerless to look away.

We thank the driver and climb out of the vehicle. It's a warm summer night, but there's just enough of a salty breeze coming off the ocean to make it bearable. Valerie closes her eyes for a second and inhales.

"I love the water," she says, tilting her head back to bask in the sea air.

"I know." When we were kids, we spent summers at the city pool, since it was cheap and close and didn't require a parent to take us down to the waterfront. But we both always wished we were out in nature. So when we went out on our first tour, we found ways to see the water. It's one of the things we used to make time for whenever we were on a new stop. We didn't have much time for hiking or exploring, but we'd try to find an hour to drive to the ocean, or a lake, or a river.

Sometimes we'd bring a guitar and write a little, and sometimes we'd just let the water center us for a bit.

Valerie's smiling like she remembers those days all too well.

"I still do that when I'm somewhere new. Try to find water," she says. "It's not the same . . ." I almost think she wants to add *without you* to that, but she doesn't. "But yeah, I try."

"Maybe we can walk on the beach after the movie," I say. The night hasn't even begun and I'm still desperate to make it last.

"I'd like that," Valerie says. "Now let's go find those magical food trucks."

She grabs my hand and leads me to the trucks, which are set up in a square like an ever-changing outdoor food court. There's everything from Korean barbecue to vegan burgers, Cajun to Mexican-Asian fusion, but Valerie makes a beeline for the gourmet grilled cheese truck.

Every moment with Valerie this summer stirs up another memory from our past. This one is of late, bleary nights on a tour bus with a hot plate plugged into the cigarette lighter, feasting on a loaf of bread and a stack of Kraft American Singles. We didn't have a ton of money coming in right away, so we tried to limit eating out on that first tour, but the results were mixed. When it was Valerie's turn to cook, she always managed to burn the sandwiches because she was never paying attention.

"I haven't eaten a grilled cheese in *years*," she admits, a little sheepish, like she remembers the charred crust as much as I do.

"Dairy is terrible for your voice, you know."

She puts her hands on her hips. "Okay, Mr. Sloane, did you learn that in music school?"

"Actually, I did," I say, grinning.

"Good thing we're not singing tonight, then," she says as we find our spot in line. "What else did you learn in class?"

I pause, trying to think of something that will make her laugh, or at least keep the conversation flowing. And then it hits me. It's a bad idea, but . . . maybe I just want to see her reaction. I step closer, lowering my voice so only she can hear.

"Breath control. I can go a long time without coming up for air."

17

+ *Valerie* +

Breath control.

A rush of heat races down my skin, my breath catching as the memories and fantasies collide and flood my senses. I can think of a perfect use for those new skills—

What the fuck is he trying to do to me?

Last night already brought us closer than ever, and flirting is one thing . . . but if Caleb keeps this up, I might explode here right on the beach.

As if he didn't just ruin me with two words, Caleb puts his hands in his pockets, casually leaning around the tall people in front of us to peruse the menu. I laugh nervously and follow his lead, trying to school my features into nonchalance.

It doesn't take long to order, and after we get our food, we make our way to the stretch of beach where they've set up a drive-in style screen and rows of chairs. Caleb guides me to a little section toward the back. We'll definitely be seen, but hopefully back here we won't be too disruptive. At least we're not the biggest names here: I wave at an actor I recognize from *Young Sherlock* with his model boyfriend, and Caleb pauses so we can greet one of the members of Jude, an all-sister indie folk trio that just started gaining some traction during our last couple of years on the scene.

Finally, we make our way to our seats and set out our meals as the movie begins, the first few bars of "One Week" filling me with the usual joy. But I can hardly savor the food or the film, because Caleb Sloane is distracting as hell.

I knew this night would mean more nostalgia, wading through memories and trying to make sense of this new dynamic between us—what it is, what it isn't, what it could be if we just let go.

I do my best to watch the movie and enjoy my food. But I can't stop watching Caleb. He's trying to play it cool, staring pointedly at the screen, but every so often, I catch him looking over at me. Every time our eyes lock, a new rush of heat pools deep in my belly.

Logically, I know this was all supposed to be just for the cameras, but my body didn't get the memo. Being near Caleb already makes me think about being *with* him, especially after sharing a bed. But now I'm thinking about how he could demonstrate that *breath control.*

Caleb was my first, well, everything, and he was always enthusiastic and eager to please when it came to sex. But we were also young and fumbling and inexperienced. We got better, but now I wonder what else he's learned in the time since we were together.

I've learned a few things too.

Goddamn it.

I hate myself for even going down this mental road, but I can't help it: I'm desperate to know what twenty-eight-year-old Caleb is like in bed. It'd be one thing if we could just go back to the hotel, hook up, and get it out of our systems, but I don't just want a one-night thing with him. It could never just be that.

Our sexual relationship was always a part of our deeper connection, and even all these years apart can't change that.

But god. I still want him. I don't know if it's fair, but I'm not going to survive this summer if I don't at least tell him what I'm thinking. He has to know where my head is at. That doesn't mean I'm just going to say it out of the blue.

The movie finishes, and even though it's the best, I barely catch any of my favorite scenes. I managed to calm myself down enough to watch Heath Ledger serenading Julia Stiles with a full marching band, because that's a classic rom-com moment that can't be ignored, but I'm still distracted after the credits roll. After a few more hellos to the people sitting around us, we recycle our dinnerware and head back over to the food trucks.

"Dessert?" Caleb asks.

"Always."

He buys us strawberry-champagne cake pops from the cupcake truck, and we wander down to the ocean, taking our shoes off to pad through the deep sand. We wander past a casual volleyball game and a family chasing a kite, but no one pays us any mind. As if in silent agreement, his hand finds mine, and our fingers lace together like they're coming back home.

The sun is setting, and it casts everything in a warm glow—the glittering waves, the sand, *Caleb*. He looks like a summer dream like this, ever the rock star in black jeans and a cutoff tee, his waves tousled with just the right amount of product. He might have walked away from this life, but it still looks good on him.

My phone buzzes, and I use my free hand to pull up a text from Wade. It's a link to Mary Kate's article, which went up impressively fast.

Wade: Good job, kid. My contact at The Network sent this to me with high praise. It's working.

Tonight has banished a lot of the anxiety from the forefront of my brain, but still, relief floods my chest at the news. I tilt my phone to Caleb, and the corners of his lips tug up in a soft smile.

"Hey, that's great." He squeezes my hand, and my shoulders relax at the reassurance.

"Do you think this is crazy, bringing the band back together?" I ask, turning to face him.

Caleb goes silent. For a moment, the only sound between us is the rumble of crashing waves. "I think that's more of a question for you than me."

"This affects you too, though," I say, releasing a long breath.

A breeze kicks up, tossing a lock of hair around my face, and Caleb reaches over with his free hand to tuck the strands behind my ear. I lean into his touch. "I thought I was perfectly content staying away, but I didn't realize what I was missing . . ." he trails off, staring at something in the distance.

"Really?" Hope tingles deep in my chest. I know we just got promising news on the *Epic Theme Song* front, but the show feels so far away when I'm doing what I really love again. I'm just scared everything I love has an expiration date. The show could get canceled tomorrow. The Glitter Bats could finish the concert and never see one another again.

"But, even more importantly"—he clears his throat—"I didn't realize how much I needed *you*."

Heat floods my cheeks. "Oh," I say, because I don't know what else there is to say. I force myself to look at him, the sunset casting a warm glow on his shoulders that makes his beauty almost impossible to face head-on. And the way he's looking at me . . . it sears right to my core.

But it's terrifying to be on the edge of *something* again. What if we jump, only to crash to the ground?

"So . . . do *you* think it's crazy to bring the band back together?" Caleb asks, shaking me out of my thoughts.

I don't know. I tug gently on his hand, and we continue walking down the beach. People are still out, but they mostly keep to themselves, tossing Frisbees, playing with dogs, corralling children. As we wander farther from the pier, it almost feels like we're alone.

I know we're not. We're out in public together tonight, and there could be photographers around. But in this moment, I let myself pretend it's just me and Caleb, and the rest of the world falls away.

"I originally planned all of this to try to save *Epic Theme Song*. I'm not proud of it, but we all know that's the truth. We still haven't heard anything concrete from The Network, and I don't know what else to do. That interview with Mary Kate was my desperate last attempt to set the record straight." I sigh. "And I don't know what will happen to my career if they pull the plug. I haven't booked any auditions. Everyone wants a Glitter Bats album, not a Valerie Quinn album. If this renewal doesn't happen . . . I think it's over for me."

After I admit that terrifying truth, we walk in silence, hand in hand. It's funny how speaking your fears out loud can make them less scary. I trust Caleb implicitly with the hard things, even now, because I know he'll hold them with gentle care.

"Can I ask you something?" he asks, finally.

"Of course." I let go of his hand and cross my arms, suddenly feeling nervous.

"Why do you want this life so much when it makes you so miserable?"

I stare down at my toes in the sand, the coarse, rough grains having already chipped away at my purple pedicure. Because that's the million-dollar question, isn't it? It's definitely one I've been hiding from for months, years, maybe since the day he left. I used to think I knew the answer—that I wanted to share my music with the world. But even that rings false when the thing I'm fighting for the most is a TV show. I love *Epic Theme Song*, but it's also the source of a lot of fear and anxiety and self-doubt.

In the end, it always comes back to him.

"I think I've been chasing the feeling of how it was with you, leading the band before it all fell apart."

He opens his mouth to interrupt. "Val—"

"No," I hurry to stop him. "I'm not expecting anything from you. I just always think if I find the right opportunity, it'll feel that way again. But it never does—or, at least, it didn't until you came back. Being the Glitter Bats again just made me realize how everything else isn't quite as satisfying." Now that I've started speaking this truth into the salt air, I can't stop. My gaze locks onto his, and I take a breath, steadying myself. "I feel like I'm so close to having everything I ever wanted. *You're* all I ever wanted. And I know you might not feel the same way, and even if you did, I can't possibly ask you to come back . . ."

He puts a steadying hand on my wrist, and I let him tug me out of my posture, linking our fingers together. His eyes are soft, solemn, and it twists something deep in my chest.

"Val."

My heart is in my throat. He hasn't called me Val in years, and I know what that means. He's going to reject me as kindly as possible, and then I will just try to survive being this close to him for another few weeks.

I can handle that. It's fine.

But instead of pulling away, he tugs me closer, reaching for my other hand so we're standing across from each other on the damp sand. Here, we're not the lead singers of the Glitter Bats. We're just

Caleb and Valerie, two people staring into each other's eyes for the thousandth time and seeing the thing we've been searching for.

"I never stopped caring about you. Not for a day. Not even a minute," he says. "Ever since last night, I've been losing my goddamn mind. It's like all of those feelings broke through a dam, and if I don't get to touch you again, I might explode."

I think he's going to kiss me then, but he doesn't. He steps closer, so there's nothing more than a breath between us. I can feel the heat of him through his tee, can feel the hard edges of his muscle and the careful surety of his fingers twined in mine. "But I'm afraid of what this will mean," he whispers, like it's a secret.

"Me too," I admit. "But I'm more afraid of spending another day wondering what it will mean if we don't."

"*Val—*"

Seizing a spark of bravery, I smirk up at him. "Kiss me, Sloane. I dare you."

A fire sparks in his green eyes, and then he's grabbing my face in his hands and drawing my mouth to his, right in the middle of this very public beach.

Our first kiss all those years ago was shy and tentative, but this is nothing like that. This is open-mouthed and delicious and a little desperate. It's familiar, picking up right where we left off, but it's also a balm, soothing the burn of the years we spent apart.

He tastes like sugar from the frosting and salt from the breeze and *him*, and I didn't realize what a craving I had until this very moment.

Caleb kisses me like I'm the perfect harmony to every melody he's written. Like we are blank pages waiting to be written into songs, and our kisses are the ink.

I slip my arms around his waist, and he groans, deepening the kiss. All I want to do is get lost in him under the peach and lavender sky, to get close enough that there's nothing between us but lips and hands and skin.

But we're not alone. "Caleb, Valerie, over here!" someone shouts, and we break apart to see a telephoto lens across the sand dune.

I bite my lip, glancing up at him, afraid of how he'll react, but he just laughs. "Well, that was inevitable."

And the thing is, it really was. All of this pretending, playing up our connection—that was all just pretense. It feels like fate brought us together again.

We go together. It just makes sense. Any time spent fighting that was a waste.

Things Between the Glitter Bats Are Heating Up!

PAIGE HART FOR *GOSSIP DAILY*

See NEW photos of Valerie Quinn and Caleb Sloane hand in hand at Kiss Me Productions' "Hot Summer Nights" showing of *10 Things I Hate About You*! The two were looking cozy, whispering sweet nothings in each other's ears, as if they were the only two people on the beach. Look how GORGEOUS they are together. Clearly two people in love, stealing glances as they tried to keep it subtle. But that fire in their eyes turned into a blaze after the credits rolled when the two were spotted walking—and smooching!—on the beach in the sunset.

That's it, Glitterbugs: after years of speculation, CalErie is CONFIRMED. We have the shots to prove it. Following a rocky start to the summer, it seems like Quinn is finally back with her one true love—and fans around the world will no doubt be screeching with glee.

Will it last after the concert? Who knows. But they sure do make a beautiful couple. Sloane has always seemed to ground Quinn, so hopefully it sticks this time.

See photo gallery below.

18

Valerie

When our driver drops us off at the hotel, my pulse is still roaring in my ears from the force of that kiss, the recent memory a brand on my skin.

We walk inside through the revolving door, fingers twined together—and even though we've entered this way dozens of times throughout the summer, everything is different. I'm not scanning the lobby for cameras or journalists. I'm not worried someone will catch me off guard. Because for the first time in six years, I don't feel alone.

I'm all too aware of Caleb's presence at my side. It's as if just by being close to him, I'm safe. Still, we're careful. Maybe it's the awareness of public eyes and security cameras, but we manage to stay decent in the elevator. We're almost stoic as we walk down the same carpeted hallway to our familiar rooms.

Everything up here feels different too. Charged. Like a fuse about to ignite. He turns to me when we reach my door.

"I had a great time tonight," he says softly, the weight of his words foreshadowing what might happen next, like there's no reason for the night to end.

"Me too," I say, waiting for his next move.

And it surprises me alright.

Because then he presses a chaste kiss to my forehead and heads over to his own door. "I'll see you later, Val."

What the hell?

I just stand there in the hall, stunned, as he flashes his key and slips inside. Finally, I collect myself enough to grab my own key from my bag and enter my room, completely confused.

I lean against the door, trying to catch my breath and make sense of what just happened. That kiss on the beach didn't feel like just a kiss. It felt like a prelude, warming our bodies up to what they do best, falling into sync in every way. Damn it, I was ready to come back here and re-chart that perfect map of his body. Now I'm completely unmoored.

Mind reeling, I start to tidy my room. I grab a laundry bag from my suitcase and ball up the used socks and underwear that need to be washed. I carefully fold the jeans, flannel, and hoodies I can wear again. I even make my bed, smoothing out the duvet and fluffing the pillows.

Because I don't know what to do with myself.

Caleb and I didn't have sex for the first time after our senior prom—we weren't that much of a cliché—but we did plan it, the way teenagers who can't keep their hands off each other do. We'd locked down protection and were just waiting for the right moment.

The moment presented itself in the strangest of ways. It was my eighteenth birthday, and we were playing a gig that night to celebrate the release of our first album, *Wanderlust*. We hadn't played in a venue that large before, especially not as headliners, and I was so nervous that it wouldn't live up to our expectations. What if no one came? What if the crowd was tough? What if I choked?

To keep from spiraling into the nerves of the moment, Caleb had suggested we plan something to look forward to after the show.

He wasn't even talking about sex—that was purely my idea—but as soon as I suggested it, he was in. I've always hated the concept of virginity, and all the heteronormativity that treats things like touching and oral as stops along the way instead of actual sex, but Caleb was a great person to experience my firsts with. He got us a hotel room and we took our time. We didn't know what we were doing, but we both went into it without expectations other than trying to make each other feel good, and that made the night perfect in its awkward, messy, imperfect way.

Sex made us feel closer than ever. We trusted each other so implicitly. And I thought after everything we've been through . . . we were heading there again.

Maybe he's wanting to take things slow. That's a rational way to handle this. We haven't been together in six years, so it's probably not the best idea to go from zero to orgasm in one night.

But *god*, I thought that's what all the loaded glances were for. And that comment about breath control? How was I supposed to take that as anything else but a come-on?

Wondering about this is going to keep me up all night. So instead of obsessing, I decide to just go talk to him. Without bothering to change, I march over to the door adjoining our rooms. It's still unlocked from earlier. I don't even bother to knock; I just yank it open.

Only to see Caleb with his fist raised, as if about to knock himself. He's still wearing the jeans and T-shirt from tonight, along with a sly smirk.

"Hi." He bites his lip, and my skin tingles with the memory of that perfect mouth on mine.

"Hi."

Instead of stepping through, he leans against the doorframe, filling the space with languid ease. "Can I come in?"

I cross my arms. "You implied the evening was over."

"Not at all. Really, I just . . ." he trails off, the heat in his gaze cooling a bit. "I needed a minute. When you're next to me, I can barely think straight. I wanted to be sure I was ready for this. Once we cross that line again . . . we can't take it back."

Caleb's right. Even though my skin is on fire and I'm practically buzzing with the need to worship his body, there's nothing casual about us sleeping together—nothing about our relationship has ever been casual. It almost feels like we're picking up right where we left off . . . or, at least, from the last time things were good between us.

And because of how it all ended, I never could have dreamed we'd get a second chance. I'm ready to grab his hand and jump off the edge.

But Caleb needs to be ready too.

"Do you need us to take a step back?" I ask.

"Well . . ." Caleb clears his throat and pulls a long strip of condoms out of his pocket, chuckling. "No."

A surprised laugh escapes from my lips. "*Oh.*"

"That's why I came prepared," he says. Then his face sobers. "But if going slow is what *you* want, I'll leave." He glances down at the foil. "Shit, this is too much."

Desire rushes down my spine. I lock my gaze onto his. "Not at all. One definitely wouldn't have been enough, with everything I have in mind."

"*Thank god.*"

As I grab him by the shirt and tug him toward me, any last hesitation goes out the window. We collide, leaving fireworks in our wake. Pressing me against the doorframe, he kisses me deeply, his hard edges pressing deliciously into my curves. I press into him, walking him backward in the direction of the bed.

Before we can even reach it, we've lost our shoes, his shirt is on the floor, and his fingers are working at the button of my shorts.

And then he pulls back, lips red, pupils blown wide.

"You alright?" I ask, breathless.

He nods. "I may not be sure of a lot of things, but I'm sure about this. I need you, Valerie Quinn." He tucks a lock of hair behind my ear. "We don't have to figure anything else out tonight. But if you'll let me, I desperately want to make you feel good."

My skin sparks with anticipation. For tonight, we can just do this. Be Valerie and Caleb. Two people so entwined in each other that nothing else matters.

"I'm going to hold you to it," I say. And then I draw his mouth to mine.

He kisses me back with tender care and wild abandon, a delicious paradox in every heartbeat. His kisses are soft yet forceful, gentle yet demanding, the heat of fire and the bite of ice, and soon we're falling onto the impossibly-high-thread-count sheets in a tangle of need.

When his fingers travel back down to my shorts, I arch my back so he can shimmy them off.

"*Fuck*," he groans. I'm wearing a maroon lace thong. It's the color you're supposed to wear under white according to every stylist I've known, but it also makes me feel empowered as fuck, and I needed that boost. "Holy hell, this is better than any of my dirtiest fantasies."

I bite my lip, overcome by the truth that we've both been desperate for this for years. "Is this a good time to tell you I'm not wearing a bra, or . . ."

"*Jesus Christ, Val*," he says. "Why the hell are you still wearing that top, then?"

He climbs up my body, sliding the crop top off my shoulders, freeing my breasts to the cool air of the room. Even through his jeans, I can feel his hard length against the softest parts of me, and I can't help it—I grind wantonly against him, like I did when we were desperate teenagers doing our best to keep our clothes on. The friction is good, but it's not enough.

And he knows it, because he knows me. He knows every sound I make, every whimper. Just like I know by the look in his eyes that he's barely holding it together. But there's also amusement there.

He chuckles, the sound rumbling deep in his chest. "Impatient much?"

"Caleb, I've been waiting for this for six years. Of course I'm impatient."

He freezes. "You've been waiting for me?"

Despite the urgency of the moment, I roll my eyes. "I mean, I haven't been a *nun*, but it was never as good. Not with anyone else."

Caleb's green eyes sober in the lamplight. "Same. No one has ever compared to how I felt with you."

I stare up at him, smirking. "You've been *pining* after me, haven't you?"

"Hey, clearly, so have you," he gestures at my nearly naked body, practically writhing for his touch, and heat rushes all the way down to my toes. "Now, can I touch you already? I'm dying here."

"*Please. Anywhere*," I practically beg. And then his fingers are wandering everywhere: grazing my throat, cupping my breasts, grasping my hips. Even with those bass-string calluses, his touch is tender, sweet, and full of so much care it makes my eyes sting. I can't believe we're doing this.

As if sensing my emotion, he pauses, rising up to brush his lips against mine again.

"You still with me?" he murmurs, his hand stilling on my waist.

"Yes," I say hoarsely. "I just . . . I really missed you. I never thought we'd be back here again."

"I'm glad we are." He presses light kisses to my temple, my cheekbone, my nose, and I giggle.

"Well, don't stop now," I say through a laugh.

"I wouldn't dream of it." And then he continues his exploration, slowly and deliberately caressing every exposed inch of my skin except the place I most desperately need. Finally, once he's charted the map of every single curve, he palms me through the thin lace of my underwear. "I can already feel how much you want me."

"I've wanted you all night," I admit.

He hisses under his breath, like he's holding himself back. "That is so fucking hot, Val."

But he still doesn't move his hand right away. Instead, he brushes more kisses across my skin, this time down my collarbone, light and teasing.

"Caleb, I swear to god . . ." I trail off with a sigh as he draws my nipple into his mouth, just a teasing taste, a tender flick of his tongue, but not enough. It sends a jolt of pleasure down my spine, and I let out an involuntary moan.

"Oh, you like that?" he asks.

"I love your mouth," I say. He should always be doing this with his tongue. Anything else is time wasted.

"I can think of better ways to use it."

And then he's drawing his mouth down past my navel, wet and hot, stopping at the last scraps of thin fabric still covering me. Like a fantasy, he grabs the red lace carefully with his teeth and drags it down my thighs, his evening scruff scratching tantalizingly against my sensitive skin.

Instead of taking them off completely, he draws my panties off just far enough, and then he buries his head between my legs.

"Fucking hell, Caleb," I hiss, throwing my head back against the pillows.

Gone are those teasing touches. He finds my clit immediately, remembering exactly where to kiss me, brushing his lips and tongue against my most sensitive spot in long, languid strokes.

After a few minutes, he finds the perfect rhythm to work me into a panting, desperate frenzy, strumming me like a guitar string.

I'm nearly vibrating with need, but it's not enough to get me there. "More," I gasp.

He glances up at me, his gaze dark and heavy under that smudged eyeliner, and grins. "If you insist."

And then he sucks my clit into his mouth and slides two fingers inside me. Tension builds deep in my core and I don't know if it's the anticipation of tonight or the literal years fantasizing about being with him again, but I lose all sense of time until I'm hovering over that sweet edge of oblivion, faster than I thought possible.

"God, Val, you're so fucking sweet." He raises his head slightly as he murmurs, before burying it between my legs once more with a moan of pleasure, like I'm the most delicious thing he's ever tasted.

And then I'm falling in earnest. I cry out, and I don't even try to muffle the sound. He doesn't relent, kissing and touching me until I've ridden out the last wave of my orgasm on his tongue. Only when I let out a shaky breath does he pull away, climbing back up to me.

When he reaches my shoulder he hovers, like he's not sure if I'll want to kiss him after that, but I reach up and grasp the back of his head, drawing his mouth to mine. He tastes like me and him and still the lingering sugar from the dessert, and I'm undone.

And so, so not *done*.

He's still in his jeans, but his erection is hot and hard at my hip. I draw my fingers down the tattoos on his pecs, down the smooth planes of his stomach, and palm him through the denim.

"We can stop—believe me, that was as fun for me as it was for you," he says. Oh, this sweet, sweet man. Always so giving.

"I want to make you feel good too, Caleb."

He exhales sharply. "I wouldn't dream of trying to stop you."

So I keep touching him. I flip him onto his back, unbuckle his belt, slide his jeans and boxers down his hips all in one go. Now that he's naked beneath me, I let my eyes linger. Finally, I memorize every inch of him, like I'm relearning the words to my old favorite song.

"Please," he breathes.

And then he stops talking entirely, because I give as good as I get.

19

+ *Caleb* +

We wake up wrapped up in each other again, but now there's nothing between us but sheets and sweat and the memories of last night.

My heart picks up as I look at Val in the morning light, gazing my fill. Sometime in the earliest of hours, the sheet slipped off her bare shoulder. I resist the urge to skate my fingers across her skin. I don't want to disturb her sleep, but I'm also afraid that if I touch her, she'll be nothing but a ghost.

It would be too easy to get used to this again. Her heat. Her scent. Valerie is everywhere, and I can't get enough. I thought I remembered what it was like being with Valerie, but I forgot the tiny details: the sigh she lets out when she wants something, the way she rolls her hips when she's begging for more, how her eyes flutter shut when she's about to come like she's trying to savor every ounce of pleasure.

I'm hard just thinking about it, and that's no way to wake her up. But it doesn't go unnoticed, as she twists around in my arms to face me with a drowsy smirk.

"We have a big day today. You can't just keep me in bed," she murmurs.

"I *could*, though."

"God, last night was incredible." She bites her lip, glancing up at me through lashes that are still a little stuck together from sleep. "Breath control, huh, Mr. Sloane? Who'd have thought?"

"It has its uses," I say, and she laughs, falling into my shoulder with an ease that twists my heart. Her hair tickles my skin, and I tug her closer. I missed this, touching just because we want to, losing track of where I end and she begins.

"As someone with real-world data, I can safely say it improves the experience," she murmurs.

I draw back, faking offense. "Are you saying I wasn't as good back then?"

Her eyes dance. "Things were always good between us. I'm saying it was even *better*, dumbass."

"If you say so," I say.

She pouts. "Aren't you going to tell me I've gotten better with my tongue?"

Val hasn't just gotten better with her tongue, and she knows it. Holy hell. "I could, but you've already got such a big head. Especially when you're *giving it*."

Valerie swats my shoulder, then rolls away from me.

"Okay, get up, you big sexy idiot. We need to check if we're trending."

My stomach drops. "Oh, right, of course." I scramble to get out of the sheets, but I can't shake the feeling of being diminished to a publicity stunt. That's not what I wanted with her. I wouldn't have done this if . . .

"I mean, we were definitely photographed. Our strategy worked. Time to see if we made a splash for that kiss," she muses, slipping out of bed and pulling on a robe.

I try to follow her lead as I tug on my boxers and gather the rest of my clothes from where we discarded them on the floor, but it doesn't remove the lead weight in my chest. Was this really just PR for her?

My stomach roils. "Right. We have to see how the *strategy* is going."

Valerie's eyes go wide, and she steps closer to me. "Oh my god, no, Caleb, I didn't mean this is just sex or anything, seriously. I just want to know if people are talking about us after last night. The press always liked me better when I was with you, and this is the first time we've ever publicly confirmed our relationship." She cackles, scrolling. "Oh! It's not *super* clear the photos are of us, but people are talking! We did it!"

I run a hand over my hair, trying to make sense of what she's saying. "So even though things are getting real between us, you still want to keep playing it up publicly for the press?" I ask.

She never wanted this attention on us when we were younger. She insisted we *never* do this, and the change is giving me whiplash. This is already getting complicated and I haven't had my tea yet.

Val nods. "Exactly! I know it's a lot, especially because we don't even know what this thing is between us right now, but I actually think it'll be easier. Now we're not totally lying. We can figure out what this all means when things calm down."

This means I still love you, I want to say, but I know it's too much, too soon. No one says those words after one night, even if that night was years in the making. I need to pull myself together.

"And I mean, we're already doing this, right? There's no point in trying to hide it now. That's when things got complicated before." Her voice is hesitant, like she's not sure if this is the right call.

And my mind reels, because I don't know the best way to handle this.

Things didn't get messy before because people speculated about our relationship—they got messy because Valerie wanted to pretend it wasn't happening . . . and I never understood why until now. It was so hard to keep track of all the secrets we were holding that our relationship became full of tension and conflict instead of joy.

I'm losing track of what's real all over again. Still, if she needs to keep the press talking, I can do that for her. Because I do understand. We're not in our early twenties anymore, and there are bigger implications for her career than just one concert involving the Glitter Bats.

Still, I can't shake the feeling that mixing our relationship and our media strategy is a bad idea. But I kiss her temple and slip back into my room to get ready, trying to stop overanalyzing everything that's happened over the past twenty-four hours. Despite the multiple orgasms we shared, tension creeps into my shoulders as I find myself alone.

Today we meet with a stylist to prepare our looks for next weekend's premiere of *Into the Dragon Realm*, an animated series Jane worked on as both composer and musical director. At first, the band wasn't on the guest list, but Jane's New York agent made magic happen. They're probably just as eager for the press as everyone else.

Jane insisted we don't need to do anything fancy to prep today, but after I place a breakfast order, I decide to spend extra time in the bathroom exfoliating and moisturizing, falling into more old rhythms like it's been weeks instead of years since I lived this life. Now that Valerie and I have made a splash, I know cameras could be anywhere. Might as well try to look the part.

I'm also just a bundle of nerves, and the familiar routine steadies me.

When we first started playing music together, we never expected to walk a red carpet. But once we got a few nominations for

Bittersweet, we started navigating the labyrinth of the awards circuit. The first time we walked a red carpet, we didn't hire stylists, didn't get outfits tailored, didn't even know how to respond to questions. It was a lot of learning on the fly, but we figured it out toward the end. For the most part.

And then we got a little media training.

Everyone else has so much more practice than I do these days, and I don't want to do anything to hurt the opportunity for good press. So I do everything I can to make myself presentable, shaving as close as I can and putting pomade in my hair, partly because I'm trying to put my best foot forward and partly because I need the extra time to process my feelings about last night.

There's nothing in my head but thoughts of *Valerie*—the good, the anxious, the uncertain. My Earl Grey and avocado toast arrive as I'm tugging on a shirt for the day, and I resist the urge to scroll on my phone as I eat. I've seen enough of what they're saying about us.

It's amazing that we're reconnecting, but I'm still nervous to start up again in front of the cameras. Last time, secrets tore us apart. This time, the press is going to know everything. I wonder, idly, if there's somewhere we can meet in the middle, so we're not hiding our relationship but we're also not allowing ourselves to be consumed. This could wreck us too.

But Valerie still needs this, and she's worth the risk. I can't say no to her. Even if we crash and burn at the end, I'm in this now. I just hope we can pull this off the way she planned.

After I brush my teeth, I finish getting dressed and head down to meet the others in a conference room. The beige space has been transformed into a shock of vibrant color. I never got used to it, but when you're famous, they bring the clothes to you. There are racks of designer suits on one wall, racks of gowns on another, and in the middle is a raised platform where a stylist, a tailor, and Wade are chatting over a tablet. Keeley, Jane, and Valerie comb through the rack of gowns, and even though I definitely took too long upstairs, I'm not the last to arrive.

"Is Riker not down yet?" I ask as I approach the rest of the band.

"I was hoping he'd be with you!" Jane says, sighing as she glances at her phone. Some things haven't changed in six years, including Riker's aggressive insomnia. Other than making a few offhand comments, we never fought about it as a group, because we all assumed his chaotic sleep schedule had something to do with his not-so-great family. His parents used to fight late at night, and he'd survived by stuffing on noise-canceling headphones and Twitch streaming past midnight. We just let him cope, offered shoulders to lean on. It was hard enough for him to focus on the band without their support. Besides, he's never missed a gig, always powering through with energy drinks and sheer will.

I might need a caffeine boost myself after the decidedly little sleep I got last night. My fingers brush against the gowns near me, some with shining and silky smooth fabric, others glittering and abrasive, but I need something to hold me steady while taking Valerie in. She looks normal in a white hoodie and a pair of leggings, but after what we got up to last night, I can't tear my gaze from her. She blushes bright pink against the soft fabric of her sweatshirt.

"Good morning," she says softly.

"Good morning." I catch her gaze, grinning a little just for her before I turn to the rest of the band. "How are we all doing?"

Keeley raises her brows. "I don't know. How *are* we doing?"

Heat floods my neck at the insinuation, but any shyness evaporates as I lock eyes with Valerie. One blazing look is enough to pull me under her spell, and my chest aches with the need to be closer to her. She bites her lip. It takes every effort not to cross the few feet between us and soothe that worried mouth with a kiss.

Jane clears her throat. "Uhh . . . that was quite the press photo."

"Right, the photo," I say. Somehow . . . I momentarily forgot we're all over the internet.

"I don't kiss and tell," Valerie adds.

My heart twists at that, and it sobers me a little. "We got caught, I guess."

"Oh my god, I fucking knew you two wouldn't last the summer," Keeley says, face lighting up in vindication.

Jane looks at me, her brows furrowed. "So . . . how much of this is strategy and how much is . . . you know, real?"

God, I wish I knew.

"We're figuring it out!" Valerie says, almost too brightly. "But that's not important right now—my stylist quit months ago, and I'm so excited to work with a new one for the red carpet!" I try not to take the *not important* personally, but ouch. It's impossible. My chest goes tight.

"Fine, but we're talking about this later," Keeley says dryly. She and Valerie return to the rack, but Jane's still looking at me, frowning.

It's all good, I mouth at Jane with a shrug.

She shakes her head, placing one of her small, warm hands on my arm. It makes me miss my sister so badly it hurts. Cameron would know what to say right now. She always has the best advice, and she has a fresh perspective since she's not in the industry. I wish I could call her, but she works today, and I don't want her to think it's an emergency.

And Valerie and I will figure it out. Her voice breaks me out of my spiral, and Jane and I turn to the others.

"You could always go with the sexy suit option, Keels," Valerie is suggesting. "Like Blake Lively in *A Simple Favor*."

"Definitely not ruling it out," Keeley says. "There are also some gorgeous gowns and jumpsuits." It goes against all of her badass girl drummer vibes, but out of all of us, Keeley is the one who gets the most excited about these events. When you're doing red carpets, it's a lot of nonstop smiling, a lot of waiting, long hours in uncomfortable clothes, but I think Keeley enjoys getting out from behind the drum set and stepping into center stage.

I've seen this woman dancing and downing tequila shots in a skintight Tom Ford gown at three a.m. like she hadn't been parading in front of cameras for twelve hours. Something about the long days just energizes her when it exhausts the rest of us, and I wish I had an ounce of her enthusiasm.

Then again, if I did, I might still be in the industry.

"I've always been tempted to take the pants route, but I can't resist a pretty dress," Valerie adds.

"Oooh, we have to find you something backless!" Keeley says, heading to the other rack of gowns with Jane close on her heels.

"Backless is good," I murmur to Valerie, who winks before following them.

"Caleb, come here a sec," Wade calls. I hurry over, and he introduces me to our team for the day. The stylist, a slender Black person with short curls and a perfectly tailored jumpsuit, introduces themselves as Rowan. They met Keeley through Bianca Martin, Keeley's still-friendly ex, and they're going to be styling us for Glitter Bats press as well as the *Into the Dragon Realm* premiere.

The tailor, a white and curvy woman with spiky gray hair, introduces herself as Jenna. She hasn't met anyone in the band before, but Rowan enthusiastically vouches for her talent.

"We're going to be working off the rack due to the timing, but with a build like this? You have *options*," Rowan says, gesturing at me. My cheeks warm at the compliment, because I'm not used to being scrutinized like this anymore, but I manage a muttered thank-you as they comb through the racks. My heart stops as I see the names on the labels. Six years ago, I wouldn't have thought twice about buying a bunch of these suits, blowing five figures in one shopping trip like the money would never run out.

Suddenly, my breathing shallows as the cost of everything in the room hits me with full force. It's probably enough to buy my mom a house. At least I'm not picking up the bill today—designers usually provide red-carpet clothes because they want them to be seen and talked about.

Jenna crosses her arms, oblivious to my mental spiral.

"We can rush an alteration if needed, though, so let's get a few quick measurements. Do you mind?" she asks, gesturing at me. The no-nonsense tone behind her question leaves no room *to* mind, but I'm grateful for the ask.

"Not at all," I say weakly. At least I remembered how to handle this part. I'm in a T-shirt and athletic shorts, something easy to change out of without any added bulk. Jenna gestures me up onto the platform, then measures my waist, the breadth of my shoulders, the length of my arms. She rattles off measurements, and Rowan takes them down. Once they've got everything they need recorded on a tablet, they both hurry over to the rack of suits, grabbing three options after some hushed consultation.

"Let's put him in the Hugo Boss and see what we have to work with," Rowan says. I'm ushered behind a screen, where I'm handed the suit and a white button-down. I strip out of my clothes and shrug into the suit.

When I step out, Riker wolf whistles across the room, apparently having finally shown up for his own fitting. I flip him off before stepping up onto the makeshift platform and staring at myself in the mirror. Rowan hurries over and takes stock of the ensemble, tugging at a sleeve here and straightening a pant leg there. Excitement ripples around me, but I don't feel it. I'm just numb. A stranger stares back at me from the mirror.

I swallow thickly. At least the eyeliner and pomade were things

I chose, so putting them back on didn't feel so jarring. Wearing a suit that I could never afford on my teacher salary just makes me feel like I'm playing dress-up, like this summer is all pretend.

"Honestly, even if we had more time, I'd put you in Boss. You're lean but broad-shouldered—hell, this suit was made for you," Rowan says, swooping in over my shoulder to smooth my lapel.

"We'll just take the hem up a bit and call it good," Jenna adds. I laugh, because the *a bit* is generous. At my five foot seven, she'll definitely need to take a big chunk off the pants like past tailors usually did, but that never really bothered me.

"Sounds good," I say. It's a nice suit, and I'm excited to celebrate Jane, but I really don't care what I look like. I'd rather skip the premiere if I could get away with it. I don't feel like the guy who wears designer suits and smiles for a hundred flashbulbs anymore.

But whether I feel like him or not, it's what I have to do.

With my look taken care of, Rowan and Jenna call Riker over and start recording his measurements. He's got them both laughing in seconds, the way he always does when he meets new people.

"Caleb looks smoking hot," Keeley half yells across the room.

"Yeah, he does," Valerie murmurs. I catch her gaze in the mirror, and it's full of so much heat that I'm not sure how anyone could miss it. But it sends a thrill up my skin, the way she's looking at me with such open appreciation. My shoulders relax a little in the jacket.

I slip behind the screen and change back into my own clothes, then place the suit on the hanger—but I don't resent the thick, expensive fabric the way I thought I would. Getting all dressed up isn't so bad if it makes Valerie look at me like that, and I know I can survive a red carpet with her by my side.

Maybe playing up our romance isn't the worst thing we could do.

PRESS RELEASE: *INTO THE DRAGON REALM* PREMIERE!

A Taylor and Tyler original animated family series, *Into the Dragon Realm*, is landing exclusively on The Network this weekend! With a star-studded voice cast including Finn Lewis, Rose Carrington, and Kyle Harris, and introducing Josie Ramirez as Hanna the Unicorn Rider, *Into the Dragon Realm* will appeal to fans of all ages who love *Avatar: The Last Airbender* and *Adventure Time*.

Catch the Comic-Con trailer here: thenetwork.com/intothedragonrealmishere.

Into the Dragon Realm is the most highly anticipated animated series of the year. It follows the story of Hanna (Ramirez) and Jamie the Singing Elf Knight (Lewis) as they journey to the Dragon Realm to save the dying magical forest that protects their kingdom. The series promises adventure, romance, and plenty of laughs. Add it to your streaming list on The Network!

Into the Dragon Realm is executive produced by Kate Taylor, Jordan Tyler, and Kyle Harris. The series features an original score and music production by Jane Mercer, a member of the Glitter Bats and composer for the hit space fantasy RPG *Shooting Stars*.

The series will premiere at the Los Angeles Carrington Theater ahead of its streaming debut. The theater was recently renamed in honor of Hollywood legend Rose Carrington, who voices Orchid the Elven Queen in *Into the Dragon Realm*.

20

✦ Valerie ✦

Tonight's premiere is a welcome break from nonstop rehearsals, but it's also my biggest test out in the world with Caleb—can we show off our relationship for the cameras while we're still figuring out how to be together?

Last time, I hurt Caleb by hiding us from the world. Now, I'm worried I'll hurt him by using him for press. But the media stuff is just a convenient way to keep the attention on the Glitter Bats and try to save my show. Sure, it's a little strange going from faking it to something real, but we've never had the luxury of figuring things out away from the spotlight. We have a second chance at honesty. So what if we sensationalize it a little? Caleb knows how I feel about him.

He has to.

At least our friends are supportive. We've been discreet, but when we slip out of Caleb's room together on the way to our morning prep and run into the others in the hallway, no one says a word about it. While we get manicures at the hotel spa, Keeley even mentions that tonight will be a good photo opportunity for

CalErie—which means she's come a long way from warning me to keep my distance.

I glance at Caleb across the salon, and he winks from where he awaits his sheet mask. It all feels so easy, falling back into feelings I tried so long to suppress. It's been all loaded glances in rehearsal, stolen kisses in hallways, a brush of fingers in a crowded room—it's so sweet rediscovering these moments with him. My heart beats faster with every look, my skin heats with every touch, and it's as if my entire being missed the familiar tempo. Like he's my metronome, and I'm finally finding my rhythm after years of drifting offbeat.

Being together doesn't make things easier, but it does make them less daunting.

We booked the salon out for the day, so after our skin is glowing and our nails are perfect, the hair and makeup experts arrive to finish our looks. As we glam up, we take plenty of selfies, posting them to social media and tagging one another like we're one big, happy, glittering family.

I almost believe it myself. Now that Caleb and I are back to . . . something, it really is feeling like old times. Long days on set for *Epic Theme Song* always left me exhausted, but something about spending hours with the Glitter Bats brings me back to life. We've been so in sync during rehearsals that we're practically one unit. Every song we return to is tight, and the rest of the band quickly caught on to "Daydreams Like This."

In the bustle of red-carpet prep, I even forgot my morning social media check. With the fate of *Epic Theme Song* still unknown, I should be full of panic, but there's a sense of calm hanging around my shoulders. If I didn't know better, I could almost believe there was a future for the Glitter Bats after the concert.

I have to keep reminding myself that's not what I want.

We manage a careful, mess-free meal, then head back to our

rooms to change. With deft fingers, Caleb helps me fasten the plunging backless gown that Keeley insisted will go viral. The color options were limited with my pink hair, but I think we picked the right piece for the event—a sparkly midnight-blue number with straps that cross in the back, a sweetheart neckline, and a slit up the front that almost goes to my hip.

It's sexy enough to make me feel like a million bucks but classy enough that it shouldn't hinder my reputation. I look like an old-Hollywood movie star. Still, my mouth goes dry as Caleb helps me ensure everything is in place, his calloused fingers brushing against the skin of my lower back.

"You look amazing," he murmurs. "Can I kiss you, or will that mess with your look?"

I laugh. "Haven't put the lipstick on yet, so we're good."

He draws me into a slow, sweet kiss, and I grasp onto his elbows to steady myself in the four-inch heels that make me a bit taller than him. Even through the thick sleeves of his suit, I can feel the curve of his biceps under my fingertips. Part of me wants to say fuck the event and fall into those strong arms.

But we need to support Jane, and we need to be seen.

He draws back, resting his forehead against mine—softly, so as to not smudge any makeup. "You ready for this?"

"Yeah, are you?"

He grins. "I have a gorgeous woman on my arm. How could it not be a good night?"

I will never get tired of this man calling me gorgeous, and warmth blooms across my cheeks in a way that makes me think we could have gone lighter on the blush. If he keeps saying nice things about me all night, I'll be glowing red for the cameras.

"Let's go," I say. Jane is arriving separately with the rest of the *Dragon Realm* creative team, so it's just the four of us for now. This is her night, not ours.

We get the text that our limo has arrived, and the four remaining Glitter Bats head into the night using a back elevator. No photographers have shown up at the hotel—fortunately, tonight isn't about the band, so they weren't prepared—but we can't miss the cell phone cameras hovering in the hands of a few of the hotel patrons as we cross through a lounge to the side door. Hopefully no one will reveal that we're staying here, because that might complicate our lives for a couple more weeks.

But it's nice that people notice us. I wonder if I took it for granted, the constant attention—it's not like I enjoy having zero privacy, but there was something nice about being beloved instead of notorious. I like making headlines for my music, not who I'm kissing.

Maybe sensationalizing whatever this is with Caleb was a bad idea, but it's too late to back out now.

We're slated for an earlier red-carpet arrival, but there's still plenty of activity when we arrive. Keeley decided on a creamy white jumpsuit, and Riker looks flawless in a burgundy tuxedo with his long hair tied back in a low knot. They go ahead of us, each taking their turn alone, smiling and smirking for the cameras before they hit the interviewers. But Caleb and I enter together like a couple, and even though it makes my palms sweat, I'm so glad I don't have to walk in alone. I've done that too many times over the past few years.

But the journalists don't miss the implications.

"CalErie, over here!" one shouts, and I bite down on my smile to keep from rolling my eyes.

"I hate that name," I whisper to Caleb through gritted teeth, quiet enough to not be overheard through the clicking of the cameras. After just a few minutes walking in these teetering heels, I won't let go of his arm for the rest of the night. I lean on him, just a little, just enough to feel like I won't float away in the chaos.

"Me too," Caleb admits, smoldering at the nearest camera. "But we're stuck with it now."

It's not such a bad thing, being stuck with Caleb.

After we pose for photos, we have a few minutes to answer questions, which is my least favorite part of the evening—they could throw anything at us, and most of them are recording footage live for their various outlets.

Fortunately, the first question isn't terrible.

"Caleb, what's it like returning to the stage with the Glitter Bats?" a more seasoned reporter asks.

Caleb smiles and turns to them, leaning toward their purple microphone, but he pulls me a little closer. Maybe he needs to be steadied too. "Well, tonight is all about *Into the Dragon Realm*, and I haven't returned to the stage yet." He laughs good-naturedly. "In all seriousness, it's great. The band is so talented, and I think everyone has just gotten better with time. It's sure to be an incredible concert."

I lean in, speaking into the microphone. "What Caleb is *not* saying is that he's the best he's ever been. The first thing we sang together was 'Midnight Road Trip' and he sounded so good, it brought me to tears."

A half-truth—I cried for a lot of reasons that night—but I mean what I say about Caleb's voice. It's aged like fine wine.

Caleb smiles, but he's looking at me. "Fans are not prepared for how great Valerie sounds either."

"It sounds like there's a lot of mutual . . . admiration here," the reporter says.

"Absolutely," we say in unison.

The reporter then switches topics, throwing out a question about Theo and *Fantastical Mysts*. Before I can even blink, Caleb apologizes and gracefully moves us along to the next reporter.

"We might be here for *Into the Dragon Realm*, but I don't think *anyone* missed that the two of you walked in as a couple. Rumors of CalErie have been all over the internet since the concert was announced, and you've been spotted in public together a number of times—most recently, allegedly sharing a kiss on the beach. Are you two officially back together?"

My mind spins as I try to figure out how to play this. We had a plan, but it's completely escaped my mind in the onslaught of flash-bulbs and rapid-fire questions. I don't know how to play it coy when I've completely forgotten how to speak.

There is so much riding on this moment.

To his credit, Caleb smirks at the camera as if on cue. It's unfair how good he is at this. "Remind me—were we ever officially together in the first place?"

The reporter's eyes widen, like they've just gotten the sound bite of the night. "Weren't you?"

And . . . then I have an idea. We share a glance, and I look down at Caleb's lips, then back up at his soulful eyes. He shrugs, almost imperceptibly, and I gently tug his tie to bring his lips to mine.

Live on the goddamn internet.

It's chaste enough, and intended for the thousand GIFs I know it will generate, but it still makes my heart race. Caleb holds me closer, dipping me a little, and in these heels I have to hang on to him for dear life, but his arms aren't bad to cling to. I get totally lost in the moment, kissing him. Even in a crowd, he makes me feel like we're the only two people who matter.

Caleb rights me on my feet and turns back to the camera but doesn't lose his grip on my waist.

"Does that answer your question?" I ask brightly, wiping the soft smear of lipstick from Caleb's mouth with my thumb.

The reporter nods. "It definitely clarifies a few things." But they don't back down. "I was going to ask Valerie about Theo Blake next, but I don't want to ruin your night."

Caleb's grip tightens as if to move us along again, but I lean into him, reassuring.

I can handle this.

"Theo and I broke up amicably several months ago and have not spoken since. Regardless of our history, or anything that has circulated on the internet, I wish him nothing but future success. *Fantastical Mysts* is an incredible opportunity, and I'm sure everyone will love it when it drops. But tonight is about celebrating my friend Jane's wonderful contributions to *Into the Dragon Realm*, not my love life."

The next group is waiting, so the reporter has to let us go without the zinger they were hoping for. However, I think that lip-lock will make up for it.

"Not that I didn't enjoy that kiss, Ms. Quinn," Caleb murmurs into my ear as we walk away, "but what's the plan here?"

My stomach flutters with nerves. Here I am, making Jane's big night about us. The video will be all over the internet in the next fifteen minutes, and everyone should be talking about the show instead. I just really wanted to take advantage of the night.

"I'm sorry, I just thought . . . yeah, that was probably bad timing." So much for being a supportive friend. Maybe Keeley was right, and it was inevitable that this summer would become the Valerie show.

Anxiously, I glance at Caleb.

He grins, but there's something tight in his gaze. "I'm sure it's fine. Besides, I like kissing you. If it finally puts those rumors to rest, well . . . two birds, one stone."

I hope he's right.

Fifteen minutes was being charitable. Within five, Keeley and Riker are heading over to us, quickly flashing Keeley's phone in our faces. We share a look, then laugh—nervously, on my part at least.

There are cameras everywhere, so Keeley slips between the two of us and grins at the closest one. Riker puts an arm around my other side, and we smile wide for the chorus of "Glitter Bats, over here!"

But that doesn't stop Keeley from hissing through her teeth. "I know you're trying to drum up press, but this is Jane's night. Don't fly too close to the sun."

I brace myself for her withering glare, but when I glance at her, she's smiling for the photographers. Still, I know this isn't the end of this conversation. I might have fucked up . . . again. And not just with the band—I can feel the buzz of my phone blowing up in my clutch, but I choose to ignore it.

As we move into the building, I nearly stumble into a server holding a tray of champagne. I apologize, taking two flutes and handing one to Caleb, then downing mine.

It's too late to take back that viral-bait kiss. Let the internet talk.

21

+ *Caleb* +

I don't know how I was supposed to focus on the *Into the Dragon Realm* premiere with Valerie looking like a goddess at my side.

Her look tonight screams Hollywood starlet. That blue dress clings to her curves in a way that's straight out of a dream, and all I want to do is find a quiet corner and take advantage of that dangerously high slit up her thigh. Maybe that kiss wasn't the wisest move, but once I'm buzzed on champagne from the trays that are being passed around on a continuous loop, I can't bring myself to be truly mad. The timing wasn't great . . . but it does ensure people will be talking about the premiere.

And Valerie looks so incredible—I can't stop touching her.

I palm her bare lower back as we walk through the crowd to the auditorium. I grab her hand as she navigates her way up the stairs. I even find an excuse to tuck her hair behind her ear, letting my fingertips linger on the soft skin of her neck as we find our way to our seats.

How did I go six years without touching Valerie Quinn? Now that I've started again, I'm not sure how I'm supposed to stop.

The pilot of *Into the Dragon Realm* is fun, and Jane's music is incredible, but if there were a pop quiz on the plot, I'd fail it. I'm too entranced by the woman next to me to register a thing. By the time we're shuffled across town to the after-party, I've sobered up, but that doesn't make me keep my hands to myself. If anything, it makes me want to pull her closer.

This isn't the Oscars, where everyone has costume changes throughout the night, and the vibe is definitely more relaxed as we slip into the private club in our designer clothes. When we first got into the industry, these nights felt like playing dress-up. I got used to it around the time *Bittersweet* hit the awards circuit, but after spending years in a classroom in Target button-downs and khakis, I feel like that eighteen-year-old kid stepping into the too-bright spotlight again.

I loosen my tie as soon as we get away from any cameras. Tonight there's a dance floor, but most people are lounging in booths or standing in groups, drinks in hand as they network and share gossip.

It's hard not to overhear that some of it is about our red-carpet moment.

We got our official photo op with Jane during the premiere, but she couldn't sit with us. At the after-party, though, we claim one of the booths as Glitter Bats territory, and Jane quickly slips away from the *Dragon Realm* creative team to join us, looking beyond glamorous in a green velvet fit-and-flare gown.

"The music was brilliant," Riker says. "You did good, Janey."

"Good, because I'm exhausted," Jane sighs, leaning onto his shoulder. He pats her red curls, which are falling out of her once-styled braid at this point in the night. "There was an issue with the last track that I literally fixed at four a.m."

"Do you need a nap?" Riker asks, shrugging off his jacket and wrapping it around her.

Keeley scowls at them. "I'm going to go get drinks."

She doesn't even take our orders, just slips out of the booth.

"What's with her?" Riker says.

Valerie just bites her lip—she hasn't missed it either—but neither of us wants to actually comment on it. We were always so wrapped up in each other, but it was impossible to miss that *something* was happening there. It's always just been hard to pinpoint. All I know is that Keeley is feeling feelings, and she's not ready to talk about them.

"Keeley's probably just tired. It's been a long summer for all of us," Jane says, taking her hair out of the braid, then fluffing the red curls with a satisfied sigh. I can't tell if she truly doesn't understand, or if she's trying to be diplomatic. Keeley was always the one Glitter Bat who could party until dawn—mostly sober, somehow. Maybe Jane's protecting someone's feelings—I'm just not sure whose.

"Well, she needs to chill out, because we haven't even started press yet," Riker says. "Maybe she's run out of edibles or something."

"Ugh, I forgot about Glitter Bats press. I just did press!" Jane says, groaning and leaning back against the booth. She's not one to complain, so she's probably just hungry. Keeley clearly anticipated this, because she shows up moments later with a pitcher of what I assume is a very pretentious beer, as well as a plate of the gourmet hot wings and parmesan truffle fries I saw on the menu board on our way in. She drops the food directly in front of Jane, but we all dig in.

"Oh my god, I could kiss you right now," Jane says, diving in for a hot wing.

Keeley clears her throat. "Calm your tits, Mercer. It's just the free food your fancy production company brought in."

"God, I missed catering," I admit. "At school, they don't feed us—and *if* they do, it's like cold pizza or soggy sandwiches." Oh the joys of being a public employee. Of course, I'd rather the money go to the kids, but it definitely took some getting used to. Good thing we had those years of greasy drive-thru meals on tour to give me an iron stomach.

Valerie wrinkles her nose as she reaches for a fry. "Ugh, pre-prepared subs, no thank you."

She hates mayo, which I haven't forgotten, because of course I haven't.

"Why would you subject yourself to that kind of treatment?" Keeley asks around a mouthful of wing. "I mean they pay teachers next to nothing, right? Seems like a strange choice coming from all this."

She gestures around the room, the sheer definition of excess. This is just one industry event for one series, and people are donning designer clothing they'll wear exactly once to get photographed in and eventually discard. There's gourmet food and an open bar and even tiny 24-karat-gold key chains with the *Into the Dragon Realm* logo etched on a medallion.

It's a stark contrast to my day job, but I didn't get into it for the money. Some of the days are hard, but for every moment I question my path to teaching, there's another where the kids remind me why I took it. Still, I'm starting to wonder if changing my career was a real choice or just my desperate exit strategy.

It doesn't matter. I made my decision.

"Maybe because he's passionate about his job?" Jane suggests. I shoot her a thankful look, because the last thing I want to do is get defensive, especially when we're all trying to have a good time.

"Sure, it's not glamorous, but I'm close to my sister and her wife, and I have a really great dog who loves exploring nature as much as I do. Plus, I like working with kids. Keeley, I sent that drumming video you made to our band director, and she absolutely lost her mind. She's got a girl drummer in her jazz band next fall."

Keeley's eyes go wide with glee. We've been squeezing in a few videos between practices, and Keeley seemed to have a lot of fun with hers. "Oh my god, that's amazing. You're welcome to give the teacher my number if she wants to set up a meet and greet over Zoom or something."

My heart warms. "Are you serious?"

"Absolutely! It's so stupid how people assume drummers have to be, like, slacker dudes who couch surf while stoned 99 percent of the time. I had a 4.0 GPA and got into Stanford, Columbia, and Brown."

"Be careful, Keeley, or you'll become a motivational speaker," Jane teases.

Keeley grins, a little pleased. "Honestly? I'd do it."

"They'd kick your ass out for swearing," Riker says.

She gapes, pressing a palm to her chest. "If I can clean up my fucking act in front of my grandma for an entire fucking week at Christmas, I can do it for one fucking hour to work with some kids."

My stomach twists, and I reach for a fry. Maybe I'm just hungry, but talking about my day job and the Glitter Bats colliding makes the end of the summer feel all too real. With only a few weeks left before the concert, it's hard to accept I'm leaving this world behind again. But what would it look like if I didn't—would I quit teaching for good? I don't see how I can have both. Something tightens in the back of my throat, and suddenly this booth feels too hot.

"Wanna dance?" Valerie whispers in my ear, shaking me out of my head. I nod, and she grabs my hand and tugs me out of the booth.

"We're still going to talk about your stunt later!" Keeley calls, gesturing after us.

"Your objection is noted!" Valerie shoots back. I follow her lead, but she doesn't take me to the dance floor. She pulls me through a maze of velvet curtains and partitions, slipping us past a door into a completely private staging room. Other than a few empty containers on the ground and a stack of unused tablecloths, there's nothing in here but party debris. We can still hear the sounds from the after-party, but they're distant. Muffled.

I feel my pulse start to steady.

"You okay?" Valerie asks, as soon as we're alone.

Even as I'm coming down from the adrenaline, my heart warms. She noticed I was starting to spiral, and she wanted to check on me. It seems we really are as in sync as we ever were.

"Yeah, I just got a little too much in my head tonight. Things will be clearer tomorrow."

"That's good," she says, leaning against the wall to steady herself in her shoes. She really does look incredible tonight. That gown is killing me.

Once I catch my breath, I smirk, noticing just how alone we are back here. "So all of that just to check on me? You didn't have any ulterior motives for pulling me away from the party?"

She grins and crowds me, putting one hand on each of my shoulders. In these heels, she towers over me just a bit, and I don't mind at all. "*Should* I have an ulterior motive?"

"I mean . . ." I trail off, punctuating the silence. "If you did, I wouldn't be upset about it."

Even in the low light, I can see a red flush bloom across her chest. "We're in public, Caleb!"

"It's less public than earlier," I say, reaching behind me to lock the door. "And I never suggested you get naked. There's a lot we can do with you remaining safely clothed."

"I don't know if I understand what you mean. You'll have to show me," Valerie says, a little breathless.

"Is that a *yes*?" I ask.

She bites her lip. "I'll consent to whatever you can pull off in this dress, because *damn*, I want you."

"I'll take that as a challenge." I sink down to my knees in front of her, smirking. "This okay?"

Her breath catches. "Absolutely."

"Good, because this dress has been giving me ideas all night," I say, pressing a soft kiss to her exposed thigh. Her skin pebbles under my lips, and she lets out the tiniest gasp. "But you're going to have to be quiet. Can you do that for me?"

She swallows thickly, her pretty throat bobbing in the dim light, and presses a hand over her mouth. My heart races, both because *fuck*, that's hot, but also because we don't have time to make this last.

"Good girl," I say.

If we were really alone, I'd take my time, tease her until she was begging for release, ensure it was really good for her—but we've already stolen too many minutes. I have no idea how long it'll be before someone tries to get in here, and I want to make the time count.

I'm a man of my word.

So I duck my head under the slit of her gown, tug her panties aside, and lick her sweet folds. She shudders, sinking back against the wall.

I swallow down my own moan because *god*, I can't believe we're doing this. It's not even the thrill of potentially being caught. She's thrilling enough.

"That's it," I say. "Just enjoy it."

She lets out a shaky breath. "That's not a problem."

I draw back, careful to cover her as I do. "I thought I said you need to be quiet?"

Valerie's eyes spark with heat. "Fine. But how will you know you're doing it right?"

I run a hand over my hair, grinning up at her. "Oh I think we both know I can do it right."

"Prove it, then," she says. But I just wait, until she finally presses her hand over that lovely mouth again.

I dive back in, and I'm relentless. She's so wet it drives me wild, and I'm a man on a mission as I start sucking on her clit. Once she starts to tremble, I slip one finger inside her. When I add a second, she throws her leg over my shoulder, her stiletto digging into my back and demanding more.

It's so hot I almost come myself. She's practically riding my face now, wantonly chasing her pleasure, and I fucking love every second.

She clenches around my fingers, writhing beneath my tongue, and the softest, muffled moan escapes through her fingertips. Once she sags against the wall again, I pull her panties back into place, then slip out from beneath her dress.

Valerie grabs my lapel and drags me to her in a breathless kiss. It's soft and wild and a little sloppy, but neither of us cares. We're just lost in each other.

"I didn't know semipublic sex was your kink," she whispers as soon as we part for air.

I lock onto those ocean-blue eyes. "*You* are my kink."

[TODAY]

@GlitterbugsUnofficial

Repost @BuzzWordCeleb: After a rumored reconnection on the beach last week, Caleb Sloane and Valerie Quinn share a hot kiss on the red carpet for bandmate Jane Mercer's Into the Dragon Realm.

@GlitterbugsUnofficial

CALERIE CONFIRMED! I FUCKING KNEW IT ALL ALONG 😻😻😻😻😻

@BatsThatGlitter

Dusting off this account because IT'S CALERIE MY BABIES LOOK AT THEM

@ValerieQuinnSuperFan

It's so nice to see Valerie happy after everything the media has put her through. She was practically glowing tonight 😭

@EpicThemeSongMemes

VALERIE QUINN NEWS! Seen kissing bandmate Caleb Sloane on the red carpet!
[Image description: Epic Theme Song *GIF from episode 1x08, "Friends That Kiss," with Valerie Quinn*

*as Wendy the Wonder standing in a kitchen in a
blue leotard and saying, "The Killers are wrong—it's
never only a kiss."]*

@BatsThatGlitter

Does anyone else think this means we're getting
more music? The band split because they broke up,
right? There could be hope!

@GlitterbugsUnofficial

Ok @BatsThatGlitter, we're manifesting this. ⭐ ⭐ ⭐

@BatsThatGlitter

Yes @GlitterbugsUnofficial (good to see you! just
DMed!) I swear I'll summon GB3 into existence by
sheer will if it's the last thing I do on this hell site.

@BitterSweetGlitterati

OMG @GlitterbugsUnofficial @BatsThatGlitter
THEY'RE BACK AND IT'S EVERYTHING WE
DREAMED! *runs to resurrect the old group chat*

@BatsThatGlitter

AHHHH @BitterSweetGlitterati
@GlitterbugsUnofficial WAIT FOR ME I HAVE
THEORIES

22

+ *Valerie* +

A week before the concert, Caleb and I are late to our first day of Glitter Bats press because we attempted to share a shower.

I'm powerless to resist him. Especially when water is dripping down his jawline, streaming down that muscled torso, soaking those strong thighs. I was the one on my knees this time, and it was totally fucking worth it. We had to race through getting ready after that, and I'm not even sure this is the right look—I chose a form-fitting tank dress and a black denim jacket, and my eyeliner is a bit crooked—but I'd do it again.

These days before the concert feel like borrowed time. We haven't spoken about the future much, after how he reacted to a potential album, and I'm afraid to bring it up again. What if he doesn't even want to give us another real chance? So instead of being disappointed, I just pretend I get to keep him for as long as possible.

This morning, it's hard to believe our time together has an expiration date. He kisses me as we wait for the elevator, and hardly lets go when the doors open and we join a few other guests on the way down.

I forgot how *tactile* this man is. He's constantly touching me, fingers brushing my wrist, a hand on my back, a kiss on my temple when no one is looking. Every time our eyes catch, he smirks.

"Don't be so cocky. All the fans will think you just got lucky," I murmur as the elevator descends to the main floor, where the conference room is set up for a VIP coffee hour with the band.

"But I did just get lucky," he whispers into my ear as the elevator stops at our destination. "And you've given me a morning that I now have the pleasure of thinking about all day."

A wave of desire pulses through my core, and I discreetly press my thighs together before we step out of the elevator. If Caleb doesn't rail me in this dress tonight, I swear to god . . .

But there's a small group of fans waiting outside the conference hall, so I push the dirty thoughts to the back of my mind and plaster on a smile until it comes naturally, while Caleb flashes a huge grin and waves in their direction.

The Glitterbugs really are amazing. If it weren't for the fans, I may not have a place in this business at all. Sometimes I forget that. So many fans followed me through my (failed) solo album and all the musical collaborations and minor guest roles I did prior to landing *Epic Theme Song*. In fact, there was a marketing meeting where one very brave intern reminded the room that I had an established fan base so I didn't need so much "image management." I hope they're still working in the industry, because we need more kind souls.

Since those fans will be joining us for a meet and greet later, we don't stop for selfies, but I make it a point to smile and make eye contact with as many as possible before we slip into the conference room. Keeley, Jane, and even Riker are already waiting, looking a little bored.

"We were supposed to be here twenty minutes ago," Keeley says.

"Hell, even I've been here for fifteen. What gives?" Riker asks.

Jane's jaw is set, and I can tell even she is holding back a reprimand.

"I needed Caleb's help with something," I say, and then I clear my throat. "Band related. I needed help with something band related."

"Valerie, you are the worst liar in the world," Keeley sneers.

"*But* we don't have time for this conversation because our fans are waiting!" Jane says, her voice at a higher pitch than usual. Clearly, we've stressed everyone out, and I don't want to add to it.

"Whatever—let's do this," Keeley says.

"*Finally!* They brought in dark chocolate orange peel scones and lavender muffins and *oh my god* the fresh donuts!" Riker says with heart eyes. He got really into baking one summer and briefly considered culinary school before the band took off, and his enthusiasm for pastries clearly hasn't dimmed over the years.

The hotel's catering manager confirms we're ready to go, and security handles the door. We don't worry about fans, per se, but we've been in this industry long enough to know that security is essential when we're mixing with the public.

It felt strange when we hired them for the first time, but now I'm just used to intimidating people in all-black outfits with radios hanging out whenever we need them. It's mostly just for crowd control, but there was a time where this one dude begged me for feet pics and wouldn't leave a signing line without trying to grab my shoe.

I was really grateful I didn't have to de-escalate that situation on my own. It's uncomfortable, the way fame makes fans put you on a pedestal one minute, and act like you're best friends the next. Fortunately, when we open the doors, the group is calm and follows the guidelines. It's all the usual: no unsolicited touching, no revealing the location of the hotel, but photos are allowed (and, in fact, encouraged).

A videographer comes in and begins to shoot B-roll of the event for the promo video. I'm still unsure of the purpose of the promo video—tickets are sold out—but I do my best to pretend they're not in the room. It's hard when you're used to playing to them on a TV set, but as we split up and mingle with the fans, the camera fades into the background.

There are only fifty fans at this event, so it's easy to move around and talk to everyone. Even though I feel like I need to be chatting and taking photos the whole time, I make it a point to grab a coffee and a lemon bar so I can take small bites while the conversation flows.

When I run into a few familiar faces, I grin. It's the college kids we saw at Magic Cupcake. They've all dressed up for the occasion, in concert black like proper music students.

"Glad to see Wade made you VIPs," I say, smiling at the three of them.

They share a look, eyes wide. "You remember us?" Whit asks.

"Of course I do! You're Whit, and this is Sophie and Aiden, right?"

Sophie bounces on her heels. "Yes!"

"Hey, friends, good to see you!" Caleb says, joining the four of us. I glance around, surprised he's joined our little group, but Keeley and Riker are entertaining most of the room with a cajon and guitar they pulled out of nowhere. Jane's still talking to another group, though, so I don't feel the need to join in yet.

"Your manager got us incredible seats for the concert, and VIP access to all fan events this week. Seriously, thank you so much," Sophie says. Just like before, she's clearly the most extroverted of the group, but Caleb, in his natural warmth, manages to draw a starstruck Whit and sullen Aiden out of their shells too. We talk about music and the industry and queer representation in media, and for a minute I realize it's been too long since I had conversations like this with fans. During all the meet and greets for *Epic*

Theme Song, I've kept my chatter really surface level—I tell myself it's to set boundaries, but it's not like you have to bare your soul to connect with people.

Sometimes just a thoughtful question, or even an encouraging word, can make all the difference. It makes me want to do better in the future.

Caleb brings out the best in me. He's always done that. I feel like I lost my way without him, and I'm finally remembering why I wanted to do this in the first place. Because knowing your art has been meaningful to someone? It's everything.

We wander back to the rest of the group, and soon Keeley and Jane are leading the room in a lively acoustic version of "Still Dancing," with Riker playing the guitar like we're at a campfire singalong. Fans are recording video with their phones.

Caleb and I stay in the background, clapping to the beat and singing harmonies.

"We're not totally committed to a new arrangement for this one, right?" I ask quietly. Our set list has been final for weeks, but we've spent these late-stage rehearsals tinkering with sounds and perfecting every detail. Even with the clock ticking, we've all agreed to be open to changes as inspiration strikes.

I don't think any of us wants the collaboration to stop.

Caleb grins at me, eyes sparkling at my meaning. "No, but I think we have now. They should do it."

Despite Keeley's accusations to the contrary, it was always really important to us that the band was about all five of the Glitter Bats, not just me and Caleb. The label always wanted the two of us to lead songs in recordings, but when we toured, we'd get away with putting Riker on lead guitar to shred on "Vampires" or giving Jane a chance to riff on a ballad. Keeley would get at least one drum solo per night.

Caleb slips his hand into mine as we watch them hit the bridge.

Keeley's brassy soprano and Jane's rich alto blend gorgeously with Riker's soft tenor melody, filling the room with warmth.

And . . . oh, I don't want to lose this.

One last show just isn't enough. I want everyone to get to showcase their wide range of talent, and that can't all be crammed into one performance. Maybe it's enough that they're all showcasing their talent outside of the band, but it feels like the Glitter Bats have unfinished business. It's always been at the pit of my stomach, a reminder of the band—my family—that fell apart too soon.

I don't know if the concert will be enough to make that feeling go away.

After the song, we mingle a bit longer, grab pastries, and wrap up. Then we have a long day of interviews, both solo and as a group. We're getting ready to record the big reunion exclusive for *Buzzword* in a few days, and do our official photo shoot, but today it's other media outlets like *Gossip Daily* and *Twenty-Two* and even a few fan creators.

Some of the interviews will happen via video call, but we're hosting a few of the creators in one of the other conference rooms. Just as we're wrapping up, Keeley and Riker pull me aside. Jane and Caleb are on the other side of the room talking to the hotel event coordinator.

"What's up?" I ask, staring between them.

Keeley raises her brows. "What are you doing?"

To buy time, I take a sip of my nearly gone coffee. "Oh?"

"Why did we have to find out from the internet that you and Caleb are involved again?" Riker says. I flinch.

"Who says we were ever together before?" I blurt, even though the band knows it was the least well-kept secret of our past.

"You were never subtle," Keeley says. "Besides, we used to stay in some really shitty hotel rooms and, you know, mattresses squeak."

I flush. It's not like I ever thought the band was clueless, but I always thought we had this unwritten rule that we never spoke about it. I guess unwritten rules are void when you haven't been a group for six years.

But I don't need their permission.

"So?"

"Just tread lightly," Riker says. "I don't think he's over you. Don't use him."

I narrow my eyes at him. "Do you really think so little of me, after all our history, that you believe I would treat Caleb Sloane like a fuck buddy?"

They share a glance. "No, but . . ." Riker trails off, frowning, like he's trying to figure out how best to call me out without pissing me off.

"We love you, but this is a terrible idea," Keeley says. "Have you even talked about what happens after the concert?"

I open my mouth to say something, anything, in my defense, but I come up empty. Before I can even try, we're being called over to go over the schedule for the rest of the day.

But the worst thing is, I'm worried Keeley is right. When all this is over, it's entirely possible I'll be alone and heartbroken. As we confirm plans for our first interview, I'm half listening.

I won't let history repeat itself. I'll fight for Caleb. This concert can't be the end of it all, even if we're not sure what any kind of future between us could look like yet.

I'm holding on to this happiness, and I won't let go without a fight.

23

+ *Caleb* +

The rest of the week goes by in a blur.

Interviews, photo shoots, VIP events with more fans. Despite what everyone hopes, it does nothing to make us feel free of Label Records' expectations.

But Valerie thrives. As we get ready for the last photo shoot—a cover for *Punk!* magazine—she's buzzing with excitement.

"My publicists just checked in—the press is so good!" she says, beaming at her phone for what feels like the hundredth time this morning. We're in hair and makeup, and she's letting them bleach her hair platinum again, with plans to tease it into a glam-rock look. I'm tolerating the extra product on my hair, the thick photo-friendly makeup on my face, but when the makeup artist pulls out a stick of Perversion, I grin.

"You did your homework," I say.

Rowan—who has been supervising all of our prep—pops into my mirror over the makeup artist's shoulder. "Didn't feel right to put you in anything else. The goal is fresh but nostalgic. We want fans to recognize you when they see these images but have a reason to keep looking—let's intrigue them."

"Sounds good."

They place a hand on the back of my chair, gesturing to my face with the other. "You're not twenty-two anymore, so I thought we'd go a little heavier on the makeup if you're okay with it. You good with mascara, maybe a smoky eye?"

I shrug. I never really tried other makeup, with the exception of basic stuff for photo shoots and red carpets. It took me a lot of YouTube videos and more than a few mishaps to even get the eyeliner right. I'm curious, though. "I'll defer to your expertise."

Rowan's eyes spark. "Oh, we're going to have fun."

They pull the makeup artist away into a huddle, and she starts taking notes as Rowan describes their vision. I take a chance to pull out my phone. It's been buzzing off and on, and I grin when I see it's not press inquiries, but the group chat with my sisters. I've been a little apprehensive all morning—I never loved being photographed—but seeing their flood of texts eases some of the tension in my shoulders.

Carrie: So Caleb, you're like famous again??? I swear, every time I'm online, someone is talking about you.

Carrie: Also. You LIED to me when you said you and Valerie weren't back together. There's no way that kiss was just for clicks. I'm not totally clueless.

Carrie: I don't think I've ever seen you go viral before. It's weird.

Cameron: Oh gosh, I forgot you were like seven when "Midnight Road Trip" dropped. He was EVERYWHERE.

Cameron: I almost gagged the first time I saw him top a Gossip Daily list of "The Hottest New Musicians We'd Most Like to Kiss"

It wasn't "kiss," but I'm glad Cameron had the foresight to spare Carrie the gory details. Heck, I wish *I* hadn't seen a paragraph of Paige Hart speculating how badly she wanted to find out if the "rumors about short kings are true."

Valerie always got the brunt of the media, but it doesn't mean the rest of us didn't get our fair share.

Carrie: EEW! That's so gross!

Cameron: It was!

Cameron: There was so much back then.

Carrie: Caleb is so boring now. I always forget he's very Google-able.

I send a selfie from hair and makeup, Riker photobombing in the background from the chair next to mine with a peace sign, his hair in foils.

Me: HEY now, I'm not that boring.

Carrie: TELL RIKER HI

I roll my eyes. "My baby sister says hi."

"God, I miss that kid. Tell her hi back, and that she should come down for the concert," he says.

My stomach twists. Of course I want my sisters here, and I set aside tickets for them, but I'm not sure I can trust Mom to get Carrie to the airport. I don't want her to do something rash like try to take a rideshare all on her own.

So I don't remind her of it in case she gets let down.

Me: He says hi.

Carrie: Does he still live by that candy store he used to post about on IG? And will you be in that neighborhood? 👀

Me: That's very presumptuous.

Cameron: IDK, if she's stuck at piano camp all summer, the least you could do is send her sour gummies.

Carrie: I'll text Riker. I know HE will send me sours.

The thing is, she's right. Out of all of us, I have the youngest sibling—Jane's younger sister, Nora, is a year older than Carrie—and the rest of the band always spoiled Carrie rotten whenever they could.

Riker chuckles from next to me, and I know she's already sent the text.

"Dude, ignore her. She's being a brat," I say, but there's no real force behind the words.

"I actually have to run home tomorrow to grab a couple jackets, so it's no trouble!"

"Oh, we're definitely sending her candy," Keeley calls from Riker's other side, where a stylist is making the finishing touches on her silky blowout.

I laugh. "I don't know how many seventeen-year-olds are getting care packages from rock stars."

"Only the lucky ones," Valerie says. I glance over her way, expecting to catch her grin, but she's scrolling her phone obsessively. I wish I could say something to make her feel better about all of this, but I know she's on edge with the concert coming so soon.

The makeup artist comes over again. "You ready, Caleb?"

"Sorry, one sec."

Me: It's my turn for makeup. Be good!

Carrie: No promises!

Cameron: UGH send us another selfie when you're done. It's unfair how good you look in eyeliner.

With that, I shove my phone away. Instead of fidgeting with my phone like Valerie or popping in earbuds like Riker, I like to watch in the mirror as I transform from regular Caleb to stage Caleb. The process has always fascinated me. It's a kind of armor, the makeup, making me feel like I'm ready to take on the crowds, hidden away behind the smudge of the pencil. I close my eyes as the artist layers on eyeshadow, trying not to flinch as she layers the powder on my lids.

"Go ahead and open. What do you think?" she asks.

I blink, barely recognizing myself. The effect is more intense than ever, like the volume dial on my face is turned up all the way. Somehow my eyes look even greener.

"It looks awesome," I say. "Thank you so much."

"Knock 'em dead out there," she says, moving her stool over to Riker. "Can't wait for the show."

Nerves flutter in my stomach. The concert is in forty-eight hours, and then my life will go back to normal. We haven't talked about the future, and I still can't bring myself to say anything about it. For now, Valerie and I are existing in this sweet, precious bubble, where there's only us. Only this. No day but today and all that jazz.

It's a goddamn Broadway tune over here.

Because I can't give Valerie what she wants. It's so clearly written on her face, the hope that all of this means *Epic Theme Song* will be renewed. I don't work at The Network, all the money from this performance is going into my sister's college fund, and I can't come back to this life the way she would need me to for any of it to be worth it.

While I wait for Rowan to come by and give me their final approval, I glance over at Valerie. She's still beaming down at her phone from under a hair dryer.

I can't swoop in and save her, but I hope my presence was enough to spin the trends in her favor. This morning, as we were tangled in the sheets and procrastinating getting ready for the day, Valerie shared the latest update from Wade: The Network is impressed and they're having talks. But once you've been in this business long enough, you know never to put your hope in "talks."

You can only put your hope in sure things—deals, contracts, commitments—and even those don't always stick. So you have to control the things you can: your behavior, your look, the projects and opportunities you choose to pursue. The rest is up to fate.

I hope that for Valerie's sake the stars align.

Rowan comes over and gives me their final approval before sending me to the next room for wardrobe. Again, I'm told the goal is to look like me but also like someone new, so I'm thrown into whitewashed designer jeans and a Nirvana tee with the sleeves artfully cut off. After some digging on a rack, Rowan hands me a leather jacket, but since I won't be wearing it in all the photos, I'm also given tattoo balm to rub on my arms.

Jane joins me then, her thick red hair in perfect curls, shimmering gold makeup on her eyes and cheeks, in a green minidress and combat boots. I can tell she's staring at my tattoos as I work the balm into my skin, her eyes growing wide and watery.

"I never really looked at them before," she says, fanning her face to stop the tears. "I didn't realize . . ."

"Yeah," I say, swallowing thickly. "I, uh, couldn't stop."

The ink tells the story of Glitter Bats in a way I can't articulate. After I walked away from this life, I still felt this unshakable compulsion to write it on my skin. There are ghosts and vampires and bats, but also broken hearts and a lipstick print of a kiss and even a minimalist outline of the old VW van we took on our first tour.

Jane—ever wise, ever kind—doesn't press me for more. She just smiles.

"It's beautiful work."

"A friend from college began apprenticing at this really fantastic shop. He practiced on me."

She opens her mouth to respond, but we're interrupted by Keeley's drawl.

"Well don't you look like a heartbreaker," she says, assessing me. Her bob is sleek and fresh, styled so her blond hair swoops into her eyes. They've got her in minimal makeup, but she's wearing the hell out of a tie-dye Wildfang boilersuit and Chucks.

"Hey, I just showed up," I say. "It's not my fault if hearts break when they see me."

"Wow, Caleb, vain much? I was talking about Mercer—she's literally *glowing*." Jane flushes bright pink, and Keeley smirks before she clears her throat. "You look good too, Sloane. You miss any of this?"

It would be so easy to say no—I don't miss being told what to wear, how to look, where to be. But I miss *this*, the easy rapport with my bandmates, the music. I'm excited to play the concert.

Excited to sing with Valerie one last time.

"Some of it," I finally admit.

"This doesn't have to be our last rodeo," Keeley says, a little softer. "We could talk about doing more. I'd be open to recording again, if we were all on board. I just don't want to force you into anything."

"I'd be in," Jane admits. "I was talking to Riker over drinks last night, and I think he'd do it too."

Keeley flinches, almost visibly, and I frown at her. She glares at me, and I raise my brows. Jane squeals, oblivious to our interaction.

"I have to take this," she gestures to her buzzing phone. "We've been waiting to hear an update from The Network on *Dragon Realm*, and this is my producer!"

"Go, go!" Keeley says, unable to stop smiling at Jane as she disappears around the corner.

"You want to talk about it?" I ask.

Keeley scowls. "Talk about what?"

"*Keeley.*"

She crosses her arms. "*Caleb.*"

"How long have you been pining after her?"

"I thought you were in therapy. We call that '*projecting,*'" she says, but her jaw is tense and her eyes are wide, like she's freaking out a little.

I raise my hands. "How is that projecting?"

"Oh, come on, you've clearly been pining after Valerie, or you wouldn't be here—you certainly wouldn't be fucking her. Dude, I love you, but watching this is so painful. You're going to go back to your boring life with your noble day job in a couple of days, and it's going to hurt you again."

I swallow thickly, because I've been worried about the same

thing. "I thought you wanted us to keep working together. If that happens, maybe Valerie and I can figure out . . . something."

I shove my hands in my pockets, leaning against the cold concrete wall. I haven't been able to get Valerie out of my head for years—I don't think I can just walk away completely again.

"Is that what you really want?" Keeley asks.

I think about life back home—working with the kids, being close to Cam and Leah, taking Sebastian Bark on hikes every weekend. It's not a bad life. I'm comfortable, and mostly happy.

But it's nowhere near perfect, and it's definitely not glamorous. I spend most of my free time doing lesson prep. Any savings I can manage get drained to nothing whenever Mom needs help. The nights alone in my town house are brutal. There's no room for Valerie in that life.

And I don't know if I can go back to a life without her.

Still, it's hard to trust that Valerie would really want to take this path if the Glitter Bats reunite for good. Would she be content making music together until we become classic rock, or are her dreams bigger than that? She'll be running back to TV the moment The Network calls. What then?

I'd be pushed to the sidelines of her perfect life. I want her to achieve her dreams, but I can't give up everything for nothing. If I knew for sure she was all in, that might change things. But maybe it wouldn't.

After finding our way back to each other this summer, losing her again would tear me apart.

"I honestly don't know," I say.

She lowers her voice dramatically, as if it's a secret. "You only have like two days to figure it out."

I sigh. "Enough about me. Let's talk about what you want—are you going to ever tell Jane you're in love with her?"

"Obviously not, because it's not true," Keeley says, staring petulantly at the floor.

"So you're just going to suffer in silence," I say, all too aware that it never works.

Her eyes snap to mine with a flash of something I'd almost call panic. "Hell yeah I'm going to suffer in silence, because what if she's not into me? I don't even know if she *likes girls*."

"Well, maybe you should just talk to her about your feelings, because you're very good at making her blush."

"I'm not the only one," she says, crossing her arms and glancing in Riker's direction as he comes around the corner. "Did you know those two are the only ones who really stayed in touch before this summer? I mean, the three of us hung out a few times, but I . . . most of the time I wasn't included. You can't tell me there's nothing . . ."

She trails off as Riker comes over. He's let the stylist cut his hair into an actual shag, and they've managed to wrangle it into messy curls with some extensions. "Why do you look like that one dude from *Stranger Things*?" Keeley asks, elbowing him.

Riker's eyes light up. "I *wish* I could be as badass as Eddie Munson. Taking that as a compliment."

"There is the whole *bat* connection," I say. "You look good." Like me, Riker is a styled-up version of himself. He's in a tight black tank and black designer jeans, and he's got a flannel half on his arms. There are black leather bracelets on his wrists, and he too has been subjected to extra eye makeup, although less intense than mine.

Riker flexes. "I know, I'm a dreamboat. Feel free to keep complimenting me."

Keeley punches his arm, and the two start trading friendly jabs. I fall quiet, letting them bicker like old times, knowing there's no real reason for me to intervene.

And then Valerie emerges from wardrobe, and she takes my breath away.

She's exuding pure sin in black leather pants and a tight black crop top, practically a corset that gives her already-perfect cleavage a distracting lift. Even in platform Doc Martens, she walks with remarkable grace. She's wearing a choker around her neck and bloodred lipstick, evoking both Taylor Swift's *Reputation* era—arguably her hottest—and something entirely *Val*.

"Oh my god, those pants should be illegal," Keeley says.

Valerie spins around slowly, and I have to swallow thickly because there's no hiding a hard-on in these jeans. Her ass looks like it was carved out of marble.

"Damn, Quinn," Keeley wolf whistles, lightly smacking Valerie's ass.

Val preens, swinging her hips. "You like?"

"Who wouldn't?"

Riker coughs, clearly uncomfortable at where the attention is going but unable to stop himself. "What is that, yoga?" he asks.

Val laughs, tossing her hair over her shoulder. "That or the Pilates."

I wrap an arm around her shoulders, careful not to smudge anything. "Whatever it is, it's working for me," I whisper in her ear.

She flushes. "Noted."

"Okay, if this is going to be a thing, we need a no-PDA rule, because I'm about to throw up," Keeley says.

"Jealous you're not getting any?" Val shoots back with a wink.

Keeley strikes a pose, tugging on her top. "I can get *plenty*, thank you."

"I think Keeley's got her sights set on someone in particular," Riker says lightly.

Keeley blanches, but Jane joins our group in a whirlwind before it goes any further.

"The Network renewed *Into the Dragon Realm* for two more seasons!" Jane shrieks. "Our numbers were already that good!"

"Mercer, that's amazing!" Keeley screams.

Jane turns and immediately throws her arms around Keeley's neck for a hug, and Keeley swings Jane around in a circle. Maybe that whole situation is not as unrequited as Keeley thinks. Riker grabs Jane for the next hug, I join in, and soon almost everyone is jumping up and down and screaming.

Valerie just blinks, stunned. But when she realizes she's the odd one out, she quickly recovers. "Wow, that's amazing. I'm so proud of you," she says, drawing Jane into a hug of her own.

But I can't miss the sadness hanging in her shoulders. I know she's trying to hold it together, be happy for Jane, but it can't be easy watching a friend get the exact good news you're hoping for.

"Come on in, Glitter Bats!" an assistant says, and we all file into the room for the first round of shots.

Valerie leads the way, but I can see that her spark has dimmed.

I wish I could shield her from this pain, the heartache of not knowing if she'll be allowed to continue on. That's the thing about this business—it'll break your heart more times than it won't. You'll hear a hundred nos for every precious yes. You can fall in love with the industry, you can give it everything, but it will never love you back.

And it's a reminder that I still don't know if I can subject myself to it all again.

GLITTER BATS IN CONVERSATION WITH MARY KATE HAMPTON FOR *BUZZWORD*

Video Description: *Valerie Quinn, Caleb Sloane, Riker Maddox, Keeley Cunningham, and Jane Mercer sit in two rows of director's chairs at* Buzzword *HQ in Los Angeles. The room has bright purple walls and a shiny wooden floor. Mary Kate Hampton sits across from them with a tablet in hand.*

Video Transcript:

MARY KATE HAMPTON: Thank you all for meeting me today.

RIKER MADDOX: Anything for you, MK.

KEELEY CUNNINGHAM: Okay, Maddox, keep it in your pants.

RM: I'm trying to be *polite*, Keels. Something you could learn from me.

[Laughter from all]

CALEB SLOANE: We're all very happy to be here, Mary Kate.

MKH: The concert is tomorrow! That must be such a thrill after all this time. How are you feeling?

VALERIE QUINN: Working together again is a dream come true.

JANE MERCER: I agree—I can't believe this is finally happening.

KC: These [*******] are some of my favorite people in the world. [*Clears throat.*] Wait, am I allowed to swear?

RM: NO, Keeley.

MKH: [*laughs*] We'll cut anything out if needed.

KC: I'll behave.

JM: Don't make promises you can't keep, Keeley.

[*More laughter*]

CS: I think we're off topic, but I'll tell you I'm both nervous and excited about tomorrow. It's been a long time since I've played music—and I haven't played in front of this many people since the *Bittersweet* tour.

MKH: That tour ended early. What happened?

VQ: It was my fault, I—

CS: [*interrupts, turning to VQ*] That's not true.

VQ: Yes it is. I'm the reason you left.

CS: You didn't make that choice for me. [*turns to MKH*] Everyone has always been so quick to blame Valerie, but I dealt poorly with a personal matter, and I left the band—which is essentially what broke up the Glitter Bats. Valerie was not responsible for my actions. I was young and stupid and letting my emotions get the best of me. Really, it's a testament to her passion that this reunion is even happening.

MKH: Were there any hard feelings when you all started playing together again?

RM: [*laughs dryly*] Yeah, there were a few.

JM: It was a . . . tense few days.

KC: I had to get my head out of my [***], but I eventually forgave everyone.

VQ: I had a lot of apologies to make.

CS: [*grabs her hand*] So did I.

MKH: Well, I think I can speak on behalf of the entire Glitterbug community when I say I'm glad to see you *all* together again.

RM: Do you run a secret fan account, Mary Kate?

MKH: I'm not the one being interviewed here.

CS: We must be a nightmare. Descending into chaos already.

MKH: This is not even close to the most chaotic interview I've conducted, but I appreciate your concern.

VQ: Is this Caleb going into teacher mode?

CS: I have excellent classroom management.

MKH: Caleb, you've been working away from the industry, which we spoke about a couple weeks ago. I'll refrain from rehashing it here, but I know fans are excited to see you back onstage. Can any of you tell fans what they can expect tomorrow?

VQ: Our lips are sealed.

RM: I think it's safe to say we have a few surprises.

JM: It's sold out, but you can still catch the livestream. The concert will be broadcast on The Network, and you won't want to miss it.

MKH: Can't wait. But for today, we have a game for you, if you're up for it.

KC: Of course we're [****]ing up for it.

VQ: We're a very competitive group.

MKH: Perfect! So the game is called . . .

24

+ *Valerie* +

City lights stream through the gap in the hotel curtains the night before the concert. I toss and turn for the thousandth time, unable to stop my mind from racing. At least Caleb is totally out, his face smooshed into the hotel pillows, snoring softly. I'd hate to disturb him with my insomnia.

A sleepless night isn't unusual before a performance, but this one feels particularly ominous. Finally, at three a.m., I slip out of bed to pee and brush my teeth again, hoping I can maybe trick myself into going to sleep with the familiar bedtime rhythm. I should have taken a gummy, but I was afraid I'd be groggy onstage. So much for avoiding that. I'll just throw back espresso like candy when it's time to go, because there's no way I'm sleeping on this performance. The adrenaline will keep me running if nothing else does.

I slip into bed, but my shoulders are taut with nerves, and I curl into a little ball, willing myself to rest.

"Val?" Caleb asks sleepily. I glance over at him. His voice is a little husky from sleep, but as he turns to face me, he's smiling out from underneath his curls in the darkness.

I wince, staring back up at the ceiling. "Sorry, I didn't mean to wake you."

"Nervous for tomorrow?" he mumbles.

I sigh, sinking into the pillows and adjusting to look at him. "It's today now."

He turns over to look at the white LED of the in-room alarm clock. "Damn, you're right." He flips back onto his side, facing me, and twines his fingers through mine. Maybe it's because it's three a.m., and maybe it's because I have nothing to lose, but I speak the words that have been stuck in the back of my throat ever since we kissed on the beach.

"I'm not nervous for the concert. I'm afraid of what happens after," I whisper. The last time we performed, it wasn't the show that went wrong—it was everything after.

He proposed. I said no. Everything was ruined. What if it all falls apart again?

"I know you're worried about what's next. I am too," he says, squeezing my hands gently. "I'm not ready to say goodbye."

"You don't have to leave, you know," I murmur, finding my courage. "We could do it. Make more Glitter Bats music. Be a band again."

He sighs, scrubbing a hand over his sleep-heavy eyes. "I wish it were that easy."

"It could be."

He smiles sadly in the dim light. "This summer, playing music, finding you again . . . it's made me so happy, but I have a life back home. Hell, everyone has established a career outside of the band. Say we all agree to do more, and then *Epic Theme Song* calls. What would you choose?"

You, I want to scream, but I know I can't promise that. I haven't earned the right. "I don't know. I think we could maybe make it work."

His shoulders tense. "I want to believe that, but you know this industry. Schedules are the one thing you can't control. If I could see the future, that might be one thing, but I don't know if I can give up my life back home for a maybe."

I do my best to smirk. "Do you need a push?"

He rolls his eyes, but his smile has softened a little. "If anyone could push me, it would be you. It's always been you."

My voice nearly breaks. "I'm not ready to give you up again."

"Val, before we get up on that stage, I just want you to know . . ." he trails off, breath hitching as he draws me closer. "I never stopped loving you, and I don't think I could if I tried."

My heart races, and this time it's with a hopeful beat. I never thought I'd hear those words from him again, and I'm completely overcome. Tears prick the back of my eyes, and I blink them away, determined to hold it together.

"*Caleb*."

And then we're grabbing, desperate, clinging to each other like a raft in a wild sea in these last precious few moments. He lets go of my fingers and slides a hand up my arm, caressing my neck, pressing his palm to my cheek. I lean into his touch, slipping my arms around his neck and pulling him toward me.

His lips brush mine in the sweetest of kisses that sparks the flame between us. I deepen the kiss, our tongues colliding. When I hook my leg around his hip and press his growing erection into my center, grinding into him, a feral growl escapes the back of his throat.

He draws back, leaning his forehead against mine. "*Fuck*, Val."

I love seeing him like this, completely undone. When we're out in public, he doesn't swear all that much. But when it's just the two of us in bed, he has the filthiest mouth. Hearing him say *fuck* is my own private kink.

"I just want to be close to you right now," I say. *I'm afraid this will be the last time*, is the unspoken phrase sitting on my tongue.

"I want that too," he says. His fingers trace down to my shoulder, and he plays with the fabric of my tank top. "May I?"

"Please."

He slips the dainty strap down my shoulder, fingering the lace, and exposes my breasts to the air. But he doesn't do more than stare. "God, just look at you." He swallows. "I never get over this view."

"I wouldn't want you to get bored of me."

"It'd be impossible to get bored of this." He palms my breast, then works my nipple into a point with a gentle touch of those rough, practiced fingertips. The bass-string calluses send a jolt down my spine, and I shudder. "You like that?" he says, a hint of smugness in his tone.

"I love your hands," I say.

"Those aren't the only things I can use to make you feel good," he says, before dipping his head down to my breast. Maybe it's the late hour, or the urgency of our circumstances, but he doesn't continue his teasing. Instead, he takes my nipple into his mouth and sucks, grazing the nub with his tongue.

A soft moan escapes my lips as the sensation sends heat between my thighs. I press them together, but it's not enough.

"Touch me," I beg.

Without stopping his attention to my breast, he trails his hand down my belly and dips into my shorts. He traces the curve of my ass down between my legs, then palms my center. This stops him short.

"Fuck, Val, you're already so ready for me."

I let out a shaky breath. "I thought I asked you to touch me."

He quirks a brow, even though his pupils are blown wide with desire. "You're so impatient. I should really tease you, get you all worked up and begging for it."

"I'm already begging you for it," I whine.

He swallows thickly, his throat bobbing. "I've never been able to say no to you."

And with that, he slips two deliberate fingers into my folds, using his palm to rub my clit in a slow, rhythmic way that makes me gasp. His long, calloused fingers press that perfect spot deep inside me, already taking me to the brink, until he pauses.

"Is that how you want it?" Caleb Sloane has figured out exactly how to drive me wild.

"Yes," I hiss. "Don't stop."

"I wouldn't dream of it."

He works me into a near frenzy, until I'm just on the edge of bliss.

"More," I say, palming him through his shorts, luxuriating in his heavy length. "I need your cock inside me. Now."

This time, he's the one shuddering. "Condom," he says, shoving down his shorts.

I scramble over to the bedside table, reach into the open box, and yank out the first condom I can grab. My fingers are trembling so much with need that I have to rip it open with my teeth.

"That is so fucking hot," he says with a sigh.

"You should see what else I can do with my mouth."

"Later," he says. "Now, I just want to feel you."

Slowly, I roll the condom onto his length, and his hips buck under my touch.

"I want to be on top," I say.

"You want to be in charge? Get over here," he says, eyes blazing as he pulls me on top of him. I raise my hips above his, positioning his cock at my entrance but not going further.

"Are you going to make *me* beg this time?" he gasps.

It feels incredible, being here with him, seeing how much he wants me. I feel powerful, but also completely at his mercy. I think I'd let this man do anything to me.

"Not tonight," I say. Slowly, carefully, I sink onto his cock, angling my hips so he's pressing against that sweet spot again.

"Valerie, fucking hell, your pussy feels incredible. God, you're so wet."

"That's how much I want you," I say, lifting my hips up and sinking down again. He hisses, and I ride him like this: slow, languid, pressing my clit into his pelvis with every thrust. When I find the perfect angle, I wrap one arm around his shoulders for leverage, using the other to hold myself steady. I dip down and kiss him again, and our tongues collide, desperate, unable to get enough of each other.

I don't think I'll ever get enough of him. Even together like this, every part of him pressing into me, I'm just craving more. I never stopped loving Caleb Sloane. He might have been the brave one to say it, but with every kiss, every caress, I hope he understands the way I feel about him.

If I spent every night like this, with this man I adore worshipping my body and peering into my soul, I'd be the luckiest girl in the world. The fear of losing him is overwhelming, and I push it away and focus on us. This. Right now.

Leaning down for another kiss, I adjust the angle of where our bodies meet. I ride him slow and sweet until I feel that spiral at the base of my spine. My palms go slick with need as I get closer to the edge.

"That's it, Val. Take what you need."

I don't need him to say it twice. I work myself into a frenzy, fucking him faster, grinding my clit against him with a hunger I didn't know I possessed. It's not long before I'm digging my nails into his skin, coming apart with a trembling cry until I see nothing but stars.

"Caleb," I gasp.

He rocks his hips into mine, faster, urging me on until he's locking us together and shuddering through his own heaving release. Once we're both sated, we collapse onto the mattress, panting. The sheets are damp with sweat, but neither of us seems to care enough to move. Once the room has stopped spinning, he goes to dispose of the condom, and then I take my turn in the bathroom cleaning myself up.

We fall back into bed together, limbs entwined, like neither of us can bear to let go. I'm worried that if I lose this contact, I won't find my way back to him again. I nestle closer, finding that perfect spot on his chest to rest my head, and he shifts, resting his palm softly on my hip as his breathing deepens.

"You should always wake me up in the middle of the night," he murmurs into my hair, just when I think he's already asleep.

"Noted," I say, even though there's a distant piece of my brain warning me that this night is all we have left. As I drift off to sleep in his arms, I think about what our life together might be like if I'd said yes after that last show in Vegas.

I wonder if this could be real.

25

✦ Valerie ✦

Morning comes too soon.

After a long, lingering good-morning kiss, Caleb escapes to his own room to shower and prep. I'm sweetly sore from the sex and groggy from sleep deprivation—but I chug coffee from room service like my life depends on it as I start to get ready for the day.

I ran down to a beauty supply store after the *Punk!* magazine shoot and bought a fresh jar of vegan dye to cover up my blond. My first instinct was to grab my signature Pink Crush, but then my eyes fell on the Lavender Daze.

All that talk from Rowan telling Caleb to do something familiar but fresh rushed into my head. I bought the Lavender Daze without another thought, and now I'm stuck with it. Maybe it wasn't the right call, but this is a change I can control, and it'll definitely keep the fans talking.

And I need them to keep talking.

Sure, I could have a professional dye my hair, but that didn't feel right going into today. I've always done this part on my own, knowing it'll get me the results I want. Rowan agreed to let me have this one thing, as if they sensed somehow how much I needed to have something under my control.

Becoming this version of Valerie Quinn one more time.

So I pour the conditioning dye into a bowl, slip on some gloves, and begin working it into my freshly platinum strands. My hair is short enough that it doesn't take long, and soon the entire bathroom looks like a violet ink explosion. While the color sets, I clean off the sink and countertops, then run a bath to exfoliate and shave my legs.

Once I'm scrubbed clean and moisturized, there are still a few minutes left on my timer before I can rinse my hair, so . . . I scroll social media. News about us is everywhere today: the concert, Jane's premiere, my relationship with Caleb. Hell, even Theo tried to reach out to me, and *Gossip Daily* has nice things to say.

And I realize—we did it.

The posts don't say anything about my reputation. I'm not being tied to Theo Blake or Roxanne Leigh or anyone else I've dated in the past. No one is bringing up old mistakes I've apologized for a hundred times. They're all talking about how heartwarming it is to see me and Caleb back together again—one comment even says it's making them believe in soulmates.

Hell, it's making me believe too. Relief washes over my skin like cleansing rain.

We accomplished what we set out to do this summer. My name is no longer associated with heartbreak and scandal. Everyone is talking about us in a good way. A few of the posts and articles and videos speculate about what's next for the Glitter Bats, and *Epic Theme Song* is mentioned multiple times. It's exactly as we planned.

If The Network wanted me to turn my reputation around, I've officially done it.

My stomach still twists with anxiety, but it's all nerves and espresso. We've rehearsed every single moment of the concert, gotten through multiple run-throughs—I even have planned where I'm standing and what I'll say when it's my turn to talk between songs.

I've got this. We all do.

Soon enough, it's time to wash out my strands, and I follow my old hair process like a ritual, taking comfort in the familiar routine. Each movement grounds me further, and I feel the anxiety melting away. The soft purple is a shock as I dry my hair, but I like how it looks. Like me, but also new. It makes my eyes pop, and I play that up as I add texturizer to my hair and put on mascara.

The stylists will make me up properly later in the day, but even barefaced, I feel like I'm on top of the world. I'm making music with the people I love tonight. Caleb is back in my life—for good, if I can do anything about it. And with how things look online on top of it all, I'm so close to having everything I wanted.

Nothing can ruin this perfect day.

My stomach growls, so I call down to the hotel restaurant and put in an order for room service. Just after I hang up, my phone rings again. It's a number that's not in my contacts, but it has an LA area code, so I assume it's just the restaurant verifying my order.

I got a little carried away with the substitutions, but I hate mayo.

"Hello, this is Valerie," I answer.

"Valerie." A familiar voice draws out the last syllable of my name in a possessive way. A chill runs down my spine. "This is Ryan Tate from *Gossip Daily*. So glad I caught you."

My jaw tenses, and I sink onto the foot of my bed. "Hello, Ryan. I apologize—you're not in my schedule for today. Unfortunately, I don't have time for an interview." There's nothing unfortunate about it. No doubt, he's trying to throw me off my game.

And the next thing he says sure does just that. "This will be quick. Any comment on *Epic Theme Song*'s cancellation?"

Panic blurs my vision, and I have to clutch the phone to keep from dropping it. "What?"

"Surely *you've* heard the news, right?" His voice is triumphant, a little vindictive. "Or . . . whoopsie, did I just spill the beans? I have a very reliable contact at The Network who confirmed they're finally pulling the plug. I wanted to give you a chance to give me your reaction, unfiltered, before the press release drops."

My hands start to shake. This can't be happening. Finally, I get my shit together enough to respond. "No comment."

"That's a shame. Good luck tonight, by the way. All eyes will be on you."

I end the call and toss my phone on the bed.

"Fuck!" I shout, to no one.

This can't be happening. I did what they asked. They sat on a decision for months, made me turn my personal life into a sensation, and then they do this. Today of all days.

Was this all a game to them? All this scheming, and it wasn't enough.

My shoulders tighten. These Network assholes are filming our concert, and they're sending some of the higher-ups, so I'm going to have to play nice with the suits all day. Even though they've just ruined my career. It's sick.

Unless Ryan was lying, I rationalize. Maybe he's just messing with my head, trying to get me to say something inflammatory—it wouldn't be the first time the press has set me up. I was just too stunned to give him what he wanted.

I pounce back on my phone, practically throwing myself across the bed. Frantically, I start scrolling social media for something, *anything*, to give me a sign. For a blissful few minutes, everything looks totally normal.

And then, in my costar Lola Martinez's stories, I see it. Lola

has snapped a picture of a giant iced matcha and a pink macaron.
In the tiniest of text, she's written:

> Just got the most terrible news. Even my little treat
> between rehearsals isn't making it better, but at least I
> tried. 😭

It *could* be unrelated, but I have to know for sure. I scramble to
a seat and start a video call.

My heart races as she picks it up almost immediately. Lola is
Mexican American, and her dark hair is piled into a neat ballerina
bun on top of her head. She's a dancer as well as an actress and
singer—a true triple threat—and I imagine by her leotard that she's
heading into some kind of rehearsal. But she doesn't look her usual
serene self.

There's something wild and stressed about her, and it puts me
on alert.

"Oh my god, Val."

"Ryan fucking Tate just called me asking for a comment
because—he claims—our show got canceled. Is it true? What do
you know?"

Her eyes widen. "I spoke with Patricia about an hour ago. My
agent has been trying to get more answers, but it sounds like we're
done."

The news hits me like a punch in the gut. "Shit."

She tosses her free hand up in the air. "They weren't even planning to call us." She swears under her breath. "They were going to
let us find out in the press release!"

I place a hand on my chest, trying to breathe. "You've got to be
fucking kidding me."

"I wish," she says. "I had a good panic about it in the bathroom,
had to take a Xanax."

"Did they give us any kind of explanation?"

Lola gestures to someone off-screen, then refocuses on me. "No, not that I could get from my agent. I know Tyler has an in, so I was going to try to call him after my rehearsal."

Tyler Rowe. I have zero desire to use his *in*, but it might be necessary to let the nepo baby call in a precious favor. "Let me know what you find out." I swallow back the tears in my throat. "God, Lola, I'm so sorry. This is all my fault."

She shakes her head. "No, you can't put this on you. They would have renewed us months ago if we really had a shot. Besides, you're like the hottest thing in LA right now. I'm really sorry you heard the news like this, and at the worst possible time, but I hope you can forget it all and focus on being incredible out there today."

My gaze goes blurry, and I blink. "God, how am I supposed to go out there after this?"

"It's hard to focus." She laughs bitterly, but her eyes are still sad. "I wish I could make the concert, but I just booked the new national tour for *Legally Blonde*, and they've got us in all-days to learn the choreography."

"That's incredible. Congratulations," I say. I hope she can't tell how hollow my voice is. Lola will be fine after *Epic Theme Song*. She did Broadway before, and she'll do Broadway again.

"Thank you," she says. "Can we talk soon? I think I'm still in denial, but I'll need a good cry later this week. I'm so, so sorry you found out right *now*. I would have called you, but I was hoping you could avoid the news for at least one day."

"It's . . . what it is," I say.

She frowns, her eyes soft and sympathetic. "Break a leg, babe." And then she ends the call.

I groan. I need to get down to sound check, but everything feels numb. I haven't booked a single audition since the *Epic Theme Song* hiatus. Sure, I can have Wade broaden my net to television now that I'm no longer tied to a show, but this feels like an ending.

My career as an actress is over.

I stand up and begin to pace, trying to make sense of it all. Is this really it?

No one wants a failed leading lady with a messy reputation. I'll be lucky to book guest-starring roles again. As soon as the news cycle for the reunion—and hell, the cancellation—is over, I'll fade into obscurity. The only thing I have left is the Glitter Bats. It's ironic, since the whole reason this reunion started was to salvage my career, and now there's nothing left to save.

It's all too much. I stride over to the big windows and pull the curtains closed, trying to shut out the world.

We tried to fix my image, and it actually worked. But maybe it was doomed from the start. My knees go weak at the realization that Lola was right—if they were going to renew the show, they would have done it months ago. Anything I did was never going to be enough.

Defeated, I sink to the scratchy hotel carpet. It scrapes my bare legs like sandpaper, but I'm too stricken to care.

After tonight, I'll be nothing more than a girl who used to be famous. Unless I can think of a way to turn it all around, all I can do is hold myself together until the last notes of the encore.

The Glitter Bats Return!

RYAN TATE FOR *GOSSIP DAILY*

It's finally here, Glitterbugs: the Glitter Bats return to the Hollywood Stadium for one night only! We know you're all excited.

It's been a rocky summer for Tinseltown's heartbreaker Valerie Quinn, whom you may have seen most recently in the yet-to-be-renewed *Epic Theme Song*, but love looks good on the pink-haired songstress. Her beau, heartthrob Caleb Sloane, is back and better than ever. Punk rock's boy next door has been quiet about his work away from the industry, but all reports say he sounds the best he's ever been. Perhaps he's getting inspiration from his new-old flame. If you missed their hot kiss on the red carpet, click *here*, but prepare to fan yourselves.

The two lovebirds are supported by jack-of-all-music-trades rhythm guitarist Riker Maddox, who was last seen filling in with Lime Velvet and absolutely shredding. (Real fans will remember that the Glitter Bats opened for LV back in the day!) Percussion master Keeley Cunningham keeps a steady beat from her drum throne, which has been installed in many recording studios over the years—you'll even see her credited as a cowriter on former flame Bianca Martin's seductive pop song of the summer, "Your Body and Mine." Triple-threat Jane Mercer rounds out the group on the keys, and the songwriter, music director, and piano genius has been keeping busy working on The Network's newest hit se-ries, *Into the Dragon Realm*.

The Glitter Bats have been busy bees apart, but they're flying back to the stage together.

We spoke to a representative for the Glitter Bats who promised an exciting show—and hinted that there will be at least one surprise in store for fans. You won't want to miss it!

Tickets have been sold out for weeks, but you can still catch all the hits streaming live on The Network. (Premium rates apply, see website for details.) And follow our Glitter Bats tag for nightly updates—I'll be sure to share juicy details as they become available.

26

✦ *Caleb* ✦

During our final sound check at the stadium, I can't stop staring at Valerie.

The purple hair looks amazing, but she looks good in any color. That's not it. There's something strange about her today. She's too enthusiastic, too cheery, too . . . different. It's like she's a louder, brighter, more intense version of herself, and it makes me feel like she's a thousand miles away instead of standing at the microphone next to mine. After waking up tangled in the same sheets, the distance puts me on edge.

She's always been fidgety, but today it's different. As we go through vocal warm-ups, she's jumping up and down on the balls of her feet. While Riker goes over his setup with the guitar techs, Valerie keeps adjusting and readjusting her mic stand. At one point, she just walks over to the edge of the stage and stares out at the thousands of empty seats, like she's looking for something.

It's got to be nerves. I know we're all feeling them. The afternoon sun above the dome is hot, and the pressure is on. But still, I've never seen her like this before. Maybe it's just my own anxiety

overanalyzing the situation, but I think that's an easy excuse to ignore my gut.

On the last run-through of "Ghosts," Val goes sharp bordering
on shrill on the chorus, and it's obvious to everyone by now that
something is off.

"Jeez, Valerie, save some for the performance," Riker says,
reaching for his next guitar.

"I don't know, we have a long-ass day ahead of us—if you took
something, I want it," Keeley says dryly, but she shoots me a nervous glance. I'm not the only one who noticed this is weird.

Valerie blinks, tossing her hair out of her face. "What? Y'all
know I'd never take anything, especially before the most important
performance of our lives! I'm fine!"

The most important performance of our lives.

My stomach twists. When did it become that? I fiddle with my
bass strap, readjusting my instrument.

I thought we were giving fans one last glimpse of the Glitter
Bats. We have nothing more to prove. The concert is sold out, and
Valerie is all over social media. Fans are arguing about whether
they want to kiss her or be her. They're praising her talent and
poise, defending her against the haters, making content about her
best moments.

Valerie Quinn is no longer notorious—she's beloved.

Everyone says nice things about the rest of us too. It doesn't
matter to me, but I know Jane and Riker and Keeley have gotten
positive feedback from their teams. This reunion is going to help all
of them.

And if I can't stay, it's the best parting gift I could give my
friends.

"Well, your vocal coach would remind you to dial it back," Jane
says gently.

Valerie laughs, almost maniacally. "Right. Of course. You're so right, I just got excited. I'll totally dial it back." Every word comes out slightly too fast, like she's a podcast set at 1.5 speed. She puts her hands on her hips, then in her pockets, then grasps her microphone like it's a lifeline.

Jane frowns but tosses her hair over her shoulder and blinks, adjusting her setup for the next check.

At least we're not running through everything, just checking levels, and we get through "Daydreams Like This" in a much calmer fashion. Still, it's almost as if I can feel Valerie vibrating, like she's pounded a dozen shots of espresso. She paces between her mic stand and the front of the stage, fiddling with her earbud, like she's not happy with the in-ear monitor. But we dialed that in hours ago, so it shouldn't be an issue. It's like she can't stop moving.

Usually our eye contact on the bridge feels warm and a little seductive, but today it's odd. Like she's trying to send me a message, but I can't sense what it is. There's a disconnect, and I want to find it before we get onstage.

We all have to head to hair and makeup after rehearsal, so I try to pull her aside quickly, but she just tells me she has to "take care of something" before she disappears.

After we're styled, we all show our nerves in different ways: Riker is obsessively checking over his iPad, ensuring he knows the changes; Keeley is fiddling with the drumstick she cracked earlier today; and Jane is playing a word game on her phone between bites of her rice bowl. Even Wade starts pacing when he comes to check in on us, and he asks about Valerie. That's when I really start to worry—she always checks in with him, if no one else.

She reappears just in time to eat half of her chicken wrap before the last VIP event—a meet-and-greet cocktail hour just before showtime. Half of this event is fans, and the other half is industry people, so we're all extra aware of our behavior.

"You good, kid?" Wade murmurs as we're ushered to the dining room the hotel reserved for this event.

"I'm handling it," Valerie says, with a nod so sharp and determined it's almost robotic.

Wade quirks a brow before he moves off to chat with one of the label executives, and I hang back to catch her.

"What was that about?" I ask.

She blinks up at me, eyes wide. "What? Oh, it's nothing! Nothing at all. I'm fine!"

"You sure?" I raise a brow. I know when Valerie is hiding something, but I also know I can't force her to talk before she's ready. Maybe it's just hitting her the way it's hitting me, that this is the last night we'll be together unless we figure something out.

I could trust that more if she would just tell me what's going on. This woman is *it* for me, and I just wish she didn't feel so far away in this moment.

She puts a hand to her chest. "I promise I'm fine! Everything is going to be fine. Better than fine. It's going to be perfect."

Everything does not feel perfect, but I get it. I feel a little uneasy too. Still, I don't know how to pull her out of this sugar rush she's been spinning through all afternoon. So I just do my best to stay by her side until showtime, even as she bounces around the room like an overenthusiastic Ping-Pong ball, moving from guest to guest with alarming speed and cheer. Every time I try to pull her away to actually check on her, she finds another diversion.

After we leave the event, change into our clothes for the show, and head to the venue, it starts to hit me that we're really doing this. Lime Velvet begins their opening set, and even in my anxiety to talk to Valerie, it hits me—we opened for *them* on our first tour. How wild that now they're opening for us. We chatted with them a bit during their sound check, and they're all still so professional and kind.

I remember, when we were first starting out, really taking that example to heart. How you treat people matters. No one is less important just because they are newer to the scene, or have fewer social media followers, or went indie instead of signing with a label. Things in the industry can really change so quickly. It's a far better experience if you treat people like colleagues instead of the competition, reaching out a hand to help others up when you can. And you never know—the people coming up behind you might suddenly be the ones in the spotlight.

Even if that spotlight is fleeting.

I finally catch Valerie backstage while Lime Velvet begins their last song. She's a knockout in a tight black minidress, her lucky bejeweled leather jacket, and platform Docs, and she takes my breath away. Now, at least, the manic look is gone from her heavily shadowed ocean eyes.

As I approach, Valerie grabs my wrist and tugs me toward her. Wrapping her arms around my neck, she draws me into a searing kiss. This isn't distant.

It's warm, and hot, and full of feeling.

I don't even care if she's wearing lip gloss; it just feels so good to be close to her again after such a strange day. I deepen the kiss, and she tastes like her pre-performance ritual of honey cough drops and herbal tea. So many of our kisses have included these subtle flavors, and I can't get enough of the intoxicating familiarity. With just the two of us like this, everything feels okay again, and I want to believe there's no reason to worry.

Valerie has my heart—and my back. If she's keeping something to herself, I'm sure it's for good reason. I know she'll tell me when the time is right.

I pull back, leaning my forehead on hers. "God, I don't know how I'm supposed to let you go after this," I whisper, admitting the fear that's been hanging in the back of my mind.

"Then don't," she says. "Trust me. We'll figure this out to-gether."

My throat tightens. I want to believe her, but worry still lingers. Instead of hiding it the way I might have when we were younger, I decide to tell her. If we're going to move forward, we need to be better at communicating. I can do better.

I clear my throat. "Do you really mean that? Because today . . . it's like you're living in a different universe. I've been so worried that something's wrong and you were afraid to tell me. You know you can open up to me, right? I want to help."

She pulls back, biting her lip. "No! That's not it. Look, I'm sorry for earlier. I don't mean to be so distracted. I just . . . I want every-thing to be perfect."

"Me too," I say. "It's going to be great."

"I know," she says, biting her lip. "It's you and me, Sloane."

"Like it was always supposed to be," I say, pressing another brief kiss to her lips.

"We can talk more after, I promise." She glances up at me, a cheeky look dancing in her eyes. "One more for luck?"

And then I pull Valerie into my arms and kiss her again.

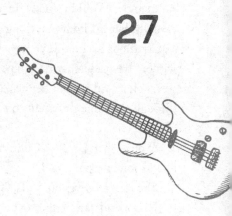

27

◆ Caleb ◆

The cheers from the crowd for Lime Velvet's last song bleed back-stage, and my mouth goes dry as I realize something is missing.

Before every set, the five of us used to stand in a circle and pass around gummy bears. The rules are simple: before you can eat one, you have to give a compliment to the person on your left—it was mostly just to hype one another up, but more than one argument had been resolved by a circle shout-out. It started before we even made it to the industry that first summer at camp, but we never missed it in the years we spent making music together.

The thing is, I always brought the candy. And when I realize I forgot, I really start to panic. I root through my bag, as if that shiny gold package will magically appear, and anxiety begins to blur my vision as I realize it's in vain. I didn't buy them.

If we miss this pre-show ritual, I don't think I can go out there.

"I got you," Keeley says, shoving a bag of Haribos into my shaky hands.

"Thank you," I say, letting out a nervous laugh as some of the tension melts from my neck.

"I just . . . grabbed some as insurance when we went to get Carrie's candy. Wouldn't be right to skip band circle." She says it casually, but if I know anything about Keeley, it's that she's just as superstitious as I am. I've never seen her play a Glitter Bats set without fresh aquamarine nail polish or the raw citrine pendant she wears on a cord around her neck, and she always takes time to run through the same rudiments on her drum pad before every sound check.

"You're such a softie, Cunningham," I say, trying to play it off like I didn't drop the ball.

She rolls her eyes but yells, "Circle up!"

Riker and Jane come over, and Valerie materializes at my other side.

"I can't believe it's happening!" Jane shrieks, clapping her hands and pressing them to her lips with barely contained excitement. "Can I start?"

I offer her the bag cupped in two hands, like it's a precious gift. She beams, the golden bronzer on her cheeks shimmering in the light, looking almost angelic with her gauzy cream dress. Keeley's eyes go wide as she realizes she's in the hot seat.

"Keeley," Jane starts. "You are the best drummer I've ever worked with. You're responsive and dynamic, and you multitask well enough to sing effortlessly on top of everything. You never miss a beat on- or offstage, and I'm constantly in awe of you."

Almost reverently, Jane pulls out a gummy and hands the bag over to Keeley, whose cheeks have flushed bright red. Keeley turns to Riker, toying with one of the buttons on her denim vest with her free hand.

"Riker," Keeley croons. "Despite your terrible taste in booze, you are one of the best people and collaborators I know. The way you anticipate our needs onstage is unmatched, and it's one of the reasons the Glitter Bats have always *worked*. You're the glue."

"Aww, you're too nice," Riker wraps an arm around Keeley's shoulders and squeezes quickly as she passes him the bag.

Riker grins, turning to his left. "Valerie! You never stop fighting for what you want, and it's a marvel. I wish I had your drive. I'm so glad you brought us all together this summer, because I'm proud to make music with you and call you my friend." Valerie reaches an arm up and boops Riker on the nose. He laughs, popping three gummy bears into his mouth before passing the bag along.

"Caleb Sloane." Valerie pulls out a gummy, then locks her eyes on mine with a smirk, and my neck warms. "This summer reminded me how great it is to work next to you. Thank you for letting me drag you out here. You're my favorite person. I can't imagine doing this music thing without you, and I hope today isn't an ending, but a new beginning." She kisses my cheek and hands me the bag, and I try to ignore the way my heart races with nerves.

This is it. I turn to Jane, who is tearing up. Even as my pulse rings in my ears, it's easy to compliment Jane. She really is the best of us. "Jane, you have taken this industry by storm, and it's been an honor to watch you grow into such a powerhouse. I'm impressed that you even had time for this reunion, but we couldn't have done this without you laying it down on keys."

She beams at me. As soon as I eat my own gummy bear, we're ushered to places by our tech crew. Usually, the pre-show ritual grounds me, but today, I'm still panicking.

This is our chance. I can't let the band down. I can't let *Valerie* down.

I've always been anxious, and then I left the industry. After all this time away, the pressure of one last performance is crushing, and even the most perfect schedule of taking my meds regularly can't fix that entirely. But I have to work through it. While I plug in, I go through the square breathing exercise I practiced with my therapist. I try it ten times for good measure. When that doesn't calm me down, I try my 5-4-3-2-1 coping technique, but I lose count of *things I see* as I stare at a chip in the black polish Keeley painted onto my nails this afternoon.

My hands are still shaking until I grab my bass—and then something snaps into focus, like the crack of a light stick in the crowd. I'm buzzing with the glow. Why am I trying all these techniques to control my brain when the music is my light in the darkness?

The Bianca Martin hit pulsing through the speakers goes quiet. The lights go down. A fog machine turns on, slowly filling the stage. There's a sharp, collective gasp, followed by screams and cheers.

It's time. We've practiced every piece of this set a dozen times, down to the minute, as if rehearsing a play, so we know our routes to each of our places by heart. We line up by the stage door.

First, Keeley steps out, ascending the drum platform to a thunderous roar of cheers. The spotlight shines right on her.

"How y'all doing tonight?" she asks into her mic. I can't see her from this angle, but I know she's shamelessly flirting with the audience, smirking and winking and strutting before she takes her seat. It's her way, and the fans love it.

Jane is next, traveling to her keyboard setup on stage left, and through the fog I see her wave to the crowd. Riker follows his own path to stage right, and he whoops into his mic after he plugs his guitar in.

Then it's our turn. Hand in hand, Valerie and I walk out onto the stage following the glow-in-the-dark tape set out by our crew. The rule is to never stare into the spotlight, but I can't help but squint and look out at the crowd. It's a sea of faces, mostly silhouetted against the stage lights, but I catch a few sparkling signs as we pass by.

The Glitterbugs are in full form tonight.

We plug into our respective cables, then turn to face the audience.

"Hi, friends!" Valerie says, before she strums her guitar once. The audience absolutely roars in response. "It's good to see you again!"

I grin, taking my cue. As I approach my mic, the rest of my lingering anxiety melts away. I know how to do this.

"Good evening, and welcome to the Glitter Bats reunion show at Hollywood Stadium!" I pause to let the cheers around the room sink in. We're surrounded by people who want to hear our music, and it's the best feeling in the world. It's why I wanted to make music in the first place—connecting with people. Telling truths.

I don't think I realized just how much I needed to be in the band again until this exact moment. On the video screen, I catch my own gaze, and I'm almost startled by how happy I look. But I flash the crowd a sly smirk as I lean into my mic again, starting us off. "My name is Caleb Sloane—"

"I'm Valerie Quinn."

"Hi, I'm Jane Mercer."

"Riker Maddox."

"And I'm Keeley fucking Cunningham!"

"—and in case you forgot, we are the Glitter Bats!" I finish. Warmth and adrenaline wash over me as I take in the moment. On this stage with these four people who are my family? I feel at home.

It's an unexpected bliss. This makes sense. Me, my instrument, Valerie at my side, my band around me. I want to live in this moment forever.

"If you're all up for it, we're going to get started with a fan favorite," Valerie says.

She plays the guitar intro to "Ghosts" with razor-sharp precision, like she was born for this moment. The fans gasp and shriek, the palpable excitement running through the stadium like an electric current. We all only have eyes for Valerie. She's so incandescent with that violet hair in the glow of the lights that I have to remind myself to layer in the bass line as the rest of the band comes in.

But thank god for muscle memory, because my fingers know exactly what to do.

Valerie croons on the verse, singing and swaying and entering that magical state that happens to her onstage. Even staying close to the mic stand, she takes up space, using every movement of her body to engage with the crowd.

And they're eating it up, singing along with every word, jumping up and down, waving their hands.

A thrill runs up my spine. I never liked the fame, but I liked knowing someone loved my song. Valerie and I cowrote "Ghosts," like nearly everything we recorded, and the audience response after all this time feels so personal.

When I jump in on the on-the-nose chorus, I grin.

ten years from now will we be here
or will we just be ghosts?
spirits of love who never call
'cause it's been way too long
oh if there's space between us then
promise you'll haunt me right
oh if this can't be our forever
let's be shades of night

It's all a cheesy metaphor—it's why Keeley calls *Bittersweet* our "goth rock phase"—and I sing it with my entire chest. I'm proud of this song. I'm proud of everything we've done, not just in the past, but this summer. It took a lot to come together again, and here we are in an arena full of thousands, proving we can and still rock together. Hard.

My chest warms as I glance around at my band, and then the roaring crowd in front of us. After the first few shaky rehearsals, we're better than we ever were. Valerie plays her guitar solo with cocky grace, swinging her hair around in a way that completely mesmerizes me. Thank god Riker is doubling my vocals on the bridge, because I almost forget my part—I can't look away from the rock goddess beside me.

Keeley takes the high harmony, giving Valerie time to regroup before the quiet chorus, and I nod my head at her.

The fans are expecting it—why make them wait?

"I've got the bass line if you want to go for it," Jane says, whispering into the monitor mic, sensing what we're doing.

I throw a thumbs-up behind my back, and that's that.

Valerie grins, and it makes my heart race. As the music builds for the cheeky bridge, Val flips her guitar around her back and steps over to my microphone. I let go of my bass as Jane takes over the line. Valerie's fingers brush against mine as she leans in, and I can't help but wrap my hand around hers on the mic. Her gaze glitters on mine under the lights.

God, I'm the luckiest person in the world.

We know exactly how to sing this together.

Valerie starts:

oh I like the way you haunt
stand behind me in the mirror
with your hands around my waist
phantom fingers touch my skin

I respond with a smirk:

oh I like the way you haunt
underneath a sheet like Casper

stealing covers from my bed
when you moaned there all night

And then we join our voices in a bright unison up the octave, leaning so close our foreheads touch:

if only memories remain
please haunt me
I'll haunt you
please haunt me
I'll haunt you (you) YOU

I adjust the mic so I can start playing the bass again, angling it carefully between us. Valerie swings her guitar around to layer her part back in, and we transpose up into the next key and bring the lead lines back into the repeated chorus. The fans go absolutely wild as our sound gets louder and fuller. I'm at the top of my range where I know my voice really pops, and Valerie sings a tight harmony instead of the unison. Even with our monitors in, I know our blend is perfect.

Like it always was meant to be.

I'm breathless with adrenaline as the final chords ring out.

After we finish "Ghosts," we stop for some audience interaction. Riker and Jane vamp on a random chord progression that Jane's calling into the monitor, and Keeley plays along on the kick drum. Eventually, they'll transition us into "Summer Sunset," but they don't even hint that it's where we're going yet.

We planned a pause here, so I grab my mic.

"Well! That was a fun start. You're all such a great crowd. Thanks for showing up tonight and making memories with us, Los Angeles!" Cheers resound as I free my mic and walk to the edge of the stage, reading some of the signs in the crowd. "I guess you're not all from LA, huh?" I squint. "Seattle—hey, that's our hometown!" The crowd roars. "Nashville, Denver, Tallahassee, New York!" I pause, turning to two fans on the left of the pit with something like disbelief in my throat. "Wait, did you two really come here from Paris *and* Tokyo?"

The sign holders shriek in confirmation, and I almost tear up. It's silly, but it means a lot that they traveled all this way to see us.

"That's halfway across the world!"

I tilt the mic in their direction. The one with the Tokyo sign leans in. "We met in a Glitterbugs Discord and we had to come!"

The Paris sign holder grins and rattles off some rapid French. I studied just enough for my college vocal classes to understand they're excited to be here.

I tilt the mic back. "Thank you both *so much* for coming!" I reach into my pocket and hand them each one of the custom purple Glitter Bats guitar picks that Wade ordered as a surprise for us tonight. The fans jump up and down.

I grin, handing out a few more as I walk past some other fans in the pit, fist-bumping and throwing peace signs and even taking a selfie with someone's phone. "You're all amazing. We love our Glitterbugs!"

"We really have the best fans in the world, don't we?" Valerie asks from her mic. "They probably want to hear another one."

I turn back to face her. "I'm sorry, I got distracted. Is it time to play the next song?"

The audience yells a few of their favorites.

Valerie places her hands on her hips in mock-annoyance, which we also rehearsed. The crowd laughs. "They didn't just come here to hang out, Caleb Alexander Sloane."

I roll my eyes. "Okay, Valerie Elizabeth Quinn, let's rock."

Riker leans into his mic. "This one's called 'Summer Sunset.' Sing along if you know it." More screaming. This song is a Riker feature since he wrote it with us, and he gets the guitar solo while Valerie plays rhythm. They've both already swapped out their guitars, which tells me I spent exactly the right amount of time up front.

Jane confirms it in the monitor talkback. "That was perfect, Caleb."

Riker launches into the song, and Valerie and I join in on the chorus, just like we planned. We settle into a groove, and the time starts to fly by, our set going without a hitch. By the time we're winding down to the last few songs, I realize, now more than ever, that I don't want this night to end.

Maybe I don't want to stop playing music with these people. Maybe I never did.

When it's time for the big reveal, I force myself to focus. Valerie and I each grab a stool and an acoustic and huddle around two mics.

"You didn't think we'd finish tonight without a surprise, did you?" Valerie asks, looking at the crowd with mock-dismay.

Their response is wonderful and overwhelming, as it has been all night.

"There's one song Valerie and I started to write together years ago that we never finished. But I'm excited to announce that we had a chance to complete it this summer, and—"

Valerie interrupts me to tell the crowd, "This is when you get your phones out."

The stadium lights up with the glittering sea of recording phones.

I continue, "—and we're excited to share the world premiere of 'Daydreams Like This.'"

I look at Valerie, and she nods, biting her lip. She leans into her own mic one last time. "This is a love song."

The fans absolutely lose their shit as we play the intro. While she begins to sing, I pretend it's just me and Valerie, and we're not in a stadium full of thousands of people. A chill rushes through me as her voice rings out, clear and true, and my skin prickles with goose bumps. She sounds perfect. This moment is perfect.

I can't believe we're really doing this.

I swallow thickly, trying to keep it together. When it's my turn, I sing every word from the bottom of my bruised and battered heart, and by the way her eyes are shining, I know she understands what I'm feeling, especially as we're singing in tight harmony on the new bridge:

> *never knew my heart could feel it*
> *'til I kissed you and I fell*
> *thought I had to keep you secret*
> *but it's too good not to tell*
> *got all my hopes and dreams*
> *now I'm finally waking up*
> *cause making it means nothing*
> *if I'm there without your love*

The applause that roars when we're finished shocks me back to reality. Time to thank everyone and head into the grand finale: "Midnight Road Trip." And then when they beg us for one more song, we'll come out with a cover of "I Want You to Want Me" that fades into "All the Lips You Kiss."

We swap out our guitars with waiting techs and plug back in, and Valerie returns to her microphone as planned. After the applause fades, we're supposed to shout out Wade and the crew and then launch right into "Midnight Road Trip."

But she doesn't launch into thank-yous like she's supposed to.

She just pauses a minute, then squares her shoulders. "Tonight has been really special. As a band, we value our fans so much. It's because of you that we're allowed to keep doing this. This industry is hard, and some days it really feels like . . . well, we're just incredibly lucky to be here with the best fans in the world. We want to make this a night to remember."

My stomach flips. But the crowd erupts, and Valerie waits for the noise to subside as I try to make sense of what this is. I glance around at the rest of the band. Keeley's face is a careful mask, but I catch the tick in her jaw. Riker's brow furrows. Jane gapes, then covers it quickly with a smile.

They're just as baffled as I am.

"Daydreams Like This" was our big surprise, the special reveal no one expected, and we sang it. We've got nothing left.

We're not supposed to pause here.

I have no idea where she's taking us, but I do know one thing for certain—this wasn't in the plan.

28

+ Valerie +

I don't have a plan yet, but all eyes are on me.

Usually, it's Caleb who vamps, and I feel a little unmoored as I scramble to arrange my thoughts. But Caleb stares at me as much as everyone else, confusion darkening his heavily lined eyes. I nod at him in what I hope is a reassuring way before unclipping my mic from the stand. I feel the weight of his gaze, but I tear my eyes away as I step closer to the pit, knowing this moment rests on me.

We have the audience for these last precious minutes, and I have to make them count.

Even under the lights, I can sense the weight of ten thousand stares on my shoulders, feel the gasp of ten thousand breaths held in anticipation. Sudden fear crashes through my veins, sharp and static. If I don't do something right now while I have their interest, this might be my last bow. I scan the audience for something—a sign, a beacon, an omen—and then my eyes fall on one poster catching the light.

Covered in glitter and ghosts, it reads:

PLEASE HAUNT ME
WITH GLITTER BATS 3!

And . . . oh. Maybe it's that simple. Maybe today's loss of *Epic Theme Song* is a gift.

There's nothing like playing songs with people you love, vamping and innovating and making it all the best it's ever been, doing this for fans who have supported you from the jump. Despite the fighting and tears, I've been happier making music with the Glitter Bats this summer than I have been with anything else I've done in my ten years in this industry.

The whole band is in sync tonight, tighter than ever before, and I don't want to lose this electric feeling. We've been dancing around this decision all summer. Someone just needs to close their eyes and leap—and I have nothing to lose, so it might as well be me.

"This concert was supposed to be a one-night thing, but the response to our comeback has been overwhelming. This summer has shown me just how much I love making memories with everyone on this stage—and all of you. The thing is: we're not ready to leave you again, so . . ." I trail off, building tension.

Casually, strategically, I smirk in the direction of the camera, projecting my expression on the big screens. "Glitterbugs, we're not going anywhere. We have so many more songs inside of us just waiting to be written. I can promise you all—tonight isn't the last you'll hear from the Glitter Bats!"

The stadium erupts like it's the literal Super Bowl, and I grin and wave, soaking it in. This is all I want—to continue the Glitter Bats legacy for years to come. I don't know why I ever thought I needed to make it in Hollywood, why I was holding on so hard to the renewal news for *Epic Theme Song*—all I need is my band. My family.

So I smile and take in the thundering cheers drowning out my monitors. This is the moment I'll remember for years to come, the moment that brought the band back together—the moment that saved my career.

But then Caleb nearly tears me away from the microphone. I stumble in my surprise, swinging my guitar instinctively around my back. His grip on my wrist, gentle but urgent, tugs me far enough back that we can't be overheard.

My heart thunders in my chest as I stare at him, disoriented, trying to figure out what's wrong. The crowd is still so intense that they drown out any sound they might hear, so at least we have an illusion of privacy away from the mics.

"What the hell was that?" he demands, his voice tight with panic.

I blink. Sure, my declaration was a little sudden, a little impulsive, but that's my thing. He knows that. Once I explain the plan, everything will be fine.

"You aren't ready to say goodbye, right?" I ask, sure he'll understand as soon as the surprise wears off. "We all want this. Let's do it."

He blanches. "What?"

Something like worry tightens my throat, but I surge ahead, because I know I did the right thing. "You needed a push. That's what you said last night."

His jaw drops. "You're taking that so far out of context . . . Jesus, Valerie, you had to know I wasn't agreeing to *this*! We haven't even talked as a band! I can't just uproot my life because you're high on the applause tonight."

My stomach plummets at his anger. This wasn't just about the applause. The concert was perfect. Everything felt so right. Caleb was having such a good time playing the best he's ever played—we all were—and I thought he'd be happy to continue. He basically said that last night.

He's just processing. Once he realizes I'm all in, he'll be fine. He can rely on me now. The band has joined us, and I look around, sure they'll back me up.

They . . . don't.

Keeley is sullen, arms crossed, glaring at me. Jane looks stricken. Riker is just weary, running a hand over his face.

Maybe it will take a few minutes for everyone to understand, but I know they'll be on board. We're so much older and wiser and we can pick up right where we left off and make things even better this time. Everyone wants this. So my announcement was a little spontaneous—but that doesn't mean it's a bad idea.

We were running out of time.

"Everyone wants to make another album, right? The timing was just too perfect to pass up," I say, squaring my shoulders despite the tremble in my voice.

They can't possibly be mad. We need this. But Caleb sighs and shakes his head, stepping back to his spot on the stage.

I wait for the others to say something, but no one does, so I stride back to my microphone, brazening past thousands of confused stares. "Now, on with the scheduled programming!"

But before I can begin the lead line for "Midnight Road Trip," Caleb leans into his own microphone.

"I'm sorry, everyone. You're all so amazing for coming here tonight, but I can't do this. Another album . . . it isn't what I signed up for when I agreed to perform tonight."

Oh god. My heart thuds in my chest as he unplugs his bass and turns to leave.

I can't let him leave. I run to him, grab his elbow, trying to root him to the spot long enough to let me explain. "Caleb, please."

He wrenches his arm away, whirling to face me with wide eyes. "No! I thought we were in this together, but after what you just pulled, I don't know how I'm ever supposed to trust you again, let alone make music."

My vision swims, and I shake my head, trying to anchor myself. This can't be happening. This isn't what I wanted.

I thought he'd be happy.

I swallow, grasping at the words I need to make him listen. "Please, let's just finish the set. We can talk after, figure everything out as a team," I say, but I'm practically begging and my voice is weak.

Those green eyes I adore stare back at me under the lights, cold and piercing. "No, Val. It's too late for that." He laughs bitterly, shrugging the strap of his bass off of his shoulders. "You made sure of it. I'm out."

Tears choke the back of my throat. "Don't go."

But then he does just that.

✦ Caleb ✦

After everything we've been through, I thought I could trust Valerie to choose us over fame, but I was wrong. I'll never be more than a means to an end for her. I can't let her keep breaking my heart.

I wait for the anxiety attack to come, but it doesn't. I'm just . . . numb. I barely feel my feet pounding on the stage floor as I hurry away.

When I get backstage, I don't stop walking until I'm past security and out of the stadium.

+ *Valerie* +

The crowd falls silent.

It's chilling, like the stadium is haunted, and instead of the ghosts being in our song they're out in the arena, looming. There are a few coughs, and even a couple boos, but other than that, it's eerily quiet under the glare of the lights. Adrenaline races through my system as I try to get my bearings.

We're still livestreaming.

I glance around at the rest of the band, but no one says anything or moves to pick up their instruments. They just stare at me, judging. But the show must go on, so I begin to play the intro for "Midnight Road Trip," determined to keep this up even without Caleb. My ears ring.

God, I can't do this without Caleb.

Riker materializes at my side, and for a moment I think he's going to grab one of Caleb's spare basses and start playing, but he just shakes his head.

"Come on, Valerie," he says.

And then he follows Caleb's path off the stage. Keeley's already gone, and Jane gives me a sad smile before hurrying to follow.

Tears sting the back of my throat, and I fumble to unplug my pack. The crowd jeers in earnest now, but I don't know how to respond. My head buzzes with anxiety, and I can't focus on anything but getting out of here.

But that's the coward's way out.

"Just a technical issue. I promise we'll be right back," I say into the mic.

I gesture at one of our stage techs, who just shrugs, but soon there is a steady stream of Glitter Bats music playing over the loudspeakers. I stumble over cords as I hurry off the stage.

Back in the greenroom, I expect to find the entire band, but someone is missing.

"Where is he?" I ask.

Keeley barrels forward, getting right in my face. "What the *fuck* was that, Quinn?"

"Where's Caleb?" I demand. I expected him to be back here, ready to lay into me in private.

But he's nowhere to be seen.

"Valerie, why did you . . . I'm speechless. What were you thinking?" Jane says.

Her question barely registers as the whole room tilts. Caleb's gone. He can't be gone. After everything we've been through, I can't believe he would just leave me like this. Again.

Even if he was mad, how could he do this to me?

He said he loved me. I thought . . . I don't know what I thought. But I never expected Caleb to abandon me in the middle of a show, no matter what I did. It's like Vegas all over again, and the kick-in-the-gut feeling of abandonment makes me want to fall to my knees. He's gone and I *need* him and—

Shit. The show.

"We have to get back out there," I say.

"*We* don't have to do anything!" Keeley says. "You went off script, and you had no right to make promises to the fans we can't keep. Didn't you realize Label is going to use this? They're going to make us record with *them*!"

I swallow thickly. I didn't think. I just had the microphone and needed to do *something* and . . . damn it. This is the one thing Wade said not to do.

But maybe it'll be okay.

It has to be. They suck, but Label Records has a vested interest in keeping things moving with as little delay as possible. Glitter Bats are hot, and we're all over the internet. We need to capitalize on our momentum. That's what I was trying to do out on that stage. We have a shared motivation.

Going to a different record company would be better, but it would also mean meetings, negotiations, contracts—and we don't have time for that. Label Records is full of sharks, but they're sharks who know how to manage a big group like this. They'll give us the tour we deserve. We might have to jump through a few extra hoops, but I know we can handle it.

"It'll be fine. You all said you're interested in making a new album." When no one reacts, I course correct. "But we can talk to Wade! We can still walk away and find another label—it just might take some negotiating. That's what lawyers are for, right? Then we'll be off and recording something new before you know it."

"I don't think it works that way." Jane crosses her arms. "What's the big rush, Valerie? Help us understand where this is coming from."

"We need to ride this hype!" The idea sounds better and better as I talk through it. Okay, Caleb might need some convincing, but Jane, Keeley, and Riker are all in the business. If we don't do this now, it's never going to happen. They'll get it. "There are no guarantees in this industry. We have a contract with Label. I know they're the worst, but it's a sure thing. How often do we get those?"

I glance around at the band. The crowd has gotten so restless, I can hear them back here. Jeering, shouting, wondering. As they grow louder, I feel like I can't breathe. I have to fix this.

"The only sure thing is how perfectly you fucked up," Keeley says.

I look to Jane and Riker for backup, but neither of them moves.

"She's right," Riker says.

Jane sighs. "Valerie, you know I love you, but you crossed a line. Making an announcement without talking it through as a band first . . . this isn't you. How are we supposed to go back out there now?"

"We play the rest of our set," I say, like it's obvious—but by the way she flinches, I know that was the wrong thing to say.

"That's essentially sending a message to the world that we're all on board with your plan, and we need to have a long conversation if we're going to think about moving forward. You made a decision for all of us. It wasn't yours alone," Jane says. Her voice is quiet, resigned, disappointed.

It hurts.

Keeley scoffs. "You just sold our souls back to Label, and we were so close to being free. I'm not going back out there."

Riker closes his eyes, sighing. "Me neither. Sorry, Valerie."

"So that's it, then?" I demand, desperation clawing up my throat. If we don't go back out there, it's going to send a terrible message to the fans, to the label, to everyone. We can't come back from that kind of negativity.

I should know.

"You're all just going to abandon our fans?" I ask, but what I'm really asking is if they're just going to abandon *me*. I don't want to be alone in this industry again, if I even have a career after tonight.

But I can't say that. I reel, trying to find something that will get them to stay. "We have to finish the show. They paid good money!"

"Hey now, you don't get to put this back on us." Riker's uncharacteristically angry, pointing in the direction of the stage. "You made a terrible call out there. Maybe we all at one point or another said we're interested, but that doesn't mean you get to decide how and when we're moving forward as a band—if at all. I have commitments. So do Jane and Keeley, and hell—Caleb has a day job! We deserve more consideration than this."

I gape, unsure of what to say but knowing if I can just *convince* one of them, everyone else will get on board. "Please, let's get out there. The news is going to be an absolute bloodbath if we don't."

Keeley sneers. "That's your fault, Valerie, just like everything else."

My blood runs cold. "Excuse me?"

"You always play the victim, and you know what? It's exhausting," she says, her voice dripping with disdain. "You treat everyone in your life like they owe you something, and once you get it, you just abandon them to climb to your next goal. Hell, you did this to us six years ago when Caleb left. You decided a solo career was the most strategic way to move forward—and instead of talking it out with us, you left the three of us alone to face the fucking *wolves* at the label. You act like you're so innocent, but you deserve every part of that bad reputation."

Jane puts a hand on Keeley's arm. "That's not fair."

Keeley whirls on her. "You know it's true!" She gestures at me, but continues to talk about me like I'm not in the room, her cheeks flaming with anger. My shoulders tense. "She thinks fame is going to love her back. Well, news flash, this industry will take everything from you before it gives you even an inch. We've all figured that out and protected ourselves, adjusted our expectations, but

Valerie is over here trying to suck the industry's dick for a pat on the head!"

I flinch. It hurts to hear her talk about me like this, especially after the day I've had, but I'm not going to back down. My intentions were good, and I was just trying to do what was best for all of us. This will be good for them too. They have to see that.

And I'm not going to let Keeley treat me like a child.

"Let's talk about this." My mouth goes dry as I glance away from Keeley to Riker, who won't meet my gaze. I look at Jane, and she bites her lip. "Please, just listen to me," I beg. They have to listen. This is all I have.

"No," Jane says, filling the silence. "There's nothing left to say. What you did is unacceptable, and I'm not comfortable going back out there." Her voice breaks, and my heart plummets. "I'm sorry, Valerie, but you went too far."

"I won't go back without Caleb. Wouldn't be right," Riker says, crossing his arms and staring at the ground. "We're done here."

And just like that, I realize what I should have known all along: nothing has really changed this summer. I can't expect the Glitter Bats to have my back. I can't expect Caleb to stay. I'm on my own.

Because no one wants anything to do with Valerie Quinn.

"Fine, I'll go fix this myself." Mind whirling, I pace back over to the stage door. "I'll tell them it's a solo set—a special surprise to cap off the night."

"No, you won't," says a familiar voice from the door. I spin on my heel to see Wade, frowning and shaking his head. Dread pools in my stomach. "I don't know what you were thinking, kiddo, but you can't go back out there. It's over."

Just like my entire career.

@BuzzWordCeleb

The Glitter Bats reunion concert came to an abrupt end, and we have questions—what's next for the band? ICYMI: Valerie Quinn announced a comeback, but then the band left the stage and did not continue the show. Our reporter on the ground is still searching for any details—and we'll be sharing them as they become available.

@GossipDaily

Glitter Bats comeback bomb from loose cannon Valerie Quinn explodes the highly anticipated reunion. Caleb Sloane has disappeared from the scene. Riker Maddox, Keeley Cunningham, and Jane Mercer refuse to comment, and Quinn's team won't respond. Will we ever know the truth? Everything we know *here*!

@GossipDaily

Outraged Glitterbugs demand a refund after the Glitter Bats fiasco, and we think they're right to do so. More from Ryan Tate *here*!

@GlitterbugsUnofficial

WHAT THE FUCK. Just got back from the concert. I'm numb.

@BitterSweetGlitterati

I have never felt so many emotions in a two-hour period. Trying to see if my therapist does emergency 10pm appointments.

@BatsThatGlitter

I'm so worried for Valerie. Everyone is giving her such a hard time, but we don't know what really happened. There's got to be more to the story.

@MakeMeMrsSloane

@BatsThatGlitter 🙄 Valerie has never been good enough for Caleb, and tonight proved that. No wonder he left after that stunt she pulled. He deserves better than some stupid, fame-hungry bitch.

@ValerieQuinnSuperFan

@MakeMeMrsSloane @BatsThatGlitter YOU DID NOT JUST CALL HER THAT, DELETE YOUR ACCOUNT

@MakeMeMrsSloane

@ValerieQuinnSuperFan @BatsThatGlitter WHY ARE YOU IN MY MENTIONS? I DON'T CARE ABOUT YOUR OPINION—VALERIE IS THE WEAK LINK AND SHE RUINED THIS BAND TWICE. I WILL NEVER FORGIVE HER FOR DOING THAT.

@BatsThatGlitter

@ValerieQuinnSuperFan @MakeMeMrsSloane Untag me please.

@EpicThemeSongMemes

> A reliable source close to *Epic Theme Song* just told us they've officially been canceled. The announcement is expected any time now. Maybe that's tied to all of this weirdness with Glitter Bats— did Valerie find out and have a total breakdown?

@WendyTheWonder99

> If The Network actually canceled our award-winning show I swear to god I will cancel my service. HOW FUCKING DARE THEY?

@WendyTheWonder99

> Link: *Sign the Petition! Save Epic Theme Song!*

@GlitterbugsUnofficial

> CODE RED: VALERIE JUST DELETED ALL OF HER SOCIAL MEDIA

@BitterSweetGlitterati

> @GlitterbugsUnofficial WHAT DOES THIS MEAN?!

@BatsThatGlitter

> @BitterSweetGlitterati @GlitterbugsUnofficial DMING YOU BOTH WHAT THE FUUUUUUU

31

⋆ Valerie ⋆

In the aftermath, Wade hands me over to security. Head pounding, I'm ushered into the back of a town car as flashbulbs spin my vision. My stomach lurches as the driver speeds away.

It's all just a blur.

Finally alone in my hotel room an hour after the concert, I pull out my phone with shaking hands. My self-loathing kicks into high gear as I realize just how much I fucked up. When you've ruined your whole career in one night, you deserve to read the comments.

And I deserve everything they're saying.

Loose cannon.

Desperate poser.

Lying whore.

The hits just keep on coming, and not in a chart-topping way. I absorb the impact of each jab, letting myself get more bruised and battered with every confused post, every scathing article, every vicious comment. Whenever the sting starts to lessen, I come back for another round.

Like social media is the bottle, and every angry word a swig. My mind whirls as I get drunk on it all.

A few fans are defending me, but I wish they wouldn't. I'm not worthy of it. Their loyalty has been misplaced in me from the beginning, and I just keep letting them down as I fall apart under the pressure of the spotlight.

The person who calls me a "stupid, fame-hungry bitch," though? I earned that. I could have prevented this if I hadn't been too single-minded to consider anyone but myself. I just clutched at the first opportunity to stay in the spotlight, not pausing to think of how it would affect the people I care most about in this world. Jane, Riker, Keeley . . . Caleb. I've lost them all.

I ruined everything.

There's nothing left to do but wallow in my misery. I don't even bother changing out of my stage clothes, but I wrap myself in the fancy, oversized hotel robe and order room service. Soon I'm eating a giant ice cream sundae like Kevin McCallister at the Plaza. But instead of watching some violent noir flick, I'm watching this violence of my own making tear my career to shreds. A few times, I drop the spoon and smear chocolate syrup on the fluffy white fabric, and I don't even care. I'll just pay for the robe.

I'm just about to order a second ice cream—it's not like I'm going to be singing anytime soon, so bring on the dairy—when I'm interrupted by a knock on my hotel room door.

My heart stops. Maybe it's Caleb.

Sure, he could have knocked on the door between our rooms, but maybe that's too intimate. Or maybe he checked out, and then thought better of it and came back to talk to me. I launch off the bed, leaving my bowl to rest precariously on the duvet, and run to the door.

But it's the last person I want to see.

"What are you doing?" my mother demands, striding into my

room. Tonight, she's wearing a too-loud floral-print designer blazer over leggings, and the stench of cigarette smoke and too much Chanel No. 9 is strong enough to make my stomach roil. She glances around the room with a wrinkled nose; all my possessions are strewn about. "God, you're such a mess." She gestures to the ice cream. "You know you need to watch your figure for the cameras, right? I taught you not to eat like this."

"Right." I flinch. She's always *watched my figure* so closely that I don't have to. When you have a parent who comments on your appearance, who expects you to look Hollywood thin, it's bad enough. It's even worse when you actually work in media.

Or, rather, *used to* work in media. My stomach churns.

She sniffs. "You'd better go run on the treadmill. They'll open the gym up for you, I'm sure."

I clench my jaw. "Fine." I have no desire to run on the fucking treadmill, but she doesn't need to know that. I just need to get her out of here.

"And it looks like a teenager is staying in here. Are those designer jeans in a ball? You know there's an entire dresser right in front of you. I taught you to fold your clothes properly, and I expect you to do so."

"Sure."

"Seriously, Valerie, what will the staff think? Someone is going to leak to the press that you're a total slob. How embarrassing that my daughter can't even keep her room tidy."

I roll my eyes at the familiar lecture. She always finds something to criticize, and she's on a roll tonight. "How'd you get in here?" Only guests can use the elevator, and we asked security to keep her away.

"I told the receptionist it was a family emergency," she says.

So she lied. Wade is going to have a meltdown when he finds out—any fan could exploit that if they learned which floor we were on. Most of our fans haven't been scary, but after tonight, they might be out for my blood.

Understandably.

"Well, good for you," I finally say, setting my empty ice cream bowl on the tray and slipping it off the bed. My instinct is to shrug off the dirty robe, but I don't want her to see I'm still in my stage clothes.

It'll just give her another thing to criticize.

She places her hands on her hips. "Now, what are we going to do about your image?"

I blink at her. "My image?"

"Of course. That little stunt you pulled has consequences, Valerie Elizabeth."

As if I haven't been working in the industry for my entire adult life. The infantilizing isn't new, but it still sets my teeth on edge. "I'm aware."

"Obviously we've had a setback, but I just got off the phone with Label Records and they want that third album, despite the negative press. They're willing to record without Caleb."

My stomach plummets at how casually she dismisses him. "I can't do this without Caleb."

I don't want to do anything without him. That's what I was trying to say tonight, but it came out all wrong. What have I done?

She rolls her eyes. "Grow up, Valerie. Plenty of other bands have survived losing a member and gone on to great success."

"This is different!"

"What, because you think you're falling in love with him again? It'll pass."

It'll pass. Like Caleb is just a summer storm that rolls through one night and leaves in the morning. But he's not the storm—he's my atmosphere. I'm not sure I can breathe without him.

Because . . . I *am* still in love with Caleb Sloane.

The realization hits me like lightning, and I want to collapse on the floor. Of course I love him. I drove him away *again*, and I don't know how to function without him. I certainly can't continue the band we created without him by my side. Even if any of the other Glitter Bats agreed—which they absolutely wouldn't now—it'd be like living every day with a hole in my chest where my heart used to be, then pouring salt in the wound.

I can't. Tears well in my eyes, and I wish I had the kind of mom who would let me cry.

But there's no appealing to emotions with Tonya Quinn. "There's no way the rest of the band will move forward, especially if Caleb isn't in the mix."

She purses her lips. "Everyone is replaceable. Besides, they won't walk away when they realize how much money is on the line."

"For *you*, you mean."

My mother raises a brow. "And?"

"You're not here because of any kind of sympathy or maternal affection." Heat rushes up my cheeks. "You only care about this because it'll get you a paycheck. Did you come here to push me when I'm down because you know it's your last chance?"

"How dare you!" Her eyes flash. "You ungrateful little bitch. After everything I've done for you all, I deserve to be compensated for managing the beginning of your careers. Hell, I should still be managing, but you insisted on hiring a baseball player over your own flesh and blood when you got a little taste of fame."

I swallow thickly, but no, I'm not going to cower before her this time. I sweep my arm in her direction. "I didn't need you to be a manager—I needed my mother!"

She juts her chin. "I was there with you from the beginning!"

"No, you weren't!" Adrenaline rushes through my body, and I let out a huff. "You were never there for me in the way I needed. In case you haven't noticed, becoming famous at seventeen absolutely destroyed me, and I can't help but think it all would have been different if I'd had your support and protection. Instead, you used me."

My mom rolls her eyes at me. "Oh, please. You wanted this life! I helped you get it." Her voice is nonchalant, but I don't miss the vein popping on her forehead.

"At what cost?" My heart races. I've never really confronted her, not like this, and now I can't stop. "You expected me to do everything they asked because it benefitted you, even if it meant crash diets or lost sleep or endorsement deals for companies I didn't believe in. Hell, you gave my very personal, intimate photos to the press without my knowledge or permission—even though I was only nineteen and it branded me a slut! But you said it made me relevant, so I stayed quiet and counted headlines. I bet that tabloid paid you for the damn photos. You turned my self-esteem into this bruised, spotlight-desperate monster who hurts everyone around her. And right now, I'm having the worst night of my life. It'd be nice if you'd, I don't know, check if I'm okay before trying to exploit me again. But you just don't understand basic empathy."

You'd think any of this would move her, but it doesn't. She just scoffs, like she's bored with the conversation, and sits primly in the chair. "Don't be so dramatic, Valerie. It's immature."

"I'm not the emotionally immature one! You're making this all about you, and I don't have the energy. We're not discussing my career any longer." I laugh dryly. "Not that I have a career left to speak of."

She gapes, rising again. "Now wait just a moment—"

I interrupt her. "No. It's over, Mom. You need to leave."

She throws up her hands. "Fine. When you come to your senses, you have Gina's number. We'll all be waiting to hear from you when you're ready to fulfill your obligations."

And then she leaves, slamming the hotel door behind her. I

wonder how many times we'll have the same conversation. She's never going to understand—she'll always want something from me. The best thing I can do is cut her out of my life. Maybe I won't even have to—once my career is gone, there will be nothing left to take. She'll go find someone else to manipulate.

My mouth goes dry as I realize . . . maybe I'm just like her. I manipulated everyone in this band to get what I wanted from them. I orchestrated this reunion for my career, and then I tried to exploit more from it. How could I have done that to my friends? To Caleb?

It's exactly what Tonya would have done.

God, I don't want to be like this.

My mind is still reeling as I collapse back onto the bed. My phone buzzes, and I brace myself for another media contact reaching out for comment.

It's probably better if I start ignoring my phone, but I don't.

Fortunately, it's not the media at all. It's a text from Wade.

Hey, kiddo. I don't need to tell you that you screwed up, but nothing is ruined forever. I just met with my team and we're going to work on an image rehab plan. We'll email you when it's ready, but don't look at it right away. We can discuss everything next week. Try to get some sleep.

Sleep? As if.

I almost call down to the restaurant and order another sundae, but my stomach lurches as I open a new tab and try to catch more headlines, and suddenly I feel like I'm going to be sick. I can't make sense of anything. It's all horrible.

So I give up and do what I always do when the world doesn't make sense—I pick up my guitar and start writing.

32

+ *Caleb* +

The next twenty-four hours are a blur.

Somehow I manage to leave the stadium, check into a different hotel, and book a new flight for the afternoon after the concert, but I'm so numb I hardly clock any of it.

I just know I never should have come to LA.

When Valerie showed up unannounced on my doorstep, I should have closed the door in her face, but I wasn't strong enough to resist her. One look at those ocean eyes and I was under her spell again. Some naïve part of me hoped this time would be different. I thought we'd both changed enough to replace our bitter memories of those final Glitter Bats days with some good ones. One last time.

I should have known it would end like this: her chasing the limelight, me running again into the night. Does she even care that she broke my heart all over again?

By the time my plane lands, I'm ready to put everything behind me. As much as I want to drive straight home, I stop at a restaurant to order pizza and fancy beer to thank Cam and Leah for babysitting my dog. Despite the heat of the summer, I tug my hood up like a shield when the guy taking orders stares a little too intently at me from behind the counter. It's all I can do to escape before I'm recognized.

When I get to their house, I hug my family without saying another word, then drown my feelings in cheesy carbs and a few beers. Sebastian Bark would not leave my side at first, and it almost felt like everything was back to normal. But after he stole some pepperoni from my pizza and hightailed it out of there, I realized that was more about the food than missing me. Even the dog I rescued can't be loyal. Still, it's nice to be home . . . whatever that means anymore.

I can't even make sense of the jumble of feelings in my chest. Anger. Embarrassment. Numb disbelief. I should have seen Valerie's scheme coming, and I'm a fool for thinking I could trust her.

We're watching an iconic episode of *Schitt's Creek*—the one when Patrick serenades David, even though it feels a little on the nose—when Leah asks the question.

"You want to talk about it?"

I groan. "Which part?"

She quirks a brow. "Wherever you want to start."

Wherever I want to start, as if it would be that easy to pick a point. My mind whirls with anxiety and a light buzz of alcohol and the weight of everything that's happened over the past twenty-four hours. The past seven weeks. The past six years. Shit, maybe more like the past ten, since we were starry-eyed teens who made that cursed deal with the demon that is Label Records.

"No," I say. "I don't want to talk about it."

Cameron crosses her arms, ever the disbelieving older sister. "Fuck that. You obviously need to vent."

She knows me too well, and I sigh. "It's just too much. I need to, I don't know, process it before I can make sense of anything. I don't want to relive all of that drama more than once."

Cameron scoffs. "You want drama? I had a bored teenager re-break her leg post-surgery today because she tried to take a shower without asking for a nurse, and the parents yelled at *me* because she's an equestrian who's 'missing competition season.' Your drama is nothing."

My stomach twists, because Cameron is absolutely right. Her work drama may be less public than mine, but she's dealing with illnesses and injuries and people on the worst days of their lives.

Leah puts a hand on Cameron's arm. "His emotions are still valid."

Cameron sighs. "I know. I just want him to talk about it, and I thought guilt was a good motivator."

"I hate you," I say, but there's no malice in it. I know what she's doing. "I mean, you saw the concert. You know what happened."

"We saw the livestream," Cameron says. "And I'm sorry. We wanted to come out there, but I was on call last minute."

"Well, you didn't miss anything," I say dryly.

Leah sighs. "Remember, we only saw what they presented to the public. The livestream cut off right after you left the stage, so it must have been a little delayed—like they were trying to control the damage. Why don't you tell us your side of the story?" she prompts gently.

I take a long swig of my beer. It's a little bitter, but so am I. "Valerie and I . . ." I don't even know how to describe it. "We got involved again."

"Oh, shocker," Cameron says. "Dude, you know it's been all over the media, right?"

I groan. "Yeah, but most of that was more like fake dating for the cameras. It was all about playing it up, trying to help her get some positive press, that kind of thing."

"Well all of those kisses looked real," Cameron says.

I lean my head against the couch, sighing. "They were."

"Wait, I'm confused," Leah says. "You pretended to date . . . but you were actually dating?"

Is it "dating" if you've been pining for your ex-situationship from afar for six years, then started hooking up again, admitted there are feelings, but neglected to ever put a label on it? "Kind of?"

"So you were sleeping with her, at least," Cameron says.

I choke on my beer, feeling the heat flood to my cheeks. "Jesus Christ, I'm not going to talk about my sex life with you."

"Why not?"

"Because you're my sister!"

She shrugs, glancing at Leah. "We have sex, lots of it. Does that help?"

"No!" I say, shuddering. I don't want to think about that either.

Leah smirks, but she doesn't help me out, just takes a smug bite of her pizza.

Finally, I recover. "I mean, how is that relevant to the story?"

"Sex always makes things more complicated," Leah says sagely.

I roll my eyes. "Yeah, fine, we were sleeping together. Better than it ever was before. You happy?"

"You are very upset for someone who's been getting lucky all summer after—what—an eight-month-long dry spell?" Cameron says.

"I've dated since Morgan! And that's completely irrelevant. Did you miss the part where Valerie tried to manipulate me into returning to the scene full-time?"

"Is that really what happened?" Leah asks, her voice soft and gentle, like she's afraid to spook me. "She manipulated you?"

I shake my head. "I think so? Things were going great, but we didn't really talk about what would happen after the concert. I mean, I told her that I hoped we could figure something out, but how does that translate to 'let's surprise everyone by announcing a permanent comeback'? She did this without consulting me *or* anyone else in the band. She didn't even tell our manager!"

I found that out when Wade texted to ask if I was okay, and if I knew what she was planning. The only answer I could give him was no.

I gasp, trying to catch my breath. Saying it all out loud doesn't exactly make me feel better, but bottling it up wasn't working. "I just . . . I can't believe I didn't see this coming. I was so stupid."

"Let it out," Cameron says. "This sucks, but it isn't on you."

"You have every right to be upset," Leah adds.

"I know!" I say, adrenaline rushing through me. I take another sip of beer, trying to steady myself. "Valerie betrayed my trust and assumed I would just go along with it, the way I've gone along with everything else this summer."

"Is that why you walked offstage?"

I sigh, running a hand through my hair, pizza grease be damned. "I don't know, maybe? I just couldn't be there anymore. I didn't want people to think I had any part in her statement."

It was all too much. I couldn't face Valerie treating me like this again—like I'm just a ticket to fame, not a person she loves.

"Don't you think that maybe . . ." Leah begins.

"What?" I demand, a little too harshly. I swallow, trying to calm my racing heart.

Leah and Cameron share a look. Finally, my sister speaks up.

"Maybe you should have stuck around to understand why she did it? At least until the end of the show? Maybe you could have worked something out."

Shame twists in my gut. Valerie betrayed my trust again, and I'm allowed to keep boundaries in place. She did the one thing we said we wouldn't do—promised another album to Label Records. But to the audience, it must have looked like I was throwing a fit. Give it two days, and I'll be on a *Gossip Daily* list of the worst diva moments in rock history. I mean, who leaves in the middle of a show?

Me.

Unless they spin it to blame her, the way they did six years ago.

I left the tour last time Valerie and I argued, and this time I couldn't even finish out the night. I'm very good at leaving her.

"Fuck, maybe," I say. "I was just so hurt and confused and . . . I ran. Again."

A familiar voice interrupts. "Does Valerie's announcement have anything to do with her TV show getting canceled?"

We all turn to the front door, where my baby sister has just walked right in, somehow without any of us hearing her arrive. Sebastian Bark and Strawberry bolt for Carrie, giving her kisses and demanding pets.

"Where did you come from?" Cameron demands, jumping out of her spot on the couch. She pulls her into a fierce hug.

Carrie shrugs when they part. "I knew Caleb would be upset, and I wanted to be here," she says, like that's a good-enough reason for a seventeen-year-old to show up unannounced at eight p.m., more than two hours away from her own house.

"You drove through the Seattle-to-Portland traffic while you were texting me? What the hell?" Cameron says.

Carrie grins, flipping her short, dark waves over her shoulder. "I used speech-to-text. I'm an excellent driver. I took an extra traffic safety course to save money on car insurance."

"We're glad you got here safe, honey," Leah says, hurrying over to hug her too. I feel completely out of my element, on the way from tipsy to drunk with my baby sister here. Carrie launches herself at me.

"Gross, you smell like beer," she says, burrowing into my shoulder. "But I missed you anyway."

"I don't like that you know what beer smells like," I say as she pulls back to frown at me. "Does Mom know you're here?"

Carrie glances at her shoes before looking back up at me. "Mom hasn't been home in three days. Your manager hooked us up with tickets, including travel, and I was going to surprise you yesterday in VIP. But Mom never showed, and I didn't want to leave on my own in case she came back."

God, I wish my mom could focus on her kids for once. It makes me want to fight to enroll Carrie in school here and make her move in with one of us, just so I can watch her, but I know that's not what she wants for her last year of high school. But Mom needs to know this isn't okay.

"I'm going to call her right now," I say.

"Please don't! I'm here for *you*."

Cameron puts her hands on her hips. "I'm texting Mom that you're here and you're safe, and reminding her that even though you're one of the most responsible kids in the world, she still needs to check on you."

Carrie rolls her eyes. "Fine. Whatever. But back to my question—do you think Valerie's stunt had to do with the *Epic Theme Song* cancellation?"

My heart sinks as what she's saying really sets in. "When did *Epic Theme Song* get canceled? I thought it was all still up in the air." That was the entire point of this charade.

She shrugs. "I don't know—it was all over the internet yesterday right before the concert started, so I assume the decision happened recently. Maybe even that morning."

Suddenly, everything starts to make sense. Valerie's strange behavior at sound check, being elusive, "making calls" when we were supposed to focus—she found out about the cancellation and panicked. But I wish she would have talked to me first before making some desperate grab for more Glitter Bats. She should have told me what was going on.

Doesn't she trust me?

"That doesn't excuse what she did," I say, but the back of my neck prickles. Suddenly, I see yesterday in a different light.

"No, but it sucks," Carrie says. "Wonderfans are pissed. We made fan art and memes and fic, covered songs, signed petitions—hell, we even got it trending in the US and France and fucking *Brazil*—but they still canceled the show."

"Don't say *fuck*," Cameron and I say in unison.

Carrie laughs. "I'll be eighteen in like two months. And you say it all the time, Cam."

Cameron sighs. "Whatever. So you're saying the show got canceled and you think Valerie . . . panicked? That's what all this was?"

"That's exactly what we think," Carrie says. "So I saw what happened and put the pieces together, and I only came down because I wanted to make sure Caleb was okay." She gestures with the keys still in her hand. "But I can drive back if you want."

"In the dark? Absolutely not. Go grab some pizza and I'll make up the guest room with fresh sheets. Sebastian Bark has been crashing there," Leah says.

"Thank you, Car. You shouldn't have come all this way alone, but I'm glad you're here," I say.

"I think you forget because you're always taking care of everyone else, but you need *us* sometimes too, Caleb."

My eyes sting, and I pull my little sister into another hug. I've been second-guessing my decision to leave the Glitter Bats all summer, drawn in by nostalgia, by the joy of working with my friends again, by Valerie's allure. But if I'd still been on the road all these years, I never would have known how much my family needed me. Or maybe my sister is right, and it's more about how much I needed them.

Everything hurts right now, but at least I'm not alone.

Where Is Valerie Quinn?

MARY KATE HAMPTON, STAFF WRITER, *BUZZWORD*

Ever since the ill-fated Glitter Bats reunion, Valerie Quinn has been noticeably MIA. This is new behavior from Quinn, who has been a mainstay in the LA nightlife scene since she moved here permanently several years ago. Even when she wasn't partying it up, she was seen slipping in and out of clubs, hanging in VIP sections at shows, and dining in celebrity hotspots. But not now.

For more than a week, Quinn hasn't been spotted at so much as a grocery store or her favorite coffee shop, much less her usual haunts. No one knows if she's even in LA. Her social media has been wiped clean. Fans are worried, and rightfully so.

If you've been online at all, you know everyone has been speculating about what's keeping her away—whether it's shame or fear or a carefully cultivated media strategy—but Quinn is the only person who can answer that question. I join many fans in hoping she's okay. When I reached out to her management for comment, the only statement I got in response is that "Valerie is taking some time."

But from what? With the Glitter Bats reunion coming to a screeching halt last week and the news of *Epic Theme Song*'s unfortunate cancellation, Quinn's schedule has opened up.

So maybe this is the real question: What's next for Valerie Quinn?

33

+ Valerie +

I've been hiding out in my apartment.

No media. No contact with the band. I don't even talk to Wade about his team's image rehab plan, but I'm following it closely enough. No public appearances, no interviews, not even a trip to a convenience store where I could be spotted by the wrong person. It's effectively a full blackout, and I follow the advice even if it's less strategy and more survival.

Or a simple lack of any desire to engage with the world.

So just as Wade and the agency wanted, I haven't been seen in public since I was on that stage. Without more *Epic Theme Song* money, I can afford to keep them on for another six months or so, and then I'll need to book something or fade into obscurity.

Maybe obscurity isn't so bad. Other than the kind person who discreetly delivers my groceries, no one who knows where I live has stopped by my place. No one's worrying about me, but that's fine.

I've spent the week poring over my old notebooks. It's like a switch has flipped in my brain, and the only catharsis I find is in the music. I'm tweaking old songs and writing new ones, and these aren't songs I'm writing for public consumption.

They're spilling out of me just because I need to write.

I forgot about the healing power of my guitar and a blank page. Other than working on "Daydreams Like This" with Caleb this summer, I haven't written anything original in years. I've sung other people's music. I recorded songs written by strangers for my failed solo career. But I haven't poured my emotions onto the strings like this since before we became famous, when I started to realize that Caleb was always more than a friend to me. All these years, and I haven't bled into a melody. Haven't pulled a new rhythm deep from my bones.

But even though exorcising my emotions is painful, it's also a release. It reminds me that I never got into this industry for the fame. I got into it for the music, just like Caleb did. Once upon a time, we had the same motives. I just got so distracted by the public attention, my face in the glossy pages of magazines, my name trending online . . . that I forgot what a joy it is to be making music for music's sake.

And I took it for granted all over again.

I let myself believe the Glitter Bats were still just a call away. Thought they'd go along with any plans to keep the momentum going, because I assumed they wanted to keep it going. I didn't think of any of their feelings, much less their own goals and hopes for the future.

The fallout with Caleb feels the worst, and it's something I'll never forgive myself for, but I'm racked with guilt about the others too. Keeley's anger, Jane's quiet disappointment, Riker's resignation—they haunt my dreams as much as the betrayal on Caleb's face does. I broke more than one heart on that stage.

So I write about it all. I write about guilt and shame, about hurting the people I care for, about chasing fame and feeling empty.

And I write love songs.

Every lyric smashes my shattered heart, but I can't stop. Every morning that I wake up and Caleb isn't in my bed, I feel lost, and I need some way to process those feelings. So I write about him. About us. About longing and desire and falling for the person who makes your heart beat faster. About being tangled in sheets at three a.m., about holding hands on a beach at sunset, about kisses that taste like sugar and promises.

It's all catharsis, but none of the songs feel like what I'm looking for.

Until one does.

My heart races as I reach over the guitar in my lap to jot the words and chords into my messy notebook. I chase that feeling of *rightness* for hours until I've captured every detail. With the ink on paper, I revise the lines, move around the chords, play with the melody until it's perfect.

Glancing over at my soft bed with bleary eyes, I realize that's not enough. There's no way I'll sleep now. I need to do more with this song, even if it hurts, even if it's all in vain. So I set up my Mac and a microphone, then stay awake past midnight to record a rough sample.

I upload it and send an email to Wade with nothing but "Thank you" in the subject line, and the music file attached:

Wade,

I'm sorry for being radio silent. Please help me figure out how to release this, and then I'm done. With all of it.

Thank you for everything.
Valerie

My eyes are tired, but I have another message to send:

Me: I owe you three an apology, and I'd like to do it in person. Can I make you dinner tomorrow night? Or rather, tonight. 6PM? I hope your phones are all on silent, otherwise I apologize for waking you up too.

When I finally wake up the next afternoon, I have three texts.

Riker: Sure.

Keeley: Fine, but I'm not going to be happy about it.

Jane: What can I bring?

Their acceptance of my invitation is more than I expect and far more than I deserve. But because I've got all the ingredients for vodka sauce in my pantry, I begin preparing the meal. I even throw together a green salad and garlic bread.

My heart flips when I hear the knock on my door, right on time. I hurry to open it, trying to settle my nerves.

"Are you going to poison us? I've had your awful grilled cheese, and this smells way more intensive," Keeley says. She's got Jane and Riker in tow, and I realize they're here as a united front. It's them versus me, and it's up to me to get us all on the same side again.

"Theo was an asshole, but his mother was Italian. I learned how to make this pasta from her one weekend," I admit.

Riker cocks his head as he steps through the door. "At least you got something out of that bastard."

Jane surprises me with a small smile. "It's really good to see you," she says.

"Thank you all for coming," I say, anxiously clearing my throat. "Wine? I've got red and white."

"No rosé?" Riker says, pouting.

I laugh, then pull the screw top out of my fridge. "Just for you, bud."

"Yes!" he says. Instead of pouring it into one of the stemless wine glasses I have set out on the counter, he drinks it right from the bottle.

"Riker!" Jane says. "What if we wanted some?" But there's no bite to it as she pours herself a glass of the chardonnay instead.

Keeley laughs. "All yours, dude."

While they all get started on their wine and relax onto the couches in the living room adjacent to my kitchen, I go to check the sauce. It's the perfect creamy color, and the scents of garlic and prosciutto and Parmesan hang in the air.

"If you cook like this for all your partners, no wonder everyone wants to date you," Keeley says. "I'd put out for good Italian."

"Noted." I laugh.

But she doesn't; she just purses her lips and leans back, examining me. "Are you trying to fuck us or fuck us over, though? That's the question."

My jaw clenches. Of course it was never going to be this easy. I didn't expect to feed them and be forgiven. Swallowing thickly, I take a sip of my own wine for courage, then turn to face my friends.

The energy in the room is tense, and I square my shoulders. I can do this.

"Keeley's right, and I suppose there's no use in beating around the bush. This is an apology. I'm not asking any of you for anything—I've already done too much of that. But I need you all to know how sorry I am for ruining the concert, and for dragging you into a reunion in the first place with sketchy motivations. I was looking for validation in all the wrong places. While that doesn't excuse how I've treated all of you, I want you to know I never intended to hurt anyone. I love you guys. And I am so, so sorry."

"Do we have to forgive you to eat the pasta?" Keeley asks dryly.

"No," I say, even though tears tighten the back of my throat.

"You don't even have to talk to me if you don't want to." My voice breaks, but I fight through the tears knowing they don't owe me any pity, keeping my words as steady as possible. "But I just hope you all know I'm really sorry, and I'm going to work on thinking about others before I make any more impulsive decisions."

Now, Keeley's the one crying. "Dude, I *want* to stay mad. What you did was bullshit."

"I know," I say, sniffing. "It was the worst. You should all hate me."

She huffs and swipes at her wet cheeks. "But I love you too much, you dumbass." She rises and pulls me into a hug, and I realize it's the first time anyone has touched me in days. I collapse into her arms and start sobbing in earnest.

"Damn it," Riker says thickly. "Now I'm crying too. You're all the worst."

Blinking hard, I lift my head and glance over Keeley's shoulder, catching Jane's eye. Tears are quietly streaming down her face too. "Of course we forgive you," Jane says. "I forgave you the second I saw the news about your show. What you did wasn't okay, but I understand you were hurting too. It all made so much sense. We should have been there for you instead of abandoning you."

"Speak for yourself," Keeley says, still holding on to me. "I only forgave her when I smelled the pasta."

We all laugh.

I pull back from Keeley. "Let's eat, then."

"And then we can talk about the future of the band," Riker says. "I think it's time."

I groan, unable to hide the shame rising in my chest. "There's no future," I say. "I'm not asking you to get back together again."

"Maybe we want to," Riker says. "You'd know that if you asked us."

I sigh, extracting myself to the kitchen to start dishing up. The others follow, and Riker grabs plates while Jane pulls the salad out of my fridge. "I think I need to be done."

Jane purses her lips. "Is that why you've been writing? Because you're done?"

"How did you . . . ?" But she's nodding at the open notebook on the counter, the one Keeley is flipping through—no privacy, but then again, I shouldn't have left it out if I didn't want it to be found.

"This is really good, Quinn. Did you write this for Caleb?"

My stomach churns, because she found last night's song.

I nod. "I sent it to Wade, thinking maybe I could record it, send the proceeds to charity or something. I just don't think an apology is going to be enough. But now, I'm not really sure I want to put it out there."

The three of them share a look and seem to decide something.

"We could produce it, if you wanted help," Jane says, nudging me gently. "I have access to a studio. Contractually, you might owe it to Label after your announcement, but at least the personnel could be some familiar faces."

My chest warms at the offer. "I don't know . . ." I say. "I'm probably just going to put my heart out there only for it to break again."

"You'll never know unless you try, though," Keeley says.

The thing is, she's right. Caleb has my heart, and if there's any possibility he would hear me out, I have to take it. Maybe it'll all come to nothing, but if there's even a chance this will reach him, even a chance he'll consider talking to me . . .

"He's worth it," I say. "I want to try."

"Oh, hell yeah," Riker says, leaning back against my counter. "Is this the moment when Heath Ledger sings with the marching band?"

I grin, letting his enthusiasm stoke the last ember of stubborn hope in my chest. "You're damn right it is."

34

Caleb

Ten days after the concert, I'm back at work and trying to be happy about it.

The kids don't start school again for another two weeks, but we have in-service days: mostly training and rehashing old procedures, all the routine stuff no one tells you about until your first teaching gig.

But it's fine. Less glamorous than anything else I did this summer, but normal is good. It's what I wanted, right?

I'm still so defeated after the concert that it's hard to say. Life without Valerie is dull and uninspiring. Now that I know what was going on that night, I constantly wonder if she's okay. I grab my phone a dozen times a day, hoping the latest notification will be from her.

It never is. The only way I "see" her is when Jane uploads another of the instructional videos we recorded to the channel, and it's one where Valerie is talking about her approach to singing harmony. Past Val grins at me from my spot behind the camera, and the flashback of joy, of being together with her in that moment, is like an electric shock to my senses. I watched it on repeat until my phone died last night. Maybe I should reach out, but I'm not sure she wants to hear from me. Maybe it wouldn't have changed the outcome, but I wonder what would have happened that night if I'd stayed. I've made a bad habit of leaving her over the years.

But I can't change the past, so I try to move on, focusing on work and my family. Cameron and I tried to remind our mother that she needs to be more involved after Carrie's little road trip, but I'm not sure she gets it. Still, I think she felt chastised enough that she'll get through this year without incident.

Hopefully.

At least I got my check for the concert. After it hit me that leaving in the middle of the show might put me in violation of my contract, I spoke to Wade. He didn't say anything about what I did, just agreed to reach out, and the check came through a few days later. As soon as it cleared, I went to my bank's financial adviser and put a chunk into a college account for Carrie. It'll be enough to get her through a couple years, and if she gets the scholarships she deserves, then it would cover her full room and board so she doesn't have to work while she goes to school.

She's already had to grow up so much, and I really want her to be able to relax and do her homework, even go to parties, make a few bad decisions. She deserves to get the college experience that I never did.

I finally told Carrie about the money over coffee before she went back to Mom's, and she started sobbing right in the middle of the cafe. It reminded me all at once that I did this for her. If nothing else came out of my ill-fated return to the limelight, at least my baby sister will be okay. She can pursue her dreams without worrying about the money, and if it all falls apart, she knows she has a soft place to land.

When Glitter Bats first started up, I had to work part-time at a bakery to pay for my own instruments, plus my share of the gas and food and hotels when we were touring. It meant a lot of late nights studying—and a dipping history grade that nearly cost me my high school diploma—but I pulled through. My dreams cost me a lot.

Carrie's path won't be easy, but if this can alleviate some of the stress, it was worth it. And I remind myself that's why I'm here today. My students need someone who believes in them. But with my mind so scattered, even meditating on my reason for becoming a teacher doesn't do much to hold my attention.

All I can think about is Valerie, and I have to force myself to focus on this meeting instead of wondering if she's okay. There's a new assistant principal this year, and he's giving us a long post-lunch presentation about a lot of logistics, mostly review from the last few years. I'm in the back with Leah and the other fitness and arts teachers, and we're pretending to pay attention but passing a doodle back and forth. When it's my turn, I add Sebastian Bark to the pretty Oregon landscape the others have sketched.

When the principal starts to talk about our contracts, my palms grow damp. I don't know why the idea of a contract I signed months ago is making me panic. I don't want to take a pill in front of everyone if I can avoid it, so I just take a long sip from my water bottle and try to relax, my fingers playing silent piano scales on the table as I absorb his next words.

"There was an error back in May when you were all sent your contracts, so those have been voided after union review. It's just a formality, but we'll be distributing your new contracts via email today. Please use Adobe Sign and return them before you head home, otherwise you'll be chased down tomorrow by Yvonne from the office and owe her coffee."

Stilted laughter echoes around the room. They've got us packed into the cafeteria, which still smells like grease from summer school, but at least the tables are clean enough. The others dutifully open their laptops to sign their contracts, but I just stare at the desk.

"Dude," Leah says. "You good?"

I swallow thickly. "Yeah, sorry, just . . . thinking."

And suddenly it hits me: I had wanted to sign that contract at the beginning of this summer, but after everything that's happened, I'm not sure it's the right thing to do now. I love this job, I really do. But every minute I'm here is another minute I'm away from Valerie. She may have hurt me—again—but that doesn't mean I'm ready to give up on her.

There's a conversation we still need to have, and I can't make any plans without it.

"I'm not going to sign the contract."

"Oh my *god*!" Leah says. I blink up at her, thinking this is a reaction to my statement, but it's not. She's staring at her phone. "Caleb, have you been on social media at all today?"

"What? No," I say, scowling. I've just made a potentially life-altering revelation and she's staring at her phone?

She sighs. "Here!" She shoves her phone in my face, and I freeze.

Valerie has posted a photo from our magazine shoot that I don't remember seeing before, but we look happy and in love, and the hope of it all makes my pulse shift into a higher gear. Then I read the caption, and it jolts me, like I'm slamming the brakes at an unexpected red light.

THE ONLY POST ON VALERIE QUINN'S NOW-SCRUBBED SOCIAL MEDIA

August 25th—

Image Description: *Valerie Quinn and Caleb Sloane on the set of their* Punk! *magazine cover, taking a selfie against a red backdrop. Caleb is smirking at the camera, and Valerie is kissing his cheek.*

My silence has been a statement all its own, and after some self-reflection, I've decided it's not the one I want to make.

While I don't love public apologies—because they're often attention seeking, false, or simply about saving face—I want to make it clear that no one but me should be held responsible for the events at the Glitter Bats reunion last week.

First, to our beloved Glitterbugs—you deserved better. On the morning of the concert, I learned *Epic Theme Song* had been canceled, and I acted out. There's no excuse. I turned what was supposed to be a celebration of our music into a selfish attempt to cling to my fame. You've been loyal, and I've been thankless in return. I deeply apologize for what I've put you all through. I hope you can find it in your hearts to forgive me, but even if you don't, it's been an honor to play music for you all. You're the best fans in the world.

To Jane, Keeley, and Riker—I want to acknowledge that I put you all through too much this summer. You were brought on this ride, and my intentions were wrong from the start. If we were ever going to reunite for good, it should have been something we decided together on our own terms. You're not just my band, you're my family, and I should never have treated my family so thoughtlessly. I love you all.

I want to state for public record that no one else in the band knew what my plans were, and I made that announcement without knowledge or consent. If there are any legal or fiscal implications as a result of my announcement, I intend to take full responsibility. My lawyer has reached out to Label Records, TicketChampion, and The Network to ensure that no one but me is held responsible for my actions.

To Caleb . . . you are the best person I've ever known. My actions this summer have been beyond careless with your feelings, just as they were six years ago, and there is no excusing all the ways I've wronged you. I can't apologize deeply enough for everything that's happened between us, but I'm sorry for all of it. I'm sorry for hurting you. I'm sorry for dragging you into my chaos, time and time again. I'm sorry for exploiting your kindness, for ignoring your needs, for asking you to pretend to reconcile a romance with me to save my image after I'd already broken your heart.

But if I'm really honest, I was never pretending. I never had to fake it when it's all I've ever wanted. You deserve every good thing in the world, and I can only hope you know the precious moments we've shared are everything to me. You make me want to be worthy of spending the rest of my life with you—I'll fight every day to earn your trust back if you'll give me one last chance.

And even if you won't, my reckless heart will love you forever. This song is for you.

Link: *stream "everything I wanted"*

"everything I wanted" by Valerie Quinn

[Verse 1]

spent all these years playing games
grabbing spotlights, made a name
lost your sunshine next to me
hustled and schemed every day
only to tear me away
from your perfect harmonies

[Chorus]

I walked away
when I should have held you
wide-eyed daydreams
left me so damn confused
searched for a place
with applause and acclaim
but it was never enough
cause you were everything I wanted

[Verse 2]

spent so many shining nights
taking in the neon sights
couldn't see them light your eyes
you're my specter, you're my ghost
and I missed your heart the most
took too long to realize

[Chorus repeats]

[Vamp]

everything I wanted
everything I wanted
everything I wanted
all I want is

[Bridge]

walking barefoot on the sand
burned grilled cheese at two a.m.
secrets shared with microphones
your keys next to mine at home

I don't need a diamond ring
if you're holding my six string
I don't even need the fame
but if you ask, I'll change my name

[Chorus]

I walked away
when I should have held you
throw out my daydreams
I'm no longer confused
don't need a place
with applause and acclaim
can't say sorry enough
you're the only one I want

can't say sorry enough
can't say sorry enough
can't say I love you enough
you're the only one I need

35

Valerie

After I publish the post, I turn off my phone for the first time in my entire life. My heart races as the screen turns dark, but then, when nothing bad happens, I'm filled with a strange sense of calm. I don't need to know what people are saying about me anymore.

I don't care.

I don't owe this industry any more of my heart. I've given them everything, and I won't let them tell me how to feel about Caleb. Because I know what's in my heart. I don't regret what I said, and I don't regret the song.

It's not perfect, but it's from my soul, and it's all I have left. Keeley, Jane, and Riker made good on helping me produce it, and we released it under Label—who, unfortunately, still owns everything I write because of my stunt. But the band agreed to send all of *our* royalties to underfunded music programs on the West Coast, and I try to take heart knowing we've done a little bit of good.

So instead of scrolling online to figure out what people are saying, I start cleaning my place. I scrub the bathroom, mop the floors, wash all of the linens. I even sanitize my fridge. When there's nothing left to clean around my apartment, I tend to myself. I take a long, hot shower; shave; exfoliate; and even put a treatment on my hair. I know it's silly to think you can wash off a mistake, but the cleaning is almost a ritual. Detoxifying my life.

I don't know what's next, and I think that's okay.

Instead of drying my hair, I comb it out and spritz the strands with salt spray, letting it air-dry as the sunset streams in through my windows. Trying not to think much of it, I slip into Caleb's old The Clash T-shirt and yoga pants just as someone knocks on my door. The only people who have visited me recently are the band, but they're all working this week, so I don't know who else it would be. Wade?

Who I don't expect is Caleb Sloane, leaning against the door-frame, looking like he was plucked right out of my fantasies.

He's wearing an old, faded Lime Velvet T-shirt and gray jog-gers slung low on his hips that leave nothing to the imagination. His hair is a little mussed, and he's got a duffle bag over his shoul-der like he just got off a plane.

My mouth goes completely dry. "Hi."

He runs a hand over his hair. "Hi."

"Hi."

Caleb's lips twist into an almost-smirk. "Can I come in?"

"Right. Yeah, of course," I say, pulse thundering in my ears. What do I do? Do I offer him something to drink? Ask what he's even doing here? Maybe he's here to yell at me.

My mind has gone completely blank with panic, but I manage to urge him inside and shut the door. We just stare, facing each other in my narrow entryway, and I don't even know where to be-gin. My hand jerks almost involuntarily to reach for him, but I think better of it and clench it in a fist.

"I almost quit my job today," Caleb blurts, without pretense.

I blink. "What? Why?"

He shakes his head, letting his bag fall to the ground. "I wasn't sure where my commitments lay, but fortunately my principal is giving me twenty-four hours to figure things out."

"What commitments are you talking about?" I ask.

With a self-satisfied grin, Caleb puts his hands in his pockets like his being here is the most casual thing in the world. "If we're going to make more music together, I want to work out the terms before I do anything else."

My jaw falls open, and I'm not sure I've heard him correctly. "What are you talking about?"

He chuckles. "You wrote an entire song. Do you really think I missed the subtext?"

I shake my head, walking over to the living room where there's more space, like somehow that will help me understand why he's here.

I know why I *hope* he's here, but I don't dare to believe it. "No, but that wasn't . . . I didn't intend . . . I'm not asking you to leave your life behind. I haven't been fair to you. I promised another album to Label on top of everything, which was the worst-case scenario! You can't just upend your entire world for me."

"That's my choice to make."

My heart warms at those words, but then I remember it's a choice I tried to take away from him. "It doesn't matter. I'm done with the industry."

"Are you?" He steps nearer to me, closing the distance between us. "Because I was already rethinking my job before I heard the song. Before I read your post, even. That all just confirmed what I was thinking."

I swallow thickly, tucking my hair behind my ear. My pulse pounds in my chest. This can't be real. "You didn't want this, though. You were very clear. I bulldozed your feelings, the way I always do . . ."

Caleb interrupts me, leaning closer. "No! I was *scared*," he says, his voice lowering. "Sure, the way you went about it wasn't cool, but I was clear that I wanted to try *something*. It just felt like you skipped past the figuring-things-out part right to a plan I wasn't ready for, and I panicked. I don't love that it's Label, but . . ."

"Caleb, no. It should never have been Label." My heart twists. "I'm so sorry I did this."

He reaches for my hand, tentatively entwining our fingers together. "I know you are, and I forgive you."

Tears sting my eyes. "You do?"

"Of course I do," he says, placing his free hand on my cheek. I lean into the touch. "Because I love you too. I never stopped loving you all those years ago, and walking away from you was the most painful thing I've ever done in my life. Twice. We have a lot of details to figure out, but I want to try. We can figure out all of the band stuff later, but I need you to know I'm here, and it's because I want *you*. Is that okay?"

"Are you kidding?" I ask. "That's literally all I want. I wasn't saying that stuff to fool anyone—I am so fucking in love with you, it's not even a question."

We just stare at each other, grinning, the setting sun casting shadows on our faces through my windows. I can't believe he's here. I can't believe he loves me.

I can't believe I'm not saying goodbye.

"So what now?" I finally ask.

"Kiss me, Quinn, I dare you," he says with a challenging smirk.

I don't need to be told twice. I grab the front of his T-shirt in my fist and draw his mouth to mine. The moment our lips touch, I melt in relief. Kissing him is like finally coming home. My knees go weak, and I lean into him.

He kisses me hard, walking me backward in the direction of

the couch. I tug him closer so our hips are flush, groaning as the thrill sends sensation to my core.

"Caleb," I gasp.

"Val," he says against my lips, barely more than a whisper.

I pull back. "We need to talk about the details. There are so many things to work out. I don't want . . ."

He blinks, drawing away. "You're right. You're absolutely right. But if it's okay with you, I think you should let me take your clothes off first. We can talk about the details after, while we eat takeout, because we'll be too exhausted to cook when I'm done with you."

Desire snaps through my veins like static. "Is that a promise?"

"Absolutely." His eyes rove over me. "Nice shirt, by the way."

I grin at him. "I stole it from the love of my life."

"Looks better on you."

"Good. I'm keeping it."

His hands tighten on my hips. "As long as I can take it off of you right now."

"I'm counting on it."

And then we're kissing again. My knees go weak as he brushes his lips down my jaw to my neck, my shoulder, and I sink to the edge of the couch with a shudder. He kneels down, kissing my breasts right through my shirt—just the hint of heat through the fabric has me writhing for more. With the help of his deft fingers, my top is soon off. He wastes no time sucking on one nipple, toying with the other with those soft, guitar-string-calloused fingers.

The touch sends a spiral of heat between my legs.

"I need you to touch me," I gasp.

He pulls away. "I am touching you."

"*Caleb*," I whine.

He laughs but reaches his hands around to support each of my thighs. Instinctively, I wrap my legs around his waist, and he hoists me up so we can keep kissing without breaking apart. He takes a few steps to the side, then presses me deliciously into the nearby wall. Our hips meet, and I grind against him, sliding against his length despite the fabric between us.

"Fuck, Valerie," he groans, leaning his forehead against mine. "If you don't stop, I'm going to come in my pants."

"Get it together, Sloane," I say, trying and failing to sound nonchalant. "You promised to tire me out."

"Oh, I didn't forget," he says. "You just need to behave."

"Fine." I stop grinding.

He chuckles. "Good girl. Bedroom?"

"Back there," I say, nodding toward the hall. Without missing a beat, he carries me back to my bedroom, where, fortunately, my bed is made with fresh linens that smell like orange blossoms. Caleb sets me down gently on the mattress, then sinks down on top of me, hovering over my body.

"It's your laundry," he says, eyes widening.

"What?" I ask.

"That *scent*," he says. "I knew what the shampoo was, but that citrus has been destroying me all summer."

I laugh. "I could buy you the detergent I use. It's gentle on the environment."

"I don't want to smell like you unless we're sharing a bed," he says.

"Are you inviting yourself to move in with me, Sloane? That's a big step."

He flushes. "That's not what . . . I meant . . ."

I pull him closer, delighting in watching him get all flustered for me. "I think we're overdue for some big steps."

Caleb's lips slowly widen into a grin, and this time it's not a smirk at all. It's big and open and dazzling, and I could get lost in his warm green eyes. "I think you're right."

"Sex now, talk later," I say.

"If you insist," he says. He slips his fingers into my waistband and between my thighs, hissing as his hands slick across my opening. "Fuck, Valerie, you feel so good."

"It's been ten days without you in my bed. I need you," I say, rolling my waistband down as he works my clit with his fingers.

"Jesus Christ," he groans, divesting me of my leggings entirely before returning his palm to my center. "I've missed you so much."

"My vibrator is just not as good," I admit with a gasp.

His eyes light up. "Vibrator? We'll come back to that later."

A thrill runs down my spine at the idea of using toys with Caleb. We never tried them when we were together before, but he's clearly game. I don't want any of that tonight, though. Just him.

"Deal," I say.

He leans down for another kiss, drawing slow circles around my clit until I'm nearly on the edge. It's too much, too soon, and I don't want to fall yet. He's barely touched me; I can't come now.

"You're resisting," he murmurs. "Just let go."

I kiss him deeper, and he slips a finger inside me, then two. My throat goes dry, and I'm panting for release, but I don't want to let it happen. Not yet.

"I want to feel you inside me when I come," I say.

"Fuck, Val, you don't have to tell me twice," he practically purrs in my ear. His voice is so hoarse and full of wanting that it's almost enough to send me over the edge, especially with his hand between my legs.

"Come here, then." I reach into the waistband of his joggers and wrap my fingers around his hard length. He shivers under my touch, and I pump his shaft softly once. I grab some lube from my drawer, stroking twice. Three times, and he's begging me for more.

"*Valerie*. If you keep touching me like this, we're not going to get to the good part."

I bite my lip, smirking. "This is good too."

He hisses out a breath as I pump him again. "I'll let you have your fun later, I promise."

"We're making a lot of promises," I say. My words are light and teasing, but there's more to them. There *are* a lot of promises we're making tonight, and I mean them with all my heart. My hand stills, even in this intimate position.

As if he can read my thoughts, his voice softens. "I'm not letting you go this time."

"Thank god, because I'm not going anywhere. You're stuck with me."

He swallows, and even though his pupils are blown wide with lust, there's a vulnerability to him.

"Good, because I really love you."

I smile. "I really love you too."

And then we can't wait anymore. I'm sliding down his joggers, climbing onto his hips, grabbing a condom from my drawer, and sliding it on him. He grips my waist and helps me ease onto his warm, hard length.

"Fuck, I missed you," he breathes, like he can't believe we're here again. Neither can I. All those nights this summer felt like borrowed time, and after everything fell apart, I never thought he'd speak to me again, much less love me. I know now that I'm never going to let this man go again.

It just makes me pull him closer. And soon I'm gasping and falling over the edge, and feeling the exquisite heat deep inside me as he falls right with me.

After, when we've cleaned up and slipped between the sheets and we're scrolling on Caleb's phone, deciding on food delivery, he presses a kiss to my temple. "This feels different," he says.

"We're different." I let out a shaky sigh. "Maybe it's because we're not lying to ourselves anymore," I say.

"But if we hadn't faked it for the cameras"—he presses another kiss to my temple—"we never would have fallen in love for real again."

I smile. "I think even without the reunion, we would have still found our way to each other again."

"Does the ever-skeptical Valerie Quinn believe in fate now?" he asks.

I snuggle into his chest. "Maybe I just believe in whatever brings me back to you."

"You give me something to believe in too." He squeezes me tight, then reaches for my chin, softly drawing my mouth to his.

EPILOGUE

✦ *Valerie* ✦

THE NEXT SUMMER

The Glitter Bats are back and things look different this time.

Vegas is the last stop tonight on our—very limited—US tour, celebrating our third album, *More to Say*. In the sold-out stadium, spotlights wash over us as we finish the last chorus of "Better Times," our latest single. Across the crowd, I can see myself on the big screen—and I'm glad I let Rowan talk me into playing with my hair color again, because the turquoise is oddly flattering.

The camera pans to Riker, shredding on his seafoam-green Telecaster. He flips his hair wildly over his shoulder and winks at the camera, confident as ever. With all the stress of last summer behind us, we get to just have fun again, and it's incredible.

With *More to Say*, we finally fulfilled all contractual obligations to Label Records, and the options for our future are endless. Caleb is still teaching, so we recorded over his winter break, and the album released in February to the most praise we've ever gotten as a band. We're seeing headlines like:

"The Glitter Bats Are Back and Better Than Ever"

"Glitter Bats Are Maturing, and So Is Their Sound"
And of course the usual:
"Are the Glitter Bats Back, or Is This Too Good to Be True?"
"*More to Say* Is a Masterpiece, but Is It a Farewell Album?"
We take it all in stride.

My heart warms as I glance around at the rest of my band. Keeley whoops as she crashes into a drum solo, and Jane bounces to the beat as she plays changes on the synth. Caleb looks over at me across the stage, and the heat in his gaze makes my pulse kick into a higher gear.

This is the happiest I've ever been.

I was nervous to come to Vegas, but it all melted away at sound check. This is where it all ended the first time seven years ago, but we're a different band than we were back then. We're closer than we've ever been before, and it feels so good to work together like this. We have all that same chemistry and sync onstage with none of the tension offstage.

And we all have a lot to celebrate.

Caleb didn't quit teaching, and I would never have wanted him to, as long as he's happy. Over the last year, I spent most of my time in Oregon with Caleb and Sebastian Bark when school was in session, and Caleb's time off brought them both to my place in LA. After Carrie got accepted to a music program in Southern California, Caleb started looking for a teaching job closer to my home base. He already has an offer for a part-time position that will give him some much-needed balance, and he has a few days to decide if he's taking it. But I have no doubt he'll land in the right place. Whether that's Oregon or California or fucking Finland, I don't care—I'll follow him anywhere.

The same way I do on this stage. When he jerks his head in my direction, I step out from my mic and go to sing the bridge at his. The crowd screams. My heart races.

If I only ever did this, it would be enough.

But that doesn't mean I'm not working. When Caleb's school year started back up, I told Wade I wanted to get back into acting, and he delivered. I had a short guest arc on a new drama series that's going strong, and I also landed a leading role in an upcoming Christmas rom-com. It was nice to be on set again.

And even better, after our fans rallied around us and our creators fought like hell, *Epic Theme Song* was picked up by another streaming service. I still want to pinch myself. Just when I'd finally accepted our beloved show was canceled for good, we got the call that Sunset Streaming+ wanted to bring us over for two more seasons *and* a movie, which means we'll get the ending our showrunner planned. We filmed season three over the spring, and it's scheduled to drop in September. I think the fans will appreciate the loving care that went into developing this next chapter.

And other than some *ETS* press, I'll have a break after this concert. I'm having the time of my life staying busy, but I plan to take Sebastian Bark for long walks on the beach, try all the new restaurants I haven't had time for, and catch up on fantasy novels.

I have another surprise in store tonight that I'm a little nervous about, but this time, *almost* all of the band is in on it—Caleb's the only one in the dark, and that's just because he needs to be this time. For his own good.

After we finish the bridge, Caleb and I drop to a low chorus. The rest of the band fades out, so it's just my acoustic and our voices. I get chills as the stadium goes quiet. When we finish the final notes, the crowd goes wild. I peck Caleb's cheek, and the cheers get even louder before I run back over to my own mic.

It's almost time for our grand finale—which happens to be "Midnight Road Trip," and I'm pretending that's not a bad omen— so I grab the mic to start vamping. But Caleb grabs his too, though he gestures when he sees me. "You first," he says, quirking a brow.

It's my turn, I mouth at him. Caleb has no idea how much I mean that, but he just nods and steps back, and I take that as a sign to continue.

I can do this.

"Thank you all for coming out tonight," I say. "You all know that Caleb and I are officially together now, right?"

"You haven't been subtle," Keeley says into her own mic, and the crowd laughs and whoops along with the band. Vegas is always a great crowd, but there's something magical in the air tonight that lights a fire in my chest.

"Right, we definitely have not. But some of you might not realize that tonight marks one year since we got back together. We were hopelessly in love with each other for, oh, four years before the band split, so that means we've really been together for five years. Isn't that wild?"

The crowd booms. One year since we made up in my apartment, but no one needs to know the details.

Heat floods my cheeks. "The thing about Caleb Sloane is he's the best person you'll ever meet. He's kind, and openhearted, and he always has your back—even when you haven't done the same. I've never met anyone like him." He grins across the stage at me, and the crowd lets out a collective *aww*.

I continue. "I'm so glad we figured out our baggage, because I can't imagine life without Caleb. I love this man with my entire heart." I swallow, gathering my nerve. "And I fully intend to do that for the rest of my life if he'll let me."

I dig around in my pocket, but these pants are too tight. Shit. I should have gone with the fanny pack Keeley suggested.

"Wait a second," Caleb says. "I have something to say."

I turn to him, and my heart starts racing.

He knows what I'm doing.

Shit.

By the unreadable look in his eyes, I have no idea if that's a good thing or a bad thing.

+ *Caleb* +

I almost missed that box in her pocket, carefully concealed by her guitar pack. But when she turned to face me, I saw it hit the light, and I couldn't let her steal my thunder.

Although it was hard not to laugh. Because I have something in my jacket too, and I'm not going to make the same mistake I made when we were younger. Striding across the stage to her, I grab my microphone and get down on one knee before she can beat me to it.

"Oh my god," Valerie says, clutching her free hand to her chest. Tears well in her eyes, and they match mine. "Are you serious?"

I bite my lip, cracking open the box. I didn't buy a flashy diamond this time—she said she didn't need one. This is a vintage gemstone, a sapphire that matches the blue in her eyes.

"Valerie Elizabeth Quinn, I'm so fucking in love with you . . ." My voice breaks as my emotions overtake me, and I clear my throat. "And I *absolutely* plan to spend the rest of our lives together. So I'm asking you again: Will you marry me?"

Even with tears streaming down her face, Valerie pauses, cocks her head, playing with the audience. Finally, she digs her own ring box out of those dangerously tight leather pants. "Only if you marry me first."

And then the crowd absolutely loses their shit as we collide and start making out on stage. Out of nowhere, confetti explodes from the ceiling, and I pull back, laughing. Valerie shrugs and pulls me in for another kiss. Long, hard, breathless. Eventually, we remember we have an audience and part, sharing the rings we found for each other.

Keeley, Jane, and Riker vamp with the crowd to give us a moment. Riker even starts reading signs to show love the way I usually do, and I could kiss him for it if I wasn't spoken for. Finally.

"I can't believe you upstaged me!" Valerie says with a laugh, brushing the joyful tears from her face.

"I can't believe you tried to propose before I could! Did they put you up to it?" I ask, gesturing at our friends.

She gasps. "The band? No! I told them I was proposing tonight. They didn't know you were."

I laugh, glancing over at Keeley, who salutes me with a drumstick. "They absolutely did, because I've been planning this for weeks! I found the ring when we were in New York!"

Of course they all knew what we were both up to tonight, and that makes this moment just that much more perfect. No wonder Riker kept smirking as I was going over the plan last week in Denver, when Valerie stepped away to take a call during our downtime.

Valerie beams. "I bought yours in LA before our first stop, but I've been saving it for tonight."

I lean my forehead against hers. "God, I can't believe we both planned this."

"I can," she whispers. "We've always been good at reading each other's minds."

"No regrets?" I ask, smirking down at her shining eyes.

"None. This is the only way I'd want to do this. Together."

I laugh, gripping her hand in mine, my chest warming as I see the ring on her finger glittering under the spotlights. It's a perfect fit—and that's because I sent Jane on a scavenger hunt with a sizer through Valerie's jewelry box months ago—and it's so satisfying to see it. I put that ring there.

It doesn't mean I'm claiming Valerie—it means I'm choosing

her. That's what love is. We've chosen each other every day since that night in her apartment, and even when things get difficult, we choose each other again.

We don't need a piece of paper to make it official, but it's obvious we both want that. We're both choosing *us*—for good this time.

She's everything I ever wanted. The rest, whether we're making music or working boring day jobs—none of that matters as long as she's by my side. I love Valerie with all of my soul, and I don't want to spend one more day as anything but hers.

And then, with a start, I realize I don't have to. I reach for her hand and drag her behind a speaker, shielding us from view as much as possible. I don't want to decide this in front of thousands of people.

"So . . . we're in *Vegas*, and my family flew out here for our last show . . ." I say, trailing off to gauge her reaction.

But the brilliant smile that breaks across her face tells me I should have known. We're older and wiser and ready for this.

"Interesting. I was thinking the exact same thing," she says. "Let's do it."

So we play the encore, laughing and jumping and trying not to kiss during *every* instrumental break. (But we can't resist.)

Once we're backstage after final bows, we alert our friends and family and head to the closest chapel. Wade calls his lawyer on retention to make sure everything is legal, and then there's nothing for Valerie and me to do but make our promises. We commit to each other surrounded by the people we love, and just about everyone is crying. It's not a typical wedding, but I wouldn't have it any other way.

Once we're pronounced "officially hitched"—thanks to the country theme Keeley paid extra for—we head to the hotel restaurant to pop champagne and celebrate our new adventure. Riker's job was to get Magic Cupcake delivered all the way from LA to celebrate the engagement, and it makes for a perfect wedding cake.

"Forever, huh?" I whisper to my wife. All night, we haven't left each other's side. We were in such a rush to make this happen that we didn't even change after the show. She's still wearing those leather pants, and I love them on her more than any bridal gown. Jane insists that we ceremoniously cut a vanilla cupcake for the dang photo op. She's committed herself to documenting the night with surprising zeal, and the only person who's been crying more than her is Cameron.

"Sounds perfect to me," Valerie says, kissing me deeply before shoving a cupcake in my face. I laugh as I get her just as good, and she chases after me across the private dining room until I let her catch me and kiss me again. Long and hard. Everyone cheers and Riker wolf whistles, and I don't think I've ever been happier than I am right at this moment.

Forever is just a new song we'll write together. With Valerie by my side, I know it'll have the sweetest harmony.

ACKNOWLEDGMENTS ✦✦

Writing is a solitary act by nature, but the community surrounding me has made all the difference in the world. The first time I tried to write these acknowledgments, I couldn't stop crying with the sheer weight of my gratitude. Becoming an author has been a dream I've held in my heart for more than twenty years, and with every milestone toward the publication of this book, I keep waiting for the pinch that will wake me up. My road to becoming an author was a long and winding one, across genres and categories and stages of life, and it was full of both heartbreak and joy. *For One Night Only* changed everything for me, and I didn't do it alone.

Thank you to my literal dream agent and professional hype woman, Samantha Fabien. You have championed my work with enthusiasm, savvy, and care, and it means the world. I couldn't ask for a better business partner in this endeavor. I also want to extend a thank-you to the rest of the fabulous team at Root Literary for their support.

To my incredible editor, Liz Sellers, thank you for seeing potential in this story and helping me bring the Glitter Bats to life! You understood my vision for this book from that first meeting, and your sharp editorial eye changed it for the better. Thank you to the rest of the amazing team at Berkley, including production editor Megan Elmore, managing editor Christine Legon, interior designer Daniel

Brount, art director Vikki Chu, copy editor Shana Jones, proofreader Michael Brown, cold reader Liz Gluck, publicist Chelsea Pascoe, marketer Anika Bates, and everyone else who helped bring this book into the world. And to Carolina Rodríguez Fuenmayor, thank you for the eye-catching, colorful, romantic cover of my dreams.

My writing community is the reason I made it here. Thank you to my dear Guillotines: Brittney Arena, Tracy Badua, Rae Castor, Alyssa Colman, Koren Enright, Sam Farkas, Jenn Gruenke, Kalyn Josephson, and Ashley Northup. You are the best friends and critique partners I could ask for! Thank you for reading countless drafts, listening to all of my spirals, and tolerating the countless pitches I've thrown your way over the years. And thank you for always reminding me it's all in the execution.

Thank you to Misty Wilson for reading the earliest version of this book and helping me find my footing. Koren Enright and Kalyn Josephson, thank you for your vital early feedback. Brittney Arena and De Elizabeth, thank you for your early reading and cheerleading—I'm honored to be on this journey with you.

I want to raise a pumpkin spice latte to my incredible Pitch Wars mentors, Heather Van Fleet and Jessica Calla. You helped me find my romance voice, and I am so grateful to you for your belief in me and my work! I constantly view the moment I saw my name on that mentee announcement as a turning point in my writing career. To the other mentors who read that book, thank you for your time and encouragement. I also want to thank the Pitch Wars class of 2021 for reading my manuscript and cheering me on through this journey.

To everyone who blurbed this book, thank you for your time, your energy, and your kind words. I'm incredibly honored!

Thank you to the Berkletes for welcoming me with open arms and providing much-needed encouragement, perspective, and a safe space. I'm so grateful for all of you.

Team Samantha, I adore you! Thank you for always cheering me on.

So many people in the book community have read my earlier work and provided vital encouragement and feedback when I needed it most. Thank you, Alechia Dow, Jenny Howe, Lillie Lainoff, Sarah Simon, Amy Stewart, Rosiee Thor, and Elizabeth Urso, for your time and talent. I also want to thank Kelsey Klosterman and Sheedy Lit for seeing something in my writing and being my first "yes" in this industry. And to Daniele Hunter, thank you for being such a kind fan of my work.

To Britt Lunsford, thank you for the buddy read that changed everything, and your constant friendship and support since.

Kaeley Scruggs, thank you for your friendship, for always being willing to talk romance . . . and for reading all of my messy manuscripts.

Thank you to Misty Wilson and Jennifer Iacopelli for the group chat. Celebrating this thing we all loved together helped me remember my love for fandom, and it made this book possible.

Thank you to Kaitlin Teague for always having tea, delicious treats, and an encouraging word to warm my heart. And to the rest of my West Pasco Library family, thank you for celebrating me from the literal first day of the long, challenging road to publication. It only took eight years!

Laurel Jackman, thank you for bonding over books with me, for the road trip to Powell's, and for believing this author thing would happen from day one—the Sharpies will be ready for you, as requested.

Andrea Hall, thank you for your enthusiasm, your constant support, and for the conversation that always makes me leave with a fuller heart.

Sarah Olsen, thank you for being so hyped for this book!

To the Eastern Washington University music department during my time there, especially Kristina Ploeger, Jane Ellsworth, and Susan Windham, thank you for teaching me what it truly means to grow—and make mistakes that won't hurt anyone—as an artist. Your lessons made the thousands of writing hours in front of my computer feel like just another practice-room session.

Kelsey Myers and Amanda Ursino, thank you for being so incredibly supportive of me as I pursued this goal.

I want to thank a few people who I know will (most likely!) never read this, because their influence on me cannot be missed. To Meg Cabot, thank you for writing the books and the blog that inspired teen Jess to become a writer. Suzanne Collins, thank you for recapturing my love of reading. Thank you to the cast and creative team of *Julie and the Phantoms* for relighting the spark of an old idea that turned into this book. Taylor Swift, Paramore, and Joseph, thank you for writing all of the songs that fueled this writing process.

Thank you to the James family for your love and support. I'm so glad you're my family.

To my parents, I love you. Thank you for telling me I could do anything I set my mind to. I took it literally.

Thank you to Obi and Neville for hanging out with me as I wrote literally hundreds of thousands of words. Since you can't read this, I'll cuddle you as soon as I'm done.

Andrew, you have my heart. There aren't enough words in the English language for me to eloquently thank you enough for loving me as I pursued this path. You held me through my tears, celebrated my wins, listened to my fears, took me on countless working coffee dates, and never doubted me, even when I doubted myself. I love you.

And to my readers: you make this possible. Thank you for taking a chance on me and the Glitter Bats. Rock on.

Photo provided by the author

JESSICA JAMES is a writer who also loves going to concerts, baking new recipes, spending time in local coffee shops, and exploring the Pacific Northwest with her spouse and dogs. In addition to writing, Jessica has a passion for singing. While she's never been a rock star, she's a mezzo-soprano with a BA in music and a healthy Broadway obsession. *For One Night Only* is her debut novel.

VISIT JESSICA JAMES ONLINE

JessicaMJames.com
⃝ X ♪ LiterarilyJess

Ready to find
your next great read?

Let us help.

Visit prh.com/nextread

Penguin
Random
House